Kitty Cameron

Back then she was the Sweetheart of Sigma Chi, beautiful and proper—except in Dan Copeland's arms. Now she's Mrs. Whitney Harris, rich, stunning, and cool. But her passion for Dan had never died . . .

Dan Copeland

Vietnam veteran, campus activist, he'd been a redheaded firebrand in love with Kitty. Now he's a feisty Wisconsin D.A. running for Congress, and looking forward with all his heart to s

Overweight, c   kout from the Bronx wh   Now she's a famous sing   still sexy—and still amazed by the power of love . . .

Benno Akkardijian

The Armenian immigrant who'd lived in Copeland's shadow—funny, bright, everybody's friend. Now, fresh from a broken marriage that finally made him his own person, he rediscovers an old friend and a new love . . .

Marcia Rose

Second Chances.

BALLANTINE BOOKS • NEW YORK

Library of Congress Catalog Card Number: 80-68222

ISBN 0-345-28670-7

Printed in Canada

First Edition: September 1981

Cover photograph by Anthony Loew

TO MAMA AND DADDY

Contents

ONE: *Daniel Copeland*   1

TWO: *Katherine Cameron Harris*   28

THREE: *Lee Rivers*   53

FOUR: *Benno Akkardijian*   80

FIVE: *William Sean Michael O'Hara*   96

SIX: *Serena Malverne De Luca*   102

SEVEN: *Florence, Italy*   112

EIGHT: *Polly Malverne*   145

NINE: *Reunion, Lee and O'Hara*   172

TEN: *Reunion, Kit and Dan*   193

ELEVEN: *Washington, D.C.*   205

TWELVE: *Larry, the Tattooed Man*   209

THIRTEEN: *Linda Goodman Barrone*   233

FOURTEEN: *Runner's World*   242

FIFTEEN: *Gladiators and Warriors*   245

SIXTEEN: *Dan and Whit*   260

SEVENTEEN: *Whit Harris and His Wife*   273

EIGHTEEN: *Big Jim*   292

NINETEEN: *Dinah Franklin*   304

TWENTY: *Klass of '70 Kum-Back Komments*   320

TWENTY-ONE: *The Harris Family*   323

TWENTY-TWO: *Whit and Kitty Reprise*   337

TWENTY-THREE: *Kit Harris's File Marked "Trivia"*   341

TWENTY-FOUR: *London, England*   345

TWENTY-FIVE: *Kit and Dan Reprise*   360

TWENTY-SIX: *Lee and Ben*   366

TWENTY-SEVEN: *Whit and Dinah*   369

TWENTY-EIGHT: *Lily Harris and Her New Friend*   376

CHAPTER ONE

Daniel Copeland

DAN CAME AWAKE all at once, filled with a child-like joy. It was an emotion so alien to his practical nature that he immediately closed his eyes to chase after the dream that had left this feeling. Too late. There was nothing but a blur of something silvery and smooth, something vague and elusive.

Then he thought of her: *Kitty*. And his eyes flew open. He lay perfectly still, staring at the ceiling, trying to remember. Had he dreamed of Kitty Cameron after all this time? Ten years ago she had filled all his dreams, sleeping and waking. And then, blessedly, the dreams had stopped. Why this morning? Of course. This morning he was flying back to Hampton College, where, after two years in Vietnam, he had found his future. Where he had found himself. Where he had found—and lost— Kitty Cameron. So, he thought, yawning and stretching out his long legs to the bottom of the bed, it wasn't surprising to find Kit haunting his dreams again. Be amazing if she didn't. As for that intense, aching happiness . . . more memories . . . old memories . . . not worth dwelling on.

With a last, jaw-cracking yawn, he pulled himself up to a sitting position, reaching automatically for the pitcher of ice water on the night table and glancing at the clock. Seven-thirty. The plane left at ten. He poured himself a glass of water and gulped it thirstily, trying to shake the feeling of loss that suddenly weighted his chest.

A slight stirring in the bed brought him fully awake. In

1

a friendly but definite way, he patted the firm rump that curled close to him. "Okay, Dinah. Up and at 'em."

The body next to him, completely rolled into the sheet, emitted a moan.

"I have to catch a plane, remember? And Big Jim is going to call any minute. And I'm starving. Dinah, have you no heart?"

A tanned arm snaked out of the covers, and the hand coiled around his arm, tugging at him. "Gimme kiss," said a muffled voice. "Otherwise, I go back to sleep."

Laughing, Dan peeled away the sheet, revealing a mass of tousled dark hair and the curve of a cheek. He bent and brushed it with his lips. "There. Any more than that and I'll never make my plane. And there's Jim; he'll be calling any minute."

The woman lifted herself on one elbow and gave him a bleary-eyed look. "I seem to remember a fairly interesting evening before we fell asleep," she said wryly. "And this morning you're all business."

A fleeting image of Kit from his dream flashed across Dan's mind and was gone. Not fair. Dinah might be older than he, but she was still a good-looking, firm-bodied woman. He was lucky to have her in his bed, in his office, and in his life. "Last night was wonderful, Di, but like the guy said, 'Time and airplanes wait for no man.'"

Dinah's lips tightened, and a look crossed her face that he had seen too often lately. It was a look that said, I love you but you don't really love me. As it happened, she was absolutely right. He had warned her from the very first: no strings. And she had agreed. Women always did. And eventually they all got that hurt, cheated look. But Dinah was kind of special. He hated to see it happen with her.

"I'll just have to try harder." She smiled, but it was strained.

"Dinah," Dan said warningly, "let's not start that again. You know I'm very fond of you. You're the best assistant I've ever had—"

"That's *not* what we're talking about!"

"That's what *I'm* talking about." Stretching his arms above his head, he yawned hugely. "There's no one I'd rather have working for me," he went on, pinching her bottom lightly, "and no one I'd rather have in my bed."

Unless I could have Kit again, he added silently. He had to admit that Kit was the real reason he was so eager to get to the reunion. He had a lot of painful questions to ask, a lot of puzzles to unravel. He had to see her alone. The dream, like an omen, had steeled his resolve. He had lost her, okay, but she owed him. An explanation at the very least.

Dinah, her full lips pursed, stared up at him thoughtfully. "I wonder sometimes . . ."

"Wonder? About what?"

"Oh, nothing . . . just . . . whether it's really *me* you're making love to."

Copeland turned to her, jolted. It often amazed him how perceptive she was, even of his innermost thoughts. She was an extremely bright woman. She deserved to be loved, but his love had been claimed long ago. It was a shame. "Not really you?" he responded lightly. "When you start to talk nonsense, you're obviously hungry. Come on, get up and get going. Your brain cells need feeding."

As she puttered around the kitchen, dressed in his old oversized Hampton sweatshirt, Dan took a large bath sheet and went into the shower. He soaped himself. He started singing: "On the shores of Lake Winnetaka stands a mighty hall . . ." Then he laughed aloud. The old school song, and those were the only words he remembered.

A few minutes later, still singing "Dah-dah-dah" in a loud voice, he stepped out, dripping. He felt good. His confusion had gone away entirely. Dinah would be all right; she always was. She was no innocent babe in the woods. And in a few hours he would be on the plane, on his way to . . . what, he didn't know. But he would settle with Kitty once and for all.

As he toweled off, he could dimly see the shape of his body through the mist that covered the mirror. On an impulse, he rubbed at the cloudiness and stared at his reflection. Would anyone at Hampton recognize him? he wondered.

Dan Copeland, the Vietnam vet and campus radical, had been a rail-thin boy with unruly, shoulder-length auburn hair, always held back by an Indian headband to keep it from falling into his eyes. That Dan Copeland had slouched about wearing faded jeans and T-shirts. The Wisconsin congressional hopeful, the "Daring D.A." who looked back at him from the mirror this morning, wore fine American tailoring. The bright hair, now darkened to the color of old copper, was regularly razor-cut for an exorbitant sum by Andy, the barber—no, these days it was Mr. Andrew, the Hairstylist. Dan had filled out, too. Those summers working on the Zuni reservation, and the years of running and playing squash, had built up the muscles in chest, arms, and legs.

He squinted at the image in the mirror, then gave himself an embarrassed smile, revealing a deep dimple in his left cheek, next to his mouth. His eyes were alert, he noted, and not even bloodshot. He and Dinah had put away a whole bottle of Rothschild Chateau-Something '57 last night, from her prize stock of vintage wines.

Patting his flat belly, he mused, "At least I haven't gone to fat. Nor gone bald." Many of the guys he knew were aging quickly. He combed his fingers through the thick hair and then made a face at himself. Enough of this. Bad enough, the way those P.R. characters had fussed over him yesterday before the taping—which reminded him . . .

Opening the bathroom door, he called out to Dinah: "Get Channel Six on, will you? I'm supposed to be on that morning show." A delicious aroma of bacon and coffee made his mouth water. He wrapped a bath towel hastily around his hips and strode out into the kitchen.

A mug, already filled with coffee, was waiting for him on the butcher block. He sipped at it gratefully. Perfect as always: strong, a dollop of cream, and one spoon of sugar.

Dinah, her dark hair pulled back into a quick ponytail with a rubber band, did something with eggs in a pan and remarked, "No, not the morning show. It'll be on the six o'clock news. *Then* they'll repeat it on tomorrow's morning show. And don't worry, I'll watch—both times."

Dan pulled out a stool and sat with one elbow on the counter. "Dinah, you're a treasure."

"So I am, so I am." To his relief, the hurt tone was gone from her voice. He didn't want to have to deal with that. There were too many other things to think about. He had been campaigning hard since last April. Now, in October, with the election only a month away, it had been day-and-night meetings and speeches and appearances and dinners. He was tired. Still raring to go, but glad for a chance to relax. Relax? He was making a speech at the reunion. Business as usual. Wherever he went, his mouth never stopped working. That was the politician's fate.

"I packed the notes for your talk in your briefcase," Dinah said. "And I had a few thoughts, so I wrote them down and put *that* in, too. And you'd better read the FBI report."

Dan groaned. "That thing? It must be five hundred pages. I'm supposed to be taking time off, Dinah."

"The hell you are, Dan Copeland, and you know it! You may think you're God's gift to Wisconsin, but when you're running against an incumbent as tough as Leland . . . well, it's still an uphill battle. The trouble with you is, you read all the polls and believe them. You know you shouldn't count on them. The very idea of taking three days off, and for what? A dumb college reunion in upstate New York, where nobody can vote for you!"

Dan shook his head and grinned. "Dinah, Dinah, you're two hundred percent pol and I love it." Then, quickly, sensing a change in her, he added, "But isn't it time for Big Jim's call?"

In answer, she pulled the white telephone over, punched out a series of numbers, and handed the phone to Dan. "Why wonder? You call him."

Dan held the receiver out from his ear, in preparation for the booming, gravelly voice.

Three rings. Then, "Hello!" The familiar voice could be heard across the room.

"Hi, Jim."

"Dan! Have you changed your mind about this crazy trip yet?"

"No, Jim. I'm going."

"Hell! I coulda had you out at the Dairy Convention."

"Jim, for the love of God, lay off. I've been working thirty hours a day for the past six months. I need these couple of days. I'm getting stale. Look, I'll be on TV twice and on the radio six times a day while I'm gone. The great electorate of Wisconsin will hardly miss me."

"If you say so, Dan." A gusty sigh. "But come back ready to move your tail, boy. 'Cause now we're really going to take off!"

Jim was always full of enthusiasm and optimism, but

something in his voice alerted Dan. "What's happening?"

There was a rich chuckle from the other end of the line. *"Money,* boy! And plenty of it!"

"Who?"

"You're going to love this! The American Health Committee!"

"American Health!" Dan turned to Dinah, who looked just as quizzical as he felt. "What're they giving *me* money for? Those guys hate everything I stand for."

"Not quite everything, Danny boy. Your stand on the FDA . . . ah . . . pleases them, shall we say."

"Huh! Maybe I ought to change my position, in that case. That's one lobby that gets its way too often to suit me."

Big Jim laughed heartily. "It's just a common case of strange bedfellows, Dan. Hell, their money's just as good as anyone's. But being in pharmaceuticals and loving good profits the way they do, they just kinda like how you've been teeing off at the high cost of FDA testing."

Dan scowled. "I don't like it. Do they have the idea I'm all for lowering the high standards of drugs? Because I'm not. But the rigidity of the FDA—they keep important discoveries off the market too long and make people spend too damn much money for medication."

"Get off the white horse, will you? You don't have to sell me, Dan. Look, American Health doesn't like you or the party very much, but they do like that one particular position. And their money will make all the difference to us. It'll buy us a call-in show the week before the election."

"I still don't like it. But . . ."

Jim chortled. "And by the way, when you're at Hampton, look up Mr. Big of the Health Committee. He's one of your classmates. Whitney Harris the Third. Know him? He's gonna be there, too! Small world, isn't it?" He laughed triumphantly.

Dan found his voice. "I'm sure I'll see him," he said between clenched teeth. "Meanwhile, set up a meeting with the P.R. guys first thing Monday."

"Will do. I'll call Dinah right now."

"No," Dan said quickly. "You'd better call Dinah later. She's not home now."

"Boyfriend, huh?"

"Yeah," Dan replied carefully. "It might be a boy-friend." He winked at Dinah, but she turned away, stormy-faced. He swiftly ended the conversation and be-gan, "Now, Dinah—!"

"Why the hell can't you admit I'm with *you?*" she de-manded. "Everybody knows we're sleeping together. Big Jim knows, too. He probably knew before anyone else. So why the big cover-up all the time?"

Dan pushed himself off the stool, unwrapping the towel from his body and slinging it over his shoulder. "Look, Big Jim knows but doesn't want to hear about it. I've explained it all a hundred times."

"I know, I know. So he was once your father-in-law for a few months. But, Lord, Dan, that was years ago. Do you think he expects you to live a monk's existence in memory of his daughter?"

"That's beside the point. Jim was a friend before he was my father-in-law. If it hadn't been for him, I wouldn't be here today. Not in any sense. I wouldn't be in Wis-consin. I wouldn't be in the D.A.'s office. I wouldn't be running for Congress. And, my dear Dinah, I wouldn't be standing in this apartment preparing for a trip, after having spent one hell of a night with you." He grinned at her, hating himself a little for being so sure of what would charm her.

Her brown eyes softened. "Wasn't it good, Dan?"

He went to her and, holding her close, kissed her mouth. "It's always good, Di. But you have to under-stand that my relationship with Jim is very complex. He loved Polly, and he went off the deep end when she was killed. He's never forgotten the horror of that day, and tough old bird though he is, he's very vulnerable where his daughters are concerned. He hasn't had much luck with them, you know. Well, never mind." He kissed her on the forehead, lightly. "I just don't want to rub it in—that I'm having the time of my life and she's gone—" He stopped abruptly. "I've got to get dressed." He walked toward the bedroom. "And you'd better do the same," he called over his shoulder. "I have a million errands for you today."

At nine-twenty sharp, they were both out on the side-walk in front of Dan's apartment, waiting for his cab.

"Why can't I drive you? It's no trouble."

"Dinah, go to the office," Dan said patiently. "Let me get started."

For a moment she stood undecided, a hand on one blue-jeaned hip. Dan felt suddenly impatient with her intensity and her constant energy. It was like this with all women. After a while he just had to back off. Even from Dinah, who knew him so well, who sometimes seemed capable of reading his mind. He could work with her endlessly, but when they were intimate and he saw entreaty in her dark eyes, he felt helpless and smothered. How could he change the way he felt about her? If he pretended—and every once in a while he considered that— but no. Once he had pretended, and the outcome had been tragic.

As always, his mind veered away from that memory. What was done was done. He would never again make the same kind of mistake.

"Tell you what," Dinah said with a winning smile. "I'll pick you up at the airport when you come back." There was an unspoken question mark at the end of the sentence.

"Yes. I'd like that."

"Good. Then goodbye. And have a wonderful nostalgic time and don't even think about the election—not too much, anyway." Standing on tiptoe, she gave him a brief kiss on the cheek.

He hardly noticed her leave, so intense was his need to be alone for just a few minutes. This was unusual. He loved crowds and excitement; he thrived on being at the center of things. He would not be able to stand politics otherwise.

But right now there was a smell to the air that he wanted to savor: burning leaves, apples, damp earth; a smell of ripeness that always made him sentimental. Thoughts of sparkling days and starry nights, the harvest moon floating large and orange in the void . . . the Hampton campus . . .

He laughed. For most men of his age, this would lead naturally to memories of football games and flying pennants, cheerleaders and freshman beanies, the chapel bells ringing out after each touchdown.

But not for Dan Copeland. No, he thought, *my* trip down Memory Lane brings vivid pictures of marching on the president's office to make new demands; hanging the dean in effigy; organizing sit-ins; lettering signs and bombasting the "military-industrial complex" from the steps of the Administration Building. Maybe, he reflected, they'll all think it's very amusing that the big-mouth campus radical comes back to his class reunion, just like any Establishment fink, and makes a speech to boot!

The cab came and he climbed in, still ruminating. Actually, it was not so strange, his going back to Hampton and giving a talk, just like all those other windy Old Boys he remembered from his college days. He had undergone a gradual metamorphosis from agitator to politician. But he was still essentially the same person, wanting to change the world for the better and willing to devote his time and energy toward that goal. It was simply that he had changed his mind about the best methods.

Back in school, he had thought that if you yelled and demanded loudly enough, you could make things come out right. At the Indian reservation he'd thought that if you helped people get the things they were entitled to, you could make things come out right. In law school, if you studied and worked hard enough, you could make changes from within the system and get things to come out right. During the year with Judge Cooper of the State Supreme Court, the majesty of the law and the wisdom of the judiciary would be enough. In the D.A.'s office, getting in there and fighting the good fight would do it. And now? Now he would make laws and be a part of important decisions. And still he was looking for the way to make things come out right.

For a man of thirty-four, he had tried a hell of a lot. And he had, so far, gone exactly where he had set his sights. There were moments when he felt like the Golden Boy, with the important doors always opening. Like this unexpected money from the pharmaceutical lobby. Little as he cared for them, it would mean a television call-in show to cap the campaign: very likely the difference between winning and losing.

"I've been lucky," he murmured aloud.

The cabbie said, "Wattzat?"

"Huh? Oh. Nothing. Talking to myself, I guess."

"Talking to yourself means money in the bank," the driver proclaimed. A stocky, middle-aged man, he squinted

9

at Dan in the mirror. "Say, you're Copeland the Daring D.A., ain't you?"

Dan grinned. "I see you read my campaign posters."

"Can't miss yours—there must be a million of them all over the place. I've got a friend says he found one pasted on the side of his prize cow." The cabbie laughed, delighted at his own joke.

"If that's true," Dan said, "I'll give a bonus to the volunteer who did it. Cows can be mighty touchy."

The cab turned into the entrance of the airline terminal. Letting himself out, the driver opened the passenger door for Dan and took the fare and his tip with a sincere-sounding "Good luck to you, D.A."

To Dan's surprise, the small waiting area at Gate 2, for the ten o'clock flight to Hampton, was completely filled. He studied the faces, wondering if he would spot an old classmate heading for the tenth reunion. He thought one woman, badly overweight but still rather pretty, looked familiar. He stared at her, wondering, until she began to color and gave him a coy, flirtatious look out of the corner of her eye. Quickly, he busied himself with his packet of tickets. The silly woman thought he was making a play for her.

Women had never been a problem for him, and there was usually a woman in his life. He liked them; liked their softness, their voices, their sensitivity, their shrewd perceptiveness. He liked all the things about women that made them different from men. And women liked him. Dinah was just the latest of his companions, and one of the best, he had to admit. It would be hard to give her up, but eventually he would have to. She was getting too deeply involved and too demanding. Still, she was so damn smart . . . It struck him then that he did not at all care for the way he was thinking about her—taking her measure as if she were a contestant, with him as the prize. Good points here, but on the other hand . . . No, it wasn't right. He was damned fond of Dinah, too fond to be appraising her with such cool condescension. Was his life in politics taking its toll? Was he beginning to think of his friends and associates as pawns, to be used if useful, to be discarded if that were to his advantage? He made a face, causing the young stewardess who had begun to check the passengers to ask anxiously, "Is there anything wrong, Mr. Copeland?"

Several heads turned at the sound of his name, and he could hear murmurings. Good. The radio spots were doing their job, not to mention posters on the sides of cows.

"Nothing, thank you. Will we be boarding soon?"

"Yes, sir, in a minute or two. And it will be a pleasure to serve you again."

Now he grinned. "Aha. You've seen me before."

"Twice," she twinkled. A nice, scrubbed, and freckled face with that straw-blond hair so typical of Wisconsin. "Both times to Washington. When you went to testify on teenage crime." She sounded so much like a schoolgirl proudly reciting her lessons that he laughed in genuine pleasure and gave her arm a squeeze.

"Atta girl."

She was still flushed with delight a few minutes later when the first-class passengers lined up to board the plane. She checked his tickets, taking a rather long time about it, and smiled broadly as she handed the packet back to him. Puzzled, he riffled through the tissue sheets to find a small slip of paper with a phone number neatly inked on it.

Sorry, little girl, he thought, finding his seat by the window. Not this time. He took off his jacket and carefully rolled up his sleeves, stowing the leather bag under the seat and tucking the briefcase beside him. There was plenty of work to be done, and if the person next to him wasn't too talkative, he would have three uninterrupted hours.

A tall Catholic priest sat down next to him, a man with an ascetic expression, closely shaved, with thin lips that turned down at the edges. He did not acknowledge Dan's presence in any way, but gripped the side of his seat with knuckle-whitening intensity as the plane taxied down the field and lifted off into the endless blue sky. Five minutes later, he was fast asleep, snoring lightly.

Dan stared out the window at bright nothingness. The priest had been frightened. And maybe I should be, too, he thought. It had been on just such a clear, windless day that a plane had hurtled down, carrying Polly to her death. Polly, and— He shivered involuntarily and, out of long habit, pushed all thoughts of Polly into a secret place in the back of his memory.

Better to think about what lay ahead. The reunion. Perhaps he should study his notes for the talk he was slated to give at the Saturday-night dinner. Was he crazy to have said yes in the first place? To go four hundred miles outside the congressional district he hoped to represent? Now, of course, it made some sense, since Whitney Harris's group was contributing. But he had made up his mind months ago. Here he was, the campus rebel, the guy who wrote his own rules, making the most traditional pilgrimage of all—to revisit his youth.

He might as well admit it. It was she who was drawing him back, the memories of her, the wondering about her, the incomplete chapter of his life entitled Kit Cameron. Now, suddenly, he could see her, complete and clear, after years of trying vainly to recall exactly how she looked. He felt weak with longing.

She had been the class of '70's reigning beauty and he'd heard a lot about her—quite enough to form a definite picture in his head of a Betty Coed, simpering and spoiled, dimpled and darling, holding court in the ivy-covered sorority house with its Greek-lettered blue and gold banner hanging from the porch roof. She had been rushed by every sorority her freshman year. Every professor remembered her name, and every male in the vicinity lusted after her. She was supposed to be a real beauty, and he could just imagine her: expensive clothes, doting parents, a date every night, and not a thought in her head. He alone, he had told himself, would be the one man not to clamor to meet her. He would disdain her.

And then he had seen her and everything had changed for him, forever. He had been put onto a job—God knew he needed the money. Although it was only waiting tables at the Zeta Phi sorority house, Bessie, the cook, was a campus legend, and he knew he would eat well. So there he was, on his first night of work, standing in the pantry behind the swinging door, looking through the little round window into the dining room. His feet hurt, and the overstarched collar of his white waiter's coat was digging uncomfortably into his neck.

Under an enormous chandelier of twinkling crystal icicles, twenty girls sat around the big oval mahogany table. And they all might as well have disappeared, for there was only one. She was slender, fine-boned, her pale skin almost translucent, her hair the gleam of silver gilt. It hung thick and straight like a satin curtain down to the middle of her back, curling neatly under at the ends, pulled back from her delicately molded face by a black ribbon. She wore no makeup, and there was not a mark on the alabaster skin, merely a very faint rosiness over the prominent cheekbones. She seemed to gather all the light to herself, to shine.

Someone called to her and she turned, facing him. Dan caught his breath. Tipped cat's eyes, green as the sea; a short, straight nose; full, firm lips that begged to be kissed. He stared at her, hardly breathing. He hadn't thought such a face was possible, outside of a painting. His mind stuttered, searching for the right word: ethereal . . . angelic . . . radiant. She looked, he thought, like a young goddess, sitting serenely within her own aura of calm, in the midst of those mere mortals—jabbering, clacking girls busily cramming food into their mouths. She wore a soft sweater, almost the same champagne color as her hair. Her fingers were long, slender, and tapered, unadorned with rings or nail polish. She ate, she smiled, swinging her head from time to time on the graceful, lovely neck to toss the hair back from her face. She was there, it was impossible not to notice her, yet she seemed completely apart from the rest.

The other girls were not so bad. Some were pretty, some not, all brimming with health, all with lots of hair, in brightly colored shirts embellished with chains and love beads and patches, all very stylish. The table seemed crowded with their fringes and feathers, darkly outlined eyes, and long, swinging earrings. And with voices! He could hardly make out individual words for the noise. Nineteen strident female voices, all talking at once. And then there was she. So . . . so perfect.

He nudged Willard Clement, the fellow veteran who had suggested this job and who had come to stand next to him.

"Will," he whispered, fearful that his voice would betray his excitement, "who *is* that girl?"

Will grinned. "The Sweetheart of Sigma Chi."

"Don't be an ass. I mean her *name*."

"What? You've been on campus a whole two months and you don't know the name of the girl who almost turned down Sweetheart of Sigma Chi last year?"

"I've heard it, but now I forget. Goddamn it, Will, just tell me her goddamn name."

Will threw up his hands in surrender. "Kitty Cameron. Katherine, if you want to be formal. Not that it'll do you any good."

"Hard to get, huh?" Why did he feel so bereft? She was probably dumb, dull, and completely self-centered. And he had better things to do than chase after the smugheart of Sigma Chi: a fraternity boy's sex symbol, for God's sake! Still, he found his eyes pulled back to that exquisite face.

"I wouldn't know how hard or easy she is," Willard murmured, sounding amused. "She's out of *our* class, man. Travels with all the BMOCs and the old-money guys in Psi Upsilon. Forget it!"

"Um," Dan said. "Just let me serve her the next course, okay?"

"Five bucks says you strike out."

"You're on!"

They were eating the main course—beef bourguignon—and it seemed to take them forever. They were too busy trying to set up some sort of dumb demonstration.

One of them, a tiny girl with a baritone voice and long nails painted in magenta glitter, was the ringleader. "We're adults," she was booming. "Not babies. What do they mean, ordering us to be in by midnight on a Friday, one o'clock on a Saturday—big deal, one o'clock!"

There was a chorus of "Yeah!" and "Right on!" The housemother, a fluttery little lady with blue-white hair and rouged cheeks, tried to regain order by tapping a spoon on her water goblet, but the sound was lost in the babble of raised voices.

"Let's burn the dean in effigy!"

"Linda makes terrific effigies, she'll do it, won't you, Linda!"

"We'll march over there—after hours—and picket her house!"

"Not *after* hours, you nit, the campus cops will drag us home before we get a chance to do anything!"

"Ladies! Ladies! Let's calm down now. We can't eat properly in this atmosphere!" the housemother sputtered, but her words were drowned.

A tall, Junoesque girl with olive skin and a mop of frizzy dark hair gave a guffaw. "What are you going to do, march around and chant, 'The dean is mean'?" Her pleasantly deep voice rose to a falsetto. "The dean is mean. The dean is mean."

It was obvious to Dan that she was putting them all on, but they thought it was wonderful. "Right on, Lee! That's the creative spirit!" In a minute, eighteen of them were practicing the chant. The girl called Lee watched, a look of half-hidden derision on her face as she lounged back in her chair. And the goddess, who was sitting next to her, kept right on eating, dainty forkful after dainty forkful, as if nothing at all were happening.

"We'll do it tonight!" That was the tiny girl with the basso voice again. "Kitty, you'll come, won't you?"

"Come on, Kit, say yes!"

"We'll call Zeta Tau and the Betas and the Tri-Delts!"

"Somebody start calling!"

"Courtney will, won't you, Court?"

But the phone rang first. The girl Lee got up, and Dan saw that, standing, she looked even taller and more voluptuous. A real Amazon. In a moment her voice from the hallway cut through the chatter like a knife through butter. "Whitney Harris the Third for Katherine Cameron!" There was a slight emphasis on the *Katherine,* as if she thought the name was funny.

Personal calls were not allowed during mealtimes, Dan had been told. Yet the blonde vision smiled at the housemother and waited patiently while Mrs. Camberson fluttered on and on in her twittering voice about house rules and that Mr. Harris knew quite well—he *was* a fraternity man, after all—the rules of proper behavior. Kit Cameron waited politely, serenely, and smiled. And in the end, she was given permission to take her call.

So, Dan thought, I was right. The spoiled darling of the entire sorority. Probably always gets her way. Will she be a challenge? Or just a bore?

When she came back, the sisters clamored for her to join their march to the dean's house. Although her face betrayed no change in emotion, Dan saw the swift flick of exchanged glances between her and Lee. They were good friends, then. And they both felt the march was childish. Maybe Kit Cameron wasn't so dumb, after all.

She gave the girls a piercingly sweet smile. "I can't really. I'm busy tonight."

They did not insist and she did not explain. He could understand why anyone would shy away from pressing her. Even with the pantry-door window separating them, he could sense the barrier she had erected between herself and the rest of humanity. Formidable and forbidding—but unbreachable? Could she be stormed and taken? he wondered. It never occurred to him that she might have already been stormed and taken. No, not she. There was something untouched about her, something virginal. Virginal! In 1967! It was enough to make you laugh out loud. Dan Copeland knew his women, and he knew all about these ultra-controlled types. Underneath, they were seething, unerupted volcanoes. Well, she'd never get the chance to break out, not dating jerks with names like Whitney Whatever the Third. What she needed was a real man, a Dan Copeland.

As Bessie piled his tray with crystal dishes of English trifle, he realized he didn't really care *what* she was like. All he wanted at this moment was the chance to drag her off to his bed, by her long and glorious hair if necessary. Ten minutes with her, that's all he wanted.

Out of the corner of his mouth he reminded Willard, "The Sweetheart of Sigma Chi is mine." He hipped the swinging door open. He saved her for last, handing out the dishes in his best style. Then, bending low beside her, he put the dessert in front of her.

"Your trifle, Miss Cameron. And may I add that I wouldn't mind trifling with you personally."

Her slim body stiffened slightly in the chair, and he felt a moment of panic. Had it come out wrong? Then she turned those bottomless eyes upon him and looked at him carefully. In an even, sweet tone, she said, "I just can't wait to hear what you'll come up with when we have Bessie's apple pandowdy."

He felt as if he were drowning in the depths of her eyes. That, and a bit shamed. He had expected confusion, a giggle maybe, or iciness. Not a wisecrack.

Her friend, Lee, the tall, hefty one with the rich voice,

laughed and murmured sardonically, *"Mene, mene, tekel, Dan Copeland."*

He whirled around to face her. She gave him a lop-sided smile, half humorous, half challenge.

"How do you know my name? And what did that garble mean?"

"Answer to number one: I work as a lowly slave at your Students' League—much too far down in the ranks to be noticed by the Head Slave Driver. I found it very funny to see the revered Head Slave Driver serving me my beef whaddyacallit tonight." She laughed again, to his discomfiture.

"Answer to number two," Kit Cameron chimed in. *"Mene mene tekel up-harsin.* The handwriting on the wall. Didn't you go to Sunday school when you were a kid?" Her expression didn't change, but her light, cool voice took on a subtle sonority as she intoned, "You have been weighed in the balance and found wanting."

He stood there, tongue-tied, like a doltish farmboy. Dan Copeland did not like to be at a loss at any time. But since his return from 'Nam, he had become used to being treated as an older, mature man. He liked the automatic deference, the automatic status. Actually, he was only a couple of years older than his classmates.

He found himself torn between whether to give a smart answer to the blonde vision—whom he desperately wanted to impress—or whether to turn the charm on Lee, who was working with his League. He was deeply involved with the League, trying to get it off the ground and make it into a force on campus, maybe even in town. He could use every willing pair of hands available. And yet, when Kit Cameron tapped him on the arm, he nearly jumped. A casual, unthinking touch like that, and the spark was rushing through his entire nervous system.

"Yes?" Anything you say, Sweetheart of Everyone's Eye. Anything.

"Mrs. Camberson is trying to get your attention."

The housemother was rosy with agitation. "Now, now, Daniel. You know the rules. No socializing on duty."

"Yes, ma'am." He left, feeling as if someone had hit him over the head. Stunned. Reeling. She was not to be believed. He hated everything Kitty stood for: wealth, privilege, snobbery, elitism, self-satisfaction, vanity, so-

17

rority life, the lot. But oh, my God, she was the most gorgeous, the most perfect female he had ever seen. She was every teenaged boy's fantasy as he fumbled with the pimple-faced reality that was his lot in life and love. Yet here she was, fantasy in the flesh, in the pale, perfect flesh, better than any imagining.

"And not for me," he exclaimed aloud, slamming pots and pans down near the dishwasher in the kitchen.

Bessie, fat and wheezing, gave him a shrewd grin sparked with gold. "You've tangled with Snow White, I see." She cackled.

Dan held down his irritation. "What do you mean, Bessie?"

"Humph! Can't fool *me*. I know your type. Used to having them fall all over you, ain't you? Well, not Miss Kitty Cameron, I'll tell you that. A cool one she is. And she's not interested."

"What does *that* mean?"

"Never you mind. If I know my boys, you'll find out for yourself soon enough. Now hand me that griddle over there, and look sharp."

At eight-fifteen, exhausted from the heavy kitchen work and the unaccustomed hours on his feet, he stumbled into the main library. A term paper had been assigned in Economics, and the library was on his way home. And there she was, at one of the big oak tables, Kit Cameron, hunched over a book, half a dozen others piled up on either side of her. Still impeccable, the low-hanging library light creating a silvery halo around that sleek, shining head. He stared at her for a long time, willing her to look up and see him, but she was oblivious. So when she had told the other girls she would be busy, it hadn't been for a date with what's-his-name (as he had assumed), but because she had work to do.

As he watched, she reached into her shoulder bag and brought out an Oreo cookie, carefully splitting it apart, scraping the vanilla filling off with her teeth. Dan gaped. He had done that as a kid. That's what all kids did with Oreos. But a goddess?

Without thinking about it at all, he walked over to her, bent over, and whispered, "Can I have one?"

Her head jerked up, a faint flush staining her ivory cheeks. Then she smiled. "Another Oreo junkie," she

18

whispered back. "Don't let it get around and I'll let you have one."

"Scout's honor." Two fingers, held up in childhood's gesture.

She dug a cookie out for him with a rustle of cellophane and began to split another for herself. The library lamp cast a warm pool of light over the two of them, enclosing them cozily. Dan flexed his mental muscles, preparing to charm her. If all went as planned, they'd be out of here—together—within five minutes.

"Excuse me," she whispered. "I have work to do." And down went that incredible face, bent over the books. A door might as well have slammed shut. The moment was over. He had been dismissed. And all he could think was, But girls *never* ignore me. He stood there, staring at the top of her head, feeling foolish. It was not a feeling he liked.

To hell with her, he decided. Just another spoiled sorority girl playing princess. Sweetheart of Sigma Chi! Well, sweetheart, Sigma Chi can have you! He marched out of the library, the books he had come for completely forgotten.

For the next few weeks he managed to play it very cool in the sorority house. He would treat her as he would treat any other girl. He would not think of her. He would not let her get to him. But she always looked so lovely and smelled so exotic, he was constantly fighting off an urge to touch her, just touch her . . . to feel the silken splendor of her hair, to see if that smooth, pallid skin was cool like alabaster, to determine if a real pulse beat in the hollow of that slender throat.

Still, he kept his distance. His only concession to this obsession with her was to make some sort of comment each dinner hour about the main course for the evening. "Chicken Kiev tonight. Watch your heart, it's instant cardiac arrest." "Feeling chilly? Red-hot chili." And when there was apple pandowdy for dessert one night, he put it down before her with the announcement: "Apple Pan-Hellenic. Nobody dowdy at *this* table."

She had always greeted his pathetic little puns with a smile, but this time she slanted a look up at him that stopped his heart and said, "I knew you'd do something clever with it."

19

She remembered! He wanted to kick up his heels and dance. She remembered the first thing she'd ever said to him, after all these weeks. He was amazed and disconcerted to find himself grinning and humming as he finished the cleanup that night.

A bitter wind was blowing across campus as he made his way home. Tomorrow was Halloween, and already the area was crowded with costumed students—costumed idiots, he thought—looking for any excuse at all to goof off and get high. Ghosts and goblins, witches and devils made ghoulish noises at him as he hurried along, collar turned up around his frozen ears. To hell with them all and their childishness, he thought.

The cold, the wind, and his irritation wiped away the euphoria he had felt in the Zeta Phi house earlier. Huh! Talk about childishness. And what about himself, carrying on like Tom Sawyer because Becky had given him a smile? Stupid, stupid, he berated himself. Even Benno, his roommate, had caught on, had been asking him why he sighed so heavily in his sleep. And when Dan denied everything, Ben grinned more broadly and said, "Then why are you blushing right now?" Blushing! Damn the fair complexion that went with red hair. He was damned if he would blush over *any* woman. Bending his head down to escape a sudden icy gust, he decided he had had enough. He was really going to wipe her out of his mind.

It didn't quite work. He kept seeing her around the campus; he couldn't help that. Now that he knew her, he could spot her half a mile away. He would go out of his way sometimes to cross her path "accidentally," hating himself because it was such a juvenile thing to do. And every time he did it, she would be walking with the quarterback, or the president of Student Government, or that big guy who headed up the Intra-Fraternity Council, Whit Harris. She always gave Dan a wave and a friendly "Hello," but dammit, she was never alone, never. After a few days of this, he deliberately kept out of her way.

It was just as well. The Students' League was his first love, and they were planning their first big demonstration: a peace march on the night of November 22, the anniversary of JFK's death. If they did it right, if they organized it well, people from the town of Hampton would come out and join those on campus. It could be the beginning of working together, of building political clout. And if the press picked up on it, the Students' League would suddenly become a real power on campus, not just another club.

For two weeks he worked at his studies by day, served dinner in the sorority house in a daze, and worked half the night at the League headquarters, which at the moment were in his and Ben's attic apartment. There were signs to be painted and envelopes to be stuffed and speeches to be written and marshals to be coached. He hardly thought of or noticed Kit Cameron; he was too exhausted. Before falling asleep the night before the march, he congratulated himself. *She isn't really that important. As soon as I got busy with real stuff, I just forgot all about her.* As he drifted off, another thought crept in: *Then why am I thinking about her now?*

It rained the night of the parade. Dan cursed and paced and kept turning the radio from station to station, until Ben laughed and said, "You'll never find it."

"Find what?"

"The magic station that says the clouds will go away and a bright moon will shine."

Dan cursed again and turned off the radio angrily. "No one will show, goddamn it. They won't show. Weeks of work and now—"

"And now the fickle finger of fate. Yeah, well, I think *everyone* will show."

Ben was right. Fulton Plaza, in downtown Hampton, was packed with people by six-thirty. The march was slated to start at seven. The rain had let up somewhat, but a fine, misty drizzle saturated the air and made the raw northeast wind even more bone-chilling. It was supposed to have been a candlelight march, and cartons of thick candles stood by the curb, soaking in the wetness, untouched. But every single person had brought a flashlight. When Dan stepped up on a box to survey the scene, they all flicked on their lights and waved them in the air, cheering. A great surge of warmth enveloped him. They knew. These people knew what had to be done and they did it.

Projecting his voice across the windswept plaza, he called, "Am I glad to see all you crazy, wonderful people

21

out here on a lousy night like this!" Then his voice was drowned out by cheers and whistles. He held up one hand and the noise ceased. "This proves it," he went on, his voice gathering strength with every word. "We can all work together. If we can do it on a rotten night like tonight, we can do *anything!*" More cheers.

"Okay!" he shouted. "Stay where you are until your marshal gets to you. You all know our Head Marshal, that fabulous fullback, Joe Rugowsky! Joe, get 'em going! Let's get moving!" The huge football player, draped in his scarlet rain poncho, was highly visible as he gave final orders to his group. More whistling and stomping erupted, and cries of "Go! Go! Joe! Joe!"

Dan stood back, watching the almost miraculous dividing of an amorphous mass into tight groups. Ben was off somewhere in the crowd, yelling in French and German, pulling the foreign students together. And there, in the middle, was the huge white silk banner of Pan-Hellenic. Dan wondered how many spoiled sorority girls would show up. Six? Three? People were still arriving, waving their flashlights. In one group were the ministers of the town's five churches with members of their congregations. And that group of middle-aged women had to be the Mothers for Peace Club. He scanned the plaza, making guesses. A thousand? Could there be a thousand people here tonight? Yes. Maybe more. A knot of excitement grew in his chest. It was going to be all right. It was going to work.

Then he heard Ben's voice from the other end of the square, amplified but distorted by the bullhorn: "Okay, everybody. Follow your marshal. We'll march around City Hall, then up the hill, ending at the Administration Building on campus. Leading us will be Mayor Cox, Congressman Pritchard, and Syracuse columnist Marjorie Lucas." There was some applause, but they were all more subdued now, recalling the tragic event they were commemorating. Slowly, slowly, the mass of raincoated bodies began to move. Flashlights were turned on and lifted up to shine into the lowering sky. Someone—a woman—began to sing "We Shall Overcome" in a powerful, rich contralto; and as the crowd moved off, away from Dan, the sound of singing swelled into the damp night air, sending shivers down his back.

Dan walked toward the end of the march. Benno, he knew, was up in front with Joe Rugowsky, but he wanted to be able to guide last-minute joiners into the line. There were quite a few of them, mostly townspeople, gawkers who had suddenly decided that they wanted to be part of it.

As they marched slowly around City Hall, a sudden shower pelted down. Ahead, he could hear squeals and shrieks, and a mass of umbrellas went up, their wet surfaces gleaming in the light of the street lamps like a herd of turtles.

Along University Place, at the turn to go uphill, the pace slowed slightly. Dan held his light down for a minute and put the hood of his slicker up over his hair. He was dripping wet but jubilant.

As the march resumed its former pace, he noticed that a new bunch had joined in at the end. Then he became aware of the high-pitched voices. Kids. Little kids, about a dozen of them, giggling and grinning, shepherded by a girl who had stupidly come out without a raincoat. She had put a scarf around her head, but it was soaked through, and straggles of wet hair clung to her cheeks and forehead. Her duffle coat was dark with rain. Poor kid. What a mess. He slowed down until he was near them and threw the beam of his flashlight on her. "Miss—" he began, and then stopped short. "You!" he exclaimed. "What —what are you doing here?"

Kit Cameron blinked into the glare of the flash. "Please! You don't have to give me the third degree!" He hastily lowered the light and moved closer to her. "What do you suppose I'm doing here?" she said. "I'm marching in your parade."

"But—but—*you?*"

Even in the semidarkness those clear eyes impaled him. "Why not me?"

"I . . . no reason. I just never pictured you doing this sort of thing, getting drenched . . ."

"Wanda, hold on to Duncan's hand, please. I don't want anyone getting lost." She turned back to Dan. "And just how *have* you pictured me? Never mind, I already know. Forever posing for the camera, or shopping for the right cashmere sweater, or giggling over a serenade. Sure! That's it, all right." She scowled as they walked along, shaking her head violently so that showers of droplets flew out around her. "You think you're so forward-looking, so rational, so—special. But you think in stereotypes, too, just like the rest of them. Pretty girls are stupid! Q.E.D."

"No . . . I . . ." he spluttered.

But she kept right on talking, her voice still low and controlled, only the way she bit off each word showing her anger. "Well, if you must know, I think this kind of march is stupid. I don't think they're worth the time—which could be much better spent, I should think, working to make real changes where all the real changes are made—within the government!"

"The government! That's crazy! The government wants war!"

"This—" She waved her hand. "This won't accomplish a thing."

"That's where you're completely wrong, my lady! This—" He waved his hand in imitation. "This—and thousands of other demonstrations just like it—will eventually *end* the war. You'll see!"

They sloshed on side by side for a few moments without speaking. Then Dan said, "And anyway, if you think this is all so stupid and hopeless, what are you doing here?"

"If you must know, my kids voted for it."

"Your kids?"

"The Morton Street Settlement House. You may not have heard of it; it's not on campus, where all the action is. But I work there twice a week as a volunteer. We were supposed to bake cookies tonight, but they wanted to pay honor to the memory of Kennedy." She added something else in a sour murmur.

"What?" His mind was busy trying to sort out all these new impressions of her. Gone the impeccable goddess. Gone the detached beauty. Gone the pristine perfection. Here she was, sopping wet, in charge of a raggle-taggle band of kids, arguing. A human being. For the first time she was a real, live person. "What did you say?"

"I said, they could pay much more honor to Kennedy by getting their parents to vote regularly. Do you know, only twenty-eight percent of the townspeople voted in the last election. How's this march going to convince them their votes count?"

"I'm telling you," Dan said grimly, "marches and demonstrations like this are going to end the war. This is the voice of the people, too, you know."

"Humph! Two or three big shots at the top, where decisions are made, are going to end this war—when they're good and ready."

"The people—"

"The powers—"

They stopped, glaring at each other. Her eyes were snapping. With the back of one hand, she pushed at the wet wisps of hair on her forehead. She was so lovely. Even now, annoyed as she was, there was something still about her . . . something still and deep and untouched. He stared into the endless depths of her sea-colored eyes.

"The people count," he murmured, quite suddenly, and without any warning, in love with her.

"Only one by one." Her voice, too, had taken on a hushed quality.

"One . . . by one," Dan repeated, and reached out for her. Somehow she was in his arms, eyes still intent upon his, her small white face tipped up, bedewed with droplets of rain. "Oh, my God," he muttered, and brought his mouth down on hers.

Her lips quivered slightly under his, soft and warm and, after a second or two, tremulously responsive. He kissed her gently, questing with his lips, feeling something like delirium sear through him. The delicate scent of her skin surrounded him, and he tightened his grip around the slender body in its wrappings of damp wool. This was it. There was no doubt at all. Holding her was coming home. How could he have thought she was all wrong for him? This was right, so right. He lifted his head, to look at her. Her eyes were wide open, searching his.

"Kitty . . ." This was the first time he had called her by name, and he repeated it for the sheer pleasure it gave him. "Kitty."

"The march. We've been left behind." Her voice sounded rusty, as if it hadn't been used for weeks.

"To hell with the march. You were right. What counts is people, one by one. And you—you're the one for me." He bent his head, eagerly seeking her mouth.

But she turned her head slightly, so that his lips found the smoothness of her cheek. "The kids. I've really got to catch up."

Dan pulled her closer, insistent. "Don't you know what's just happened to us?"

She gave a shaky little laugh, pushing at him gently. "I know what's just happened to me. I've been kissed—and very nicely, too."

"Don't *do* that!" His voice was fierce. "Very nicely kissed is not what was happening. What was happening is that you're mine now. *Mine!*"

Kit's face tightened. "I belong to no one." Her body, so pliant and yielding a few moments before, became ramrod-stiff. He could feel her quiver with the need to be free. He dropped his arms, suddenly conscious of the cold, the wind, the wetness, and he shivered.

The cool little sorority-house smile. The pleasant little sorority-house voice. "You're supposed to make a speech, aren't you? You don't want to be late for that." As if nothing at all had gone on between them.

She moved off, half walking, half trotting, toward the straggling end of the parade. By taking long strides he was able to stay with her, but they didn't speak. Not until she had found her knot of children did he grab her arm, force her to look at him, and grate, "Fight it all you want, Kit. But you belong to *me*."

He dropped her arm angrily and plunged into the heart of the crowd. He would have her, he *would* have her, if it took him till the end of the spring semester!

"This is Captain O'Brien. We are ahead of schedule and will be landing at the Oswego County airport in ten minutes. The stewardesses will collect your glasses. Have a good day."

Dan blinked and shook his head. That rain-filled chilly night had been so real, so alive. That first kiss seemed still warm on his lips. But it was so long ago now, light-years away, the dream of a dream. He had vowed to have her if it took him the whole next semester. He smiled sadly at the self-confident, impatient young man he had been then. He had spent the rest of his college years trying to claim her. The pattern had never changed from that first kiss. She had always come to him eagerly, longingly, only to retreat in the end. Something inside her had always been afraid to let go. She had loved him, he knew she had loved him. Why had she always fought it so violently?

Even in Italy . . . but he could never bear to remember Italy. It had been glorious, glorious, but that afternoon in Florence had signaled the final defeat, the final negation of his love. Since then, a vital part of him had been locked away where no woman could reach it, not even the woman he had married.

Lights flashed at the front of the cabin. Dan automatically fastened his seat belt and put all depressing thoughts firmly into the back of his mind. It was normal, he supposed, to find yourself in the past when you were on your way to a class reunion. But you didn't have to *stay* there.

The priest next to him stirred and stretched.

"Feeling better, Father? We're coming down now."

A groggy smile. "Over, is it? Thank God." He crossed himself. "Fast asleep is the only way I can manage a plane trip."

They chatted for a few moments about fear, while Dan's mind raced ahead. He knew she would be there; he had had the lists checked months ago. Of course, Whit would be there, too, and that might prove awkward. But at such a huge gathering there ought to be a few minutes when he could arrange to see her, to touch her hand, to look into her eyes, perhaps even to speak with her.

What would she say? How would she be? Would she look at him blankly, seeing him as just another face from the far-off past, as nobody special? His stomach knotted and he chided himself, only half amused. For all these years he had been constantly "on stage." Courtroom trials, newspaper interviews, TV shows, speeches, debates, confrontations, the works. He could wheel and deal with the best of them. He could spout statistics off the cuff, or come up with a joke to relieve the tension.

Come on! he scolded himself. You're a successful man. A comer. Perhaps the next congressman from the Eighteenth. And after that? There's no limit.

But even as he lectured himself, his palms were damp with nervous sweat. Talk about fear, he thought. Worse than a roomful of antagonistic reporters, worse than summing up for an unfriendly jury, worse than trying to convince a heckling, hostile crowd—worse than all of these together was the sick anticipation in the pit of his stomach at the thought of seeing Kit Cameron again.

CHAPTER TWO

Katherine Cameron Harris

SHE FELT NOTHING. For one horrible moment there was no sensation of having a body at all. Kit pushed herself bolt upright, splashing steamy water all over the redwood planking of the bathroom floor, and wiggled her legs. The sudden clutch of panic dissolved and she tried to laugh at herself.

"Sitting *too* quietly," she murmured. The water in the new sunken hot tub was 105 degrees Fahrenheit, very relaxing. Perhaps too relaxing, she thought. She'd have to watch it or she'd fall asleep and drown.

Whit would be appalled, of course, she thought wryly. He'd paid many thousands of dollars to have this wing built onto the old mansion. It was supposed to be hers, her private space, but he casually brought all his business associates through to point out the open shower with the drain hidden cleverly in the floor; the raised redwood section with the tub built right in; the narrow, floor-to-ceiling windows; the clever way his architect had joined the bathroom to the dressing room. "She gets the most spectacular view on the North Shore," he would say proudly, "yet there's complete privacy." And he would crowd them into the tiny garden—*her* garden!—created in the corner between the wing and the original house.

No, it would not do at all to have an accident in one of Whit's latest acquisitions. Not to mention the damage that might be done to one of his other belongings: herself.

No more of that, she scolded herself, and looked out one of the windows, at her much-vaunted view. It certainly was spectacular. If she looked one way, she saw past the ancient hemlocks and spruce, down past the leafy tops of the oaks and maples—now scarlet and gold—to the rolling lawns and the formal gardens glowing at this time of year with yellow and russet mums; down, down the carefully tended slopes to where the Harris land ended abruptly at the edge of a cliff. Below there were, suddenly, sand dunes tumbling over a narrow beach and the salt water of Long Island Sound.

If she turned the other way, she was gazing at a miniature Italian garden, walled in stone and cozy. A two-foot-tall stone cherub sat plumply among the dusky pink geraniums, forever beating his stone drum and smiling impishly. Over all curved a grape arbor, now covered with large, round, almost black Concord grapes. Today was so unseasonably warm, she had opened one of the sliding glass doors, and the rich, pungent smell of the grapes wafted in to her.

Whit had planned a Henry Moore, large and overwhelming for that space, but she had insisted on a small garden. "And I want my angel there." Her husband had made a face—things generally had little value for him unless they were old or famous or high-priced—but he had not pressed her. In the end, she had to admit, Whit never forced anything upon her, including himself. It was something to be grateful for.

"There's a lot to be grateful for!" she said aloud, annoyed with herself. She had a life most women only dreamed of. "And all you can do is . . ." She did not finish the thought, but stood abruptly and stepped up out of the tub, stretching her hand for the thick, lush towel that always hung, neatly folded, on the heated towel bar. She dried off carelessly, reflected in the wall of mirrors opposite, but she refused to look in that direction.

Kit Harris never looked at herself in a mirror if she could help it. It was an old habit. She had been told too often, for too many years, how beautiful she was, until it seemed to her that people never spoke to her of anything else. She knew that being beautiful made some things easier for her, but she was unable to feel gratitude for the genetic accident that had made her the way she was. She had never known anything else, and it had always made trouble in the end . . . much more trouble, she was sure, than it was worth.

And anyway, she knew what she would see if she looked at the reflection: a small, slender body with skin the pale creamy white of the true blonde, still firm-hipped and high-breasted. Only the slight curve of the belly revealed that this woman was over thirty and had borne a child.

Absently, Kitty smoothed lotion onto her arms and legs. Pale skin might look ethereal, but it had its drawbacks. It burned in the sun, chapped in the wind, reacted to rough surfaces, and had to be cared for constantly. Lily, luckily, had escaped that fate. As much as she looked like her mother—and even Kitty could see the astonishing resemblance now that Lily had outgrown her baby plumpness—thank heavens she did not have moon-child skin. Lily browned like a cookie, and her little nose was splattered with freckles. Kit's hand paused as she pictured her daughter, and she smiled.

"You're still a beautiful woman, Katherine." Her husband's penetrating baritone behind her gave her a start, and she dropped the lotion bottle. After all these years, she still couldn't accustom herself to Whit's sudden appearances. For such a large, muscular, booming man, he moved very silently, as if on cat's feet.

"You startled me," she said, picking up the bottle and reaching for her robe on the back of the chair. "I thought you'd left ages ago." She gave his reflection in the glass a smile.

Whit was an imposing man, looking somehow much more solid and settled than a thirty-two-year-old man usually did. There hung over him the specter of middle age, ready to envelop him. This impression had nothing to do with his smooth, closely shaven face, which was only lightly creased at the corners of his eyes from hours spent on the tennis court or the golf course. Rather, it was his air of total command. He always seemed to fill the entire room, wherever he was. Her spacious bath had, in a moment, shrunk with his presence, leaving barely enough room for her.

Involuntarily, she took a step or two back and then covered the movement swiftly, saying, "You look marvelous. Whatever it is you intend to convince them of, I'm sure you'll be successful."

His eyes flew to his image in the mirror, as if to reassure himself of her appraisal. He needn't have, she thought. He always looked impressive—always had, even in college when everyone else made a point of appearing scruffy. Unlike many men, he cared deeply about his appearance and spared no expense to ensure that the image was exactly the one he wanted. She knew that the gray pinstriped suit he wore, for instance, had been cut and fitted by an English tailor flown over from London. The glossy shoes were one of a dozen pair made from his last by an expensive Italian bootmaker. The pale yellow shirt was pure silk, custom-made, and monogrammed; the tie, a blend of gray, yellow, and gold, had his family crest woven into it. He liked to say that a man his size needed careful tailoring. Sleek and well fed, that was how he appeared to her, and she often thought—but never said— that it was a good thing he was so active or he would become quite fat.

Having checked himself over, he gave a nod of approval and answered her remark. "Don't you worry, it'll go well. I've done my homework."

"You always do," Kit murmured.

He came closer. "I know I'm always away on business. We've hardly seen each other these past months. But once the Washington meetings are out of the way . . ."

"By tomorrow, I hope."

"Tomorrow?" He frowned.

"The reunion at Hampton," Kit said. "You haven't forgotten! Our tenth reunion. I'm going in an hour."

"Oh, damn! Yes, it *had* slipped my mind for the moment. And I have to go, don't I? There's that presentation. Too bad." He took a small leather notebook and a gold pen from his inside jacket pocket and scribbled a few lines. "I could better use my time at Burning Tree, playing golf with Senator Crawford. I'm sure he's the key to that bill we're interested in . . . Well, it can't be helped."

Kitty busied herself with the bottles on her dressing table. "Wouldn't you like to go just to see it all again? After all, we did meet at Hampton."

He laughed. "Women! So sentimental!" Her head still down, she winced a little, sensing what was coming next. "It's a good thing," he said, "that *I'm* the president of Harris Pharmaceuticals and *you're* in charge of advice to the lovelorn."

She knew he despised the column she wrote. But why was that the only thing he ever mentioned, when he was well aware that she wrote other things, too? Better things. A familiar knot formed in her stomach as she bit back the bitter words she longed to say.

He padded up behind her and wrapped his arms around her waist, bending his head to nuzzle damply at the back of her neck. "God, but you're lovely," he said. "There isn't a man I know who doesn't envy me my beautiful wife." He chortled, and his voice dropped to a husky whisper. "But *I* have you, Katherine, don't I?" His big soft hands slid up, under the open front of the robe, and curled around her breasts. Kit held herself very still. He kneaded her flesh casually, in almost the same way that he would fondle a new cashmere sweater or the latest horse for his stables. All she had to do, she knew, was to shrug away from him and his hands would drop. He had already registered his ownership, and the ownership was what gave him his pleasure. In spite of her disinterest, her nipples hardened under his fingers, and he immediately pressed his loins heavily into her back.

"That's right," he whispered. "It's been a long time." His hands left her breasts and crept down to the tender skin of her belly. She held her breath so as not to reveal her panic.

But he sighed gustily and released her. "Wish I had time . . ."

Kit gave a shaky laugh. "Can't fit me into your schedule?" It was meant to be a lighthearted joke, but the words came out tight and hard.

"Hey!" Whit took hold of her shoulders and turned her to face him. "You know this is an important meeting."

Might as well let him think I'm disappointed, Kit thought, putting a sulky look on her face.

"I said I'd make it to the reunion and I will," Whit went on. "I'll meet you at the dorm on Saturday before the big game—no, wait a minute, make that Saturday evening. That way we can still get in nine holes at Burning Tree. And then you and I can have Saturday night, eh? Just the two of us. And we'll do some of that Good Stuff."

He consulted his watch. Instantly the softness of desire was wiped out of his eyes. All business once more, he leaned over to kiss her. Kitty deftly turned so that his lips landed on her cheek.

Whit stepped back. His voice sharpened. "Now, see here, Katherine. Don't imagine I haven't noticed how you've been blowing hot and cold lately—and mostly cold, I might add. I'm a patient man, as you well know, but there's a limit. I can't help being busy. I don't know what's wrong with you, but whatever it is . . ." He shook his head and finished in a quieter tone. "You're my wife, Katherine, and you have . . . obligations." He looked her over carefully and smiled. "It will be my pleasure to remind you of them, Saturday night." He picked up his attaché case and was out the door as soundlessly and swiftly as he had appeared.

Kit didn't move for a moment or two after he had left. How like Whit, she thought, to consider *his* pleasure only. She had just been given her orders: You, Katherine, my personal possession, will submit to me, Whitney Harris the Third, on Saturday night according to my schedule of events for the evening.

Oh, *damn!* She belted the robe firmly about her waist, knotting it tightly, as if she could tie herself so he could never reach her again. Why, why did she feel this way all of a sudden? Why, after ten years of a marriage she herself had chosen, of lovemaking which—while never exactly ecstatic—had certainly been satisfactory, did she find herself shrinking from his very touch? Lately, she had feigned sleep on those rare occasions when he slipped into her room at night, and had breathed a sigh of relief if he left instead of sliding under the bedclothes to insistently kiss her awake.

She padded barefoot into the large dressing room with its neatly banked closets in which her wardrobe was carefully arranged: blouses, then shirts, skirts, then pants, then jackets by color. Cream, putty, cinnamon, mushroom, ivory, all her favored pale neutrals, and one section of everything black. She shook her head as she surveyed the array of elegant and expensive clothing. Her wardrobe was under the exclusive care of a sharp-eyed Frenchwoman named Anne-Marie. Her personal maid! Kitty still couldn't quite get used to the idea of servants; she was forever feeling guilty about them. Hating them, almost. Her whole childhood Mama had fussed over her clothes and her body and her hair, until she'd been thoroughly sick of it. When she had finally managed to escape to Hampton, she'd been delighted to do for herself without other eyes constantly measuring her and looking for tiny flaws.

She sighed, chose lacy underwear and panty hose from a drawer, and began to dress. It *was* nice to have lovely things; of course it was. One of Whit's great joys, when they were first married, had been to take her to Tiffany's or Henri Bendel's and order her to pick out anything she wanted, anything at all.

What has he ever done for me that wasn't generous? she chided herself. He's been so good to me, and to Lily. I must never forget how well he took care of Lily, how different everything might have been if he hadn't wanted me so badly.

Drifting into the large bedroom with its lacquered Japanese furniture and huge tropical plants, she eyed the corner screen hiding her desk, typewriter, and armoire stuffed with office supplies.

"I ought to write myself a letter," she said, smiling at the thought. As far as her friends knew, Kit Harris wrote articles for the Sunday edition of *Newsday,* the large Long Island newspaper, on all kinds of topics: old mansions, the favorite dog breeds, a little-known library filled with treasures, the best beaches—all having to do with Long Island.

But her favorite writing was a secret, to everyone but Whit. Only he knew that Kit was "Trudy," author of "Tell It to Trudy," a wildly popular daily feature of the newspaper. Like Ann Landers and Dear Abby, Trudy answered all kinds of questions and gave advice on all kinds of problems, in a tart-sweet, relaxed style.

"Dear Trudy," Kit murmured as she began to dress in the chamois suit and silk shirt laid out by Anne-Marie. "I have been happily—no, make that *nicely* married—no. I have had a perfectly satisfactory marriage for ten years. As a matter of fact, I proposed to my husband. He knew I wasn't madly in love with him, but he wanted me so badly—no, leave that out. We made a bargain; he got what he wanted and I got what I wanted. And now, Trudy, suddenly out of nowhere, I seem to want . . .

something else. And I don't know what that something else *is!* I feel . . ."

But she didn't know how she felt. Smothered. Stultified. Standing still. Cornered. Trapped. Restless. But *why?* None of those was true. She didn't even see Whit half the days of the week; he was forever off on business trips. Her money was her own; she was free to travel or take up yoga or invest in a gold mine or do whatever struck her fancy. He paid all the bills and asked very little in return. That she be his hostess, that she not disgrace him, that she run the household (but the servants really did that, and very well, too). And that she sleep with him. That had never bothered her before. Whit Harris's drives were mostly toward money and power. His physical demands had never been very great. And he was far from repulsive: big and blond and strong and athletic. She often caught avid looks on the faces of other women at the country club as they watched him at tennis or on the dance floor. But lately, for some reason, she could not bear it when he thrust into her body, burying his head in her shoulder, moving mindlessly in a regular rhythm until he was done, never looking at her, never saying a word until afterward. And then it was always the same word: "Good," in the same, self-satisfied tone.

"Dear Trudy, he's never once asked me if *I* thought it was good," Kitty said, and then laughed shortly at herself. What would Trudy answer if some other woman had written that letter? "You say you made a bargain. A marriage is not supposed to be a business deal. Looks to me as if both parties are being cheated."

Cheated. She did not like the sound of that word. I've always been honest with Whit, she told herself, and then flushed deeply. Well, not always, perhaps. But I've always kept my side of the bargain and I always will.

There. That was settled. No more nonsense. On Saturday night she would have a few drinks and go obediently into her husband's arms. And now she would check over the clothes she would take for the weekend.

They were carefully, lovingly, laid out for her appraisal: costly, rich, beautifully tailored things. She fingered a cashmere shirt absently and then threw it from her. What was she doing with all these . . . things? And what did they *mean?* She paced nervously at the foot of the bed, glowering at her beautiful clothes.

Anne-Marie came to the door. "Madame, you are not happy with the selection? You would like something different? The Givenchy instead of the Norell?"

Oh, for God's sake, Kitty thought in irritation. Who cares? But she smiled at the maid and replied, "No, it's lovely, Anne-Marie. Pack it just as it is. And have it in the car by eleven o'clock."

"I *know* at eleven," Anne-Marie said in an aggrieved tone to her mistress's departing back.

She watched the slight figure turn the corner with a graceful movement, shoes and jacket still in hand, and start down the long, carpeted corridor. Anne-Marie shook her curly head and tightened her lips in disapproval. Just look at how Madame had thrown down the beautiful cashmere—as if it were a piece of trash! And she was usually so caring of her lovely things. Madame was, Anne-Marie knew, a great lover of beauty, beauty of *any* kind. If a flower in the gardens were trampled or broken accidentally, she would pick it up tenderly, frowning at its death.

But she had been very different lately. Yes, Anne-Marie decided as she deftly folded each item on the bed into its own sheet of rustling tissue paper, there had been a change. Once so busy that she always seemed to generate energy, now Madame would often stand very still, gazing into some inner space, lost in a world of her own. Then she would sigh deeply and shake her head, as if to say *"Non"* to her own thoughts. At these moments, the maid had discovered, Madame would hear nothing, not even her own name.

And she would become irritated—at *nothing*, Anne-Marie thought, automatically placing the folded garments neatly into the leather suitcase, saving the top space for the Grecian-style silk nightgowns and the simple robe of heavier silk. Anne-Marie loved Madame's underclothes: all silk and all of the same ivory tint as her skin, and just a shade lighter, perhaps, than her hair. She loved to choose Madame's clothes, but lately Madame—formerly the most gracious, the easiest, of employers—could not be satisfied. She would try on four different outfits, discard them all, then pick up the first one from the pile on the floor—from the floor!—and put it on, muttering to herself.

There were other signs, too. Anne-Marie prided herself on her perceptiveness. As she often told the other servants, "Me, I am *française,* and the French, they miss nothing." Her sharp eyes noted the many times Madame shrank away, ever so slightly and ever so delicately, from Monsieur. They had never been what one might call a *passionate* couple. They were both cool, correct, pleasant; theirs was a truly civilized marriage. But something was happening . . . not to Monsieur, *non;* he remained, as always, strong and calm, a true man of affairs. But Madame—her beautiful, serene, contented mistress—it was obvious she was having a *crise de nerfs,* and Monsieur, like all men, was blind to it.

Anne-Marie surveyed the layered suitcase, mentally checking off each item in it, nodding to herself with satisfaction. Of course, she mused, in a situation like this, one usually looked for another man, especially a younger, beautiful man such as the gardener's new assistant, the dark and muscular Raymond with the wicked brown eyes. But Anne-Marie had watched very carefully, and Madame had shown no interest in Raymond nor in any other man. No change in the daily schedule. No long lunches, no unexplained late evenings out. If anything, Madame worked even longer hours at the typewriter, sometimes late into the night, without a bite to eat. It wasn't a love affair, then.

Packing the lovely old ivory-backed brushes—antiques that Monsieur had found on a business trip to England—the maid was suddenly reminded of a little scene that had taken place several weeks before.

Dressing for an evening at the country club, Madame had uncoiled her splendid hair, letting it hang loose and shining like satin all the way to the curve of her derriere.

She had waved Anne-Marie away with a smile. "No, let me." And she had brushed her hair herself, pulling it back behind her tiny ears and tying it with a ribbon—a ribbon!—like her child, Lily!—and then had said, "Well, Anne-Marie? What do you think?"

Think? What *could* one think? And then she had rummaged through her bookcases in the other room and come back with a big book of red leather—her yearbook, she had called it—and opened it to show Anne-Marie the little picture of herself taken in 1970, the face exquisite but unmarked by life, a tiny smile like the Mona Lisa, and the hair worn long and shining and childlike, just as she had arranged it now.

The maid's dark eyes snapped with pleasure as she recalled her response that day. *"Non,"* she had said unequivocally. "It is attractive, of course, but it is not you, Madame. You are a lady of . . . *importance, vous comprenez?* Monsieur, he would not approve, I think."

"Indeed?" Madame had eyed herself in the mirror—a bit sadly, Anne-Marie had thought. "No, no, of course not. Not me. Not any more." And she had quickly coiled her hair back into its usual Psyche knot, revealing the slim column of her neck.

Nothing very dramatic; yet it seemed to Anne-Marie that the fixing of the hair had hidden something else, something *très important*. Ah! Then perhaps Madame feared the passing of the years. She was leaving today for a reunion with her classmates. Perhaps she looked deeply into her mirror and saw the passing of the years. Silly *petite!* A woman became only more beautiful with experience! Any Frenchwoman knew that. And Anne-Marie, just a bit past twenty-nine, gave herself a knowing wink in the mirror.

Kitty trotted down the thickly carpeted curved stairway, humming a little under her breath to break the heavy silence. The house was hushed, as very large houses have a way of being when they are not filled with people. Usually she reveled in this pool of quiet, but not this morning. Too many unbidden thoughts were rising to the top of her mind. It would be much better once she had picked up Lee in New York. And then . . . reunion. The picture-postcard campus with its lush lawns and cobbled walks, ivy-covered buildings of mellow old brick, columned fraternity houses, wide streets bowered with lines of ancient trees. She smiled, heavy with nostalgia. She had been very happy in college, her four years of freedom. It would be so good to see them all: Lee, the other sorority sisters, maybe some of the professors . . . Benno might be there, Benno and— A face, a particular lean and chiseled face, edged into her consciousness, and from habit she pushed it swiftly back. The forbidden face that brought with it forbidden memories. Silently, she recited her litany: I am rich, I am cherished, I have a wonderful daughter and a wonderful job, I'm healthy and in my right mind, I have everything.

"Everything," she announced in a loud voice as she came to the bottom of the long staircase. She could hear, from somewhere at the other end of the house, a muffled drone. Mrs. Decker, hard at work with the vacuum. Delicious smells wafted from the direction of the kitchen, where Cook was doubtless turning out a masterpiece that only Lily would be home to eat that evening. If, in the way of nine-year-olds, she did not suddenly decide that *veau cordon bleu* was not to her taste and that she would much rather have a plain hamburger with french fries: "Please, Cook, please, please, please, you do them so well."

Unexpected tears pricked at the corners of her eyes. Damn! What in the world was the *matter?* "I have everything," she repeated stubbornly. This was an incantation which normally dispelled all gloom or irritation. But nowadays the magic spell refused to alleviate her confused emotional state. It was like trying to paint over a rotten surface, with the ugly, damaged spots underneath always seeping through.

Skipping her usual quick survey of the beautiful rooms she had decorated with such care, she headed for the breakfast room at the back end of the house. Lily should still be there, if she hadn't gone riding. A bad cold had kept her from school most of this week, and although she seemed better, Kitty had heard her coughing in her sleep last night. So she had left a note on the child's night table that she should stay home on Friday, too.

Actually, she was glad for the excuse; she wanted a chance to see Lily before she left. Why it was so important to see her daughter before this particular trip, she did not know. The most obvious reason she refused to think about—and besides, he would most likely not even be there. She had read in *Newsweek* magazine that he was running for Congress; surely a college weekend was low on his list of priorities.

No, there was something else about this weekend trip, something more portentous and worrisome. Even though she was traveling only three hundred miles upstate, it seemed farther away than the moon, perhaps because of her feeling of going far away in time. Which is longer, she wondered wryly, ten thousand miles or ten years?

Lily had not gone to the stables, although she was dressed for it, in jodhpurs, boots, and a shetland sweater. She sat at the verdigris wrought-iron table with its thick glass top, an enormous, mostly eaten breakfast spread out in front of her. Kitty saw the remains of a peanut butter sandwich, a banana skin, the crumbs from a slab of chocolate cake, and an empty carton of plain yogurt—all this besides the portion of eggs and sausages prepared by Cook. At the moment Lily was busily chewing on something, her head bent, totally absorbed in "Tell It to Trudy," the latest craze at her school.

"Good morning, baby."

Lily's face, a miniature of her own, tilted up, and she grinned. "Hi, Ma. You're all dressed up." She took another huge bite.

"Not so very. What are you eating *now?* After all that."

"Bagel and cream cheese."

"Lily!" Kit laughed and went to give the child a hug. "You're going to get fat!"

"No, I'm not. I'm growing."

So you are, her mother thought. How the years flew by. She caressed the soft, thick, tawny hair, remembering the fine pink fluff it had been when Lily was born. But she knew better than to say what she was thinking. Lily was, at the age of nine, the consummate cynic; her most common response to anything these days was likely to be "So what?" or "Yuck." Instead, Kit pressed her fingers on the smooth scalp and massaged; and Lily moved her head in response, saying, "Yum. That feels good."

For a few minutes they remained in silent closeness, two identical faces, the one creamy pale, the other as lightly browned as a biscuit.

"How do you feel today, baby? Cold nearly gone?"

"It's rotten. It's *never* going to go away. I'm going to have this cold *forever!*"

"I promise you, Lily Dilly, that by the time you are accepting your Nobel Peace Prize, you won't still have this cold. But do you feel really awful? I hate to go away for the weekend if you're not well."

Lily's demeanor changed dramatically, an impish sparkle appearing in her hazel eyes. "What, and keep you from your college ree-YOON-yun? With all the old people?"

"Old!" Kitty made a face.

Again the voice changed. "You gonna see all your old boyfriends there, Ma?"

To her surprise and dismay, Kitty felt hot color climb in her cheeks. "Don't be ridiculous."

"Old boyfriends can be disappointing."

"Ha! The voice of authority! Who says?"

Lily waved the newspaper. "Trudy. There's a letter here today about a woman whose old boyfriend moved in across the street, and he's getting *very* friendly and she wants to know what to do."

Kit finally recalled the letter; she wrote her answers days before they were printed. A woman from Roslyn, in a very exclusive neighborhood. "And that's what Trudy said? That old boyfriends can be disappointing?"

Lily scanned the column and read: "'Since he seems happily married and you say you are, it's time to cut the fantasies and come back to reality. What's over is over, and old loves revisited'—she stumbled over the last word —'tend to be disappointing.' "

"Mmmm. Very wise of her," Kitty said, trying not to smile.

"Really? *All* of them?"

"All of who, sweetie?" Kit poured herself a mug of coffee from the silver pot and sipped it.

"All your old boyfriends. Some of them must have been nice."

"Daddy was my boyfriend," Kitty said lightly.

"I know that. But Daddy says you had *tons* of them. He says you were Sweetheart of something, I forget the name. He says he had to fight them off with a club." Lily giggled.

"Daddy likes to exaggerate."

"Well?" Lily demanded. "*Are* you?"

"Are I what, baby?" Kit took a last sip and put the cup down on the table. It was nearly eleven. Martin had probably already brought the car around.

"Are you going to see any old boyfriends?"

"I really don't know. I haven't the slightest idea who I'll

41

see . . . except for Aunt Lee, of course." And maybe . . . but it didn't matter, even if he were to come. It didn't matter. It was all so long ago and far away, a different time and a completely different life. And she should remember what Trudy said about old loves revisited. Trudy, after all, was a wise old bird. She had to smile.

"But if you *do* see one," the child persisted, "will you kiss him?"

"Lily! What a question! Come give me a kiss yourself. It's time for me to leave."

The little girl eagerly leaped from her seat and flung herself at her mother, snuggling into her. "I can't kiss you, Mommy," she said in a muffled voice. "I'll give you my germs."

Kitty bent her head and kissed the strawberry-blonde hair. "That's okay. You give me some of your germs, and I'll bring you something really icky from the reunion, okay?"

Lily was still giggling as Kitty hurried down the hallway to the front of the house. She stopped for a word with Mrs. Decker, who was now surveying the huge living room for specks of dust which might have escaped her eagle eye. Kitty particularly loved this room with its huge fieldstone fireplace centered on one wall, and opposite, a double set of French doors leading onto a wide brick and stone terrace. It was mostly honey-colored, filled with comfortable down-cushioned couches, warm lights, and a collection of sculpture gathered from the four corners of the earth.

In a way, she was reluctant to leave it: not just this room, but the house, her life, her child, the familiarity of everything. Stop this! she thought with disgust. Say goodbye, like a big girl, get out the door, and *go!*

Outside, the air was fresh, warm with sunlight, and fragrant with leaves, drying grasses, and turned earth. It smelled as the campus always had, each year when she went back to school in September. And, as had always happened at the beginning of every school year, a small knot of sickly-sweet anticipation lodged itself just under her ribs. A new start, when anything might happen!

The long silver Mercedes-Benz was in the drive, its motor humming quietly. Martin opened the rear door and she slid onto the leather seat, sinking back gratefully into its padded comfort. The car pulled smartly away with a crunch of gravel, down the curved roadway toward the big iron gates. Kitty turned to look out the back window. Perhaps she would see Lily's golden-red head at the window; but there was nobody in sight, only thick, slanted rays of sun highlighting the swirling dust kicked up by the car's wheels.

Soon the automobile was cruising swiftly along the highway, heading for New York City, a matter of perhaps an hour and a half. Kit stared blindly out the window and began to relax. It struck her that here, in the opulent back seat of the car, she was truly alone, truly private. There was a telephone in the Mercedes, of course, but it was up front and only Whit ever got calls on it, anyway. Martin was, at best, a phlegmatic man. It would take an emergency to make him speak to her.

She could allow herself to say it now. "Dan." There. The memory she had been fighting off for—how long? Since the alumni office's reunion announcement last Christmas? She couldn't remember exactly, and it didn't matter, not really. He had been haunting her.

All those years ago in Italy, the summer after graduation, she had made her decision, and that decision meant that Dan Copeland could not and must not ever again be a part of her life. How she had wept that morning in Siena's main square, sitting alone at a cafe table, the sweep of the enormous shell-shaped piazza facing her. She had never again been able to visit Siena, nor Florence either, the two loveliest cities in all of Italy. They were too full of bittersweet memories.

But she had successfully excised all thought of him from her life. And when he crept into her dreams, she would force herself to awaken. She would pace the floor so that she wouldn't fall back asleep to find him there yet again. Lily took up a great deal of her time, as did all the entertaining, the running of a very large house, the decorating, her articles, and the advice column. Her life was completely filled. She had made sure there was no room for Dan Copeland.

Yet now it must be faced. Today might very well be the day she would see him once more—not in blurry memory and not in the chaos of a dream, but Dan himself, real, alive, the dark eyes flashing beneath the copper-colored brows. Dan, tall and lean, vibrant and compelling, his voice a rich basso, the kind of voice that rumbled in your ear when you were lying with your head on his chest. The insistent intelligence that made such logical moves, that thrilled and hypnotized and—almost—made you forget where you were and who you were. Her breath caught in a piercing ache as his face, vivid and complete, flashed in front of her. Had she made a mistake, the mistake of her life? Oh, if only he hadn't been so domineering—and if she hadn't been so stubborn and single-minded! How differently everything might have turned out!

It had all seemed merely ordinary at the time: a clear, warm Saturday evening, full of the scent of early-blooming roses and evergreens. It was still light. She was strolling home from the bookstore, daydreaming about the coming trip to Italy with three of her sorority sisters. She wasn't even thinking of graduation or of graduate school or of anything very serious. The big oaks and maples rustled a little in the breeze, and as she rounded the corner by Fraternity Row, there was the sudden, tangy, delicious smell of just-mown grass. A quiet time of day, especially since everyone except seniors had already gone home for the summer.

And roaring out of University Place, a Yamaha motorbike painted in psychedelic colors broke the sweet silence and came to a spluttering halt beside her. She didn't even have to look to know who it was. Dan, in chinos, boots, and a blue and white helmet, giving her that sassy grin, as if he knew damn well how the sight of him always started her heart pounding.

"Hi, babe. Hop on and let's go."

The familiar exasperation flooded through her. For three years, in spite of anything she might say, he had always assumed that she never had anything to do, or that if she did, it couldn't be nearly as important as being with him.

"Nothing of the kind," she retorted. "I don't remember you calling me for a date tonight." He never did, which was the thing she hated the most. He just turned up. And every time he did, her heart turned over. Now he swept the helmet off, allowing the long, shaggy red hair to fall to his shoulders.

"I'm asking you now." He smiled at her, the dimple next to his mouth flashing. "Dates are for fraternity boys, my love, not for the likes of you and me. Can the middle-class manners and come have some *fun*. I've got a full tank of gas." He reached out and traced the line of her cheek softly with one finger.

Kitty shivered a little at his touch. How did he manage to do it to her every time? "I'm sorry," she said, "but as it happens, I *have* a date tonight."

The finger continued its light caress. "With Witless, I presume. The original Mr. Square. Will he bring you a gardenia in a little white box? I have something better." His deep voice teased, and he leaned over, precariously balanced on the motorbike seat, to bring his lips close to her ear. "I have something a *lot* better."

Kit's heart began an irregular thumping. "Don't," she murmured, unwilling to trust her voice further. Instantly, the impish gleam disappeared from his eyes, and she hated herself. "You can give me a ride home," she relented, as much to see the smile return to his face as to sit behind him, her arms tight around his slender waist, her cheek nestled against the hard muscles of his back.

In a moment they were off with an earsplitting roar. It was only a minute or two to the sorority house, but when they approached it, Dan put on extra speed and swerved around the turn to go up to Hillside Park. "Dan! Stop!" she yelled, but if he heard her, he gave no sign; and she was certain that she could hear his maddening, self-satisfied laughter above the awful noise of the engine. There was nothing she could do; she should have known he'd pull something like this. When he finally stopped this thing, she was going to give him what for. She had a date, made *weeks* ago, with a man who knew how to treat her. Dan, as usual, thought he could just ride right over any-one's plans or ideas or arguments—and that the person would love him for doing it. The big bully!

Hillside Park was not a manicured formal garden, but natural rolling woodland, with stands of young spruces and rock-sheltered nooks hidden by shrubbery. From one of the higher rises, where Dan was heading, you could see a slice of sparkling lake far below. He pulled up to a

copse of birches surrounded by soft new grass and turned
off the motor. The sudden silence was stunning at first.
Then she became aware of the chorus of birdsong filling
the air.

Kit slid quickly off the bike and glared at Dan, who
was balancing the machine between his legs.

"For a guy who fancies himself so sensitive to other
people," she gritted, "you show no consideration at all
when it comes to *me*."

"Why can't you ever be spontaneous?" he countered,
dismounting and propping the bike against a tree. "Here
we are, in one of nature's most beautiful spots, on a beautiful spring evening, and I even brought a picnic. And all
you can do is carry on like a spoiled sorority girl!"

"You know I can't stand this cave-man routine of yours
—being dragged off whenever you feel like it! I'm sick of
it! Now take me home! This time I'm *really* mad!"

"Really?" He smiled and held out his arms to her.
When she refused to respond, he came toward her, saying, "Don't you know this is home?" and scooped her into
his embrace.

For a minute she stood stiffly, resisting with all her
might. She loved the feel of his body; she seemed to fit
into him just right. His clean smell surrounded her senses;
his hands were big and warm on her back. She squinched
her eyes shut, willing herself to stay strong, but she was
painfully aware of every inch of him . . . of his cheek
rasping against her . . . of his lean, muscled body, so thin
but so strong.

In spite of herself, her arms crept up around his neck
and her head tilted back. His mouth came down, warm
and demanding, parting her lips with his tongue. When
he lifted his head for an instant, she had a blurred sense
of his eyes burning hotly into hers, and then he was kissing her again, almost brutally exploring her mouth. One
hand curved around her buttocks, drawing her tightly to
him, while the other hand pressed the back of her head.
He lowered her down onto the grassy knoll, his mouth
moving from her ear to her neck to the hollow of her
throat. She made a sound that was half sob, half plea.

It was always like this. They came together like metal
and magnet, clinging as if some law of nature forced them
together. He aroused something elemental and fierce in

her, an overpowering maelstrom of greed that her fastidious soul rebelled against. She was forever struggling against this utter loss of self, this desperate need of him, this degrading submissiveness.

He unbuttoned her shirt and nibbled at her collarbone, moving quickly down to the soft swelling of her breasts. She moaned, giving in once more, thrusting her hands under his shirt to rub his bare back. Impatiently, he pulled her shirt off, kissing her feverishly. Her senses swam and she drew his head closer, gasping. She felt his hand, warm and strong, on the tender flesh inside her thigh, and this time, she knew, there would be no stopping. A heavy throb of desire pounded in her ears and filled her senses.

For a moment the reverberations seemed to be coming from within her own body. The caresses stopped abruptly. Kit looked up at him. His eyes were wild, his teeth bared in a snarl.

She struggled and grasped his shoulders, shaking him. "Dan. What is it? What's wrong?" His face was frightening, so intent was the feral glare in his eyes.

Then he shuddered. "I thought it was gunfire. Stupid guns!" Once more he turned, intent upon her body, murmuring, "Relax. It's only the fireworks."

"The fireworks—the *fireworks!* Oh, my God!" She put both hands on his shoulders and shook him again. "Stop! Dan! I've got to get back. I *mean* it!" The weight of him was pressing on her. "Dan, stop!"

Pushing his long hair back from his flushed face, he rolled over and sat back on his haunches. "What is it this time, Kit?"

Frantically, she pulled on her disheveled clothing, buttoning her shirt with fingers that shook. "I should be with Whit right this minute at the fireworks. I told you I had a date. He was picking me up at seven-thirty—what time is it?"

"Oh, for—! Quarter to eight."

"I've got to get back. He'll be frantic!" What am I doing? she asked herself, ashamed. A moment ago I was on the verge of making love with Dan, and here I am, worried about my date with Whit. What's the matter with me? Why does he do this to me?

Dan sighed and put a proprietary hand on her shoul-

47.

der. "Come on, babe, forget Witless and those stupid fireworks. It's too late, anyway. And besides, I need you. Much more than he does. He doesn't turn you on. He doesn't really appreciate you, that cold fish."

"Oh, really?" She inched away from him, stood up, and tucked her shirt into the skirt. Not looking at him, she added, "He wants me to marry him."

Dan threw his head back and hooted. "Marry? *Him?* I could see him arranging a merger, maybe, but a marriage? What did he want in return, Kitty? Stock options?"

"Dan, what a horrid thing to say! You don't know him at all, but that doesn't stop you from making up your mind, does it? Well, I don't care what you think of him. It just so happens I have a date with him, and I'm going to *keep* it!"

Dan slid to a sitting position, knees up and arms around his legs. He grinned at her, as he always did whenever she became angry. "Well, I'm going to have my picnic now, so I guess you'll have to walk. You oughta be there by . . . oh, eight-thirty."

Kitty glared down at him, speechless.

"And anyway," Dan went on in a different tone, "you and I have serious things to discuss. I'm not taking you back to campus until we've settled this."

Her heart sank. She had been avoiding the subject for weeks. It was going to be the Peace Corps routine all over again. There must be a way of ending the discussion before it got started.

"Well," she said briskly, "I picked up my plane tickets to Italy this afternoon."

"Goddammit, Kit." He came abruptly to his feet. "Both our applications are in."

Avoiding his gaze, she said, "*I* never applied. You had no business putting my name in. I told you a hundred times that I didn't want to join the Peace Corps!"

"Forget what you told me. You don't know what you want. Once we're out of this phony-baloney-college-rah-rah atmosphere, you'll see that I'm right. My God, Kit, it's the most exciting opportunity in two hundred years to make real changes, and all you can say is, 'I'd rather help people one by one.' Of all the self-centered, out-of-date attitudes! Wake up, Kitty, wake up and join the world!"

His hands grasped her shoulders, digging into the tender flesh.

Her voice was cool and expressionless. "You're hurting me."

He dropped his hands, and his voice took on a deadly calm. "I'm hurting you? You're hurting *me*, Kit. After three years, isn't it clear to you that you're mine . . . that we belong *together?*" He bent his head to kiss her, but she pulled away angrily.

"That's your answer to everything. You'll kiss me and I'll forget everything else. Well, maybe you're right. Maybe I *do* forget everything else when you're holding me. And maybe I don't like it! I think that's how you *prefer* me: melting away and mindless. You don't just want us to be together; you want to conquer me, to *own* me!"

He laughed shortly. "I'm a man, babe, and that's how men are."

Kit felt her resolve harden. "Not all men," she said tightly. "Whit gives me space. *He* isn't forever trying to mold me and change me and teach me and control me. He likes me just the way I am."

Dan shook her. "Then you really are a dummy. Can't you see he thinks of you as a goddamn *asset?* He has a calculator for a heart, and pretty Kitty Cameron, the Sweetheart of Sigma Chi, is definitely on the credit side. He doesn't even know who you are. *I'm* the only one who knows you. Do you tremble when he holds you? Do you kiss him the way you kiss me? Of course not! Does he even kiss you at all, I wonder? There's not an ounce of blood in his veins, only accountant's ink!"

Damn him for knowing there was no passion with Whit. "Maybe I don't *like* constantly trembling in someone's arms. Maybe I *hate* it! Maybe I prefer being left alone!"

"Yeah, and maybe you like being the only virgin on campus. You want me. I know it and you know it. You want me to believe you'd rather be left alone? I've never forced you. For three years I've felt you melt under my hands and still you always say no. Why in hell do you think I've put up with it?"

"I've often wondered!" she flared. Her heart was hammering. When he became intense, his dark eyes blazing, she felt as if she were dissolving inside. There was in Dan

Copeland an implacable will that she feared would overpower her completely if she ever softened.

So she stood, irresolute, half of her longing to slip into his embrace, the other half crying to be free.

He must have read something in her eyes, because he reached out for her once more, pulling her to him until they were belly to belly.

"Don't you see, Kit? You must have figured it out. You think Witless gives a damn who you are under that angel face and incredible body? I'm your man and you're my woman—it's as simple as that. We're right together and we have to *stay* together."

"Oh, Dan, we always fight like this. It's always the same. It's *never* been right, not really. We're so different. I like knowing what's going on in my life. I *like* having dates and going to nice places and having doors opened and getting flowers and all that stuff you think is stupid. You're always too late or too early, and sometimes you forget me altogether, arguing politics with Ben."

His face was so close to hers that she could feel the breath warm on her skin as he whispered, "Kitty, don't do this to us. With the rest of them, you're a Barbie Doll. You're only real with me. You *must* go to India with me —I've got it all planned. You *can't* say no."

She turned to ice. Without pulling away from him, she replied in a remote voice, "*You've* planned. *You've* decided. Well, *you* go. I have my own plans!"

"Oh, babe!"

"Leave me alone."

"And let you go waste your life with that overstuffed pompous ass, Whit Harris? Never!"

"Not that it's any of your business," Kitty said, feeling suddenly very weary, "but I'm not planning to waste my life with *any* man. I'll make my own way."

How easy, she thought, shifting on the car seat, to make such sweeping statements at the age of twenty-two. She had been so sure of her future then. And look at me now, she reflected wryly. Seated in Whit's car, driven by Whit's chauffeur, dressed in clothes Whit had paid for, living a life that was orchestrated by Whit. She gave a bitter little laugh. Life was full of unexpected quirks.

Take Lee. Ten years ago Lee Rivers cut classes regularly, didn't give a damn what anyone thought of her, made her own rules, and slept with whomever she wanted to. If anyone was ever a nonconformist, it was Lee Rivers. And look at her today: her picture on magazine covers, slimmed down, dressed in the very latest styles, two gold records, the very picture of an American success story.

The last time Lee had telephoned, two weeks ago from Paris, she had laughed and said, "What are you wearing to the reunion?" As if Lee Rivers had ever cared what was "proper"! Kitty laughed now, just thinking of the get-ups Lee used to wear in school. She had always been an original. She still was. Oh, it was going to be so good to see her again, to talk for hours about men and love and life. It had been over a year.

She remembered how, in college, she and Lee had solemnly agreed that it was stupid to depend upon some man to give you an identity and a meal ticket. They would never fall into that trap, they had vowed. And not a year after graduation, Kit was married with a baby, and Lee was living with a freaky guitar player. Anyone writing an ending to their stories then would have said that Kitty would live happily ever after and Lee would end up in the gutter, half starving. How wrong that writer would have been.

Because there she was now! Lee sat on the edge of the Grand Army Plaza fountain, a red rose stuck behind one ear. Trust Lee not to wait like a lady in the Plaza Hotel lobby. She looked completely relaxed, a huge pair of sunglasses hiding her eyes, a silver Sportsac at her feet; dazzling in a voluminous tunic of iridescent pearl-gray silk, triple-belted in silver, and matching harem pants, tight at the ankles, and silver strapped sandals. Who else but Lee Rivers could get away with such an outrageous costume—and before lunch? Kitty couldn't help grinning at the sight.

How glamorous she looked—just like all the publicity pictures. Her hair had been cut into a halo of tiny, fluffy curls. To think that this chic apparition had gone through four years of college with long, thick, frizzy hair and wearing patched jeans and an assortment of wild shirts. She had been twenty pounds too heavy, and now she was long and slender and elegant.

Impatient, Kitty tapped on the glass separating her from Martin. "Stop right here, Martin!" The driver instantly pulled over and she jumped out, yelling, "Lee! Lee! Over here!"

The haloed head turned, and there was that familiar lopsided grin. "Hey! Kitty! Rah, rah, rah!" The words seemed to precede her as she ran as fast as she could in the impossibly high heels.

Watching her old friend come toward her, Kitty received a blurred double image: the old Lee, an overripe hippie, with this glamorous, lean creature superimposed. She had to keep reminding herself that *this* was really Lee. But no matter how many times she saw her— on magazine covers or in the flesh—it still came as a surprise. Her dear old friend who had found her own way, had done exactly what she wanted to do, and had made it in a big way. Just *look* at her!

Kitty, too, began to run, and in another moment they had flung themselves into each other's arms in a tight bear hug. And she was enveloped by the scent of Lee's exotic perfume.

Squealing together in delight like a pair of schoolgirls, they pulled apart, smiling broadly, looking each other over, grasping hands. Kitty could only marvel. Lee was the true embodiment of success: glowing, sophisticated, fulfilled, completely in charge.

Lee shook her head slowly and in her husky voice said, "Oh, it's incredible. Kitty Cameron, you never change!"

Without warning, Kit burst into tears.

CHAPTER THREE

Lee Rivers

LEE WAS DUMBFOUNDED. What in hell did I *say?* she wondered. What's going on? What should I do? She squeezed Kitty's hands, thinking rapidly. It was so incongruous, this elegant woman in her expensive, hand-tailored suit, sobbing in the middle of Manhattan like a heartbroken child.

Besides, Kitty didn't do this sort of thing. Lee had lived with her for three years, had been her confidante, had watched her deal with all kinds of things—from finals to desperate boyfriends to her father's sudden death—and hysterical weeping was simply not her style. She had always seemed to mirror in her behavior the way she looked: pale and silvery, almost ethereal, sliding through life with an almost weightless competence. Kit would not have imposed her emotions on anyone. Not even on me, Lee thought, and I was her best friend. There were always signs when she was deeply affected by something: two bright spots of color high on her cheekbones, and sometimes, if she was really upset, a small, quivering muscle at the base of her jaw. And if she suddenly threw herself into a frenzy of useful activity, you always knew she was busy working out an inner turmoil.

It was strange, and moving, too, to watch that exquisite face crumple. What could it be? Lee put a hand on Kit's shoulder and patted. "Is it anything you want to talk about?"

Kitty gave her a shaky smile, even though the tears continued to pour from her eyes. "Oh, God, I'm so embarrassed. But I don't seem to be able to stop. I'd *love* to

53

talk about it, but I don't know *why* I'm carrying on this way." She sniffled.

"It's not my new hairstyle, I hope."

Kit began to laugh and dug into her bag for a handkerchief. "Oh, my Lord, Lee, you look absolutely gorgeous! Now I really believe you're a star. And that outfit! I wouldn't have the nerve, yet it's just right for you."

"Whoa! You wouldn't be changing the subject—in your very charming way, of course—would you? I mean, Whit hasn't taken to beating you lately, has he? Or anything like that?"

"Don't be silly!" Kitty had brought out a gold compact and was patting powder onto her already perfect nose. "I must be overexcited at seeing you after so long, that's all."

Not so long, Lee thought. It was only last year that they had met in Madrid, while she was doing a concert tour through Spain. Something was going on in Kit's life, but from the old days she knew enough not to probe.

"Sure," she said lightly. "People usually burst into tears at the sight of me. I'm used to it."

Kit gave her a sharp glance, then smiled. "The car is waiting. Where are your bags?"

With a grin, Lee hoisted her Sportsac. "My years of wandering have taught me how to think small when I'm packing. This is it. Are you impressed?"

"Terrifically." Kit led the way.

"All right, let me guess," Lee said. "It's not the maroon Caddy. And it's certainly not the pink Rolls—I think Whit would probably die first. So it's got to be the Silver Mercedes."

"One hundred percent correct. But don't let Martin hear you call it a Mercedes. In chauffeuring circles, it's a *Benz*, you know."

The stolid Martin came to meet them, putting a finger to his cap in salute, and took Lee's bag as if it contained the Crown jewels.

Settling into the back seat next to her old roommate, Lee remarked, "This is the life, kiddo. After years of either riding pillion on a motorcycle or squeezing into a VW beetle, I must say I love these wonderful oversized automobiles. At last, room enough to stretch my legs out." And she did just that. "One of the percs of fame and fortune, you know, is they always lay on a big car. It didn't take me more than four or five minutes to become completely accustomed to luxury." She laughed.

"You earned it," Kitty said shortly.

"Yes, I did. But then"—Lee eyed her friend—"so did you, I think."

Kitty seemed not to hear the last comment. Instead, she called Lee's attention to the horse-drawn carriage lined up at the entrance to the park, all the horses gaily decorated with fanciful plumes or multicolored flowers. Lee dutifully looked. She loved New York in all its variety. No other city in the world could offer so many different kinds of people and neighborhoods and scenes. As the car turned smoothly into Columbus Circle, she spotted a team of tiny football players, no more than eight or nine years old, wearing red jerseys with shoulder pads and trotting solemnly behind their determined-looking young coach. "Okay, men," he was yelling. "Remember to wait for the green."

Both women began to laugh at this, and each said at the same moment, "Remember Jock Standish and the Colgate game?" which sent them into gales of laughter.

Wiping her eyes, Kit said, "Speaking of Jock, you know that Courtney's on the welcoming committee."

"Ugh. You mean *she'll* be the first one we see? I'm glad you warned me. I can just grit my teeth and put on my best frozen smile."

"You have to feel sorry for Courtney, Lee."

"Sorry! That little snob did her best to get me, all three years we lived at the house."

"But you have to remember that she was only president of our sorority because nobody else wanted the job. And she *knew* it."

Lee shifted in her seat. "Isn't it funny, Kit? When I saw you in Spain, we never once mentioned college. But because we're on our way to the reunion, that's all we're talking about."

"Yes." Kit seemed about to say something else, but changed her mind. A moment later she asked, "Why the rose, anyway? I certainly would have found you without it."

"I'll be the tall, skinny gal with the rose in her teeth? No, it wasn't anything like that. *Better*. Would you believe that somebody, somewhere, keeps track of where I go? And keeps sending a single red rose to whatever theater I'm going to play?"

"How romantic! Who?"

"Romantic! I think it's pretty weird. I mean, if some guy is crazy enough to wire roses all over the world, even to Melbourne, you'd think he'd show up at least once, wouldn't you?"

"It's a secret admirer, Lee. What every woman longs for."

"Not this woman. You know me better than that, Kit. You always were one for elegant gestures—but give *me* the real stuff every time. As I'm sure you recall." They grinned at each other. "Yes, you recall, all right. All those years helping me get my big butt out the window, and then covering for me with Mrs. Camberson and some of our more prissy sisters. You were the best roomie in the world, Kitty." She gave her friend's hand an affectionate squeeze.

"Thanks, but you're changing the subject. I want to hear more about your traveling roses."

"It gave me the creeps, actually, to realize that some guy was following every move I made—and I didn't even know who he was, or what he thought he was doing. I began to dread the damn things. And I used to *love* roses."

"Well, I see you're carrying this one around with you."

"Well, it's a bit different now. A week ago, in London, one came with a message."

"A message! Don't keep me in suspense!"

"Handwritten. I got all excited, trying to remember people's handwriting—oh, hell, I really mean Bill O'Hara's —until I realized that it had been wired and the scrawl I was studying so hard was the *florist's*."

"But what did it *say?*"

" 'Play, Gypsy. Sing, Gypsy. See you at reunion.' Isn't that a gas?"

"I can see why you thought it might be Bill O'Hara. He always called you gypsy, didn't he?"

"Among other, more interesting things. No, what really brought him to mind was the fact that the roses only started arriving after my first gold record. It would be just like him to forget my existence until my name hit the papers. And then try to cash in."

"I never could understand what his big attraction was."

Lee smiled broadly. "You've just said it. His big attraction."

"Oh, Lee, there must have been something else."

"That's all I can recall! Of course, everything's a bit dim now. Ten years is a long time." Her voice faded. "As a matter of fact, most of my past seems a long time ago. But certain occasions are still sharp and clear in my memory. Like the night I came visiting you, drunk and depressed and horrible . . ."

"Drunk, yes." Kitty laughed. "Oh, boy, were you looped! But not horrible, Lee. You were quite civilized . . . considering."

Lee had walked all the way from the train station with the wind howling through the darkness and the icy rain stinging her cruelly. She had stumbled through innumerable ankle-deep puddles. Within ten minutes she was completely soaked, her hair hanging in wet strings over her face.

In a way, she was enjoying this misery, sloshing through dimly lighted and unfamiliar streets, stumbling into potholes, sobbing a little from too much Scotch she had put away in a Third Avenue bar an hour or two before. "Misery is my name and misery is my game," she sang loudly, making up the tune as she went along.

Somewhere, there in the darkness, was Kitty's house. Whoops, Whit's house. Her head was spinning, and she was wondering if she had got out at the right station. Oh, of course, that nice little man had told her this was the way to the Harris place. How many Harris places could there be on Mystic Point?

A car, splashing her as it went by, lighted the desolate landscape briefly: thousands of trees, shrouded by sheets of rain.

"Idiot!" she hollered into the night. And began to cry. Because it was she who was the idiot, letting that prick Larry talk her into dressing up like a poor man's Dale Evans. Country and Western music! Since when was she a Country and Western singer? Why had she let him talk her into such a dumb idea? It was a dismal failure. The record that was supposed to make them a million had never even been played by the d.j.'s! "Never even been played!" she shouted into the rain-lashed night. "Because it was a stinkeroo! You hear that, Larry? A stinkeroo, ole buckeroo!"

He'd had her hair bleached platinum blond, an ugly ashy shade, and piled up on her head, each separate hair teased and sprayed with goo until it felt like plastic. He'd had her sewed into a too-tight white satin dress covered with spangles and cut down to her navel. Then he'd had her put into a makeup chair and plastered with glop and three different pairs of eyelashes. And for what? For nothing! Because the d.j.'s had taken one look at her and laughed their silly heads off. And they'd never played "Losin' at the Rodeo of Love," not even once. And she didn't blame them. What a dumb idea!

She stumbled on, tipping her head back, letting the rain beat at her. Let it wash off all the junk, let it pour all over her. She'd never wanted to be a phony cowgirl . . . it was all Larry's fault, and she had been crazy enough to listen to him.

"Serves you right!" she muttered, and suddenly threw up into the sodden road.

Feeling wretched, but somewhat more sober, she plodded silently the rest of the way. Just as the station-master had said, the Harris place was two miles straight down the main road, unmistakable with its huge iron gates. She pushed them open, slipping and sliding on the slick pavement.

Endless time later, she pounded the lion's-head knocker on the big white door. She could see the pinkish glow of firelight on a crystal chandelier inside, as well as glimpses of paintings and ornate moldings. She didn't care what any of it was, except that it was inside, warm and dry and safe.

To the astonished-looking housekeeper who opened the door, she said, "I'm Kitty's friend. Really I am. Tell her it's Lee." And a second later, so it seemed, Kitty, fastidious as usual with her hair knotted up and a floor-length creamy robe belted neatly about her waist, came running out to the hall.

"Lee! My God! Come right upstairs with me and get

into a hot tub. Mrs. Decker, bring a pot of coffee to the green bedroom, would you?"

Lee sagged in relief onto the solidity of her friend's arm and allowed herself to be piloted up a long, carpeted stairway, through long, carpeted, silent corridors, and into a large, luxurious bathroom, the outsized tub already filled with steamy, scented water.

"Magic," she mumbled.

Kitty laughed. "Not magic, it's my bath."

She never saw those disgusting fake-cowgirl clothes again. Kitty simply tore them off and they disappeared. Soon she was lying back in deliciously hot water that smelled of exotic flowers, letting it soak into her chilled body. Through half-closed eyes she saw the storm raging against the window.

Later, in a cheerful green and white room, tucked into a soft bed, she lay against satin pillows, telling Kitty the whole sad tale and feeling like a fool.

"They even changed my name, can you imagine, to— now get this—Honey Doll Dalton!"

"Oh, Lee! How awful!"

Lee began to laugh. "I can't help it. It's so dreadful, it's funny. If only it hadn't happened to me! I can never show my face on stage again. I'm ruined!"

"You're not ruined. You're young and you're talented, and this *isn't* the end. You made only one mistake."

"Yeah—the whole damn thing!"

"Lee, *listen* to me. You already said it—you listened to what's-his-name . . . Larry. I know you better than anyone. You've never paid attention to other people's ideas of who you ought to be! My God, at school nobody could tell Lee Rivers what to do or how to behave! And they all respected you for it. Yes, in the end, no matter how mad you made them, they all ended up admiring you because you were always *yourself*."

Lee groaned. "Don't remind me of the olden days when I was myself and not"—she giggled—"Honey Doll Dalton. Did I tell you that they had a press party tonight and nobody showed up?"

"You told me. And all right, nobody showed up. Good. Now you'll never have to be Honey Doll Dalton again. It's the end."

"The end!" Lee echoed in a sepulchral tone. "You just said it. It's the end of my career, that's what it is."

"No. It's the end of foolishness, that's all. Tomorrow, after you've had a good night's sleep, we're going to sit down and talk, and you'll decide where you ought to go from here."

A week later she and Kitty were driven to Kennedy Airport, knowing only that the next stop was "somewhere in Europe." They were riding slowly through the maze of curved roads in the huge airline complex when Lee said, "Kitty, ask the driver to stop at the next intersection." And as the car pulled to a halt, she looked up at the crowded signposts. "Here goes," she muttered, and closed her eyes. "I'll go to the second airline from the top. What is it?"

Kit protested but finally replied, "BOAC."

Lee opened her eyes and said, "It's an omen. London."

And that had been the real beginning. London had made her a name.

"You were quite a reasonable drunk," Kitty was saying. "Not at all like some I've entertained. Having business associates to dinner makes for some strange goings-on."

"Here I am, babbling on about myself. Let's talk about important things. How's Lily? Still the image of her mother?"

"Can't you come back home with me when this weekend is over? She'd love to see you. You're the wonderful far-off aunt who sends the magnificent presents and is a celeb to boot."

"Oh, Kitty, I can't. I'm stealing this weekend as it is. Don't you have a picture? It's not the real thing, but it's the best I can hope for."

Kitty produced a color snapshot from her wallet. Lee studied Lily's smiling face. There was something about it, something familiar that wasn't Kitty. "She sure looks like you," Lee said, "and yet . . ."

"And yet?"

"And yet she doesn't. I seem to recognize something in the smile, but I can't quite place it. Isn't that strange?" She glanced up and was amazed to see a red spot glowing on both of Kit's cheekbones.

"Everyone says she's a miniature of me. I don't think

she likes hearing it any more. She'd rather look like herself, or like Farrah Fawcett or Brooke Shields. Actually, I really think she'd love to look like Carol Burnett, she's her favorite. You know kids her age—one day she wants to be a TV star, and the next day she's madly in love with her horse . . ."

How you babble on, Lee thought. I wonder why. She looked once more at the picture. What *was* it that was nagging at her? The child had a nice, broad grin, a couple of teeth missing, and a dimple on one side of her mouth.

"Oh, and her hair never got dark, isn't that nice? It's that same glorious strawberry blond. I always longed for red hair when I was a kid. Some hope! When your real name is Leonor Margarita Luz de Rivera y Lopez, your chances of having red hair are zilch. Remember Dan Copeland's hair? I always coveted that—the hair, I mean, of course. Oh, dear, is he still a sore spot with you?"

"Not at all. I haven't thought of him for ages."

Lee gave her former roommate a shrewd look. There was something evasive in those cat's eyes. If this reunion has made me remember O'Hara, she thought, then surely Kitty's had at least a *thought* of Dan Copeland. He was a part of her life for three whole years, and when Dan Copeland had been a part of your life, he'd be awfully hard to forget.

"He was quite a guy," she said. "What's happened to him, do you know?"

There was such a long pause that for a minute she thought Kitty hadn't heard her. Then, "Lately? Apparently he's in the thick of things out in Wisconsin. I saw him mentioned about six months ago in a *Newsweek* article—"

"*Newsweek!* What did it say?" Lee laughed. "Is he still getting himself arrested?"

"No, it's just politics. He's running for something."

"Huh! Another radical gone Establishment."

"Not exactly. He's a D.A. out in Madison and he's called the Daring D.A., apparently because he keeps taking on lost causes. Whatever the Establishment wants, he's always pulling in the other direction. The only thing that's saved him so far is that he keeps winning. Now he's running for Congress, and *Newsweek* thinks he's going to pull off a tremendous upset. But I don't know the details.

It was one of those twelve-young-candidates-and-how-they're-going-to-do things. He only got a brief paragraph."

Of which you have memorized every word, it seems, Lee thought. "Kit?"

"Mmmm?"

"I can't believe you just forgot all about him. It was a long-running thing between you two. You ever have . . . regrets?"

"Regrets! He was impossible! Arrogant, bossy, egocentric, single-minded! You know that, you knew him. And besides," Kitty quickly added in a much calmer tone, "why should I have regrets? I have everything."

"So have I, Kitty," Lee said sharply. "But that hasn't kept *me* from having regrets. Oh, hell, I'm sorry. It's none of my business to call you down. But it always seemed a damn shame to me that it didn't work out between you two. Copeland may have been impossible, but he was far and away the most interesting guy in our class. Maybe you were too deep in the forest to see the trees, but he was something special. I mean, with all due apologies to Whit. Have I put my foot in it again? No? That guy was terrific. I never could understand what your problem was. He loved you!"

"I don't know what makes you say that, Lee. *He* certainly never did."

"Oh, crap. It was obvious to everyone. You broke his heart."

Kit gave a bitter laugh. *"What* heart? Never mind, just let's not talk about him anymore, okay?"

"Sure," Lee agreed, but she was thinking, Sure, Kit, no regrets. Not much! Funny, isn't it, the way old hurts never seem to heal, not really, not completely. Years later, you nudge at the spot and it still gives a twinge.

Like Bill. Professor William Sean Michael O'Hara. The minute she had seen him lounging by the lectern in English 404: The Irish Poets, she had known he was something special. Oh, man, she had thought, I wouldn't mind having *his* shoes under my bed!

Lee Rivers liked men and liked sex, and she had always been utterly honest about that. She knew her open attitude turned a lot of men off, that they found it shocking and threatening. She didn't care. At the age of barely sixteen, after her first sexual experience, she had looked in the mirror and promised herself that she wasn't going to take a guilt trip over it. To the devil with what people thought. To the devil with romantic nonsense. In the barrio, girls of sixteen were already getting married and having babies—ending their lives before they had barely begun! She wasn't going to fall into that trap, either. She always told her boyfriends, "Look, I like you, I like sleeping with you. But I don't need that romantic trash. I figure you'll respect me tomorrow morning, so don't worry about it."

Not that she slept with just anybody. No, she picked and she chose. She knew what she wanted when she saw it. And walking into English 404 that September morning, she wanted what she saw.

He had been leaning back negligently against the desk, legs thrust out and crossed at the ankle. His feet blocked the way, so that each student had to stop and submit to being looked over. He wore an Irish fisherman's sweater over tweed pants and smelled marvelously of lime water and pipe tobacco. Lee came close and stopped, deliberately. He looked up from the pipe he seemed engrossed in reaming and impaled her with his bright blue eyes. When their glances met, Lee felt a little shiver go down her back. Those were true bedroom eyes, taking in every detail of breast and hip and thigh even as they appeared to be gazing into her face. His mobile lips parted a bit as he smiled, showing a glint of white teeth.

"Your feet," she said, her heart thumping crazily.

"Yes? What about them?" His voice, lazy and light, matched the sensual Celtic look of him.

"They're in my way." She wished she had taken more trouble with her hair this morning. She felt as if he were adding her up and making a sum of her; it was suddenly, urgently, important that it be the correct sum. She positively itched to put out her hand and smooth away the lock of curly dark hair that fell over his forehead.

"Perhaps I'm wanting you to stick around for a minute." There was a tiny lilt in his voice. "You're a lovely sight for eight o'clock of a Monday morning."

"Lovely!" she snorted. "Nobody's ever accused me of *that* before—especially not at eight o'clock of a Monday morning." She mimicked that slight lilt just a little.

His voice dropped. "Ah, but I can see beneath the shapeless clothes you wear. It's a shame to hide a body like that, a dreadful shame for a gypsy princess."

The color climbed rapidly in her cheeks, and she looked around. The classroom was filling up, and it seemed to her that everyone could hear. "Let me by," she said. "People are listening."

"I'll let you by." He lazily moved his legs. "For *now*."

She hardly heard his lecture for the blood pounding in her ears. He was so beautiful. He moved back and forth at the front of the room like a lazy cat, reciting poetry. The rest of the class, she dimly noted, was rapt upon his words; she heard nothing but his opening statement: "I understand there's a rumor around campus that I'm a gunrunner for the IRA." Lengthy pause. "Well, it's true. But not during class hours." The class laughed. Lee just stared at him. She could picture him leaping through the craggy rocks on the coast of Ireland, a gun stuck into his belt, a wild ocean thundering below.

For two weeks, three mornings a week, he blocked her way. And each time he caressed her with those teasing eyes and made some comment about her baggy clothes. He took to calling her Miss Gypsy. In defiance, one Friday morning she borrowed a black silk turtleneck from Courtney Wills, the rich bitch of the sorority, who said in her sweet, little-girl voice, "But won't it be awfully tight, Lee?"

"I certainly hope so," she answered, delighted at the silent "O" of Courtney's pursed mouth.

And it certainly was tight, revealing in exact detail the heavy, round breasts and prominent nipples and emphasizing the slope into her waist. She struggled into a pair of jeans that had shrunk rather too much and added a wide leather belt. There! she thought, twirling in front of the mirror, seeing how the pants outlined her buttocks and clung to her firm thighs. No missing me this time. Her body was beautifully proportioned although heavy, but it was usually well hidden beneath the loose, comfortable tops she favored.

He wants to see, she told herself. Okay, then let him see it all, damn his Irish eyes. If nothing else, it ought to shut him up once and for all.

His eyes widened when she strolled in that morning.

For a change, he said nothing at all, merely stared at her.
Well, she thought, I certainly shut him up. Deliberately,
she took a stance in front of him and looked him in the
eye. "Top of the morning, Professor O'Hara," she cooed.

"Good . . . ah . . . good morning to *you*, Miss . . .
ah . . ."

Lee grinned. *"Rivers,* Professor. Lee Rivers, English
404, Monday-Wednesday-Friday at eight o'clock, third
row, fourth seat, remember?"

He cleared his throat, muttering, "I'm hardly likely to
forget, now, am I?" And he pulled his feet back without
the usual banter.

Was it her imagination, or was his usually glib tongue
not quite so silvery today? Did he stumble a bit? Was his
rendition of Yeats ever so slightly off? It could be her
imagination, but she was sure she had shaken him. He
avoided looking at her; still, she sat, deliberately holding
her shoulders very straight so that her breasts stood high
and proud in the snug shirt, scribbling busily at her notes,
and smiling a secret smile to herself.

At the end of the class period he said casually, "Will
Miss Rivers please stand back for a minute or two?" He
still hadn't looked directly at her.

While the rest of the class collected belongings and
drifted out the door, they stood at opposite ends of the
room, avoiding each other's eyes.

Finally he crooked a finger at her. "Over here, please."

"Sure." She ambled forward, swinging her hips, until
she was right in front of him. "Well?"

"You've overdone it, you know. Definitely overdone
it."

"It's all me, Professor. No artificial ingredients."

"I mean—"

"Look, you kept saying you wanted to see. Now you
see."

He licked his lips, fussing with his pipe, head down.
"And what if . . . what if I said that now, having seen,
I'd like to touch?"

"I'd say, where and when?"

Now he looked at her, startled.

"I find you very attractive. Hell, every girl in this class
is drooling over you. *You* know that."

"Very flattering words, Miss Rivers, I'm sure . . ."

Lee became irritated. Coy men made her sick. It was so unnecessary. Why did all these tiresome little games always have to be played out, when really it was so simple? I want you, you want me, that's the story, let's get on with it.

"Well, I'm going to be late for class," she said abruptly, and started away. Too bad. He was some hunk of man, and he certainly came on strong, but it was nothing but talk, after all.

She hadn't taken three steps when she felt his hand grasping her arm. "Gypsy girl. Wait a minute."

Twenty minutes later she was in his bed, lying beneath him, her legs tightly wrapped around his muscular buttocks as he thrust into her, a wide, delighted grin lighting his face. He was an expert, tireless lover, enthusiastic and eager to please. He never stopped talking: tender words, funny words, sweet words, erotic words. And when they had finished, nearly an hour later, he didn't pull away from her, but held her in his arms, saying over and over, "My wild little gypsy, you really love it, you really love it."

"I really love it," she agreed. So he wasn't just talk, after all. He was quite marvelous, in fact. In fact, she would have to give him an A plus. She traced his profile with her fingertip, along the smooth brow and the snub nose, past the narrow, sensuous lips, and down to the cleft in his prominent chin. He was really something special, something *very* special.

After a while she stirred. "I really have to go now. I have a voice class."

O'Hara groaned. "No, no, my gypsy. Stay. I don't have another class until one, and I haven't finished with you yet."

She wriggled out of his arms. "Sorry. I'm a scholarship student. I have to keep my grades up. And who said anything about being finished? We've only just begun, haven't we?"

He propped himself up on one elbow and watched her as she dressed. "What kind of a girl are you, anyway?"

"An honest one. Why? Did you miss having the interminable seduction scene? Do you feel cheated out of the thrill of the chase?"

He grimaced. "Ouch. Must you be quite so straight out?"

"Yes," Lee said. "That's the way I am. I liked it, I liked it a lot. I'd like to do it again."

"A gypsy look," he commented. "And a gypsy's lust for life. Well, I'm willing, God knows. But when? I'm not a once-a-week man, Miss Rivers." He paused and then laughed hugely. "Here we've just finished making love, and I'm still calling you *Miss*."

Lee brushed her hair hurriedly. "I guess that proves you still respect me," she joked. "And don't worry about when. I'm an expert at sneaking out of the sorority house at night. Just call me. It's Zeta Phi."

He sat up quickly, all attention. "Absolutely not! I can't be calling you on the phone like a college boy. Nobody must know about this, absolutely nobody, do you understand?"

"I understand," she said dryly. "I understand perfectly."

"No, you don't. It's a bit . . . sticky for me this semester. That misbegotten Students' League, or whatever the hell they call themselves, has badmouthed me in their stupid evaluation book! All lies! But once that kind of thing gets around, it's hell on wheels. You don't know what the English Department is like—backbiting, mealy-mouthed old ladies, the lot of them! If it ever got out that I was carrying on with you, it could ruin me. For the love of God, I'm up for tenure!"

Lee eyed him distastefully. There was panic in his eyes, even though he kept his voice light and lilting and devil-may-care. In his fear for himself, it hadn't occurred to him that she would be kicked out of school if their affair became known. Selfish so-and-so. But so what?

"Don't sweat the small stuff," she said. "So you won't call me. We'll arrange something else. I'm very discreet." She gathered her books together. "Unless it's not worth the bother." She grinned at him, rolling her eyes.

His answer was to leap off the bed and pull her close to him. And instead of pushing him off and getting to class, where she belonged, she strained toward him, all else forgotten. The minute he touched her, she was ready to give up everything.

From the very first time she was hooked on Bill

O'Hara. After all her dispassionate talk about not getting involved and just having fun, she found herself becoming obsessed with him. It wasn't only the sex, although that was a big part of it. He was funny and shrewd. He had a sharp eye for people's foibles and something witty to say about every big name on campus. He made her laugh. He really knew and loved poetry and could recite with such feeling that tears would come to her eyes. They met only at his place, and those three small rooms became the center of her existence. He was her special secret, and if anyone in the sorority house wondered why she played and sang "Bill" so often, nobody asked.

Funny that it was Kit—cool, virginal, self-contained Kitty—who gave her the word one night as she was preparing to climb out the window and make her practiced way down the heavy trellis to the lawn.

"You're not being very clever about this, you know," Kit said evenly, glancing up from her psychology text. "Don't you realize that everyone in the house is wondering why you aren't dating? Why the phone never rings for you any more?"

"Let them gabble, the silly geese."

Kit sighed impatiently. "Don't *you* be a goose. Obviously it's one of the professors. Everybody's talking and guessing and making bets. You're going to ruin it for yourself." She paused, then added delicately, "He must be terrific."

Lee stopped short, hesitated, and then burst out with the whole story. Kit, she knew, would never make moral judgments. She chose not to sleep with her boyfriends—okay—but it never occurred to her to criticize anyone who did.

She listened with her usual calm, nodding from time to time. She was a trustworthy confidante. And when the story was out, it was Kit who suggested that Lee ought to start dating again. "Not real dates," she said. "With guys who are just friends, so the girls will see them coming to pick you up. It'll stop them talking, at least."

And she had been right. Lee began to make a point of bringing fellows into the house, of being seen dashing off with this one or that. Who had to know she was only going to a political meeting or a lecture or as far as the library? She had even asked Ben Akkardijian to pick her up for a Students' League meeting, using the excuse that she was bringing a coffeepot and coffee and needed help. Ben had stared at her, taken completely by surprise. They were long-time antagonists, she and Benno, and normally she wouldn't ask him for the time of day. He was always telling her she was too aggressive with men, and he delighted in making cracks about how unfeminine she was. Ben, with his big nose and bad skin, telling her how to act with men! "After you've had your first woman, Akkardijian," she told him once, "*then* come to me with your expert advice." And had the pleasure of seeing him at a loss for words, for once. To be seen with Ben might cause some conjecture, but better for her sorority sisters to whisper about Benno than to guess about Bill.

Not that her relationship with Bill was perfect—far from it. Before Christmas vacation started, they had a long, lovely, passionate night together. "Are you sure you have to go home, my gypsy?" he asked. "Why can't you stay here with me?" He would not let her leave; and by the time she had let herself into the house early the next morning, Bessie was already busy in the kitchen with breakfast.

And then she came back from vacation a day early. He didn't answer his phone or his doorbell, so she slid a note under his door, impatient for the next day, when she would see him in class.

He ignored her totally. She couldn't believe it. He refused to so much as glance in her direction, and at the end of class he hurried out, head averted. She ran to the door, but he had already disappeared. All that day she kept calling him, but his phone went unanswered. All that night she lay in her bed, twisting and turning, burning with her need for him, crying silently so as not to wake Kit.

On Tuesday a letter came for her. It was written in his backhand scrawl, pages and pages of self-flagellation, scraps of poetry, and paeons to their lovemaking, all flung together incoherently and all adding up to *goodbye*. She read through this mess once, twice, and yet again, trying to make some sense out of it. What *was* he going on about? "I know you are suffering, sweet gypsy," the letter concluded, "but my suffering is more profound. Because you are losing so little (only me), while I am losing the best thing that ever happened to me. I am losing *you*."

She crumpled the last page in a fit of fury and threw it across the room, only to run and retrieve it a moment later, smoothing it out frantically.

She phoned him immediately, and when he heard her voice, he hung up. She called again, letting it ring and ring and ring, counting the numbers off, her heart thumping fiercely. After thirty-seven rings, he answered and said in a choked voice, "Let it be, gypsy. Let it be." She banged the receiver down and began to weep wildly.

She couldn't stand it. What had gone wrong? How could he just change like that, from one day to the next? It was humiliating. Never to see him again, never to feel his arms around her, his lips on hers. "No, no, no!" she stormed, banging her fist into the wall of the phone booth.

She cut his class for the rest of the week, trying to forget him by working very hard at her long-neglected studies. But by Sunday it had become unbearable. She flung herself out of the house. She simply couldn't stop thinking about him and she knew she had to see him, to find out why he had suddenly dumped her. Dumped her, while protesting his undying devotion! It was crazy! Steeling herself for a snub, she rapped at his apartment door.

He was unshaven and bare-chested, wearing a pair of rumpled chinos and reeking of whiskey. In the background she could hear his favorite recording of melancholic Irish songs. Faced with the reality of him, she felt her legs begin to tremble and a terrible weakness in the pit of her stomach. She couldn't speak.

"The gypsy princess," he said sadly. "Don't make it harder for me, Lee, please."

She found her voice. "I didn't understand one word of that letter. I want you to tell me what you meant, that's all."

"Meant!" He ran a hand over his stubbled jaw. "I meant I must give you up." He stopped. "Oh, God, I was just getting used to being without you . . ."

"*Why* do you have to give me up? I don't understand!" Her voice trembled, out of control, and to her horror, tears began coursing down her cheeks, choking her. She squeezed her eyes shut.

"The poor darlin'," he murmured. He pulled her close,

so that her wet cheek was against his chest, where she could hear the urgent beating of his heart. "You've been tortured enough, little gypsy. I can't go on this way. I want you too much."

Then his mouth was on hers, avid and yearning, and it was all wonderful once more. "Stay with me, Lee," he said huskily, "no matter what crazy thing I do. Stick by me, my gypsy girl."

She promised with fervor, her heart lifting with the thought that the terrible separation was over. Clinging to each other, they made their impatient way to his rumpled bed, leaving a trail of clothes behind them.

But that was only the first time he sacrificed her to his guilt. Twice more during the year, similar letters came in the mail. Twice more she was driven to despair, certain each time that it really was ended; and two more times she went to him in tears to renew her vows of devotion in a frenzy of frantic lovemaking.

Years later she would question why she had allowed herself to be put through such pain and humiliation over and over again. She thought of that period in her life as one of fever, blurred and frenetic in the living, and becoming clear only after the temperature had gone down.

The simple truth was, she accepted whatever he did because she was addicted to him. He was more dangerous than any drug. She lived only in the present tense, never thinking any farther ahead than to the next time she would see him.

One evening in May, as they lay in bed listening to a recording of Russian gypsy music he had found—"just for you"—and sipping at wine, he asked casually, "What are you thinking of doing after graduation?"

"Ugh. It's only three weeks away, isn't it? I don't know . . . I haven't thought." She pulled at the hair on his chest and laughed. "I haven't thought very much about school or anything else, O'Hara. As you well know."

He chuckled. "I've managed to keep you busy right here, haven't I? I'd hate to give that up. Why don't we just continue, but on a full-time basis?"

Her heart stopped. He couldn't mean— "Full-time? What . . . what do you mean?"

"I'm not teaching this summer. Move in with me, why don't you? We can spend all day and all night, every day every night." His voice became husky, and he began to fondle her with lazy, practiced ease.

"You mean . . . live with you?"

"I guess that's what it means, doesn't it? Of course, you're thinking that it'll be boring for a gypsy girl."

"Boring! Oh, Bill! It'll be heaven!"

"But the minute you're bored, you can leave."

"But, Bill, people will know!"

"It doesn't matter any more, don't you see? After graduation, you won't be a student any more." He grinned.

Her mouth went dry with excitement. Suddenly there was a future, and Bill O'Hara was its name. She flung herself upon him, tickling him and kissing him all over his face.

The last weeks of school were hazy and indistinct in her memory. She was totally focused on June the second, Sunday, the day her class would graduate and she would be with her love forever. She moved about as if in a dream, handing in term papers and taking her finals, but all the while she was really somewhere else. Several times she caught Kitty looking at her with concern, and once Lee snapped, "Stop it, for heaven's sake! I *know* what I'm doing!"

The night before graduation was warm and sweet, the sky sprinkled with stars. The sorority house had emptied early, with everyone going to see the annual Harris fireworks. Just the time to bring a couple of light bags to Bill's place.

He had been shut in for nearly two weeks, grading papers and final exams. They hadn't slept together in all that time. Pure torture. But he had told her, very seriously, that he needed these last weeks to finish his work. "You must not tempt me, little gypsy. Remember, I'm under the gun this year. Everything has to be turned in on time. It'll be hard, I know, but we must have no contact, understood?"

She hadn't wanted anything but to hear his voice for a few minutes. Five days before graduation, she hadn't so much as caught a glimpse of him. So she had called, and his voice had been like ice. "I thought we had an agreement. If you really care for me, you'll keep your word. I told you . . . after graduation." She had apologized profusely, but that strange conversation had unnerved her.

Whenever she thought of it, a cold knot formed in her stomach.

But, she reminded herself tonight, he had said after graduation. Graduation was tomorrow; surely he had finished all his work by now. She would come to him, out of the night, and after all this time without her, he would be eager and passionate.

She took a leisurely shower and washed her hair. She had bought a flounced skirt and an off-the-shoulder blouse—a kind of gypsy costume—especially for him, and she smiled at her reflection after she put it on.

She went sailing down the broad staircase, humming an Irish ballad, loving the feeling of being alone in the sorority house. At the bottom of the stairs, she looked around the shabby, comfortable place where she had lived for the past three years. It occurred to her suddenly that she was leaving it, that she would never be back. She really loved it all, she realized, dumb traditions and dumb regulations and dumb girls—all of it. For a moment she stood absolutely still, framed in the living-room doorway, torn between a sadness at the end of all this and a great spreading joy of going to her love.

"Lee." The voice, where none was expected, made her jump. And there, perched on the love seat in the far corner of the living room, impeccable in white flannel slacks and a navy blue polo shirt, his thick straight hair neatly brushed back from his forehead, was Whit Harris . . . looking, she thought, like someone out of an old 1930's college movie.

"God, Whit, you scared me! What in hell are you doing *here*?"

"Boiling," he said. There was a smile on his lips, but it didn't reach the cold eyes. He was really angry; but Whit Harris never let his emotions go public. "Katherine is already a half hour late, and I have no idea where she might be. She's never done this to me before, never." He glanced at his wristwatch. "Now I'm beginning to worry. Do *you* know where she is?"

As Lee started to speak, a fusillade of explosions bounded and rebounded outside. Whit's mouth tightened. "The fireworks started fifteen minutes ago, and damn it, Father is going to be furious. Not that I blame him," he added belligerently. "After all, the Harrises have sponsored the graduation fireworks for years. It's a family tradition, and I should be there."

Lee gave her luggage a covert glance. She'd have to stay with him until Kitty showed up. Dammit. There was Bill, half a campus away, almost within reach, and she was stuck. She could never think of what to say to Whit, he was so bland and conventional.

"You needn't wait," Whit said. "I can see you're on your way somewhere."

If you only knew where! she thought, with the delight her secret always brought her. Well, why shouldn't he know? Soon everyone would. And it would be worth it just to see the shock on his smooth face.

"I'm on my way to move in with Bill O'Hara."

"*Professor* O'Hara?" he blurted, color staining his cheeks.

"The one and only." She grinned, enjoying his discomfort. "We've had a thing going all year, only now it's going to be out in the open."

"Lee, I'm not sure that the administration would allow an extralegal arrangement like that."

"Oh, pooh. The administration won't have a thing to say about it. After tomorrow, I won't be a student any more."

"I think you should be warned that O'Hara—" He stopped, head turning, all alert at the spluttering sound of a motor scooter pulling up in front of the house. Lee ran to the door, nearly bumping into a flushed, windblown, and disheveled Kitty.

"Where—"

"Never mind. I'm so late. Oh, Whit, I'm so sorry. Can you give me five minutes?" And Kitty scooted up the stairs without waiting for an answer.

"That takes care of that," Lee said. "I leave her in your capable hands." She bent for the bags, unwilling to waste any more time listening to Whit's cautions and dreary opinions.

Copeland was still outside the house, slumped over the handlebars of the bike, the very picture of dejection. As soon as Whit had said Kitty was late, she knew it had to be Copeland. Whenever Kit Cameron didn't move according to schedule, it was because Dan Copeland had showed up.

"Still here?" she taunted him. Dan was not in her good graces, not since he and his cohorts had done that hatchet job on O'Hara. "You might as well leave. She has *other* plans for tonight."

He moved his head slightly, slanting a look up at her. "You don't have to tell me. I know." His usual spunk was muted, and the sharp words she had on the tip of her tongue went unsaid. The guy was miserable. In her own glow of happiness, she could find room to feel compassion, even for him.

"I'll give you a job, Copeland. You can ride me over to Bill O'Hara's."

Now his head jerked up. "O'Hara! At this hour, *you* of all people are going to see a professor? And a lousy one at that!"

"Never mind your unfair prejudices, Dan. Don't say anything else about him to me. I'm *moving in* with him."

The lean face, deeply shadowed in the faint light of the street lamp, was unreadable, but she thought she saw a smile. "Oh, Christ save us! You're *not!*"

"On the contrary. I *am*."

"All my good sense tells me not to take you to such an unholy assignation."

"That's cool. I'll walk." She picked up the bags once more and started out. Almost immediately, Dan revved up the motor and drew alongside her.

"Okay. What the hell, I don't have anything better to do. I might as well give you a lift to your doom."

"Mind your own business!" But she stowed the bags on the small rack at the rear and climbed on.

It took only a minute or two to reach the small apartment house. Bill's place was on the ground floor, and the first thing she noticed was that the windows were dark. A small chill ran down her spine, but she thought, He probably fell asleep, poor baby. All those finals.

Nonetheless, she scrambled from the bike, her heart pounding unevenly, and ran to the front door. Even in the dark her finger went unerringly to the bottom bell, and she punched it with impatience. No answer. Again she pushed it, and again and again. It usually took Bill only an instant to press the buzzer that let her in. What was the matter? She banged on the nearest window, then pushed the bell again.

She was not aware that Dan had come up behind her until he spoke. "You forgot your bags, lady. Something wrong?"

"He must have gone out somewhere . . . although he said he'd be grading papers. Well, maybe he went to The Pub. He wasn't expecting me . . . oh, *damn*."

"And you took a shower and everything."

"What does *that* mean, Copeland?"

"Nothing, nothing. Just that you smell so nice. Well, want a ride back?" He let the bags down with a thump.

"Wait a minute." She pressed on the bell with all her strength, letting it ring continuously. She could hear its strange, echoing, lonely sound inside the apartment.

Suddenly the front door opened, letting the hall light out, making her blink. It took a moment to realize that the silhouetted figure was a woman, Bill's next-door neighbor.

"Let up, will you? That bell is driving me crazy. And it won't do you any good, anyway."

"Do you know where he went?"

"Yeah. Ireland."

Lee's heart stopped beating for a long horrible moment. "Ireland," she repeated in a hollow voice, not believing it. "Ireland."

"Took off early this morning, said he'd be back in September."

Numbly, stupidly, she backed away from the voice. "Did he . . . did he leave any messages?"

"Not even a forwarding address. Of course, he *did* say he wanted to live the life of a gypsy wanderer, but then, he's *always* saying stuff like that."

A sick, stunned feeling hit Lee like a physical blow. She turned away from the door, afraid she would wretch, and walked straight into Dan Copeland's rangy body. One arm instantly went around her, and he patted her back as she moaned into his shirt, "Oh, my God, what am I going to do? He said he needed me. He said we would be together all the time."

"That bastard!"

"Why did he do it? How could he?"

"He's no good."

"He's wonderful. He loves me."

"He loves only one person—himself."

In a frenzy, she began to beat at Dan with her fists. "Shut up! Shut up! He loves me! He loves me! He loves me—" She burst into wild tears, digging her fists into her eyes. "I want to die!"

The next thing she knew, she was being propelled down the sidewalk and hoisted onto the seat of the motorbike.

"Rivers," Dan said firmly, "we've both been done in. What we need is a drink." He gunned the motor and sent the scooter flying through the night.

He brought her to his place, a dimly lit, thoroughly messy attic in an old commercial building. She had been there plenty of times, but always for League meetings, when the place had been jammed from wall to wall. It was strange to see it empty. He steered her gently to one of the big mattresses on the floor that served as couch, bed, or study. It was the neat one, its Indian coverlet tautly tucked in. The other one was a complete mess of books, papers, crumpled bedclothes, and assorted laundry.

"Where *is* your slobby roommate?" She couldn't take Benno Akkardijian tonight. She couldn't take him at any time, actually. He was a pain in the neck, either putting her down or coming on strong in a hostile way. If Ben was going to be around, she absolutely refused to stay here.

"Spending the night with his relatives in a fancy hotel in Syracuse."

She took a tumbler of whiskey from Dan and sipped it gratefully. It was strong and aromatic, and it filled the hollow space inside her with an instant warmth.

Dan took a large gulp of his own drink and settled down next to her, reaching behind to arrange a pile of pillows against the wall. From outside there came the faint sound of rockets exploding.

"Stupid fireworks!" he grunted.

"What do you have against fireworks? They're fun."

"Fireworks," he said tightly, "remind me of Vietnam."

"Sorry," she mumbled, "I forgot."

"*And* of tonight. And it's what they did to me tonight that I'm about to drown in this wonderful one-year-old Scotch."

Later, when she thought about it, she realized that Dan Copeland had been as vulnerable and wounded that night as she. She was so accustomed to thinking of him as tough and well defended. But they drank steadily, the glasses filling up almost magically as soon as the last drop had disappeared. And they told each other everything.

"Here's to your misery," he toasted.

"And here's to yours, Dan."

"And here's to your pain."

"To yours."

"And here's to Witless Harris, the guy in the white hat."

"And here's to bloody Ireland, may it sink beneath the sea."

"And to Kit, my lost love—but not forever!"

"And to Bill O'Hara, may he rot in hell!"

"You're really finished with him?"

"My God, Dan, I've *got* to be. I'm going to get out of this part of the country so fast, nobody will see anything but my dust."

"Smart girl. Have another."

"Thank you. Love it."

He put on a jazz record and lit new candles when the old ones burned down, and she remembered being suffused with the wonderful peace of forgetfulness. Bill O'Hara became a teeny, tiny figure, hardly visible, hardly worth thinking about. But even in her growing stupor she knew that the pain would return tomorrow. By this time she and Dan were lying side by side, their glasses balanced on their stomachs.

"How you feel?" he asked, his words slightly slurred.

"Lonely, that's how."

"Yeah. Me, too."

They gazed at each other, and she watched as his eyes suddenly focused on her. "Lee," he muttered, and she heard the clinking of the glasses as he moved them carefully onto the floor. She watched his face blurrily, her heartbeat quickening as he pulled her closer to him. "Lee," he said again, and this time it was a question.

Not another word was spoken. She snuggled into him, glad for the comforting warmth of another human body, glad for his gentle hands, glad to forget her pain for just a little while longer. The whiskey was a buzz in her head and their lovemaking a desperate smothering of thought.

When it was over, he put one big hand on her cheek

and said, "Lee, I'm sorry. It was unfair. You had an awful lot to drink, and so did I."

"Don't be stupid. I'm not exactly a virgin, you know." She laughed bitterly. "We both needed . . . something."

"It was a very nice something."

"For me, too, Copeland. But we both know we're just ships passing in the night."

The next morning, without waiting for the graduation ceremony, she boarded a bus for Chicago, leaving Hampton and memories of Bill O'Hara as far behind her as she could.

Bill's letter, filled with his usual self-pitying phrases—"You're too good for me. I don't deserve a woman like you"—she knew them by heart—didn't catch up with her until August. At which time she carefully tore it into a thousand pieces and—

"Lee! You haven't heard a word I've said. Where were you?" It was Kit, half laughing.

Lee made an effort to come back to the present. "Not *where*, Kit . . . *when*. The closer we get to school, the farther back in time my mind goes."

Kitty smiled. "Yes, I know. Not a car but a magical time machine. I've been wandering around in 1970 myself. And I wonder—"

"Yes?"

"Nothing."

Not nothing, Lee knew. Whose arms wound around Kit in memory? She was sure she knew. And what, she wondered, would her old friend say if she knew that Lee had just been recalling those same strong arms?

But, of course, that didn't count. The night with Dan Copeland had been medicine for her hurts, nothing more. And if she was completely honest with herself, it was O'Hara who was haunting her. Yesterday, in her cozy London flat, Bill O'Hara had been merely an old flame she wouldn't mind seeing again at reunion. And now she was sitting here, quivering with the memory of him, anxious with anticipation.

She must remember who she was. Who she was *now*, not who she had been so many years ago. The man-crazy little coed who had melted at the touch of that professional Irishman, that lecher, didn't exist any more. The

Lee Rivers returning to Hampton was a strong, successful woman of the world.

But she was not sure that she believed herself. Just recalling those long sessions of love with him, remembering his voice, husky with fatigue and desire, saying, "It's amazing, I want you *again*," made her begin to tremble.

Have I really changed at all? she wondered. Have ten years counted for anything? Or would she discover, back in the old setting, that all the work and the effort and the pain hadn't made a difference? That, inside, she was still insecure and vulnerable?

"And scared," she said aloud. "You know what, Kitty? I just realized that I'm scared of this reunion."

The two women stared at each other for a moment, then smiled tentatively.

"Me, too," Kit said. "And probably for the same reasons."

CHAPTER FOUR

Benno Akkardijian

THERE IS NO PLACE in the world, however exotic or dramatic or heroic, quite so enchanting as the Cherry Valley in upstate New York. Route 20 winds its leisurely way among rolling hills, and a vista of fields and pastures dots the hills. Clusters of cows, spotted black and white, graze peacefully, and sometimes, far off in the serene distance, there will be a bright yellow harvester moving majestically through the neat rows of crops. The farms spread out on either side of the highway, their dates of founding—1856, 1794—laid out proudly in the barn-roof shingles, often with a pair of initials as well.

At three-thirty in the afternoon, the bright red BMW sports car was almost alone on the highway. A mile ahead, a silver Mercedes-Benz sped along; otherwise the road seemed deserted.

Would you look at all those "Antiques for Sale" signs, Ben Akkardijian thought with distaste, glaring out the window of the sports car. Every single farmhouse for the past fifteen miles had its own commercial invitation to come browse and buy. It was a sign of the times, and one that he loathed. All these farmers, unable to make a living from the land any more, forced to sell off their great-grandmothers' quilts and their own old crockery! He remembered them so well from ten years ago: active, thriving, piling into campus at harvest time to hire extra help.

Ten years ago! Hard to believe college had been over that long ago. Harder still to believe that he was actually on his way back to Hampton. He laughed out loud and asked nobody in particular: "What do I think I'm doing, going to play with kids my own age?" And answered himself: "Just doing what I feel like doing. And today I feel like a reunion." He wondered if Copeland would show. Dan's career had taken him far from Hampton College, in more ways than one. And wasn't he running for something or other? He was probably too busy to travel so far just to play nostalgia games.

Taking a sudden, sharp curve with insouciance, Ben rolled the window all the way down, letting in the tangy air, crisp with the scent of ripening apples, and thrust his elbow out. He felt good. That was all there was to it. He felt damned good. "Free at last, free at last!" he intoned, and once more laughed. Yesterday, when he had arrived home from the job at midnight and finally picked up the mail, there they had been: the final divorce papers. His freedom! Studying the wordy legal phrases, he had realized it was truly over, the end of a long, lousy, fruitless, futile five years, and had felt as if someone had lifted a ton of chains from around his neck.

He had tried; God only knew how he had tried to make it work. But Helena de Blaine Reed Akkardijian—of Bryn Mawr, the Junior League, Yale Law School, and the firm of Thorpe, Whitehead, and Franklin—was too tightly scheduled and too damn proper to make a marriage.

One Christmas he had given her a golden partridge in a living pear tree, and she had said, "Oh, Benno, when will you grow up?" Her gift to him had been a chic Gucci attaché case with his initials in gold, eminently suitable. If he put his arms around her on a lazy Sunday afternoon, nuzzling into her neck, she would invariably shake him off. "Can't you wait until we're in *bed?*" If he made a joke during one of those endless meetings at Thorpe, Whitehead, and Franklin—something to relax them all, nothing nasty—she would glare at him. If at the end of a busy week of work he got into the car with her and said, "Let's go to the beach right now and have a wonderful weekend," she would be disgusted. "Without reservations? Without clothes? Without making plans?"

It had taken him longer than it should have to realize that his petite and pretty wife simply did not approve of him. Didn't approve, and planned to change him. Why had she married him? He asked her once, close to despair, and Helena thought a moment—she never spoke without thinking first—and then replied, ticking the points off on her fingers: "You were bright. You were exotic. You were charming. You were rich."

"Were?" he cried. "It's only been three years, Helena. Surely I'm just as bright and exotic and rich and whatever now—maybe more! Look at me: I'm terrific!" And he did a little soft-shoe number across the living room. He should have known better.

She shook her head sadly. "I thought your lack of tact and love of silly jokes was just . . . youth. I thought, once we were married, that you would grow up. Basically, you're sound, you know."

"I'm not a municipal bond, Helena, I'm a man."

"A man who doesn't know how to behave with clients." She pursed her slips.

"Maybe I hate it at Thorpe, Whitehead, and Franklin. Maybe I find it dull and lifeless and stupid."

"Nonsense! It's one of the finest firms in Philadelphia. And you *were Law Review*. Only Wisconsin, of course, but *Law Review* is *Law Review*, after all."

At that point he walked out of the room. It was hopeless. Helena saw things in black and white. There were no shades of gray in her experience. And my entire life, he thought, only half amused, is a big gray blob. Why am I in Philadelphia? Because I wanted to stop competing with Dan Copeland, and Philadelphia is far away from Madison, Wisconsin. Why am I a lawyer? Because Dan wanted to be a lawyer and I didn't know *what* I wanted to be.

The only decent and exciting part of his life as a lawyer were the two nights a week he gave without pay, to the storefront law office. There, at least, he felt he was helping people in a real way. And while there, he looked around the neighborhood with its crowded rooming houses and stinking, rat-infested apartments. Once these had been a row of neat town houses, not luxurious, perhaps, but solid. Under the grimy, peeling paint and filthy windows was simple, fine architecture. In idle moments he found himself daydreaming about owning one of those houses and bringing it back to life.

When he realized he was spending more time fantasizing about buildings than dealing with trusts and contracts, he went out and bought three of them, right across the street from the storefront. The first three began as a secret from Helena, but soon he found himself deeply involved with contractors, landlords, tenants, architects, the building department, and the thousand and one details of renovation. There was no more time for the law. So he told her what he was doing. She went white with rage and would not speak to him for days. After he quit Thorpe, Whitehead, and Franklin, she moved out of their bedroom into the den.

Even when he became successful, when he had turned a whole block of ruined real estate into beautiful apartments, she was not satisfied.

"Your hours are erratic, you bring those filthy workmen home at any time you please, and the place is cluttered with your blueprints. I cannot live this way—and furthermore," she added, "I don't understand how *you* can. It's ... grubby."

He laughed without humor. "I'm probably the only husband in the entire United States whose wife *really* doesn't understand him. And I don't even have a secretary to sit on my lap and hear all about it."

"I'm serious. Is that your answer? Another of your infantile jokes?"

"I'm making a bloody fortune, Helena, and what's

more, I love what I'm doing. Real estate is what I was meant for. Tell me what it is you want from me."

"I want you to stop playing games with your life and do what you were trained to do, in a proper way."

Ben stared at her thoughtfully for a moment. What a pretty, soft-skinned little woman she was, neat and polished. But he fancied he could see the gleam of metal under her creamy, unblemished skin. "I'll never be able to do or be what you want, Helena. Can't you accept me the way I am?"

After a pause, she consulted her watch. "Very well, then. I'll be out of here by—oh—five-thirty tomorrow."

He knew she would be gone, not at five twenty-nine or five-thirty-two, but at five-thirty sharp; and this knowledge made him feel very, very tired. She was leaving him, the woman he had thought he loved, the woman whose body he had eagerly sought night after night, and all he could feel was weariness.

They had been married a little over four years the day she had neatly packed and neatly moved out of his life. It wasn't until she had gone that Benno had realized that all during his marriage he had been tense. He had also been underweight, his nose jutting like the prow of a great ship from a gaunt, hollow-cheeked face. So he had begun to run every day, had grown his mustachios, had eaten hugely. Then he had looked around, and to his surprise, there were women in Philadelphia who thought he was cute. *Cute!* There was Martha Hillyard, one of his architects, tall and rangy and understated. There was Susan Lucarelli from the contracting firm. And Penny, the dancer, Penny Fortune, who had dragged him to the barber for a thirty-four-dollar haircut. "Now you're gorgeous!" she had chortled. "And mine, all mine!"

Benno gave a gusty sigh at these reminiscences and shifted into fourth. No, Penny, darling, he thought, not yours all yours. Nobody's. It was good, very good, to have women in his life and in his arms, but he had learned his lesson. "Think single!" he told himself, pushed down on the accelerator, and thumbed on a tape of *Grease*, singing loudly and slightly off key along with the music.

The siren blasting right behind him startled Benno. The police motorcycle pulled up alongside, and the burly cop gestured him to the shoulder of the road. He pulled over, a bit guilty but puzzled.

Leaning out of the window, he said with a grin, "I'm innocent, Officer." There was no answering smile from the blank square face, reddened from the sun and hidden behind huge dark goggles.

"In a hurry, sir?" The voice was thick and gravelly and deceptively calm.

"Me? Not especially. Why? Was I going too fast?"

A bleak smile. "You passed me about three miles back, going eighty. I think I'd better see your license."

"Sure. Sure." Eighty! And he hadn't even realized. He glanced around, trying to remember from college days where the speed traps were located. If this was one of them, he would be stuck for hours seeing some small-town judge (after being kept waiting a frustrating hour or two) and then be given a lecture and a stiff fine. A very stiff fine.

"Officer," he began, "I'm on my way to Hamp—"

"Akkardijian!" the cop exclaimed, holding the license at arm's length as if it might bite him. "Jee-zus, of all the people—"

"Huh?"

A meaty hand was thrust through the open window. "Don't you remember me? Joe Rugowsky. I sat behind you in Marketing 110—and I copied a lot of your test answers. And I helped out some with the Students' League."

Ben shook the huge hand with pleasure. "Killer Joe! Of course. My God, what a coincidence. To be picked up for speeding by the meanest fullback the Hampton Gladiators ever had!"

"Aw, I never was really mean. I liked the sport—the body contact and all. But that name—Killer Joe—I never liked that, you know? It made my mother worry."

"So you're a state trooper, Joe. Who would've thought it? I always thought you'd go pro."

"I did, but I got hurt my first season." Rugowsky glanced again at the license. "You coulda knocked me over with a feather when I saw that name. Akkardijian. How many guys could be named Akkardijian? I asked myself. I remember you. But I couldn't believe my eyes. Jee-zus, have *you* changed!"

Ben eyed the beefy frame, all muscle and a yard wide, and smiled. *"You* haven't."

"Naw. I keep in shape. But *you* . . . you were a real skinzo, and with that mop of brillo hair. And now . . . I'll bet you're a big shot, right?"

"Thanks. I'll have to tell my barber."

Joe Rugowsky grinned and took off his helmet. Ben began to laugh. The man was almost totally bald, with just a Santa Claus fringe of sandy hair above the ears. The trooper laughed with him. "Remember what a head of hair I had? That's what ten years of marriage can do." He chortled heartily at his own joke.

"About my ticket—"

Joe scratched his head. "We'll forget that. Lucky for you I didn't start writing it. But, Jee-zus, go slower, will ya? We're stationed up and down the road—special for the reunion crowd." He smiled. "Lots of dough, ya know."

"Thanks, Joe. I won't forget it. Will I see you at the reunion?"

"You bet! Maybe not tonight, but tomorrow for sure, at the football game. Me and the missus." He glanced at the empty seat next to Ben. "You single?"

"Divorced."

"Sorry to hear it."

Gunning the motor, Ben thought, You're the only one, then. "See you later, Joe." He waved and pulled back out onto the highway.

God, Joe Rugowsky. How many times had he watched Number Fifty-six, scarlet on gold, ramming into the enemy, sacking the quarterback, lifting the ball carrier off his feet and dropping him to the ground? Every single Saturday he had gone to the Hampton football games, not really to see them play, but with his arms full of political petitions for or against one thing or another. He could remember the chants from the stands: "Go! Go! Joe! Joe!" "Killer Joe! Hit 'em low!" He could almost smell the mustard at the hot dog stand, mixed with beer and a distant aroma of burning leaves and the heady scent of soap and cologne from the group of giggling freshmen placard girls as they went rushing by. Ah, the girls of 1970, with their long, straight, shining hair and their floppy jeans and their love beads and their scrubbed faces —would there ever be girls like that again? For an instant Helena's cool, perfectly made-up face flashed before him. Had she ever been a free spirit, marching in parades, clumping around in snowdrifts in clogs, sitting in all night for the cause of ecology, slouching on floor pillows in somebody's apartment drinking cheap wine and exchanging jokes? He couldn't picture any of it.

He had always gone after the girls he couldn't have. Like Kitty Cameron. How he had built fantasies around her; it made him laugh to think of it now. She had sat next to him in sophomore English—the most beautiful girl he had ever seen in his life: poised, lovely, super-cool, supremely fair. And smart, too. All of his puns and wisecracks that semester had been for her benefit alone. And she had seemed to like him, too. When he had showed off, she'd laughed. She had even had coffee with him a couple of times after class. And then Copeland had seen her and walked right off with her.

And who could blame the girl for preferring Dan Copeland to the short, skinny, dark-complected kid with too much hair and too much nose—and too much mouth? What a mess he had been! He had imagined himself quite the devil, with his bush of curly hair, collarless Egyptian shirts, and tooled cowboy boots. Where else, he had figured, would they ever find a half-Italian, half-Armenian, the son of an impoverished *principessa* and a filthy-rich Armenian trader who had lived in Cairo, London, Paris, St. Moritz, and on the Riviera—and had been the table-tennis champion of Egypt for 1964 to boot?

Oh, the deliriums of youth. When he had got on campus, he'd discovered that everyone had bushy hair and boots and foreign-made shirts. The old man had wanted to send him to an Ivy League college with a trunkful of hand-tailored suits and a brand-new Ferrari. But he had refused, wishing to show his father that he didn't need the Akkardijian money to make it. He had found odd jobs and let the monthly checks remain uncashed, stuffed in with his socks. As far as anyone knew, he was just another hard-up foreign student.

His first year at Hampton had been one of aimless drifting. He hadn't known what he wanted to do; he'd only known he didn't want to be like his old man.

And then in his sophomore year he had met Copeland,

standing on the endless line stretching back from the Physical Education desk.

The armory had been hot and stuffy, smelling of dust and sweat from a thousand bodies as the students of Hampton went through the twice-yearly agony of registration for classes.

It was four-thirty, Ben hadn't had lunch, and he had been forced to sign up for two eight o'clocks. He had three Saturday classes and hadn't been able to get the Poli Sci professor he wanted, and if there was one thing he did *not* feel like doing, it was standing in a mile-long line for two hours just to sign up for a dumb gym class.

He turned to the guy behind him and grumbled: "Could I use a beer right about now!"

"You and me both." The guy behind him, Benno noted, looked a bit older than the rest of them. It was hard to say exactly why he gave this impression; he was dressed like everyone, in jeans and a T-shirt, but there was something in his eyes, something wary and experienced. "Hold my place and I'll run out and get a couple of cans."

"Hey! Great! But *you* stay and *I'll* run out."

"Why? I'd just as soon go."

"No, no, I'll do it," Ben insisted. They looked at each other for a minute and then burst into laughter.

"After you, dear Alphonse," Ben said.

"No, after *you,* my dear Gaston." Then he stuck out his hand and added: "Dan Copeland."

"Ben Akkardijian."

They shook hands.

"Listen, Ben, I'm new this year. Is it always like this?" Dan gestured out over the chaotic scene, the lines of tired faces, the scruffy floors, the bleak stone walls.

"Yeah. Always."

Dan Copeland's deep-set dark eyes bored into his. "Half a mile from campus, in the world's most depressing building, with lines that last all day long. It stinks. Why don't they use the gym?"

"The gym? Don't be ridiculous. They just spent half a mill putting in some kind of super floor. Regular shoes mark it up. No, we can't use the gym."

The dark eyes flashed. "Oh? Half a million? On a

floor? That you're not allowed to *walk* on? Man, I can't believe it! Is Coach Brewster the king around here? To hell with people—right?—it's property that counts. Well, we'll see about that. Get fifty or sixty kids, and we can completely surround the gym so nobody can get in or out!"

"Wow!" Ben cried. "Not even the first day of classes for you—and already planning a revolution!"

Copeland grinned. "Yep. The Dan Copeland Doll. Wind him up and he organizes the masses."

"Gotcha. What's your plan?" Ben rubbed his hands together in anticipation. "A little demonstration here in the armory? A speech? A march? A kneel-in? What'll it be?"

Copeland looked around at the crowded scene. "I'd say we should do what the Army always did in 'Nam: Pull back and avoid further losses."

Benno grinned. "Do you mean what I think you mean? I hope?"

"This standing on line to sign up for Volleyball 242 A or Archery 317 is for the birds. Let's get out of here. I'll stand you to a beer."

Dumbly, Ben said, "But they don't let you graduate without your four years of Phys. Ed."

Copeland laughed. "Oh, really? They *don't?* Wanna bet? The Dan Copeland Doll. Wind him up and—'"

"—he protests the Phys. Ed. requirement for graduation," Benno finished with a flourish.

"Right on! Let's split."

Together, they strode past the weary, straggling lines and out the door, to find it raining hard. They huddled in the doorway.

"This damn climate!" Ben muttered. "I'll never get used to it. Can you organize something against the constant rain around here?"

"Sorry, that's not in our line."

"Our? You mean there's more of you?"

The lanky redhead laughed again. "Yeah. I've been in Hampton all summer, working and making up a freshman Philosophy course. A bunch of us who are sick and tired of being pushed around by outmoded rules have been meeting a couple of times a week. We've decided to call ourselves the Students' League, and we're going to change a lot of things around here."

"You mean, a club?"

"Club!" Dan snorted. "No, clubs are for kiddies. The League is going to have political clout around here. Wanna join? You seem like the kind of guy we need."

"Are you kidding? Give me action every time!"

"Great! I'll fill you in over some beer action. Let's go!"

Three hours and many beers later, they had drafted a petition to the head coach on seven bar napkins. Two senior girls—reporters from the campus newspaper—were sitting with them, giggling at their jokes while scribbling down all the "demands." By the time they had emerged it was almost dark. And it had been decided that Ben would share the rent and the space in Dan Copeland's attic apartment.

Glancing at the speedometer to make sure it wasn't above sixty, Ben laughed shortly. That had been the beginning with him and Dan Copeland, a chance meeting that had changed everything. If he hadn't met Dan that day in the armory, would he have continued with his charade of being a poor foreign student? He doubted it. Another six weeks, left on his own, and he would have been cashing the checks and accepting the car and living the soft kind of life he was accustomed to. One year of "poverty" had been enough.

Certainly the boy who had thought the table-tennis championship of Egypt was the apex of accomplishment would never, left to his own devices, have become politically active. He would have joined a fraternity, dressed elegantly, and picked his dates from the blondest, richest, prettiest girls on campus.

It was a joke, really. When he had married, that was whom he'd picked—the blondest, richest, prettiest woman in Philadelphia. Some things just didn't change, no matter how smart you thought you were.

Never mind what might have been. What had actually happened was that Dan had said, "Let's go," and he had followed; and that's what he had kept doing for the next six years, dammit. Dan Copeland first, and Ben Akkardijian right behind. They had done all the planning and plotting together for the marches and the demonstrations, but it was always Dan who had been in the public eye. It was Dan who had given the speeches and rallied the students. And it was Dan who had been elected president of the League and Ben who had been the veep. They both decided on pre-Law and they had both got A's, but Dan had set the curve and Ben had been number two. And when they had handed out the history prize, Dan had won it over Benno by one vote.

And the girls. There had always been plenty of girls. Ben had had the reputation of being a wit and a comedian, without a serious bone in his body. He'd known, after a while, that girls were not going to fall down and beg him for dates, the way it seemed to happen with Copeland. But he had discovered that if he got a girl away from the others, where he could turn on the charm and get her laughing, he wouldn't do badly at all. Then why had he always felt that he was getting Copeland rejects.

Of course, when he had gone after Kitty Cameron, he hadn't had the chance of a snowball in hell. He'd known that. As soon as Dan set his sights on her, she'd just been Ben's pal. An interesting one, that Kit. Usually, Dan Copeland's girls had hung around, mooning and trying to get his attention. But not Kit, she was cool. She had made him suffer plenty. Ben recalled vaguely that she had married the summer after graduation—one of those rich business-school stiffs. At the start of law school, Dan had been very tight and uncommunicative for weeks. Even after he had begun to act more like himself, he'd never again mentioned her name. He'd just thrown himself into his studies with even more fervor. And he'd come out number one in the class, hadn't he? Leaving Akkardijian runner-up as usual.

Well, it was his own fault. Dan had been his leader. When he had called that August to say that the Peace Corps plan had fallen through and that he was joining Ben in law school, Benno had been delighted. He'd felt sure it would be an active and interesting three years. It would be like old times.

And so there they had been, in Madison, Wisconsin—roommates once more. Madison, Wisconsin: what a laugh! What business had Benno Akkardijian, via Rome, London, Paris, and Cairo, in the Midwest? It was so *cold*. For three winters, shivering in twenty-below spells that lasted for weeks, he would plaintively say, "Let's switch to the University of Cairo. They're swimming there right now, Dan. They're sitting under beach umbrellas, sweating. Heaven!"

But of course they had stayed, both of them. And the old pattern kept repeating itself. Daniel Copeland, number one and editor of *Law Review*. Assistant editor and number two: three guesses, and the first two don't count. He should have pulled out after the first year, or at least after the second. He hated being second-best, and even worse, he had come to the conclusion that law school was really not for him. But then, it was unthinkable that he should not study with Dan and discuss politics with Dan and plan the future of the world with Dan.

It took being beaten out for the job with Judge Cooper —by Dan, of course—to make him really angry. By that time Dan was already engaged to Polly. And when Dan, grinning with triumph, said, "Out here, buddy, it's us poor-but-honest types who get the top jobs," that did it for Ben.

He stiffened at that crack. "Hey, man," he protested, "I thought we had that all out back in Hampton. Look at me—have I changed any since you found those checks? Do my old man's bucks make me any different. When you cut me, do I not bleed? When a chick looks my way, do I not turn on? Isn't it about time you came off it?" He slammed out of the apartment and was halfway down the stairs when Dan caught up with him.

"God, I'm a stiff-necked ass, Ben. What a rotten thing to say. Can we forget it?"

"Yeah, we can forget it, I guess. But you've got a lousy nerve. You're marrying into plenty of bread, and I don't notice it bothering you."

Dan said, very quietly, "It's bothering me. It's—never mind. It doesn't give me an excuse for bugging *you*. Look, I'm sorry."

"You're sorry and I'm splitting. I'm taking that job in Philly, where it's the rich-but-honest types, like *me*, who get the good jobs."

Just ahead was a familiar crossroads, a dairy farm on one corner and a shiny aluminum diner on the other. And, just as it had ten years ago, the crooked signpost read:

HAMPTON, 7 MI. He swung the car to follow it, down bumpy county road 37.

Almost there. And with that thought, the realization that he was looking forward to it, to all of it. Hoisting a beer at The Pub, maybe; seeing how the rest of them had turned out; and, let's admit it, showing them all how well, how very well, funny little Benno Akkardijian had done.

He grinned to himself. And it would be a kick to see their faces when they finally recognized him. It was quite possible that nobody would know who he was. Rugowsky had been blunt enough to blurt it out: "Have you changed!" It was certainly true. Any resemblance between the skinny, bushy-haired boy and the dark, mustachioed man was purely imaginary.

Of course, back then, when he had first come to America, he had thought he looked pretty exciting and wonderful. It was the old man's looks that had embarrassed him. So foreign and different, with his prow of a nose and his swarthy skin, always blue with the heavy beard no matter how close he shaved. He had thought Pa's thick blue-black hair greasy-looking, and the huge handlebar mustache with the curled-up ends a joke.

When Pa had demanded to know, at the end of his first year at school, why he let himself look like such a bum, he had almost snapped back: "You should talk! You look like Omar the Rug Dealer!" But he had known better. His father, short as he was, was powerfully built, and his answer to a fresh remark would likely be a swat to the side of the head with his thick right arm.

So he had kept his thoughts to himself. If the old man didn't realize how strange he looked, that was his tough luck. Well, the last laugh was on me, Benno reflected. The *Bulletin* had recently run a story about his latest project, and when he had glanced at the page and seen the fierce Arab face staring out at him, his first reaction had been one of surprise: What's the old man doing in the paper?

Of course, it wasn't Pa at all, but the fresh-mouthed son, who now had to eat his words—or his unspoken thoughts, at any rate. Funny, how he had looked into his shaving mirror twice each day and hadn't seen it. He was the image of his old man. It was as plain as the nose on his face! And that made him laugh aloud. The nose on *his* face—the proud, bladelike nose—was the plainest sight for miles around! Once he had been self-conscious about his nose, but no more. Women, at least, seemed to find his looks extremely attractive.

Yes, it would be interesting to see how they all reacted when they realized who he was. Especially since he wasn't expected; he wasn't on any of the lists. This had been a spur-of-the-moment decision, the kind, he thought ruefully, Copeland used to be so famous for. It would be terrific if Copeland showed. Wouldn't it? What if nobody came? Someone at a recent dinner party had told Ben about his tenth reunion. "Only five other people from my class showed up," the guy had said. "And not one I had ever known. The joint was packed with Golden Oldies, the fifty-year folks, who tottered around and called me Sonny. God, it was a nightmare!"

Well, nightmare or beautiful dream, here it was: Hampton, New York, sprawling back from the shores of Lake Winnetaka, its splendid old college lifting roofs and spires above the sleepy town.

It was past four o'clock, and the lowering sun cast a red-gold haze over the quiet street, gilding the old frame houses under their venerable maples. Ben smiled. It was still a pretty little town. Even the main street looked the same, a line of tiny shops, immaculate and neatly painted, its boulevard planted with scarlet and gold mums. Soon he was climbing the Iroquois Street hill, and there was the VA hospital and the Saxony bookstore, St. Anthony's church and the K. of C. hall right next door. Then the haughty row of old Victorian mansions, embellished with turrets and towers, bay windows and broad porches; liberally garnished with gingerbread trim; and, on each, a big sign lettered in Greek. EX. AΔΩ. ZΦ. Fraternity Row. At the very top of the hill, at the end of the line of fraternity and sorority houses, stood majestic old Major Hall, the original Hampton Academy, where in 1854 students could be educated in Greek, Latin, Hebrew, and the Scriptures for two shillings a term.

Benno turned right, onto University Avenue, and was immediately flooded with memories. University was the main drag of the campus, and there, directly to his right, in all its pseudo-Georgian glory, was the Administration Building with its large, tree-planted brick plaza. Students were sprawled around, as they always had been, chatting and catching the last warm rays of the afternoon sunshine. A red Frisbee sailed silently through the air. And there were plenty of bikers, wheeling along the sidewalk where they weren't supposed to be. He slowed and on impulse pulled to the curb and got out, strolling up to the plaza. There he turned and looked out across the street to Major Hall and the quadrangle beyond, lined with buildings.

It was here, right here, that he had stood at Dan's shoulder when they'd protested the rigid control of the gymnasium. On this very spot, during the first sit-in against the war, he had held up a heavy sign for two hours until his arms had gone numb. This was where the League had held all its sit-ins and stand-ins and kneel-ins. Once even a love-in, where everyone had sat around holding each other. For that one, he recalled with a smile, the administration had called the local police, and he and Dan had spent the night in a crammed jail cell with thirty others.

He laughed to himself. How did we ever find the time to study and get all those terrific grades? Every week there had been another cause, another demonstration, another rally, another mass meeting. The poor deans! But, by God, it had been fun! And anything—*everything* —had seemed possible.

It was strange to be standing here, looking at buildings that held so much of his youth, and to feel so distant from it all. They were the same buildings he had looked at ten years ago. They were brick and stone and mortar, and would never change. It was life that had changed. We lived in another world back then, he thought, a world of challenge and confrontation when the student voice was heard loud and demanding throughout the country. We knew we could change everything, and all we changed was ourselves. The students on the streets look so different now, with their preppy clothes and short haircuts. They seem so serious, so self-possessed. Nothing is left of the passions of the sixties and seventies, nothing.

He stopped a young man in aviator glasses and asked the way to Enders Hall. He received a careful and complete set of instructions and was addressed as "sir."

With a sudden feeling of distaste, he hurried back to

the car. And maybe we didn't even change ourselves, he thought. Maybe it was just time that made the changes.

For a moment he considered turning the car around and heading right back down Route 20. Why bother revisiting something that was dead and gone, unrecoverable? But what the devil, he was already here. And it would be good to see Copeland, if Dan were coming. He pressed down on the clutch and started the ignition. Who knows, he mused, carefully pulling out, he might even find someone in the class of '70 he had missed the first time around.

CHAPTER FIVE

William Sean Michael O'Hara

ASSOCIATE PROFESSOR WILLIAM O'HARA stood by the plate-glass window of Jordon's Sporting Goods, looking in. He might have been staring at the elaborate display of hunting knives laid out on a big brown bearskin, but his gaze was really on his own darkly reflected image. Were those wrinkles under his eyes, or just the ravages of last night's late hours? He squinted, but the imperfect glass would not reveal any details. All in all, he decided, smoothing the rather long, wavy dark brown hair back from his ears, not bad. Could pass for thirty-five, no problem. He liked the long thick sideburns; they filled in the hollows under the cheekbones and drew attention to the cleft in his chin. He thought that women fancied a cleft chin.

Behind him, three coeds bounced by, chattering in their inane way. "Hey, Professor," one of them called. O'Hara gave them a jaunty wave of the hand without turning, automatically pulling in his stomach muscles. Cute. Very cute, in their shetland sweaters and blazers and skirts. It was nice to see all those skirts on campus, to see firm young legs and thighs again. He turned his head slightly to eye the brunette in the trio. Was she in one of his classes? He'd seen her somewhere. Maybe she was worth a little extra attention. She waggled her bottom, knowing full well that he'd be watching her. They were all the same, all of them. But so young, lately. Too young? he wondered.

His latest, Jennifer, with the Prince Valiant haircut and the Rubensesque body, had patted his cheek this morning and laughingly said, "I just love older men . . . unresolved Oedipus, I guess." What had she meant, older? Had she meant older than twenty? Or had she meant—he refused to face the words—"middle-aged." To hell with her. Forty-four was the prime of life for a man. I'll bet—giving himself a smile in the wavery glass—she's never been to bed with anyone nearly as good. What do those boys know about sex? Women preferred a man who knew what he was doing.

A bright red sports car went by. O'Hara turned from the shop window to look at it. The driver was a bit younger than he, dark, with Zapata mustachios. He looked well off and sure of himself, driving with one hand, the other arm nonchalantly crooked out the car window. Maybe I should try a mustache, O'Hara mused. They look good. Sexy. The car slowed by Iroquois Street, then signaled and took the turn up the hill toward campus.

Watching it, O'Hara felt the familiar surge of anger. That car, he knew, had set that fellow back twelve thousand dollars, maybe more. How did he get that kind of money? How did they all make it, somehow, when he with his brains and his looks and his charisma was still stuck here in this backwater? That little BMW was an O'Hara type of car. He'd look good in that car . . . he'd look *right*. Life was a bitch. His classes were always in great demand; they had to turn the girls away. They'd never had to cancel him out for lack of registration, not once.

Still, his tenure had been late in coming, and then it was only by the skin of his teeth. He was still, after so many years, only an associate professor. Somebody in the department had it in for him.

He knew why. It was all the fault of that bastard Copeland. He'd never forget the year 1970, not as long as he lived. That arrogant young nit with his scraggly red hair and his big mouth! Copeland had been in one of his classes, just one, but he had made himself felt. A royal pain in the class. O'Hara laughed to himself. Not a bad joke, that. He'd have to use it in his next lecture. All the vets had been an irritant, but Copeland had thought his time in Vietnam made him God's special gift to the campus. He, Bill O'Hara, would gladly have gone to fight for his country, but he'd been too young for Korea and too old for 'Nam.

The trouble with Copeland was, he thought he had a mission. He was going to clean up the world—starting with Hampton. O'Hara's fists clenched and unclenched as he remembered it. *Professor Profiles.* They had had the temerity, Dan Copeland and his hippies, to pass judgment on all their teachers. Not only to pass judgment, but to write it, print it, and distribute it to every student before registration in '69. Each dean's office had got a copy, and each department head.

He'd never forget *that*. Harry Cohn had called him in to say: "Of course, the administration isn't going to take any action simply on the strength of student complaints, but it doesn't look good. It says here that you flirt with your female students and are often absent without warning, unavailable for conferences, and more interested in showing how well you can recite than in covering the poets in the curriculum."

Secretly sweating, he had bulled his way through *that*. "I should hope," he had said very calmly, "that you wouldn't pay heed to the maunderings of those who nearly failed my course. Sour grapes, that's all it is. Hell, Harry," he had added, puffing on his pipe, "they shouldn't call that damn thing *Professor Profiles*. They should call it *Pick on Your Professor*." He had laughed—it wasn't a bad quip—but Harry Cohn had not. It was probably Harry who was holding him back—Harry, who was bald and unhappily married and running to fat.

Nevertheless, it was Copeland he really blamed. Things hadn't been the same since that report had come out. He had felt the change in the department almost immediately. Many of his colleagues, who had invited him over for dinner or coffee in the past, stopped doing it. Certain people seemed to avoid him. Lots of things. All because of one fucking bastard who had thought he knew how to save the world. Damn Dan Copeland. He probably believed O'Hara had long since forgotten. But, he thought ferociously, Bill O'Hara *never* forgets. Never.

The big blue and silver bus pulled up with a squeal of brakes, and he boarded. It was a crime, he thought, that he should be forced to take the city bus when other men, less intelligent men, were driving around in sports cars. He looked idly out of the window. There was a big, hand-lettered sign on the Omega Alpha Phi home. WELCOME, OLD GRADS, it said, TEN WONDERFUL YEARS: 1970–1980. He snorted softly. 1970 had been one helluva year for him. He had been glad to see the back of it.

Still, it hadn't been all bad. That was the year of Lee Rivers. Some broad, that Lee! His dark-eyed gypsy girl, always ready to go. Nothing coy about *her!* It had been a relief, not having to talk about undying love or make promises he never meant to keep. Never even that old, old question: "Where is this leading us?" And the sex had been spectacular . . . so good, he had stupidly asked her to move in with him. Him! with a long-planned trip to Ireland all paid for. But the words had just tumbled out. Proving once and for all that a man in bed with a woman is likely to say *anything*.

And hadn't he considered himself lucky to have escaped! When she wasn't with him, he could see clearly that she was just another girl, not very pretty, overweight, and without any class . . . a bit of a slut, even. Look how easily she had fallen into bed with him. She had all but thrown herself on the classroom floor. And he was going to *live* with someone like that? Impossible. Couldn't he just picture her sitting at faculty teas and acting the hostess when it was his turn to have the department over for Christmas?

Shit, how was he to know that she'd become a superstar? He had heard her sing, and she was damn good. But she had looked such a mess. Who would have guessed, in his wildest imagination, that the frizzy-haired chubby would become svelte and chic and appear regularly on the pages of every slick magazine? From all the photos, she was a knockout now.

He'd begun to think he'd made a mistake, maybe. Still, her name was on the list of returning grads for the reunion. He'd checked at the Alumni Office last month and charmed the woman behind the desk into showing him the class of '70 list.

Why shouldn't he still have a chance? Star or no star, she was still the same. Round heels like that never changed. And she had really been hung up on him in 1970, hadn't she? Couldn't get enough. Climbing out of the sorority-house windows at all hours. He had only to snap his fingers. That wouldn't have changed, he'd bet on it.

It was worth a try, by Jesus. On his lap was a shiny box containing a new Harris tweed jacket with suede elbow patches and a Fair Isle sweater. The clothes always got 'em. That rugged-romantic-Irish-poet look. He could see it all: the crowded cocktail party, the lights dim, the air filled with the buzz of conversation. She'd be standing amid a crowd of admirers, and he would just stroll up casually and stand there, fixing her with his eyes. He'd have a pipe in his teeth—lit? maybe not; the smoke might get into his eyes—and he'd let the cowlick fall over his forehead the way it always did. She'd feel his eyes on her, and pretty soon she'd glance over and there he'd be, looking exactly the way she remembered him. Hell, she *must* remember him. Nobody could have responded the way she had and then just forget it all. Sure, she'd thought of him. She had shed some tears over him, he wouldn't wonder.

No reason they couldn't pick up where they'd left off all those years ago. And if now she was rich and famous and sought-after, what difference? He was going to be smart about it; he was going to act as if she were just the same old Lee Rivers.

The bus bumped its way around the corner to College Place, and, by God, there was that red BMW he'd seen in town, parked by the Admin Building. O'Hara craned his neck as the bus went by and saw that dark fellow striking a pose on the plaza, acting as if he didn't realize that every romantic little coed nearby had her eyes plastered on him.

Some life that guy must have. Expensive car, expensive

clothes. You could even see that the haircut was expensive. Time for O'Hara to get a piece of that action. Lee Rivers ought to be able to afford him easily. And the new course they'd given him this year—Elizabethan and Petrarchian Sonnets—it was a royal pain . . . too damn much preparation. It was all he could do to keep up with the class. At his age, it was time to start taking it easy. How nice to settle down with a rich bitch and let her pay the freight. And she'd get her money's worth, that he could promise. He'd be glad to go to stud. Whatever she wanted. Hell, if he were a goddamn stallion, they'd pay thousands for the same kind of service. So why not?

The bus stopped at the corner of College Place and Hampton Avenue, the last stop before it turned around and went back down into town. The doors wheezed open and the other passengers, like so many sheep, filed to the rear door. He never paid any attention to signs that ordered "alight at rear of bus"—or to any other orders, for that matter. Orders were for dull, unthinking masses of humanity, not for Mrs. O'Hara's boy.

He shoved to the front of the bus and bounded down the steps, plowing into a woman getting on who was too dense to see him coming. A woman thin as a rake, in a cheap flowered dress of the type he hadn't seen since the fifties—almost to the ankle, buttoned right up to the throat, long sleeves—and wearing, of all the damn things, spotless white gloves. A flimsy canvas briefcase bound in bright orange vinyl went flying out of her hand, onto the sidewalk, where it burst open. Papers skidded every which way: photographs, a sleazy paperback romance, another pair of white cotton gloves, two Hampton alumni magazines, and a thick black Bible stamped with gold lettering. He stood and stared. Every item was carefully encased in its own plastic bag, closed with its own green wire twist. Even a used brown paper bag was carefully, precisely, folded and sealed in clear plastic.

"Stupid!" the woman hissed. "Look what you've done!" Her face was thin, pale, tight, with pinched features. Spots of color rose rapidly in blotches, and she glared at him with ravaged eyes of a pale, bottomless gray.

Even so, O'Hara gave her his famous smile. "Madam, a thousand apologies. Please. I'm so sorry. Let me pick it up for you."

"No, you don't, O'Hara. I'll get it. It's mine!" She turned away from him, almost in revulsion, and stuffed all her plastic-covered trash quickly back into the case, snatching the case up and hugging it to her flat old-maid's chest as if it were her baby. Then she pushed by him, every muscle in her body tightly clenched.

Tight-ass, he thought. His heart was thumping painfully. Who was she? Where had he seen her before? She knew his name. Could she once have been a student of his . . . could she have been, God forbid, one of his *girls?* "Jesus, Mary, and Joseph!" he exclaimed aloud. Not her! Not *her!*

He started for his apartment, filled with uneasiness. She had got to him, the crazy old cunt. Once she might have been an eager little coed—pretty, even. She might have been all blushes and flirty looks, charmed by the handsome young professor. He might have taken her into his bed. And now look at her. Was this to be the pattern for the rest of his life? That all his sweet young things would turn into grotesque old women and come back to haunt him? He shuddered.

It was a sign to him. It was time to get out of here, get away, start a new life.

And for that he needed, and had to have and would get, Lee Rivers. Whatever it took to get her.

CHAPTER SIX

Serena Malverne De Luca

SERENA HEADED FOR a seat in the back of the bus. Her feet hurt like crazy; it was an effort not to wince every time she took a step. But she needed to be alone. How much had O'Hara seen? Sweat collected at the nape of her neck and crept down her backbone. Ugh, filthy. She needed a bath and she needed a drink—oh, sweet Jesus, she needed a drink. But not now. She sucked in her stomach and sat straight in her seat. Surreptitiously, she felt in the briefcase, her head bent close to the opening. Thanks to O'Hara, everything was messed up. Now she had to put it all back where it belonged. She could hardly bear to see the chaos inside the bag. She hated mess, hated it. A wrinkle in a cushion could drive her mad. Swiftly, her fingers scrabbled in the familiar interior, lifting and rearranging until each item was precisely where it should be. She smiled at the leather heft of her prayer book. Just to have her hand on it gave her peace. Then she zipped the briefcase firmly closed, tightening her lips as she did so. She had glanced down, and she could see very clearly, even under the wide skirt, that her thighs had splayed out. Standing up, it looked all right; her legs were neat, without bulky curves, without fat, the same all the way up. They *looked* all right. But they weren't. They were *fat*. As soon as she sat down, she could see the flesh oozing out to the side. Fat! She would have to cut down further on her calories. Eight hundred a day was too much.

She looked out the bus window, unwilling to dwell on her gross flesh any more. And then she smiled. Ha! hadn't O'Hara looked . . . well, frightened when she called him by name. Yes, frightened. Good! Give him something to worry about, the whoremaster, always too busy womanizing to pay attention to his work.

She'd taken his course in Celtic Literature, and she'd held her breath as his cat's eyes raked the room the first day of class. She'd heard about him, how he picked one or two girls from his classes every year and . . . But she knew nothing of that, only that he was beautiful, so tall and slim and sure of himself, a little smile curling at the corners of his heavy lips, his eyes thickly lashed in sooty black. Often he invaded her dreams, and she would wake sweating and scared, her heart hammering. It was always the same dream, the same one she dreamed about Dan Copeland . . . But that had been before he had married her pretty Polly. She probably hadn't dreamed that dream about Dan Copeland; she was remembering badly. William O'Hara, though, she remembered him, all right. How she had adored him, even though he seemed never to remember her name. She learned his schedule and she followed him, just for a glimpse of him. Once she said hello and he smiled, his eyes crinkling. And then one day she managed to get right behind him at a rally, almost touching him with her body. Someone called his name and he turned, nearly falling over her, hopping about in an effort not to fall. "Fat sow!" he'd spit out. She wanted to sink into the earth, disappear.

That had been her awakening. No wonder Dan Copeland had married her sister. Polly was slender. She, Serena, was fat. She knew about fat. She knew that fat people were crazy and weak, out of control. When she gazed at herself in the mirror now, it was as if she could still see the fat, slopping over the clean, neat bones, soft gushy waxy dirty.

Bill O'Hara had come into the Alumni Office just last month, sucking around, smiling, wanting a look at the reunion list. She was in charge of all the lists; she made sure they were kept up-to-date and correct. She could have told him exactly who was coming. All he had to do was ask. But he'd rather pretend, he'd rather shake his curls at her and call her "darlin' girl." She didn't have to, but she showed him the list and tried to see who it was he was looking for. She knew the one person whose name *she* wanted to be there, and it was. Dan Copeland. Dan Copeland, who had murdered her sister.

Tears stung at the corners of her eyes and she blinked them back. It had been almost seven years, yet her grief still choked her as if it had just happened. Sweet Polly! who had never hurt anyone, crushed and broken in the middle of a hay-stubbled field.

Polly should never have gone that day. Serena had told her not to go. "A woman who's pregnant," she had said, "doesn't go traipsing across Wisconsin in a small plane."

And Polly had laughed. But then, laughter had been Polly's response to almost anything. "I'm not worried, Rena. You'll be with me, so I know I'll be safe."

She still dreamed about it, constantly. Every detail was sickeningly clear: the plane suddenly sinking—heavy, stonelike, a dead thing—and Polly screaming, "Oh, no, no, no, no!" The awful noise as they scraped and crunched through the treetops. The awful, sudden silence as the engines died, and then the frightening impact as they crashed into the earth.

The pain in her head always woke her, tears streaming from her eyes. In her dream she never saw Polly, but as soon as she was awake, she pictured her as she had been then: the slight, almost childlike body with that small swelling at the stomach, lying peacefully sprawled, looking asleep. Only the twisted angle of the neck showed something horribly wrong.

Never, never would she forget! When help finally arrived—who could tell how long it had been?—they found Serena outside the torn plane in the sun-flooded field, holding her dead sister's limp hand, screaming into the empty woods, unaware of the blood that oozed from the wound in her own skull. She was the sole survivor.

Serena groaned aloud, and a passenger near her on the bus gave her a startled look and would have spoken, but she turned her head away. As soon as she got home, she'd have a drink. Just a little one. Her head never seemed to clear until she'd had a nip. She took one in the morning and another with lunch, and that usually was just fine. It wasn't as though she were *drinking*. Just a little nip to clear her head, was all. And anyway, who was there to say, "Don't you think you've had enough"? Not Carmine De Luca. Her husband, ha, some husband. But he'd gone, banging out of the house last year saying he couldn't stand it. "You crazy bitch!" he'd bellowed. "You're a drunk!" Then coming over all high and mighty, telling her she had a problem, when he'd been the one who turned her to drink in the first place.

"I've got a problem, all right," she'd said to him. *"You."* Good riddance to him.

She'd just curl up in her favorite chair and have a couple of nips, and pretty soon the crass material world would become a distant blur. And then she could rise to another astral plane, where she could talk to the spirits. But first she had to blot out this existence. She would throw the I Ching, or maybe lay out the Tarot. The Tarot spoke so much more clearly. Her aura was good. The cards always gave her a message.

Hadn't they given her one the day she'd seen his name? Dan Copeland would be in Hampton for the reunion weekend. As soon as she'd seen that name, her heart had begun to race. She had had a presentiment; she had thought she might faint. There'd been an important message waiting for her. That night she had put out the cards with trembling hands. The Hanged Man had appeared, just as she had thought he might, telling her, "Dan Copeland is evil and must be destroyed."

She had made a solemn vow to Polly, kneeling in front of the sideboard, where votive candles always burned, lighting up the framed photograph of her sister smiling her pretty little smile, her eyes as calm as death. "I'll get him, Polly," she had whispered. And then, to make it final, she had taken out her scrapbook, the one with all the pictures and the snapshots and the newspaper clippings from all the years that she had known him. She had no picture of the first time she'd seen him, no, only the one in her head, and that she would never lose.

She'd been just a frosh; Polly was still back home. Pa had decided to try sending her to a fancy boarding school not too far away. Dan Copeland was a big wheel, you heard his name everywhere, he was a senior that year and maybe the best-known man on campus. She had first seen him striding across campus, jaw jutting and eyes narrowed. He was tall and slim, his chest neatly outlined under the T-shirts he always wore, his thick coppery hair pulled back in a ponytail. And then she'd heard him, at a rally to decriminalize pot. She hadn't gone to it; she was coming back to the dorm from the library, and there was a crowd around him on the Admin Building steps. His voice was magical, deep and thrilling. She didn't hear a single word but stood stock-still, staring up at him. His eyes glittered; she watched the bunched muscles move near his jaw. They cheered him, they laughed when he joked. Serena stared at the ropy muscles in his arms that moved when he moved; she stared at his long legs, planted firmly apart, and at the bulge in his jeans. She stared up at him and her heart began to pound painfully. She would find out where he lived, she would let herself in, she would strip herself naked; and when he came home, she would be there in the moonlight and he would stop, agape, unable to believe his luck, and she would reach out and then she would . . .

But no, of course, she didn't. He was so far above her,

and when she went to work at the S.L., stuffing envelopes, she listened to the gossip. He was brilliant, he was smart, he was in love with a cold blond beauty who gave him a hard time. She saw Dan Copeland once or twice, quite close to her at the S.L. office, but she didn't have the nerve to speak; and, of course, he never even noticed her.

And then he was graduated and gone, to the Peace Corps in India, the gossip said, and she dropped out of the Students' League because who cared if Dan Copeland wasn't there? And then, in '72, Pa sent Polly to Hampton, too. Serena often wondered how he had managed that, but she was used to Big Jim's managing just about anything he cared to.

She and Polly had been home for the Thanksgiving recess on a bitter cold day in November, walking on the main drag in Madison. And there, incredibly, he was! Walking down the street right toward them. "Look, Polly," she said, trying to keep her voice steady, "there's someone from Hampton." Someone! Ludicrous. Only the most perfect man in the whole world. Someone, indeed! "He was president of the Students' League my freshman year, Polly, and then he graduated. I wonder what he's doing here."

He was still a presence, striding down the street, jeans tucked into leather riding boots, a six-foot muffler wound around his neck and trailing streamers behind him. The long copper-colored hair had been cropped to shoulder-length, the face wasn't quite so lean, and he now sported a thick mustache and neat pointed beard.

"Oooh, he's *cute*," Polly said. "Let's take him home with us."

"I didn't know him *that* well, Poll. I was just a freshman, licking stamps and stuffing envelopes. *He* was really important!"

"But, Rena, you can't just let someone from Hampton walk on by without saying *something*. Oh, yoo-hoo, hello!"

Serena felt color staining her cheeks, but Polly never cared what she did or said in public. She was used to being little and cute and adored. And, sure enough, when he whirled around, his eyes almost immediately crinkled into a smile of pleasure.

"Hello," he said. "Do I know you? I hope?" He laughed.

Polly giggled. "Not really. But my sister, Serena, worked for you in the Students' League at Hampton."

His eyes shifted to her. She felt uncomfortable and gawky, as she always did when boys looked at her. She was big and broad, like her father. But it was even worse, its being Dan Copeland. Dan Copeland, who had filled so many of her dreams her freshman year, who—in her dreams—smiled down at her and looked right into her eyes and spoke of his love.

Now, in real life, he smiled down at her and looked right into her eyes—she thought her heart would stop beating—and said, "I'm afraid I don't remember you. You must have been one of the freshies—" He grinned ingratiatingly. "Freshmen, of course, being beneath the notice of us big guys."

His voice was so nice, deep and friendly. And the smile was warm and accepting, not condescending at all. She relaxed. She found she could even speak. "That's right. I was one of the worker ants."

He laughed. "Well, it's good to see someone from old Hampton. How is it there these days? Any sit-ins—or am I hopelessly out of style?"

But he, she thought, could *never* be out of style. She could no longer remember what any of them had talked about. She couldn't recall a single word she had said. But it must have been okay, because they had chatted, the three of them, for five or ten minutes there on the windy sidewalk. His eyes kept wandering to Polly, of course, cute little Polly with her rosebud lips and her round blue eyes and the tendrils of curly yellow hair peeking out from under the fluffy angora cap. But he wasn't mean about it, like some boys. He didn't make her feel left out and alone.

And then Polly asked, "Why are you still at school when it's vacation?"

And he laughed and said, "Law students don't get vacations."

And Polly dimpled and giggled. "But you can't have Thanksgiving dinner *alone*."

Her heart was hammering so, Serena could barely hear her own voice as she took a deep breath and said,

as fast as she could get it out, "Whydon'tyoucomeand-
havedinnerwithus?"

Yes, it had all been her fault. She had actually *liked*
him. She had been fooled, as they all had been fooled.
Because—as she knew now, too late—it hadn't been the
meal. It hadn't even been Polly's dimpled charms that
had captivated him. No, it had been the charm and power
of the Malverne name, her father's political clout. He
was always an ambitious one, that Dan Copeland, and
everyone in law school would have to know who Big Jim
Malverne was. Dan Copeland was *still* using their father,
to this very day, to further his own greedy ambitions.

Her pigheaded father, who thought he was so smart!
How delighted he had been, in the end, that his darling
little problem named Polly was infatuated with Dan Copeland. Never thought to look, to see how Serena might be
feeling, no, of course not. Always had him in mind for
Polly. Why, the day after Thanksgiving, wasn't he on the
phone to the dean of the law school, and didn't he hang
up, beaming? "That's one smart fella you girls brought
home," he said, rubbing his big hands together, as pleased
as if he'd invented Dan Copeland himself. "And Polly
likes him. Now, let's see if he likes her." She could have
told him they *all* liked Polly, so cute and helpless and gig-
gly and flirty. Not at all Dan Copeland's type, but she
didn't have to be, did she? With Big Jim as his father-in-
law, he could go just about as far as he wanted in Wisconsin. So both sisters returned to Hampton after Thanksgiving recess, but Polly stayed only long enough to pack up
her things. By the end of January, Dan was taking Polly
out regularly, and right after law school graduation, they
were married.

You'd think Jim would have learned his lesson when
Polly was killed. Not an hour after the burial, though, he
had ignored most of the mourning guests, talking politics
in a corner with Dan and a couple of county leaders. Disgusting!

That night after everyone had left, she laced into him.
"That man murdered Polly and you know it!" she
screamed.

He patted her in an offhand manner and said, "Now,
Serena. Don't carry on. It was an accident. Dan's just as
cut up as we are."

"Why did he have to have her there? It was just a speech, a stupid speech!"

"Now, Serena. Try to understand. Dan's going to be an important man one of these days. Wives are expected to be with a politician. God almighty, *you* know that. Polly knew it. She *wanted* to go. So don't start making up things."

At this point, Serena became very cold and still, as if all the blood in her body had stopped moving.

"Polly wanted to go," she mimicked in a voice of ice. "You know Polly was never even capable of deciding to cross the street!"

Big Jim moved to her in one giant stride and smacked her across the face with his big hand. The words grated through his clenched teeth: "We agreed years ago that we'd never talk about that!"

Tears coursed down her cheeks. "Secrets! Secrets! It wasn't any secret at Hampton, you know! She was flunking —she was flunking *everything*—no matter how hard I tried to help her—" Serena broke down completely, erupting into harsh sobs.

"That's another thing that will never be discussed!"

She wiped the wetness from her face and gulped back the tears. Weakness in *her* only irritated him. Trying to steady her voice, which came out in a half whisper, she asked, "What did you have to promise Copeland to get him to marry her?"

This time his arm shot out without thought and he backhanded her across the head, sending her sprawling against the sideboard. He had never before so much as put a finger to her in anger. Breathless and shocked, she glared up at him. Their eyes, so alike, pale gray, shadowed beneath heavy black brows, locked and held for a moment. He loomed huge in front of her, baleful and implacable. She hated him.

When Ma had died, she was thirteen and Polly was just going on ten. He had told her then that from now on she was in charge of her little sister. She hated it and she was scared, but she did what he asked. She had always looked after Polly, always tried to watch over her. But Polly was always a handful, a slippery little devil. In school they kept pushing her along from grade to grade, even though she never learned how to read very well. She was never interested in anything in school, really, except boys.

Serena tried, but she couldn't keep her eyes on Polly all the time. Not when she was trying to become valedictorian of her class and had to do her homework and do it right. She tried to tell Jim that Polly was too much for her, but all her father said was to stop complaining. Her feelings never counted.

And then, after all the years she'd put in, taking care of her sister, protecting her, keeping her safe, when push came to shove, she didn't count at all. Big Jim had happily handed Polly over to a man, and the bastard had let her die. And now her father was mauling *her*, his only remaining child, instead of the man who deserved it.

After a minute or two, Jim gave a shudder and held out his hand. "I'm sorry. I'm upset. Come along now. Get up. We're *both* upset. Don't you think I miss her? Christ! But we've got to go on, we've got to go on."

Not she! She would *not* forget! And as for him suffering, that was a laugh. Even when Ma died, he had gone right on with his life, his rallies, and his meetings. If anything, there had been more of them. She wasn't taking *his* hand. She turned her whole body away, rejecting everything: his words, his hand, himself. The room rang with silence. And then she heard him clump his heavy-footed way out of the room and out of the house.

It was the last time she had seen her father. She had gone back to school, but she couldn't concentrate, and before the semester was out, she had quit. She had never graduated. Instead, she took a room downtown and began to hang around. That's where she'd met De Luca, in a bar. He thought it was pretty nifty that she got regular checks from a father she never spoke to. He wanted to buy a gas station. Well, she had bought him his gas station; it was still there, on the Auburn road, and he and it could rot in hell for all she cared.

To hell with all men, that was her philosophy. She recalled very clearly how she had finally gone to Dan, protesting that Polly shouldn't take that plane. And he had laughed, saying, "Polly loves to watch me do my number, don't you, Poll?" And Polly had snuggled up to him, smiling and preening and giving Serena a look that said, *Stay out.* Polly didn't need her any more; she had her handsome husband instead. And so she had died. Twenty years old, dead, and the baby with her.

The bus jolted around the big curve and hit a bump. Serena's fingers tightened convulsively on the handles of the canvas bag.

Dan Copeland had killed her little sister, her helpless little sister, just as if he had pointed a gun to her head and pulled the trigger. And now he would be repaid. She smiled a tight little smile. Dan Copeland would be at the reunion, but before the festivities were over, Dan Copeland would be punished.

CHAPTER SEVEN

Florence, Italy

ENDERS HALL sat in a corner of the campus, the oldest dormitory at Hampton, built sturdily of brick now faded to a soft rose, and laced with climbing ivy. Alone of all the dorms, it had wide lawns on all sides, fenced by huge boxwoods. A brick path in a herringbone pattern led up to the large door, which was sheltered by a pillared veranda across the front of the house with oversized leaded-glass windows on either side, their sills nearly at floor level. It looked like the main house of a grand estate, an impression soon disrupted by the college tennis courts on one side, the busy main library directly across the street, and, on the other side, a parking lot which at five-thirty on the first night of reunion weekend was already nearly filled.

Inside, the main floor glowed with light. The reception area had been cleared of its proctor's desk and the bench next to it to make room for three long tables, smiling host-esses behind each, facsimile copies of the *Daily Hamp-tonian* from graduation day ten years before, room assignments, maps of the campus for forgetful alums, and name tags.

At the very first table Courtney (Wills) Standish sat, patting her hair from time to time, greeting all comers. She had placed herself so as to see each newcomer arriv-ing. On her left shoulder, a large silver badge announced that she was CHAIRMAN, WELCOME COMMITTEE; in front of her, in neat rows on the table, were the all-important name tags, complete with old yearbook pictures, for each class member who had signed up for this reunion week-end.

"Hi, there," Courtney greeted each alum. "Welcome." Her voice sounded enthusiastic, and it was. At home in Skaneateles, she was always heading up committees. Some people were just natural organizers, that's all. Here at the first table she saw everybody *first*. There were quite a few celebrities from the class of '70, she was proud to say, and she was going to get to talk to each and every one before anyone else got a chance. Tucked into her bag was a copy of the Saturday-night *Well-Kum-Back Dinner* menu, all ready for autographs. She figured she'd say it was for her kids; who could refuse that?

"Hi, there," Courtney said brightly, flashing her famous smile. When she had been head cheerleader her senior year, everyone said her smile could be seen right to the top of the bleachers. "Jen Gladstone, isn't it? How nice to see you and how nice you look!" Half of her hanging out, Courtney thought, and why a *red* dress? No one wore red any more. With that blotchy skin, it just made her look sick. And anyway, it was too tight. And much too dressy. Her own silk wraparound, now, was much more suitable.

"Still with Mom and Dad? How convenient." Of course still living at home. What man would want her? Could hardly meet your eyes, and always giggling.

"Hi, there! Murray Fenton, isn't it? Welcome. How nice to see you and how well you're looking." She scrabbled in the piles of name tags to find his. Still a nobody, living in Hampton, a car salesman, she'd heard. Well, that's what happened to English majors without talent. Thin-ning on top, wasn't he? And his *clothes!*

Murray Fenton gave a big hello to Jen, who immediately turned scarlet and giggled nervously. "I should call Mom. She worries. She shouldn't, but . . . oh, well . . . I can—is there a phone?"

Now, wasn't that enough to turn anyone off? But not Murray Fenton. There he was, offering her a dime for the pay phone and trotting along after her. Maybe he wasn't married; maybe he was desperate.

Where were all the *interesting* people? Courtney shifted on the hard little folding chair and consulted her brand-new Bulova watch. Real gold, of course. Say what you would about her Jock (and she could tell you plenty if she wanted to), he wasn't cheap.

She had thought this job would be exciting. She'd worked very hard to nudge Susie Hazlitt out of this table and onto beer mugs and campus maps. But so far, what good was it? A parade of the class losers! People like Murray and Jen and Hal Bradford—wouldn't you know he had been the first one in!—with his second-rate job at a second-rate ad agency in Albany! Thought he was such a hotshot reporter ten years ago, lording it all over everybody!

"How you doing, Suze?" she called over to the beer mug/campus maps table.

"Just fine. How many do you figure so far?"

"Twenty or twenty-five. But we're supposed to get a hundred, and that doesn't count husbands and wives."

Susie Hazlitt had gotten so dumpy since graduation. Courtney sucked in her flat stomach and eyed herself with pleasure. The dress was a genuine designer original; the shoes had cost one hundred and fifty dollars and matched the color of the dress exactly. She sighed, patting her long pageboy bob carefully. It had been worth the day spent at Elizabeth Arden in Syracuse to know that she looked smart. She would have nothing to be ashamed of tonight. Yes, it had been worth every penny. Jock had squawked and screamed bloody murder. Yet he thought *nothing* of dropping a hundred dollars every Sunday on a football game.

The front door opened, admitting a crowd of people. More like peacocks, she thought. Wouldn't you know, the New York City crowd, as theatrical as ever. My word, are they still sticking together in that clubby little group?

Let's see, now, Chris dated David but married Bud . . . Lyla used to date Bud but married George . . . but now is married to David . . . Who is Norma married to? . . . and Fran . . . ? Who can remember? They're all alike and switch around all the time. God, what icky makeup, those ugly dark colors, brown and purple. And . . . David with frizzy hair? David? Oh, my dear, he must have had— oh, it can't be—a perm!

She hastily looked away from him, hoping he wouldn't make any conversation with her. What in the world did you say to a man with a permanent wave, for corn's sake?

"Hi, there, everybody! Welcome. How nice to see you."

They crowded around, messing up the neatly arranged in-alphabetical-order name tags to find theirs. She would have some job straightening out after they went on. David with a perm! Where was Jock? Jock should get a load of that! She knew what he'd say: "Guy's a fairy." But . . . he was married.

They were putting the tags on each other, carrying on and laughing loudly just like in the old days, leaving the rest of the world out. Courtney kept the bright smile on her face with effort. Really, it wasn't very nice of them, at a *reunion*.

Norma flashed her a smile. "Good to see you, Courtney. And that's a sweet dress."

Sweet! *Smart,* that's what it was. "It's a Diane Von Furstenberg," she said in an offhand manner.

"Really? I love Diane Von Furstenberg." Only Norma pronounced it "Dee-*on*."

And Lyla chimed in: "Jock must be doing well. My entire wardrobe is from a thrift shop in the Village." She gave a little twirl. Courtney could believe that: Lyla was wearing, of all things, a man's tuxedo, pants and all, with a ruffled pink shirt. It should have looked ridiculous, but somehow Courtney thought she'd seen something just like it in the latest issue of *Vogue*. She wondered which village Lyla meant. It sounded very "in."

"Oh, that's very smart," she said as they turned to go into the living room.

"Thanks!"

But she couldn't help hearing Chris say, "Amazing, isn't

it? Ten years, and still the same little small-town snob."

Courtney flushed. They had *always* been mean.

But she didn't have time to think about that, because there was Jay Shulman right behind them. He'd become a big-time producer in Hollywood, she'd heard. Certainly looked it. Look at that tan—and his *suit!* Must have cost five hundred at least—and the Gucci loafers! Oh, my! he just smelled of M-O-N-E-Y. And to think how she had snubbed him back in '68, when he had tried to date her.

"Hi, there, Jay Shulman. Welcome. How nice to see you, and you're really looking *terrific*."

What a smile he had; funny, she had never noticed what a terrific smile he had when they were in school together.

"Little Courtney Wills, for God's sake. I'd know you anywhere. How's the cheerleading business?"

"Oh, Jay, you're silly. I don't do that any more!"

"I know, sweetheart. But you should, you know. It was a great act and you were the star!"

"Oh, Jay!" She rummaged frantically in her bag for the menu. Where in the world *was* it? "It's nice to know you remember me."

"Oh, I remember you, all right." She gave him a sharp look, but he was smiling, as friendly as could be. "Doesn't everyone?"

"Well . . . but head cheerleader . . . I mean, everyone saw me all the time. So naturally everyone remembers me."

"You're very lucky. On the Coast, you're only as memorable as your last multimillion-dollar epic!" He laughed.

She didn't know what she was supposed to say to that, but luckily two more people came up and she had to greet them. Jess Barrone, a surgeon now, married to her sorority sister, Linda Goodman. Linda Goodman Barrone, of course. Oh, my, how pale Linda looked . . . was she sick? "Hi, there," Courtney said, smiling.

Jess was busy clapping Jay on the shoulder. "Hey, there, big man," he boomed, "how's show biz?"

"Jess. Good to see you. Show biz is shufflin' along."

"Hear you have a couple of good projects in the works. If you ever need to get rid of a few points—if it's a sure thing, of course, ha-ha!—I've got a few bucks lying around."

"I'm doing a remake of *My Fair Lady* with an all-black cast right now. Harry Belafonte's probably doing Professor Higgins."

"A nigger *Lady?* Do you really think it'll work?"

Jay pinned on his name tag and grimaced. "I've got two million says it will."

"Well, just let me know if you start going broke—ha-ha! Of course, I'll have to check with the little woman! Right, honey?"

Linda Barrone winced slightly as her husband squeezed her shoulder, then smiled wanly and echoed: "Right."

Jay gave her a pat on the arm. "Join me inside and I'll give you a drink . . . both of you."

Courtney watched all this avidly. Was Jay making a pass at Linda, a married woman? In front of her husband?

Brightly, she said, "Stick around for a minute, you two. Linda, you'll want to see Buffy. She's supposed to be helping me here. Of course she's a half hour late! You remember ole Buffer, don't you? *Always* late. But always with—oh, my word, just *look* at that, will you?"

Through the front door, shouting out loud da-*DAH's,* came the Mortons, Buffy and Sparky, crazy as ever! Courtney couldn't help laughing out loud; weren't they just the limit! And she laughed even more at the stupefied looks on the faces of both Barrones. Who could blame them? *She* saw Sparky and Buffy every Wednesday of her life over bridge, and she knew what they were like. But to the rest of the reunion, it would be a hilarious surprise. Sparks was wearing a giant red pleated skirt (it had to be enormous to get around his belly!) and an old yellow letter sweater. He had stuffed his front to look like huge bosoms, and his great hairy legs were sticking out of the skirt—it was a riot! He had got a cheap blond wig, all frizzy curls, and he was shaking Buffy's old pompons. Buffy, absolutely red in the face from laughing, was got up in his old football uniform, even the helmet. And look, wasn't that adorable, she had stuffed the sleeves with big round biceps!

When everyone had turned to stare at them, they began singing the alma mater at the tops of their voices. Courtney glanced around. Even Jay Shulman had stopped dead and was gaping at them. Oh, they were such a riot!

They sang their way right up to her table, where she applauded them vigorously. "Oh, you two! you are just unbelievable! Here are your tags. You go right into the living room and do it again. Everyone who's come so far is in there. And see if you can spot Jock. He's *got* to see this! Doesn't he, Linda?"

"Say, where *is* old Jock?" It was so funny to hear Sparky's voice from under that wig. "Never mind, don't tell me. He's where old Jock *always* is: at the bar."

As they moved away, singing, Courtney thought that perhaps it wasn't so adorable the second time around. And it was obvious she'd get no help from Buffy *this* evening, dressed like that. Was she just supposed to sit here and sit here until every last person had arrived? Such a bore—but who was *that?*

The man, swarthy as a pirate, wavy hair as black as pitch, handlebar mustache, thick eyebrows, deep-set, glinting dark eyes, elegantly and expensively dressed, stood by the front door with a pigskin case at his feet. He was taking his time, looking around, smiling a little, easing leather driving gloves off his hands. Just like a scene in a movie.

Who *was* he, acting as if he owned the place? From our class? Then why couldn't she remember who he was? She remembered *everyone*. She struggled to think of his name as he strutted straight for her table. Who *was* he? "Hi, there. Welcome. How nice to see you. Now, don't tell me your name, it's right on the tip of my tongue, I'll think of it in a sec . . ."

The dark man smiled at her. "Robert Redford?" he suggested. "Burt Reynolds? King Kong?"

"Oh, silly! Don't tease me when I'm trying to think! I *know* I know you." But she didn't, that was the problem.

"I'll give you a hint," he said. "You used to see me at the sorority house, Courtney."

"Oh, dear!" She racked her brain; something about his tone of voice brought back a hint of memory.

He reached out and patted her shoulder. "Don't look so stricken, Courtney. It's Benno Akkardijian."

"Benno!?! Oh, my goodness! But you're so good-looking!"

"*But?* Whatever do you mean, Courtney?" Yes, of

course it was he. She remembered that constant sarcasm now.

Luckily for her, at that embarrassing moment she caught sight of Lee Rivers and Kitty Cameron coming in the door. She grabbed Benno's arm and exclaimed, "Oh, look who's here! I knew she'd come! I just knew it. Lee Rivers—she had the room right next door to me— Yoo-hoo! Lee! Kit! Right over here! Welcome, welcome!"

Lee looked just like all the pictures in the magazines: tall and skinny and *chic*. Who would have guessed she would turn out to be such a big star—and so stunning? And Kitty Cameron: Of course, she had *always* been a beauty. Wouldn't you know, she still looked twenty years old . . . not a line, not a mark, not a single sign that ten years had passed.

In a moment they were both standing across from her, smelling absolutely delicious, and they all began chattering away like a bunch of teenagers. Lee wasn't at all standoffish and didn't put on airs. It was hard to believe she was the popular singer whose posters were plastered all over her own daughter's bedroom. Kitty was rather quiet, but she had always been a deep one. Benno neither moved or spoke, but stood, arms folded across his chest, that same little smile playing on his lips, gazing raptly at the two women. It was a good joke on them because they, no more than she, had not been able to recognize him. Oh, what a good story for little Courtney!

Finally, during a pause, he said in a mock-plaintive voice, "Won't someone take pity upon a poor neglected classmate? It's *my* reunion, too, you know. I know a lot of time has gone under the bridge, but you might recognize the nose, at least." And he turned his profile on them.

Both Lee and Kit whirled around at the sound of his voice and in unison shrieked: "Benno!" The next minute he had Kit Cameron—Kit *Harris*—wrapped in a big bear hug, while Lee smiled her funny half smile. Then he released Kit and turned to Lee, his arms spread out for another hug. They both took a couple of steps and then stopped, only shaking hands.

"Well," Benno said, "you may have become a star, but my nose is still bigger than yours."

"Oh, yeah? Well, I can still eat off the top of your head."

He grinned. "I dare you to take off those preposterous high heels and say that."

"I never undress in front of strangers."

"You seem to forget. I'm no stranger."

"No." Laughing. "But you're getting stranger and stranger every minute."

The three of them groaned and then laughed together, turning away. They were leaving! Oh, how Courtney wished that Buffy hadn't decided to get dressed up! Then she could come out here and take her turn as she was supposed to. At the very least, it would be nice if Jock would leave the bar and drift in and stand with her for a few minutes. Fat chance, but still . . .

"Who's that? I can't place him," Courtney said quickly, hoping to keep them around for a few more minutes. She gestured to a neatly dressed man standing quietly by the entrance.

Kitty looked around and then laughed a little. "Oh, that's Martin. He's waiting to take our bags up to our room."

Courtney stared at him again. The chauffeur! And he was as well dressed as most of the men here tonight. Well, Whit Harris always *had* had plenty of money. Old money, the kind that has Martins around all the time, quietly waiting to do your bidding. Some people had all the luck! She fought back a wave of resentment and turned back to her old sorority sisters, bright smile back in place. But they had gone inside—and she hadn't even remembered to get Lee's autograph!

"Remember this room?" Lee asked Kitty. "I was so damned impressed by it when I was a freshman. Of course our whole apartment in the Bronx would have fit into one of the beau parlors."

They all laughed. The beau parlors were a series of six bays, each one carefully decorated to look like the stage set of a miniature living room. This was where you went with your date, in full view of the living room proper, to be "alone." They had often wondered whose notion of privacy these little alcoves had catered to back in 1902, when the dormitory had been built.

"I always stayed at least five feet away from my date,"

Kitty recalled, smiling. "Anything closer was sure to get the housemother all upset."

"Remember her? The old dragon? Mrs. Argonette!"

Ben, an arm lightly around the back of each woman, snorted. "I can remember Mrs. *Dragon*ette. And not with a great deal of affection, I can tell you. 'Young gentlemen! Young gentlemen! Time!' " he mimicked, falsetto. "God! Nine o'clock curfew!"

"It was such a relief to get into the sorority house our sophomore year," Lee said. "Where a person could at least sneak out of a window at night."

"Is that for publication?" Ben wanted to know. "Remember, you're a personage now. If you're overheard admitting peccadilloes around here, you might well find yourself quoted in tomorrow's tabloids."

Lee gave him a shrewd look. "You're right. Perhaps for the first time in your life."

Kitty cried, "Oh, come *on*. It's been ten years. Don't let's fight tonight. I'm having lovely memories. It was *fun* coming to Enders, a college girl at last. I loved it. Remember the shaving-cream fight our first Halloween, Lee?"

"God, yes. Were you a mess! Perhaps for the first time in *your* life." She laughed. "And wasn't that the year of the panty raid?"

Benno chortled. "No, that was '68. The last gasp of male chauvinism, ladies. We staged the very last panty raid in college history. I got seven. But Dan . . ."

"Oh, are you still in touch with Dan?" That was Lee. Kitty was suddenly busy examining the art work on the wall, the work of graduates of the class of '16.

"Not really. Not since he got the clerkship in Madison. That was before he was D.A. I decided then that if I ever wanted to come in first, I'd better put some real distance between us. Even hero worship has its limits."

"Benno! What a strange idea!" Lee backed off a bit to stare at him. "Did you *really* think of yourself as second-best? And of Dan as a hero?"

"Well . . . wasn't I? Wasn't *he*?"

"Funny, I always thought of you as a completely cocky, self-confident bastard."

He smiled somewhat sadly. "And all the time I was only an insecure, self-denigrating bastard."

"But hell, you were the brains behind the throne, Benno. The Prime Minister to Dan's King, the . . ."

"The Eleanor to Dan's Franklin D.," Benno offered. "The Woodstock to his Snoopy."

Again they laughed.

"Look," Kitty said, "they have the same slipcovers. It hasn't changed in the slightest."

"Don't be silly," Lee objected. "They probably dug up all the ten-year-old covers from the basement storage room and put them on just to make us all feel nostalgic. You just watch, in a little while someone is going to ask us to make a nice big contribution to the slipcover fund."

"As the last of the male chauvinists, let me fetch you a drink. Two whats?"

They decided on stingers, "just to make things difficult for the bartender," and Benno headed for one of the white-covered tables, sparkling with bottles and glasses and surrounded by chattering, laughing, drinking alums.

Lee and Kitty stood for a moment, surveying the scene. It was a very impressive room, running the entire length of the dormitory, the long wall boasting eight oversized leaded-glass windows hung with heavy blue silk draperies. The old parqueted floors were gleaming with fresh wax. Three large but threadbare Oriental rugs divided the huge space, each one with two sofas and chairs, slipcovered in a blue and white print. Mahogany tables held shaded lamps and ashtrays and dishes of nuts. At either end of the room was an Adam fireplace with a huge wooden mantel over which hung an enormous old gilt-framed mirror, reflecting the room, the other mirror, and its reflection of the room, over and over, endlessly, into infinite space. A glance into either mirror and you saw thousands upon thousands of people, splintered and broken, repeated and echoed and re-echoed, smaller and smaller and smaller.

Kitty shivered a little. "I never did like those mirrors," she admitted. "I always used to try not to look at them."

Lee snorted. "All I ever knew was their practicality. If you looked in that mirror from Number Two Beau Parlor, you could see Mrs. Argonette before she came into the room. Even then, Kit, you were the romantic and I the realist."

"Romantic? Yes . . . perhaps." They headed for a seating arrangement in front of one of the fireplaces. Because of the unusual warmth of this October, there was only a tiny blaze flickering in the huge grate. All the draperies were drawn back, and the windows had been left wide open.

Lee looked at the big sofa and realized that she felt too restless to sink into squooshy down cushions; she noted that Kit made no move to sit, either. Nobody was sitting, anywhere in the room. People stood, or strolled, or gathered into little groups. Everyone kept glancing at the entrance, and there was a general feeling of expectancy.

Me, too, Lee thought. I'm dying to know for sure who is Mr. Single Red Rose, even though I think I know. Here she stood, the very picture of calm, she was sure, with her heart hammering away nervously. And there stood Kitty, whose slender fingers wound a silk scarf around and around, her eyes flickering from corner to corner. What could she possibly be anticipating so nervously, complete as she was with everything a woman could possibly want? And yet she had cried so unexpectedly. She had said she was scared. Kit, scared? Lee would find out everything tonight when, for a little while anyway, they would be roomies again.

So they stood, chatting idly, until Ben came back, somehow balancing three glasses on one arm. He handed them around, and Lee sipped gratefully at the frosty, burning drink. A little alcohol really helped when you were on edge. Of course, she thought, the real question was, why was she on edge? what in the world did she expect? Don't answer that, she told herself with amusement.

"Question for the evening," Benno announced. "Who would you most like to see here tonight? And who least? Lee, you begin. You've got a big mouth."

"You may have become all rich and terrific-looking, my dear Benno, but you're still a royal pain."

He turned to Kitty, who had become very quiet. "Okay, Kit. Over to you."

She thought for a moment. "Who the most and who the least? Well, it's the same person."

"Oh, really, Kitty? Who?" Lee asked.

"I'm not saying."

"Male or female?" Ben prodded.

"I'm not saying."

"Vegetable or mineral?"

123

"Oh, Benno! I'm not going to tell. It's an unfair question, anyway."

Benno grinned. "Okay, then, I'll go first. The person I'd most like to see tonight is my old roomie, Dan Copeland. And the person I'd least like to see I won't mention by name, but she's standing right next to me." Lee gave him a playful elbow in the ribs. "Don't be so fast on the draw, Rivers. Maybe I meant Kitty."

"Sure you meant Kitty!" Lee slanted a look over at him. "And I'll thank you to have a little more respect for a star. Why else make it, if not to lord it over wise guys like you?"

"Never mind all that stuff, Rivers. I'll give you my respect when you've earned it."

Kitty was laughing helplessly. "Ten years!" she said. "Ten years and you'd never know it. What a pair of babies! If you were both nine years old, I'd know exactly what's going on. Lily would certainly know."

"Lily?"

"My daughter. When a boy hits her and trips her and insults her and picks on her, she knows he has a crush on her."

There was a strange little silence, broken by Lee, who declared gaily, "The person *I* most want to see tonight is a mystery. I don't know who he is, but I really want to see him." She struck a pose. "I call him . . . Mr. Single Red Rose."

"Oh, that's a great story," Kitty said. "Tell him. Who knows, maybe it's Benno." She laughed.

Lee thought she looked much better, not so withdrawn and pale. She told her story as dramatically as possible, with funny asides to get Kit to laugh, and ended by saying, "And the last one came to the Plaza last night —again, it was a stop that had been publicized—and there was another message. 'A rose is a Lee is a Rivers. See you at reunion.' Isn't that wonderfully mysterious and romantic?"

Benno threw up his hands. "Don't look at *me!* I'm not such a cheapskate to send only one flower. And the only poetry I know is, 'The boy stood on the burning deck . . .' Not very romantic. No, no. I'm the guy who's been sending the diamonds. Didn't you get them?" He widened his eyes in mock innocence.

Lee laughed. "Sure, I did. But when I saw they were from you, I assumed they were fakes and I gave them to my dresser. My glass is empty, by the way. And so is Kitty's. Hint, hint."

Kitty looked at her glass as if surprised to see it. "I'll go this time," she said.

But a booming voice held them where they were. "Lee Rivers! The class celeb!" It was Dr. Jess Barrone, his wan wife trailing after him. Lee gave her a keen look. She recalled Linda Goodman as a very competent, upbeat, singing-in-the-morning kind of girl when they had lived together in the sorority house. Wanted to be a doctor, hadn't she? What happened?

But Jess had her grasped firmly around the shoulders with one hand while he reached out to shake hands with the other. "Hi, there, sweetheart! How does it feel to be rich and famous? I'll tell you one thing, kiddo, nobody would have guessed you would make it big. Whew! you were some mess, remember?"

Lee felt every vertebra in her spine stiffen and the smile freeze upon her lips. She drew herself back from his touch and pointedly ignored him. "Linda, it's been so long! Did you ever get to medical school?"

Barrone seemed completely oblivious to her anger. He squeezed her shoulder and laughed loudly. "Hell, no, she didn't go to medical school. Why become a doctor if you can marry one?" Lee glanced quickly at Linda, but there was no expression on her face at all. "Have you seen the New York crowd?" Jess continued. "Gawd! would you believe what's become of *them?*" He lowered his voice ostentatiously. "David's a dress designer . . . you know what *that* means . . .

"And would you believe that one of those broads is a *lawyer*—and one is a *doctor?*" He brayed hostile laughter. "I'll tell you one thing: I wouldn't have a hen lawyer and I wouldn't have a hen doctor and I wouldn't have a hen accountant, either." He paused for effect, looking from one to the other for agreement. There was silence. Lee thought of several choice things to say, but she decided against them. Poor Linda. How could she *live* with him? What did you say to a man like that? What could you *do* —other than punch him in the nose?

Benno suddenly crowed like a rooster at the top of his

voice, causing several dozen heads to turn in their direction. Then, an arm on each shoulder, he led Kitty and Lee away, into the middle of the room, saying loudly, "Excuse us, we're going to have a hen party."

Lee and Kit stared at each other, their eyes filled with the same outrage. At the same moment they both burst out with: "That—that—that—!" and then began to laugh helplessly, tearfully, "Poor Linda!"

Of course, they had attracted a great deal of attention, and once Lee had been spotted, they became the center of a flurry of activity. Lots of "hellos" and "how are you's," and lots of campus maps waved around for autographs. Lee resigned herself to it; she was an old hand at this sort of thing. She smiled and smiled and signed her name again and again. But it was a relief when an outburst of applause at one end of the room drew everyone's eyes away from her.

"Hey, everybody," Benno yelled, "it's Sparky and Buffy. You should see their routine! The fickleness of fans," he added as everyone turned and headed for the newest happening.

"You're a pal, Akkardijian. Would you like to earn your good-deeds badge and get me another of the same?"

He left with a bow, saying that he might be a while. He wanted to see if Copeland had arrived, and since he had come at the last minute, he ought to see about getting a place to sleep. "Unless," he leered, "you'd like to offer me the comfort of *your* bed, Ms. Rivers."

"Don't be an ass! All I want from you is a drink." Watching him leave, she remarked to Kitty, "I don't want to miss the Madcap Mortons doing their number. I mean, things like this are the stuff memories are made of, right?"

But Kitty had gone rather pale again. Now that the glass was out of her hand, she was once again twisting the silk scarf.

"Are you all right, Kit?"

"I'm hungry. We never had lunch, remember. You go watch Sparky and Buffy recapture their youth, and I'll go stuff myself with canapés. I'll meet you over there in ten minutes."

Lee picked up a handful of peanuts from a dish—she

was starving, too, she realized—and ambled to the edge of a crowd of some fifty people gathered around the fireplace, shrieking with delight and clapping. As huge as this room was, it was becoming quite noisy as more and more alums came in and had their tongues loosened up by the drinks. And perhaps more than tongues, she thought, noting poor plain old-maid Jen Gladstone, all decked out in red taffeta, leaning heavily and provocatively against a short, balding guy whose name she couldn't recall but who certainly had a wedding ring on his left hand. Oh, well, who cared? Maybe Jen Gladstone would carry home some truly wonderful memories from this reunion. And more power to her!

She found an empty armchair off to the side of the rapt little audience and leaned against its capacious back, running her hand idly along the well-worn and familiar slipcover. She had probably boned up for some of her exams curled up in this chair—and had probably hated every single moment of it, too! She laughed at herself.

Sparky and Buffy were, by this time, standing on a table top, running through the entire repertoire of cheers and songs from '69–'70 Hampton football season, complete with high kicks and jumps. Lee watched, fascinated, wondering just when the spindly Queen Anne legs of the table would give way.

But only half her mind was on the rather childish high jinks by the fireplace. Was he going to show up or wasn't he? Who else could Mr. Single Red Rose be? Still, not many of the faculty chose to join in these reunions. Would he have the guts to be conspicuous, her brave, brave boy who had run off to Ireland to escape her?

When she smelled the Irish Heather pipe tobacco, she knew. Without turning around, she knew that Bill O'Hara was there. Not only there, but right behind her, pipe clenched in his teeth as always. She stood as casually as possible, waiting, every muscle tensed. Any moment now he would put his hand on her. She stood, painfully conscious of the presence she *knew* was there. Her skin was prickly with the anticipation of his touch. Endless moments passed and nothing happened. Vexed, she turned around.

There he was, leaning negligently against the back of the matching armchair, his long legs thrust out in front of him, teeth clenched on the pipe, gazing off into space, giving her a profile. He was cradling the pipe in one hand, puffing gently. In a split second, she had cataloged him completely: Fair Isle sweater, Harris tweed jacket with suede elbow patches, Bill Blass jeans, very tight. His thick wavy hair was a bit shorter, a bit grayer at the temples, but he was the same. The same! untouched by time. She felt sure that if she looked into a mirror now, the svelte woman of the world would have changed back into the dumpy kid who had trembled at the knees when he smiled at her.

She found her voice. "O'Hara!" She pitched it low enough so that only he could hear.

Slowly he turned, brow wrinkling, gazing at her with a question in his eyes. "Bill!" she insisted, and then his face cleared and he gave her that old crooked lazy smile.

"La Belle Dame Sans Merci," he drawled. "Come on over here, gypsy girl."

Without thinking very much, she obeyed, drawn by his eyes and by the intimate shading in his voice. When she had come close enough, he murmured: " '. . . beautiful and fierce, sudden and laughing . . .' "

"Maud Gonne," Lee said quickly.

"Good girl. You haven't forgotten what I taught you then." His indolent blue eyes lazed over her body. "Nor have I."

Incredibly, her knees were trembling. How could he do this to her? She was a different person from the dumb and dumpy kid who had thought it was so sophisticated to sleep with her professor! But, it seemed, she was still mesmerized and enmeshed by old passions. I am Lee Rivers, she told herself fiercely. And yet her body continued to quiver and her heart raced alarmingly.

"You haven't changed!" she finally managed.

He took the pipe from his mouth, stuck it into a pocket, and gave her another wry smile. "I said, come over here, girl." He reached out, curling his hand around her hipbone, and pulled her to him until they were thigh to thigh. She at once became breathlessly aware of his rising excitement.

"Down, boy!" She laughed feebly. "I hardly know you." She tried to disengage herself without attracting attention. "O'Hara! For God's sake! We're in public!"

"Don't move away now, or there'll be cause for gossip for the next ten years."

It was the same, it was exactly the same. The lost years were melting away. "Why did you go to Ireland without a word to me?" she demanded.

"Oh, how I suffered for that! The nights that I lay awake in my bed and cursed you for haunting me. Yet . . . 'Why should I blame her that she filled my days with misery?' " he quoted. "If you only knew how often I've regretted that flight." Now both his hands were on her waist, pressing her against him. "And remember, you lost only me. I lost a great deal more—you." He bent to her lips, kissing her so lightly she couldn't be sure she felt his touch at all, and whispered against her mouth, "You know what you're doing to me . . . even after all this time. Be a shame to waste any more time. I'm taking you home with me."

Lee pulled back, shaking her head to clear it. "Let me think, O'Hara. And anyway, I'm staying with Kit tonight; we've had it planned for months."

He threw back his head and laughed. "Have you forgotten how to climb out of a window, then? Come, come, gypsy girl, I'm not budging from here till you say yes."

There was just no use fighting it any more. "Oh, dammit, O'Hara, yes. Yes, yes, yes."

How *could* she? Kitty thought, aghast and just a little disappointed in her old friend. She had been watching them for quite a while, wanting to interrupt but not quite daring to. It was funny—no, *pathetic* to see that old phony in his brand-new, squeaky-clean, Irish-professor costume, using the same old moves. Couldn't Lee see at last what a poseur he was? Just the ticket for an inexperienced girl who thought she knew everything—but *Lee?* Had she even forgotten what she knew ten years back? She had called herself "Coed of the Year" then. "I'm trickier than most," she had said more than once, "so it's lasting just a little longer than usual."

And now just look at her, simpering and blushing like a virgin schoolgirl involved in her first seduction. By rights she should be either squirming with embarrassment or laughing right in his face. But no. As Kitty stared at them, she saw Lee's hand reach up to rake tenderly

129

through his carefully waved and arranged hair. I can't watch this, Kit thought. I can't believe it and I certainly cannot watch one minute more.

Feeling like an eavesdropper, she turned hastily away and picked up a drink—she didn't know what it was and didn't care—from the buffet table. One sip and she put it down. She wasn't thirsty. She wasn't hungry. And yet she kept feeling that she needed *something*. Restless, she skirted the edges of the room, keeping away from the roving groups that moved about, backslapping and bear-hugging. She felt as if she had been talking nonstop ever since she had picked Lee up, and all of a sudden she felt drained. I shouldn't have come, she thought. It was a mistake to come here.

How could Lee? How *could* she? Maybe it was meaningless to be true to yourself, to grow into a whole person and face the world on your own terms—if it all could be wiped away in an instant with the touch of one man's hand!

But she didn't want to think about it. Frantically, she looked around, trying to evoke some kind of nostalgia—about this room, this place, herself. But the girl who had come here from a small town in Virginia in 1966 was a stranger to her.

That girl had been a runaway. Yes, a runaway, running from the role forced upon her by her loving mother. But Mama had never realized. Mama had been delighted with the Hampton catalog, with its reputation as a fine old institution and its male/female ratio.

"Why, look here, honey," she had drawled with delight, "there are three men for every girl." And, of course, she had had to add, "You won't have any trouble, darlin', not with your looks. Remember, it's just as easy to love a rich man as a poor one."

Mama hadn't known how that had made her cringe inside. Since she was three months old, her mother had been promoting her. Promoting her and pushing her. An accident of genetics had given her a face considered exquisite, and it almost immediately had become the epicenter of her mother's life.

Pretty little Kitty Cameron had modeled for the local department store. Her face had appeared regularly in all the Beautiful Children Contests—and had won. She had been the little girl chosen to light the annual downtown Christmas tree, sitting sweetly on Santa's lap. To solo in the church choir, standing near a beaming minister. Three times she had been chosen Miss Town of Davisville and had ridden, dressed in yards of tulle and a gold tinsel crown, on the lead float, next to the mayor. And always in the background, yet very much *there*, had been Jasmine Cameron, Mama.

Kit had hated it. Every minute of it. Had hated the constant fussing and the constant hair curlings and the constant costume fittings. She'd hated being singled out, stared at, like the town freak. Had her proud mama ever known, ever guessed, that all the men had pawed at her and pinched her bottom and squeezed her—all under the guise of "just bein' friendly"? When she thought of all the times she'd been forced to smile politely, when really she'd been longing to kick someone's shins, she wanted to scream. But how, in a small town in Virginia, could a little girl kick the minister or the mayor and hope to be believed? It had taken her years even to realize that she should have been *angry* with those men. What she had felt for most of her childhood was shame, as if somehow the way she *looked* had been to blame for it all. She had longed to tell Mama, and once she'd even tried. "Oh, pooh," Mama had said, fluffing up her hair and retying the pretty pink ribbon, "that doesn't mean anything. Mayor Perkins is a friend of your daddy's, honey. He's just bein' friendly."

Oh, Mama. Could she really have been so naive? No, she had just chosen not to see. Because if she'd seen, she'd have had to give up the prestige of having the prettiest girl in town. How Mama had eaten it up. She had gloried in the attention. And the young Kitty had gritted her teeth and through the years had learned how to avoid the unwanted intimacies, and had counted the days until she could take charge of her own life. And there had grown around her that air of inviolability, that silent signal that warned: "Don't touch." The boys back home had finally gotten afraid to ask her out, and the girls had resented her.

Hampton—so far away from home—had been like a refuge. Nobody had known Kitty Cameron there. There, she could make a fresh start. She would never again be Pretty Kitty Cameron.

To her dismay, practically the first thing that happened had been that Sweetheart of Sigma Chi contest. One of the girls at Enders had sent in a snapshot of her, and suddenly a committee of grinning fraternity boys had appeared in the living room, come to sing "She's the Sweetheart of Sigma Chi" because she had won.

She would have burst into frustrated tears that night if it hadn't been for one of the boys, a freshman like herself, who had come over to talk to her.

"Maybe you don't understand, Katherine," he had said earnestly. "You're the first freshman ever elected. You *can't* say no. It's a special honor for the class of '70." He had been tall and big and blond and handsome and very, very sincere.

She had sighed. "What will I have to do?"

"Just come to our dance and look beautiful. That shouldn't be difficult. I'd be honored to escort you, but I think the president is supposed to do that. He's a very nice guy, pre-Law, head of the debating team . . . and engaged to a Theta Beta. So, you see . . ."

"I don't like this," she had whispered.

And he had whispered back, "But you'll be Sweetheart of Sigma Chi. Every girl on campus will envy you. And besides, if you refuse . . . the girl we ask will always know she was second choice."

What a thoughtful boy, she had thought. Such lovely manners. She had looked around the living room then, noting all the waiting faces. Worse than being serenaded would be to make a scene. So she'd smiled and said: "I . . . I'm overwhelmed." And relief had swept over his face.

That was how she had met Whit Harris. He'd called her the next week and asked her to have coffee. He had been very careful in his courtship, very careful and very methodical. She could almost have guessed his next move. There had followed many weeks of "casual" dates: coffee, or a few beers, or a game of bridge at the Student Union. Then he'd escalated to a Sunday brunch, a movie, a concert. First only on weekdays, then on week nights, then on Sunday. It had taken him months to arrive at a

Saturday-night date with dinner, dancing at The Pub, and a hesitant kiss at evening's end.

She smiled to herself, remembering. That was Whit: seeming rather stolid and predictable, when he was really being shrewd and smart. He had told her at the end of their freshman year that he intended to marry her, and she had told him she would never marry. He had persisted and she had insisted, all the way through school— even though she'd always dated other men. And in the end he had got what he wanted. Not in the way he had planned, of course. She wondered often if he had ever regretted his bargain. Whether *he* had ever felt . . . cheated.

She had wandered, lost in her thoughts, to one of the big mullioned windows, and now she looked out at the purple-tinged dusk and leaned her forehead against the cool pane. There was a heavy lump in the pit of her stomach, like a scream growing inside her. Had she cheated *herself?* Had it all been one long ten-year cheat? Was that why she had been feeling so off balance and restless lately? She willed the uncomfortable sensations away, smothering them with a skittering of trivial thoughts of unpacking, of arrangements, of Whit's presentation. She closed her eyes. Oh, please, just let me not *think!*

"Kitty." The voice sent a shudder through her. She had not heard it in over ten years, but she knew it by heart. *This* was what she had been waiting for. She opened her eyes and instantly saw him reflected darkly in the wavery glass, and all the breath left her body.

Gripping the windowsill for dear life, she forced herself to stay calm. When she thought her voice was under control, she said to his image, "Hello, Dan."

From across the room he had seen that silver-gilt hair, even though it was pulled back and up, in some kind of Grecian coil. Like a beacon in the night, it drew him. He saw no one else as he pushed his way through the clusters of drinking, laughing, joking classmates. He had learned, at dozens of political functions, the art of looking in-a-hurry, very-busy, not-able-to-be-disturbed—all without hurting anyone's feelings, of course. So he waved when he heard his name called, grinned, and kept going, turning his head toward the voice but not really focusing.

Kit. He hurried toward her. And here he was—here

she was—at last. Close enough to touch. The same elusive spicy scent seemed to live in her skin. If he bent only a little, he could put his lips into the soft curve of her neck, just under her ear.

She turned around, and it was all he could do not to gasp aloud. He hadn't really remembered how beautiful she was. Hadn't really remembered how being with her could set all his senses aflame. And yet his voice had the practiced, cool polish perfected by years in politics.

"How are you, Kitty? You look wonderful." Her eyes were still the clear green of sunlit water.

"So do you. You're heavier, I think. And you've cut your hair." The same cool voice, the same enigmatic smile, the same composure that surrounded her like an invisible cloak. He knew, dammit, what passion lay hidden behind that mantle of calm. He wanted to shake her, grab her, somehow tear through.

"Yes, well, ponytails are out of style. And you know what a stylish gent I've always been." He laughed.

"It becomes you—the short hair, I mean. You look . . . successful." She smiled at him, a spark gleaming through deep water. "But that's not fair. I *know* that you're successful."

"That article!" He grimaced. "But you, Kitty. Tell me about you. How have you been since the last time I saw you?"

He regretted his choice of words immediately, as their eyes locked for a long breathless moment. He recalled only too well the last time he had seen her. He could see her yet: bare, glowing skin and a disheveled tangle of pale hair, the coarse Italian sheets rumpled in mute testimony of the emotional storm just passed.

Kitty's expression changed. Her whole face seemed to tighten as a faint rosy flush climbed over her cheekbones. He longed to pull her close, to murmur that it was all right now, it was fine. Even now, he would tell her, that afternoon remained the most perfect time of his life.

But she dropped her eyes from his for an instant, and when she looked back at him, they were blank. "I've been just fine. I— But tell me all about your career. It sounds *fascinating*." Her voice was bright, light, social. Like his when he made the rounds at a political shindig.

Dan took a deep, exasperated breath. "Goddammit,

Kitty," he exploded. "I *don't* want to make small talk with you. All I really want—"

"Dan. Don't."

"Don't. Don't. The most overused word in your vocabulary, even after all this time."

"Dan. Please. Don't do this to me."

"Don't do *what?*" For God's sake, I'm only trying to talk to you. Surely"—his voice took on a tinge of sarcasm —"surely a talk with you is long overdue?"

"Please." Unconsciously, she was wringing her hands, even though her face was as smooth as ever. It touched him, and at the same time infuriated him. She'd always done this, always backed off, looking so vulnerable that he hadn't the heart to push or press—not too far. He grasped her arms and shook her a little.

"*I'm* saying please. It's *my* turn to say please this time. You owe me, Kitty."

"Owe you? What are you talking about?"

"You know damn well." His heart was beating very rapidly; he could feel it pumping blood into his face. "You're the one who disappeared . . . ran away. I came back to the *pensione* the happiest man on earth. And what did I find? An empty room. You owe me an explanation!"

"Dan, you're hurting me."

With an effort, he let her go, so abruptly that she staggered back a little. He expected her to turn and flee, but she stood very still, rubbing at her arms with her hands, looking at him with those great green eyes. Just looking.

A bit more softly, he said, "*Tell* me. What did I do? What happened? My God, ten years! It's been ten years. Surely you can talk about it now, Kitty!

Still she gazed at him, her eyes full of confusion, telling him nothing. Her lips, the lips he had never quite been able to erase from his memory, were trembling slightly. Stepping forward suddenly, he wrapped his arms around her, and bending swiftly, crushed his mouth against hers.

The last time he had kissed her, dusty bars of afternoon sunlight had been slanting through the heavy shutters of her room in the *pensione*. Sleepy sounds drifted up from the sluggish river below. Italy. Florence in the afternoon, after love.

She had never dreamed she would see him again, not after their big fight in Hillside Park the night before graduation. He had left her in front of the sorority house, a bitter set to his lips. And the bitter words: "I hope you don't live to regret this. I know I will." Yes, it had hurt, to think she'd lost him forever. No man had ever affected her the way he did. When he touched her, even casually, she was aflame from head to toe. It was terrifying. As much as she wanted him, she knew it would be her destruction to give in to her feelings. She would be enslaved. And Kit Cameron would be no man's slave! Never! Better to give him up than to spend the rest of her life in thrall.

Yet on that sticky July morning, the air already sodden with wet heat at eleven o'clock, how her heart had hammered, as she plodded slowly across the San Trinita Bridge, to see the tall, lanky frame she knew by heart, slouching against the giant front door of Pensione Marcolini. She would have run, but she could not be positive it was really he. His face, half hidden by large sunglasses, came more and more sharply into focus, until she could tell that he was staring at her, watching her approach across the bridge. Usually he was so aggressive; it wasn't like Dan Copeland to stand still and wait. And yet he was—just standing there, waiting for her. And she was *so* happy to see him.

It had been a little lonesome being by herself, even in this most glorious of cities. She had started out to travel with three sorority sisters, but in Rome she had become sickened by Courtney Wills and her constant longing for a "good ole American hamburger" and her constant complaints about how inefficiently they did things in Italy. Besides, the other three liked to sleep till noon, then go out (complaining because nothing was open in the afternoon as it was in the States), and then dance the night away. She wanted to see everything and didn't give a snap for dancing with boys who pinched your bottom black-and-blue—especially if you were very blond. And this seemed to make Courtney extremely cross: "Kitty's made another conquest," she'd smirk.

She had gracefully—she hoped, gracefully—extricated

herself, saying she wanted to take some pictures in Florence. How the other girls had groaned. "Dull old Florence? Oh, *God,* Kitty, nothing's happening there!"

And so she'd been alone in the lion-colored city, the Renaissance jewel. And there, suddenly, was Dan, lean and long-muscled, his mane of red hair pulled back in a ponytail. She walked toward him, but did run in the end —ran the last few feet and dropped all her parcels to throw her arms around him. Which, of course, changed in a few seconds from a friendly hello to a searing, heart-aching kiss. Ah, she was hungry for him. She clung to him, leaned into him, rubbed her forehead against his bristled jaw.

"What are you doing here?"

He chortled. "Kissing you."

"No. Really. You're supposed to be in India."

"No Peace Corps without you." He nuzzled her neck, murmuring, "You smell wonderful."

"Then what will you do?" She struggled to pull back, so she could look at him, but he only tightened his grip. "Dan!" she laughed.

Still holding her tightly, he pulled his head back and stared down at her. "Law school. Wisconsin. But first I had to see you. I called the sorority house and spoke to Bessie, since she always knows *everything,* and she was kind enough to tell me that your last postcard came from Rome. So I flew to Rome."

"Oh, Dan! So much money!"

He kissed the lobe of her right ear, then nibbled at it gently. "I found your sisters at American Express. Courtney has the kind of voice you can hear two miles away. And here I am."

Kit leaned against his rangy body and sighed deeply. "Yes," she said with contentment, "you're here." Inside, she was bubbling with delight to think that he had flown all the way across the Atlantic just to see her. It was different from being on campus, where he would appear suddenly and announce that they were doing something. Dropping in on Florence, Italy, was an entirely different kind of thing. It was . . . exciting. And it pleased her, too, knowing that he'd never do this for anyone else. Other girls were too easy. Only she, Kit Cameron, had the strength to withstand his charm and blandishments. And he had come all this way, chasing her!

"So, Kit, now that I'm here—how are you?"

She laughed again. "If you really want to know—hungry!"

Dan released her, smiling, and bent to pick up a large battered knapsack from the pavement. He waved it aloft, announcing: *"Ecco, signorina! Lunch!"*

"Oh, Dan! Wonderful!"

"Salami, two kinds of cheese, a fresh loaf of bread, and the cheapest wine I could find."

She clapped her hands. "A picnic! Where shall we have it? In the Piazza della Signoria? On the Ponte Vecchio? No, too many crowds buying jewelry. Or maybe . . ."

"I thought," Dan said, "we'd go up into the hills, where we can overlook the city."

"I've got a better idea. It's so hot, and I've already walked all over Florence this morning. Let's go up and eat on my terrace."

They both laughed over her house *chiave:* the medieval key of heavy iron, a great ornate affair fully three inches long which looked like something out of a fairy tale. It really did fit into the front door's oversized keyhole, it turned easily, and it opened the huge wooden door onto the dim, cool, marble-floored hallway.

Dan hefted the knapsack over his shoulders, loaded his arms with her packages, and followed her up the three flights of well-worn marble stairs.

The reception area, a dim-lighted room filled with dark medieval furniture, was empty save for two British spinsters studying a street map of Florence and sipping from cups of tea. They looked over and called out, "Good morning, Miss Cameron. Hot again, isn't it?" and went right back to their maps.

The proprietress poked her head out of the dining room and flashed a gold-toothed smile. "Signorina Katerina, *buon giorno. È una lettera per lei."*

"Ah, sì? Chi è?"

"In càmera." She grinned more broadly, nodding her gray head toward Dan. *"Ah! un amico Americano! Bene, bene!"*

"I get the idea she approves of my presence," Dan said, following Kitty down the long stone corridor.

"Yes, Signora Marcolini worries a lot about my dull social life. I don't know quite enough Italian to be sure, but I *think* she was trying to fix me up with her nephew the other night at dinner." They laughed.

She had a corner room, with large windows looking over the Arno River and across to the central city. She could even see the top of the golden dome of the Duomo poking up from a sea of coral tile roofs. The massive eighteenth-century furniture was all mahogany, old-fashioned, and beautifully polished: a huge bedstead, an oversized armoire, a marble-topped table, and several chairs. On the bedside table stood a china pitcher and bowl. Each morning Tina, the maid, knocked on the door at seven-thirty and came in with a bowl and a pitcher filled with steaming hot water, two linen towels laid carefully over the top.

The room was high-ceilinged, spacious, and always cool even in the worst heat. The uncurtained windows—there were three of them—had two sets of shutters: heavy solid ones on the outside and lighter, slatted ones inside. When they entered, the noontime sun was flooding in, and Kitty immediately pulled the slatted shutters across the opened casement windows. The smooth tile floor took on a striped pattern of light and shadow, and the glare in the room softened to a golden glow.

"There's the terrace, that door over there," Kitty said, and picked up the knapsack. "I only have one glass."

Dan grinned. "We'll share." Without warning, he pulled his T-shirt up over his head and threw it onto a chair. Kitty stared at him. "I'm sticky," he explained. "Is there any water in that pitcher?"

"It's cold, I think."

"Great."

She watched as he washed his chest and arms, unable to take her eyes away. Dan was slim, almost too thin, but his arms and shoulders were powerful. He was smoothly muscled. His skin was fair, the chest lightly covered with a mat of dark russet, curling hair. But where the sleeves and neck of the T-shirt ended, the skin had been burned to a dark copper color, sprinkled with freckles. The blue jeans slid down on his hips, revealing a slender waist and the tops of his knobby hipbones. He soaped himself with a wet towel and her sliver of soap, then rinsed carefully, whistling all the time, seeming unaware of her eyes on him. She loved the way he looked, so lean and tight and strong.

When he had finished, he turned to her with a grin. "Too skinny, don't you think?" Kitty flushed and he laughed aloud. "Hey! I like when you look at me. It makes me feel good." And when the heat intensified in her cheeks, he strode over to give her a hug. "Hey, babe, that's why we have eyes. To look at each other."

Kit managed a smile. "I'm starving, aren't you?"

"As a matter of fact, yes. Let's eat."

They sat in a shady corner of the tiny terrace, nibbling at the salami by turns and cutting pieces off the wedges of cheese with his Swiss Army knife—"I've had this since I was a Boy Scout"—and sipping the heady red wine from her one glass.

"A Boy Scout!" Kitty marveled. "You, a Boy Scout? I can't picture it!"

Dan leaned back, hooking his arms over the wrought-iron railing. A slice of bright sunlight lit the golden hair on his arms. "God, I was the original All-American Boy. Didn't I ever tell you that part of my life story?" He snorted derisively. "Eagle Scout. High school basketball star. Honor student. Yes, I was one of the chosen . . . until I went to Vietnam and got—"

The pain in his eyes troubled her. "Got what, Dan?" She reached over to put a hand on his arm, which he instantly covered with his own hand.

"Got? Got . . . got shot at, mostly. Got to thinking . . ."

"Dan? I know you were in the war, of course. And yet . . . I've never *realized* it. You've never talked about it!"

He smiled at her and reached for the tumbler of wine, sipping at it. "No. I just make speeches about it. That's all it was good for."

"I—it was very stupid of me. I've been . . . terribly naive, haven't I?"

"Never mind that," he said. The blank look was gone from his eyes, replaced by something softer and warmer. "We're here together, it's summer in Italy, and come over here this minute." With a lazy arm, he pulled her onto his lap, holding her close.

Kitty felt a bit dizzy. The sun was a bright dazzle in her eyes and a warm spot on the side of her face. The wine she had drunk was bubbling in her head. His arms were hard and safe around her. She thought for a moment that if he were not holding her, she might float right off the terrace. Her thoughts were delightfully muzzy, drifting about like so many clouds in the sky. She closed her eyes and relaxed against Dan. Dear Dan, how nice it was to be held like this, without demands, surrounded by the clean, crisp smell of soap and sun and skin.

When he began to kiss her softly on her neck and shoulder, she rubbed her cheek against the thick texture of his hair. After a moment, it seemed natural and right to turn her head, to kiss him sweetly on the side of his face, along the lean, hard-boned curve of his cheekbone. And then she slid her lips along his face, to meet his avid, hungry mouth.

She was lost, her senses swimming. She could not believe her hunger for the touch of him: his lips, his tongue, his hands. Without knowing quite how, she was standing pressed to him, clinging, pulling him even closer in an effort to meld herself with him, to melt into him, to become a part of him.

Still kissing her, he scooped her up in his arms and carried her back into the dim shadows of the shuttered room. He laid her on the bed. "Kitty," he murmured against her parted lips. "Kitty. I need you so."

She moaned a little. A piercing sweetness was coursing through her. She felt soft, pliant, yielding. When he pulled the loose voile shirt over her head, she did not resist; when he bent his mouth to her breasts, she shuddered a little and cupped his head in her hand, holding him to her. Somewhere in the back of her mind a small protest struggled to be heard. But desire drowned all thought. She did not want to think. She wanted to give herself completely to these insistent sensations.

His naked body was a bar of heat on her flesh, and she gasped. "Look at me, Kit." She obeyed, trembling. His face was close to hers, his dark eyes tender. "It's going to be beautiful. I won't hurt you. Don't be afraid. This was always meant to be . . ." She nodded, looking deep into his eyes, lost in them. His hand caressed the satiny skin of her thighs.

Eagerly, her mouth sought his once more and she clung to him, half in desire and half in fear. "Dan! Dan! Please!" She did not know what she was pleading for, but it did not matter. One hand was under her, guiding her to him, and then he was deep within her. A cry was wrung from the very depths of her soul.

It was endless time, time without end, nothing in the world but heat and long-denied desire. He left her once, to open the shutters to the flaming sunset. But he came back to her again. And again. And she held her arms out to him each time, impatient for his touch, his scent, his untiring passion.

The sky was deep lavender, a pale sliver of moon riding high above the dark roofs, when they lay gazing into each others' eyes, exhausted. Dan smoothed the hair back from her ear. "Years from now," he said, "when you're a beautiful old lady, you'll be able to tell your grandchildren: 'The first time I made love, it was spectacular.'"

Spectacular. She closed her eyes. She couldn't look at him. Spectacular? He had seen her, clawing and screeching like an animal beneath him; had gloried in her wild need of him; had reveled in her uncontrollable lust. It was obscene! She remembered his eyes, smoky with desire. She remembered . . . she could not bear to remember. She freed her hand from his and turned away, throwing an arm over her face. She had given in to him. No, worse, she had begged him for more.

He reached over, shaking her arm. "Kit? Kit? What's the matter?"

"Nothing!" Can't he see I need to get myself together? she thought. That I need to be left alone?

"Baby, baby! Don't worry. I'm not going to leave you. You're really mine now. It's what I've always wanted. This is *it*. You and me." He jumped out of bed and stretched. "Oh, God, I feel terrific. First thing, I'll go get my stuff at the hostel and bring it here."

Kitty turned over. "Here?" She stared at him.

He grinned down at her. "You don't imagine I'll be able to stay away, do you?"

She was unable to think of what to say to him. He had always been relentless.

Dan took her silence for submission. "It'll be great, Kit. You'll come with me to Madison—you can go to grad school while I'm in law school. And every night, my dearest Kit . . ." He bent to kiss her swiftly, repeating in a whisper, "Every night . . ."

It was all she could do not to scream. His sweet words and his whispers and his sensuous, stroking hands: only to take possession. And she had let him. God help her, she had *wanted* him. And now he was trying to take charge of her life. He doesn't love me, she thought.

She would have to be clever. She managed a smile and pushed him away playfully. "Go on. I need a long, quiet bath. We have plenty of time later," she lied.

He paused, thoughtful. She had, briefly, the horrid feeling that he could read her thoughts. "Kitty, I—" he began, then shook his head. "I don't have the words," he said. "Isn't that funny? Me, the speechmaker. But when it comes to you—" He sat on the edge of the bed and gathered her into his arms, tenderly kissing the top of her head, while she held her breath and tried not to seem stiff. "I waited a long time for you," he said softly, "but you were worth the wait."

As soon as the door had closed behind him—"I'll be back in less than an hour," he promised—she went into a frenzy of activity. Drawers open, suitcases out, clothes flung in, a sweep of the hand emptying the top of the dresser. Breath sobbed in her throat. Panic squeezed at her chest. She had so little time. If he came back and she was still here . . . She must leave, run, go as fast as she could.

Signora Marcolini looked worried and began to argue, but in the end she accepted the fistful of crumpled lire Kitty hadn't even bothered to count and let her go.

She took the train to Venice, leaving there after two days when she caught sight of a Hampton classmate on the *vaporetto*. Then to Milan. She began to miss Dan, to think that her running away had been stupid, childish, maybe even a bit crazy. She was dreaming about her childhood every night—strange, lurid dreams with strangers handling her and Mama just standing by, not seeing any of it, not hearing her cries.

143

It was a fevered time, those next three weeks in Italy after she had run from Florence. She spoke to almost no one, spending her days wandering through museums and churches, staring at the art works blindly while she groped for some understanding of herself.

When she went to Siena, the lovely walled city atop its hill, August was at its worst: hot, damp, and breathless. Every morning she vomited her breakfast. Every night, as she struggled to fall asleep, she wrote a letter to Dan in her mind. And then, suddenly, she realized that it was neither the heat nor the food that was making her feel so strange. And she knew that she would never write that letter to Dan—she couldn't, not now—that she would have to erase him from her life forever. It was only then that the tears finally came.

Dan lifted his lips from hers. She was dizzy and had to clutch at his shoulders. When she looked up at him, he was smiling.

"Are you remembering, too?"

"You *never* loved me!" The words burst from her.

He stared at her, disbelieving. "How can you say that? I loved you so much, for so long!"

Stubbornly: "You never told me."

"You can't mean it! *That's* why you ran away? Disappeared? And . . . married?" He choked a little on the last word. "When I think of the agonizing weeks I spent looking for you—"

"I can't explain it. I was young . . . inexperienced. I thought . . . I felt . . . Men had always been after me, and I couldn't tell, I wasn't sure . . . It was—oh, never mind. It's too late now."

He grasped her shoulders. "No!" he grated. "Not too late. Never too late!"

"Oh, Dan, you don't understand. It's more than just you and me. It's—"

"What?"

Kit tried for a light smile. "I know this is a night for nostalgia, Dan, but what we had . . . is over and done with. All in the past."

His hands tightened. "I just kissed you. Don't try to tell *me* it's over and done with. Not for me it isn't. And not for you, either," he said fiercely. "I've never forgotten you. I've never stopped wanting you. I want you now, this minute. Oh, no, Kitty, this time I'm not letting you go!"

CHAPTER EIGHT

Polly Malverne

"YOU STLL SCARE ME, Dan," Kit said. She did not look especially frightened; the clear green eyes were blank, unreadable as ever. She didn't try to break away, but her entire body had gone still.

Dan dropped his hands. "And you're still pulling away," he said bitterly. "Trying to make me feel like a monster."

"Oh, no! Not that! You know I never thought that! A monster? Far from it." She murmured the last three words, lowering both her voice and her eyes, and then looked straight at him again, taking a deep breath. "You always thought you could overpower everything . . . and everybody. And I always tried to tell you, you can't *do* that. Not to me."

"I *never* forced myself on you. If you were ever overpowered, Kit, it was always with your cooperation. Always," he added meaningfully.

Now she flushed deeply. "That's not what I was talking about and you know it." She dropped her gaze again and turned her head away slightly, so that the thick lashes cast dark fringed shadows over the delicately prominent cheekbones. The blush receded, leaving a faint pink stain on the porcelain skin.

Dan sucked in air. "You're so lovely," he breathed.

Kit backed away from him, a frown tight between her eyes. "That's not what I want to hear. It doesn't make everything all right. It doesn't make *anything* all right. Have you ever seen who I *am*, me, the person who lives behind this damned face?"

"Kit! How can you say that? I've always known. I'm . . ."

He reached out a supplicating hand, but she twitched her shoulder away. "Nothing's changed, nothing!"

"You're damned right, Kitty. Nothing that *matters*. I still want you, and what's more, you still want me."

She smiled a tight, social smile, yet he noticed her hands were clenched into fists. Between her teeth she said in a low, intense tone, "I don't think you want the whole room to hear you."

"To hell with what anyone hears!"

An excited voice called out: "The same old Dan Copeland! Here I've been looking all over the place. I should have known to follow my ears and listen for a declamation!"

Both Dan and Kit turned with a start. It was Benno, striding rapidly over to them.

Dan allowed himself to be grasped by the shoulders, while he slapped his old friend's back. His anger and frustration faded into the background. "You've never looked better," he said frankly, taking in the elegant clothes and the self-assured posture. He laughed. "As a matter of fact, you've turned into a man of distinction."

"Much to everyone's surprise, huh? Well, if you want a real surprise, you should see Rivers. She's done a before-and-after number that's unbelievable, right, Kit? Where is she, anyway?"

"I—she was talking to someone . . ." Kitty said lamely but the two men were not really interested. They stood grinning at each other.

"So, Benno, old buddy. What created this momentous change in your physical self?"

"A long, sad story—and one I promise you'll hear before the weekend's out. Right now I'm wallowing in the past. Have you noticed how the same groups are forming? Most of them haven't seen their old college friends since graduation, but put them back on campus and they automatically revert to the way they were ten years ago. You two, for instance," he said with a sly look. "I swear, the very last time I saw the two of you together, you were tearing into each other with the same words and exactly the same expressions on your faces."

Dan laughed without humor. "It's the same argument."

"Oh, really?" He leered. "And I thought we were all big boys and girls now."

Torn between amusement and irritation, Kitty gave him a playful slap on his arm. "Some things never change —as I was just pointing out to Mr. Copeland," she said dryly. "Including wise-guy Armenians." Carefully avoiding Dan's eyes, she flashed them a smile. "I'll leave you two old roommates alone to catch up."

"I'll see you later, Kit." Dan's tone was firm. "So don't run away."

Another brilliant and insincere smile. "Run away? But I just got here. I'm only going to talk to Trudy." Gracefully she turned and melted into the crowd.

Dan and Benno looked a question at each other. "Trudy?" Ben said finally. "I don't remember anyone by that name."

"The devil with it!"

Ben gave a mock sigh. "So. She still has the power to shake you up after all this time."

Dan grimaced. "I hope I've shaken *her* up. She needs it. She's so insulated, though, I'm afraid it'll take an earthquake to shake her free."

"And I know I'm looking at the Great Earthshaker himself," Benno laughed. "Funny, we think we leave the past behind. But apparently it lives on intact, inside."

Dan shook his head. "Not everything, Ben. Just . . . certain unfinished things that I'm going to finish. Oh, hell!"

They stepped through the open French doors onto the wide rear terrace facing the tennis courts. On this clear, warm night the courts were brightly illuminated with bluish floodlights, and in the otherworldly glare, two young blond girls—both wearing ponytails and crisp tennis whites—played a silent, expert game. There was no moon, but the velvety sky was sprinkled with bright stars, and the scent of newly cut grass was in the air.

For a few minutes they leaned on the low stone balustrade and watched the coeds as they rallied, crouching, running, stretching. From this distance their movements almost resembled a dance.

"My dream girls," Benno said. "Did you know that? I always yearned after the high-class blondes. High-class brunettes didn't come into it. Blonde or nothing."

Dan laughed. "The failing of many a Levantine throughout history."

"Humph. But I made the Big Mistake. I wasn't satisfied with the fantasy; I had to go and marry it."

"Married! Somehow it hadn't occurred to me you might be married. You don't look married—whatever the hell that means."

"You're not as dumb as you look, my man. I'm *not* married, not any more. Free as of yesterday, not to put too fine a point on it."

"Sorry."

"You're the only one, then. I haven't felt this good since we got engaged. And I'm sure that Helena has very efficiently wiped the whole sordid mess right out of her memory bank. I can hear her now: 'Ben? Ben who?' " There was a moment of silence, broken by Ben's gently clearing his throat. "On the other hand, not all marriages are bad, I guess— Have I stepped out of line? Sorry, I shouldn't be badmouthing marriage, to you of all people. Remember, I haven't seen you since the day of Polly's . . . funeral, and you weren't much in the mood for talking then."

"Were you there? My God, of course you were. Stupid of me . . . I'd forgotten. Or very efficiently wiped the whole sordid mess right out of *my* memory. I wasn't myself after Polly's accident. In a daze of shock—or guilt."

"Guilt! Come on, Dan. Why do you think they call them accidents? Because they happen *accidentally*. Get it? There's no blame. You haven't been spending all these years agonizing?"

Dan waved an impatient hand. "No, no, I don't blame myself for the plane crash. I just never should have married her. I blame myself for that. You know what I'm talking about, Ben; you were there for most of it—the beginning, anyway. I'd be a liar if I said I think of her all the time. But she haunts me. If only I'd been more honest or less ambitious or *something*—agh! It makes me sick."

"You're too hard on yourself, old buddy. She was an adorable little thing and she worshipped you. And you were trying to get rid of Kitty's ghost—oh, yeah, I knew that. And look, you made Polly happy. A lot of men wouldn't have bothered. And a lot of men, I might add, have married for worse reasons. Me, for instance."

"At least you had reason to think you were in love with her."

Benno sighed. "We both made the same basic mistake. Thinking if *one* person in a marriage loves, it's enough."

"Maybe. I salve my guilt by telling myself that at least she was happy, she loved me. But did she? Was she capable of it at her age and in her . . . situation? Why didn't I see *before* we were married? That's what I keep asking myself. What made me so blind?"

"You didn't want to see."

"Right. I didn't want to see." Dan was silent for a moment. "You have no idea, Ben," he said, "how I hate Thanksgiving . . ."

He hadn't believed his incredible luck. Just because he had gotten restless and come downtown to see an afternoon movie—something he normally never did—he had happened to be walking along State Street at the same time as the Malverne sisters. If there was one man worth knowing in the state of Wisconsin, it was Big Jim Malverne. Politically, he ran the whole show. That was the word. And when you were a politically inclined law school senior, with your eye firmly fixed on the future, an invitation to Jim Malverne's home for Thanksgiving dinner was worth its weight in straight A's.

"Couldn't you say you'd bring a friend?" Benno complained, only half kidding. "Come *on*, buddy, there are two sisters."

"Only one of them's worth considering . . . and anyway, those girls aren't the point, for Chrissake. The point is—"

"Enough, enough. I know what the point is. And I'm sure you'll make the most of your golden opportunity."

"Was that nasty?" Dan asked, laughing, but he didn't care. Let Benno stew. He didn't need luck. He had *money!* This time it was Copeland's turn.

When the day dawned, gray and bleak with the promise of snow hanging heavily in the smooth white sky, it occurred to him that he didn't know what to expect. A lot of family—squalling babies and noisy little kids, frosty maiden aunts and belching uncles—as had been the case at all the Thanksgiving dinners of his own childhood? Maybe they always asked lots of law students. Then he shrugged, put on his one jacket, and stood shivering at the bus stop as heavy wet snowflakes began to fall, ready to make the most of whatever the day offered.

Serena herself, flushed and sweating a bit, opened the door when he rang; immediately he was engulfed in a blast of warmth and fragrance and hearty male laughter. Serena, looking blocky and awkward in a flower print dress, her long, thick black hair already coming out of an elaborate topknot, stammered a little. "Oh—oh—it's you. Good. I mean—come in, it's late, but no, no, not *too* late. Come in and I'll introduce you to my father."

Big Jim Malverne sat enthroned on a huge brown leather La-Z-Boy recliner that seemed totally out of place with the chintz slipcovers and dainty flowered wallpaper. Every lamp had been turned on and the room blazed with light, hazy with low-hanging tobacco smoke. Dan blinked; it was somewhat overwhelming: the noise and the light and the sheer bulk of bodies on every available seat. And all male. No, not quite all. Perched on the arm of Big Jim's chair, like a bright tropical bird in the midst of all the somber-colored suits, was the younger sister, Polly, all decked out in red velvet, her hair a froth of yellow.

"Here's Dan Copeland," Serena said loudly, and abruptly left him standing alone in the entrance to the room as every head turned toward him. Dan swallowed hard and took a quick look around. Ohm'god, there was Dean Richmond from the law school. And the guy next to him looked awfully familiar, his face had just been in the papers. And there was Senator Fairchild, and across the room a judge, and there— He just stopped. It was mind-boggling. The entire power structure of the state was here, in this comfortable, old-fashioned living room with its bowls of fruit and crystal candy dishes and cut-glass decanters everywhere.

Jim grinned at him. "Come on over and meet everyone," he invited, sticking out a big, meaty hand. Dan marched up to him and found his hand engulfed, shaken, and relinquished with quick warmth. "Dan Copeland," Big Jim announced. "Editor of *Law Review*." Dan hardly heard the introductions; he already knew most of the names, as did everyone in Wisconsin. A drink was pushed into his hand, he was told three off-color jokes, and before he knew it, the feeling of awe had faded away and he was right at home.

A bar had been set up, and trays of hors d'oeuvres or dishes of nuts were everywhere. People carried on interesting conversations in every corner. Faces just drifted in and out, out and in. A gaggle of young children ran and shrieked. But Dan focused on the wheeling and dealing.

Then suddenly, Big Jim stood up, and as if on a prearranged signal six of the most important men in the room followed suit. With a grin, Jim said, "Be back in a while, folks. A little unfinished business. Keep on drinking!" And they disappeared into the next room and closed the double doors.

Sipping his Jack Daniels, Dan roamed the first floor. The house was big and sprawling, a maze of added-on wings and hallways. He discovered a twittering covey of wives and daughters ensconced in a television room. When he said, "Whoops! Excuse me!" there was a lot of giggling, but most of them turned right back to their needlework. At one point he found himself in a kind of pantry, suddenly face to face with Serena, who colored vividly and dropped a dish of pickles, which he helped her retrieve. She was all breathless blushes, muttering over and over how clumsy he must think her. Her eyes never once met his, and suddenly it flashed upon him: She had a crush on him! He looked her over. She looked exactly like her father. Funny, Big Jim looked handsome and powerful. On a girl, though, it was just mannish. Poor girl.

"My face," he told her with a smile, "often makes babies cry and girls drop pickles. I should have stayed in the other room."

"Oh, no—" she began. "Oh, really! No! I'm glad you're here . . . I mean—"

"Oh, Rena, who dropped pickles all over the floor!" The voice came from so close behind him that Dan gave a start. And then a little hand came to rest on his arm.

Polly. "Come on, Dan Copeland," she said, tugging at him. "It's no fun in here. Let Rena pick it up. I need someone to help me put out the place cards. I can't read her printing, and you'll know who they all are."

"Me!" Dan exclaimed.

But Serena shooed them both away. "I'll finish, I'll finish, I'm just so clumsy," she kept saying. So he went, accompanied by the fragile-looking little blonde who chattered on and on about what they would be having for dinner.

She led him into a game room and they played pool. She played very poorly and he was quickly bored, hoping someone would drift in and rescue him. But she seemed to enjoy it, and he could figure no way to quit without hurting her feelings. They played until a dinner bell called everyone in for the big feast.

Polly sat herself right next to him, ignoring the card which indicated Serena was supposed to be there. Since the older sister said nothing, Dan decided to ignore it. Covertly, while everyone was busy eating, he eyed Serena Malverne. Working in the kitchen had put a dewy finish on her skin, and her eyes were bright. The Indian-like hair had slipped completely out of its old-maidish knot and lay in a thick bluish-black shining fall over her shoulders. If she lost about thirty pounds, he thought, she wouldn't be bad. Not bad at all.

There were twenty-seven at table, with two heavyset local farm women acting as waitresses, coming out of the kitchen with huge serving dishes and setting them down on the table. After that it was every man for himself: turkey and oyster stuffing, liver stuffing, bread stuffing, and corn stuffing; a goose and a roast beef; relishes and pickles and chow-chow; white potato and sweet potato and dumplings and pancakes; cranberry sauce and piccalilli; squash and beans and succotash; four kinds of homemade bread and Parker House rolls and biscuits and johnnycake and Yorkshire pudding; sweating pitchers of cider, draft beer, and lemonade. Everywhere was the glitter of glass and silver and polished gold-rimmed plates with hand-painted flowers; the glow of big white damask napkins and the flash of silver platters.

The platters were passed, emptied, refilled, and passed again. And while the food was disappearing, the conversation never stopped. The talk was lively and serious, punctuated often with what the governor said yesterday and what the legislature had better do tomorrow. Listening as hard as he could, Dan tried to follow all the conversations at once. On his left: gossip about why a certain bill was doomed to die in committee. On his right: the dean explaining why a new law was not constitutional. Over there, near the head of the table: three men who looked like someone's jolly uncles, quietly killing the career of a budding politician who didn't do well with the right folks, was too arrogant and Eastern, and would be quietly shunted aside.

Here, right here in Big Jim Malverne's dining room, were all the movers and shakers, stuffing themselves and making decisions for the whole state. This, Dan told himself with delight, was *it:* the epicenter of life. This was the Students' League for grown-ups. This was where he belonged. Well, he reflected, he was here today, anyway. The idea was to get invited back, to let Big Jim know who Dan Copeland was and what he stood for and what he could do. He'd do just about anything. He'd volunteer for Jim's club, take any kind of job, even as a gofer.

He glanced again at Serena, sitting stolidly, pushing the food around her plate with a fork. She looked up at him and colored, looking away immediately in confusion when their eyes met. Yes, she definitely had a crush. In a way, it made him uncomfortable; he wished he found her attractive. But if dating her was the price of admission to Big Jim Malverne's inner circle, then so be it.

The men stayed at table, smoking and drinking coffee laced with brandy, then just brandy, until two in the morning. As Dan was preparing to leave, having been offered a ride by the dean, Polly—in a fluffy blue robe and slippers—came racing down the stairs.

"Oh, Dan, I want to say goodbye. I'm supposed to be asleep, but Serena can't see me. She's asleep." She laughed as if it were the best joke in the world. "You *will* come back to see us again, won't you? Say you will." She turned as Jim came out into the entrance hall. "Make Dan come back to see us, Daddy. He's nice. Not like all those politicians." She wrinkled her nose and her father laughed delightedly.

"From what I hear, honey," he boomed, "your 'nice'

153

Dan is something of a politician himself. Isn't that so, Dan? You certainly sounded like one at the table."

Dan grinned and blinked bleary eyes. "I've—ah—been known to get involved, yes, sir. It's what I love."

The big man eyed him for the merest second, his look shrewd. Then he thrust out a meaty paw. "Well, if you can, why don't you come on out for Sunday dinner and we'll talk? Maybe we can find something for you to do, eh? *Besides* being nice to my girls!" And he laughed.

Dan went for Sunday dinner. Soon he was going out to the big house several times a week to talk law or politics or just to listen as Big Jim wheeled and dealed with the powers in the state. As he said to Benno, who wanted to know what the big attraction was that took him away so often and did she have a sister, "Nothing like that. It's politics. Reality. After the rarefied atmosphere in school, it's like breathing fresh air."

It was funny, Ben's insisting on a woman being in the picture. He himself thought that Jim Malverne wasn't being nice to him just because he was your bright young *Law Review* editor. He figured being a bachelor, able-bodied, and ambitious probably made him very attractive, and that Big Jim was using politics as a piece of bait to reel in a husband for the ugly-duckling daughter. He doubted Serena, with her heavy-footed shyness, would easily find a man for herself.

But it didn't turn out that way. The two sisters went back to Hampton. Dan went home for a visit at Christmas, and when he returned, there, to his surprise, was not Serena, but pretty Polly. She had quit school and come back for good. It completely changed the shape of his evenings at the Malverne house.

Before, it had been just he and Jim and the other men. What a pleasure it was to watch Malverne in action! He'd sit in his big old worn leather desk chair, tipping it way back, staring up at the ceiling through the inevitable rank fog of cigar smoke, running one stubby hand through his thick steel-gray hair as he talked. His bullhorn voice he used like a musical instrument, softening it, making it angry or sweet or jovial, as needed. The gray eyes were pouched and the broad face lined; the once-muscular short body had developed a belly. But his voice was forever young. Dan had done more listening than ever before in his life; and Big Jim, seeming not to notice most of the time, would occasionally prove how aware he was by dropping a shrewd wink that said, "What a good game this is, isn't it?"

Now Polly was always around, curling up next to her father and wrapping an arm around his shoulder, or bringing in a fresh pot of coffee, or sitting at Dan's feet with her curly head almost leaning on his leg. She reminded Dan of a kitten, soft and warm and playful. She flirted with him and he reciprocated, as one would with a friend's kid sister. Well, she looked like a child. Her body was small-boned and narrow, with slight curves, and her heart-shaped face was dominated by round, guileless, bright blue eyes. Like a good-natured child, she was full of giggles and hugs, apt to say anything that popped into her head. And a happy little head it seemed: To Polly, the world was full of wonder and delight. It soon became natural for him to hug her hello when he arrived and often to find her cuddling close to him as he sat in his accustomed spot on the enormous sofa.

Late one Sunday afternoon, when he and Jim were alone after several hours spent with two members of the State Senate, Jim tipped back his chair and said to the ceiling, "She's crazy about you, Dan. You aware of that?"

Taken aback, Dan spluttered: "But . . . but who do you mean?"

The chair came down with a bang. "Polly! Who the hell else? My old aunt Minnie?" He roared with laughter.

Quickly, Dan reorganized his ideas. "She's a sweet girl. But I've never even . . ."

"Very protected," Jim said. "Naive, even. But I know I can trust you, Dan. You know, she's been turning down dates lately to hang around here with you. Maybe—Polly! Get in here, honey!"

When she came into the room a minute later, Jim asked, "How'd you like to see a movie today?"

She clapped her hands. "Terrific! Dan has to come, too. Come on, Dan, you just work and study all the time."

Jim smiled at her. "Why, honey, Dan's going to *take* you. How's that suit you?"

For a brief moment Dan had the cold feeling that the shape of his future was looming up before him, threatening to engulf him against his will. And then he shook himself mentally. It was just a movie—a *movie,* for God's sake. And his date was a very appealing little girl who, let's face it, was too young for him. If her adoration sometimes made him impatient, it just as often soothed him, made him feel like a pasha. Why not take her to a movie and hold her soft little hand for a while? And, to be truthful, he didn't at all mind pleasing Jim.

"Don't you want to come along, Jim?" he asked.

The deep-set eyes under their straight black brows glinted at him with amusement. "Not this time, Danny boy. 'Course, if you want, I'll come along next time . . . Why don't we just wait and see?"

Dan was a bit surprised at how much fun it was, holding hands like a teenager, munching popcorn, and laughing at the antics of *Young Frankenstein.* And when they were back at the house, standing inside the front door, and she tipped her head up, saying, "Aren't you going to kiss me good night?" he laughed and bent his head casually to the rosy lips.

But it wasn't the teenager's kiss he had expected, not at all. Her lips parted under his, and the slight body pressed ardently against him as her arms wound tightly around his neck. Her little tongue darted expertly into his mouth and he broke away, slightly breathless and not knowing whether to laugh or spank her or kiss her again.

"Whoa, there," he said, grinning down at her. "You're moving too fast for me. I usually don't kiss on a first date."

Her expression was dead serious. "But I've been wanting and wanting to kiss you—ever since Thanksgiving, and here it is February already. That's not fast." And standing on tiptoe, she offered her mouth to him once more. There was no denying the delicious softness of her, the frank sensuality hidden behind the baby face. Still he hesitated, and then she quickly moved one little hand down to his groin, to the bulge she had aroused, and announced: "You want to. I can tell." At this, half amused, he gave in, wrapping his arms firmly around her, and kissed her again.

This time he did not pull away. She smelled of flowers, and she knew instinctively what to do with her hands, her lips, her tongue. He had not had a woman in months, and this woman was melting, sensuous, frankly eager, initiating every move of the age-old game. It was she who pulled him up the wide stairs and into her pink and white room at the back of the house lined with shelves and shelves of teddy bears and dolls. She who pulled impatiently at her own clothes, and then at his. And she who, annoyed with his gentle, careful caresses, begged him to "do it now. Now, *now.*"

When it was over and he lay, drained, on his back with her small body curved into his, he could not quite believe it had happened. If Jim ever found out—!

Polly snuggled closer into him. "Oh, Dan," she sighed. "I do love you so much."

"Oh, now, Polly, listen. Just because two people— uh—"

"Oh, I know all about sex. It's fun. I've done it *lots*, only don't tell because it's a secret."

"Oh, don't you worry, honey, I won't breathe a word," he agreed with meaning.

"You don't have to love me back. That's okay. Only don't go away, Dan. Because I just love you. I do, I do, I do. This time it's different. I don't want it to be a secret any more."

He lay there, on the sheets printed all over with a pattern of Cinderella and the Prince, and felt a cold, sinking sensation take over his body. "What—what do you mean, Polly?"

"Marry me, Dan. Oh, say yes. It'll be such fun, and we can do this every single night, as much as we want." Her hands darted over his body, caressing, fondling. "There" —triumphantly—"you see? Oh, let's get married, say you will!"

"Polly. Listen. Just because I—" He gave up, his mind desperately thinking ahead. He would have to extricate himself from this situation quickly, or it would all be over: his relationship with Jim, his promised job as clerk to a judge, any political career here. Jim adored this daughter . . .

"I said you don't have to love me back," Polly was chattering in her usual way. "Just let me love you. And I promise I'll stop doing this with the Becker twins. And with Mike Stapleton and everybody. It'll just be for *you.*"

Ohmygod, was all his brain was good for. He dared not contemplate what games she might have been playing with the Becker twins, whom he had seen around the house, two skinny sixteen-year-olds. They often went horseback riding or skating with Polly. And then? *Ohmygod!* And Jim knew nothing of this, nothing! It would kill him. What was worse, he might choose not to believe it and to focus his rage on Dan! Dan Copeland, despoiler of virginal eighteen-year-old little girls? Oh, God! He had a future here. Was it all to be thrown away because of a child who looked like Shirley Temple and acted like Mae West?

"Polly, honey. Now, look, I'm . . . I'm very happy that you love me . . . No, don't start that now. I want you to listen. Marriage is very serious, don't you understand me?" She nodded, her big round eyes glistening in the darkness. "We have to give it a lot of thought. And in the meantime, we can't do this any more."

"Not any more?" Her whole voice was a pout.

"No. This was wrong. That's why it's a secret, understand? And if you love me, Polly, you'll do as I say."

"Okay, Dan. I love you. I'll do what you say. No more. After tonight!" And in a gale of giggles, she threw her body on his, wriggling against him, and bit his neck.

"Polly. No."

Against his ear, she whispered, "Or else I'll scream and scream. I *will*." As he abruptly stopped pushing her away, he could feel her soft ripe lips on his earlobe, curving up in a smile. "Good. And now you lie still and I'll do lots of nice things. It'll be fun!"

In the weeks that followed, no matter how hard he tried, he could not get the memory of that night out of his head. It was half fantasy, half nightmare. He had been scared nearly out of his wits—that she would make noise, that they would be discovered, that Jim would be furious, a hundred different things—but none of that had interfered in the least with the excitement the lascivious nymph in the bed had been able to arouse.

She kept to her part of the bargain, though. When he was at the house, she was the same old Polly—a funny, adoring, adorable little girl who snuggled and cuddled and charmed everyone in sight. How bad would it be, after all, to be married to her? One, Jim would be delighted. Two, she would look good in public. Three, she wouldn't interfere, because she wasn't interested in what was going on.

And four, she wouldn't complain about the kind of life he'd be leading, because she'd been brought up in a household where politics was part of the air you breathed. There would be no fights, no emotional struggles, as there had been—oh, God, how there had been!—with Kit. It certainly wouldn't hurt to be part of the Malverne family. And in any case, Kit was irrevocably gone, and he would never again love *anyone* the way he loved her. And—he had to grin at himself—he would never lack for a complete and satisfying sex life. So why not?

He began to take her to the local dances and fundraising functions, and soon they were considered a couple. One evening at a dance Polly whispered to him, "I've been very good, Dan, like you said. So when can we do it again?"

He was surprised to feel his loins tighten at her words. Without really thinking about it, he replied, "Not until we're married." She squealed with delight, hugging and kissing him, and it was done. It was over. It was the future.

Of course, when he was studying for finals and spent all his time in the apartment, it bothered him a bit that he really didn't miss her. Not even physically. But what the hell. Jim couldn't be happier. Polly couldn't be happier. And he certainly wasn't *unhappy*.

Benno didn't approve, not at all. "Bit young and naive for you, isn't she?" he said when he heard the news. "Bit . . . simple?" Dan told him to mind his own business.

But Benno kept sniping away about it. "Talked with your fiancée this evening," he'd say. "She had a lot of intelligent things to say about the state of her hairdo."

"Shut up, will you? Polly's not an intellectual. I don't need one. She suits me."

"Huh! *She* suits you? Or her old man suits you?"

"Buzz off, Ben." He went storming out of the apartment to cool off. And when he came back, nothing further was said.

But the tension grew between them, and when—as Big Jim had promised—he won the appointment as Justice Cooper's clerk for the next year—Benno had applied, too —they had an enormous battle, with Benno taunting him that he was marrying Polly for the Malverne money and the Malverne influence and not for "her considerable

charms, which I could add up on one finger of one hand."
They hardly spoke after that, and Benno never came to
the wedding, although he had been invited.

When Serena came home from Hampton at the end of
May, she drew Dan aside and demanded: "What are you
marrying Polly for?"

"I don't know what you mean." He eyed her uneasily.
There was something implacable about her, something
steel-hard and, perhaps, steel-sharp. She was more than
ever the image of her father, stocky and short-legged like
him, and with the same stubborn set to the jaw.

"You know what I mean," she said. "You know perfectly well. I just hope you realize what you're getting
into."

"Serena, I don't think this is something I need to discuss with you. You're not Polly's mother, for God's sake!"

Color blotched her cheeks. "That's what you think! I've
been watching over her, taking care of her, practically her
whole life. I'm the nearest thing to a mother she's got.
And I know her better than anyone. Listen, Dan, she's
helpless, she's really like a baby, she—"

He cut her off with a wave of the hand. "I don't know
why you're getting so excited. I intend to take very good
care of Polly . . . and she's not as helpless as all that. A
bit overprotected, maybe."

The pellucid eyes sparked. "You've bought Jim's line,
you've swallowed it whole! Dan, listen, you must listen—"

"Polly's fine. I understand that this has all happened
very fast and that it's come as a shock to you. But really,
you must stop. The date is set." He smiled, trying for a
lighter touch. "Soon we'll be related. Let's not fight."

To his dismay, her eyes filled abruptly. "Jim always gets
his way. But you'll be sorry. You'll *all* regret this!"

Dan straightened up from the balustrade and stretched.
"You and Serena both tried to tell me, but I've always
been too damn cocksure to listen."

"That makes two of us." Benno laughed bitterly.

Dan stared out at the patch of light over the tennis
courts, at the two lithe girls moving about in their separate
little world. "She was truly helpless, Ben. Not just a femi-
nine act, the sort of thing that's done to make a man feel
big and strong and superior. There was something . . .

wrong. Something I believe Jim couldn't face. I *have* to believe that he really saw her as a slightly immature, over-protected girl; that he didn't know. He's been father, mentor, associate; he wouldn't have tricked me like that.

"She couldn't do anything. Decide what to wear. Get a meal on the table. The simplest things put her into a tizzy. But— She was pregnant when she died, did you know that?"

"Oh, God. No!"

"A week after the wedding, I knew I had made a dreadful mistake. I never had the time to really take care of her. She couldn't be left alone! We'd taken a little apartment in town . . . Within the month, I'd moved us out to the big house, to Jim's! It was the only way; at least the servants were there to do everything."

"If you knew all this," Benno said, "why did you let her become pregnant?"

Dan laughed shortly. "She forgot to take the pill . . . of course she forgot. She was pregnant almost immediately."

"What a mess."

"Yes. A grand mess, and one of my own making. I was too ready . . . too ready to think only of my career. I guess I didn't *want* to look at her too closely, I don't know. And so here I am, ten years after graduation, looking pretty good to the world. But when you add it all up, the woman I married is gone, the woman I want won't have me, and the child I might have had was killed before it had a chance to be born—"

He stopped abruptly as the air became filled with a sudden, intense explosion. With an incoherent cry, Dan flung himself onto the bricks of the terrace, his arms tightly wrapped about his head, his heart racing. He lay there, rigid and unthinking, as wave after wave of heat raced over him.

After a shocked moment, Benno bent over him. "A doctor!" he cried. "Get a doctor! Someone!" In a panic, not knowing what to do, he lifted Dan's wrist, feeling for a pulse. By the time the last syllable had left his lips, there were half a dozen people, strollers on the terrace, clustered closely around them. "Dan! Dan!" Ben yelled. He pushed Dan's shoulder, frowning as the big, muscular body rolled easily onto its back. *Where* was the pulse?

His friend's face was gray and bloodless, with a slick shine of sweat.

Then the empty, staring eyes began to blink rapidly. Dan shook his head and struggled to get to his feet. "Hey!" he protested. "It's okay, it's okay. What—? Don't worry. I tripped, that's all." His voice was a bit thick and he was pouring sweat. It was obvious that he had fainted.

Dan wished them all away, the downpressing faces encircling him, with their worried eyes and furrowed brows. What had happened? It had all gone too fast to think about. There had been the explosion. *Danger!* So he had dived for the ground. Lying there, he had been aware of wet stickiness on his face and chest and back, oh, God; half lost in the past, he had assumed it was blood. He had been hit and was bleeding to death! Now, befuddled though he was, he realized it was sweat. Simply sweating, that's all. And the weapon had been nothing more than a car or a truck, backfiring into the quiet of a Hampton night.

"I'm a doctor!" It was Jess Barrone, the hearty social manner wiped away. "Everybody back. The show is over!" His eyes were intent on Dan's face all the time, and without glancing away, he barked: "Linda! My bag!" and snapped his fingers impatiently. Somewhere in the background there was a flurry of activity, and then Linda Barrone, pale and nervous, scurried from out of nowhere with a small black leather case. Barrone grabbed it from her with a grunt and then ignored her, although she stood, irresolute, watching every move. "You scraped your chin," he said shortly, and wiped at Dan's face with antiseptic. His touch was amazingly gentle and deft. The sting of the alcohol was the first awareness Dan had that he had actually been hurt. Must have really thrown himself hard onto the brick flooring . . . funny how, when the adrenalin was pumping, pain was totally blotted out. Now he could feel the little pulsation that told him he'd broken the skin.

Barrone finished, snapped the bag closed, and handed it back without a glance into his wife's waiting hand. Again, like a wraith, she seemed to dissolve into space, disappearing silently. Wiping his hands fussily on an oversized linen handkerchief, the fleshy doctor gave his hearty social laugh. "Well, Copeland, I see you still have the knack for getting yourself into trouble, ha-ha."

Benno fisted his hands. "Back off, Barrone."

"Take it easy," Dan interjected. "He didn't mean anything. I'm glad you were here, Barrone. Thanks for coming so fast."

"Wait'll you get my bill, ha-ha!" But he took the hint and moved off, asking loudly whether someone might fetch him a martini.

As soon as the doctor was out of earshot, Dan gave his friend a punch on the arm, laughing. "Akkardijian to the rescue! Just like old times, Ben. I'd forgotten how nice it always was to have you right behind me . . ."

"What the hell *happened*? Who's after you, anyway? Jesus, it was just a backfire!"

"Hey. Come on. Don't you remember when we were roomies?"

"Sure. The nightmares, the night sweats, the yelling and screaming. Who the hell could forget that? You were a barrel of laughs, fella, yelling, 'Kill! Kill!' into my ear at three in the a.m. But . . . well, it never happened the three years at law school. I guess I figured the dreams were all over. That the war was water over the bridge, in the past, all that kind of stuff."

"Well, it was," Dan said. "It was, goddamn it. This is the first time in . . . God, I don't know, *years* that I've pulled that kind of stunt. Don't ask *me* what the hell happened. Beats me. Maybe it's all this reliving of the past, or something . . ." His voice faltered.

Quickly, Ben declared, "Buddy, what we both need is a good, stiff drink. You wait here and I'll go get it."

Dan leaned on the balustrade again. He still felt a bit shaky inside . . . not that he'd admit it to anyone, or let it show. You couldn't do that and keep your image intact for very long. "Bulldozer Dan," they'd called him back in his undergraduate days. And they'd been right. He'd trodden on a lot of toes, political and emotional, male and female. Oh, Lord, the girls . . . He'd loved Kit, but that hadn't meant he had to live like a monk. Many was the night he'd hung a towel on the doorknob to let Ben know there was a woman with him. A lot of girls, even then, had hung around just so they could be laid by the campus big shot. The night of the first big demonstration in '67, the night he had claimed Kitty, in fact, he'd come home to find a naked girl in his bed. He hadn't kicked her out, hell, no. In fact, they had both had a wonderful time. But he'd always kept all his real emotions for Kit, who wouldn't have him . . .

And then Ben appeared in the doorway with two clinking tumblers, and he found himself reaching out eagerly for the whiskey. He'd drink up first—this would stop his knees from shaking—and then he'd go up and change.

The upstairs hallways were dimly lit and completely deserted—almost ghostly, Dan thought, without the noise and bustle of the students who normally lived there. The floor creaked beneath his shoes; his elongated shadow fled silently ahead of him. He felt much more uneasy than he was willing to admit. The scrape on his jaw throbbed, and he could still feel that stab of panic that had shot through him on the terrace when for one horrible second he had been sure he was being shot at. He tried to laugh at himself. It's been a long time since Vietnam, he told himself, but the malaise persisted. He didn't like the utter silence, and he fought not to look back over his shoulder. Come on, fella, he told himself. You're just up here to change your shirt. Don't make a war story out of it.

Then the breath caught in his throat as he spotted another shadow, a grotesque of a human shape creeping along the wall. He was being followed. Why? Someone was quietly edging up the carpeted stairs after him. Swiftly, Dan flattened himself into an alcove near the top of the stairway, scarcely breathing, and waited, hands curling in readiness, as the shadow shifted, squeezed in, and—rounding the corner—became attenuated.

The soft footsteps padded closer and closer as the shadow on the wall opposite stretched in weird patterns. He could hear the other figure's soft breathing, and then it was walking directly past him. He leaped with a low grunt, locking his arms tightly around the upper torso, squeezing. There was a kind of scream, quickly choked off.

The body he clutched so tightly was small, warm, slight and soft and— "Kitty!" he gasped, and let go.

Her voice was a shaky whisper. "D-Dan?"

Putting now-gentle hands on her shoulders, he turned

her to face him. "Oh, Kit! Don't be scared. I had no idea it was you . . . I thought . . ." He pulled her in close.

Kitty's arms went instantly around him and she buried her head into his shoulder.

"I was so worried, Dan!" The voice was muffled. "I didn't dare show it or say anything. You—lying there, so still. And you looked so white, going up the stairs. I just didn't care what anyone thought—I had to see you!"

He put a gentle finger under her chin and tipped her head up, looking intently into her eyes. They were shiny with unshed tears, and as he watched, one droplet escaped, trailing down the pale cheek, leaving a faint trail of gleam.

"Ah, Kitty, don't cry. It was nothing. I'm sorry I frightened you—I guess I'm a little nervous. But everything's fine."

"Everything's *not* fine. Everything's a mess. Don't you see? My life has been all neatly arranged: everything planned for, everything settled. And then you come back into my life and . . ." She paused, lips trembling.

He felt suddenly breathless, his heart thudding painfully. "Yes, Kitty? *And?*" His grip tightened. She winced but did not flinch, and even in the semidarkness he could see the intent emerald glitter changing the look in her eyes. Under his impatient grasp, her body was quivering as if shaken by an internal storm. "And?" he insisted, his voice a trifle hoarse.

She took in a ragged breath, hesitating. Then she burst out: "Oh, God, Dan, the wasted years, all those wasted years!" and strained into him, standing on her toes, lifting her soft mouth, and pulling his head down.

The throb of pain at the side of his face was washed totally away in the sweep of excitement that coursed through his body. All rational thinking fled. She loved him! She had come to him! The long battle was over—and this was to be his sweet triumph! He crushed her to him, aware of nothing but her—the shape of her body where it curved into his, the scent of her perfume, faintly musky. His mouth avidly explored the warmth of hers, the curve of her neck, the tender skin of her eyelids, savoring the sweet taste of her, the promise implicit in her shivering sighs. The surging of his own hot blood sang wildly in his ears as his hands eagerly sought the soft, yielding secrets of her body and she sank against him in surrender. He was drowning in desire, his senses swirling around a single vortex that was Kitty, Kitty, Kitty.

From somewhere out in space he felt her whisper. "My love, my love," against his neck. With an arm around her slender waist, he half propelled, half carried her down the hallway.

"Kitty! Oh, yoo-hoo! Kit Harris!" The shrill soprano echoed up the stairwell, coming closer with each word. "Oh, Mrs. Whitney Harris the *Third*. Kitty!"

Dumbstruck, they sprang apart guiltily, staring at each other with glassy, unfocused eyes. Then Kit began to giggle uncontrollably. "Oh, no!" she groaned and giggled some more.

Dan shook her. "Shhh. Who the hell *is* that?"

"Who else, Dan, darling? Courtney."

"Dammit!"

"Yes, dammit. Oh, my dearest, don't look so desolate. Later . . . later." And she formed her lips into a silent kiss.

Courtney appeared a moment later at the top of the stairs, shielding her eyes as if looking into a bright light, and peering down the hall at them. "Oh, *there* you are," she burbled, hurrying forward. "Are you all right? Buffy said she saw you going up the stairs—as white as a sheet, Buffy said—and I thought maybe you had to barf or something. I mean, everyone's getting so drunk down there, but"—she came to them and gave Kitty a narrow-eyed scrutiny—"you don't look drunk at all."

"I'm not," Kitty said. "Just felt a bit warm. Thought I'd change into something lighter."

"You *do* look warm," Courtney said brightly. "I'll come with you and we can catch up on things—the kids and stuff. But you've got to come back down, Kitty, 'cause everyone's asking for you. We're going to have a sing-song—remember when we used to have one every Sunday night? Remember Whit? He never *could* hold a tune. Come on, you'll miss all the fun."

"Well, Dan," Kitty said, a smile playing on her lips, "I don't want to miss all the fun. Do you?"

"Not me," he agreed solemnly. "I'll go change, too."

Courtney gave a little shriek. "Oh, silly me! I forgot to

ask you how you feel, Dan. And here I am, just going on and on."

"Don't worry about it. I hope everyone's forgotten."

"Well, you know, they're all so tight by this time, I wonder if any of them can remember which reunion it is." Courtney giggled. "You'll come, too, won't you, Dan?"

"I'll come and sing my heart out, Courtney, just like in the olden days."

As she and Kit went off down the other corridor, he could hear her say: "But he never used to come, did he, Kitty? Now, why do you suppose he said a thing like that?" He couldn't hear Kit's answer. I'll ask her later what she said, he thought with relish. When we're alone. Afterward. There were too many other things they had to catch up on first. Oh, he'd go back down and stand around the piano and act as if he were recapturing his youth, but no number of college songs could compete with the secret that sang through all his being, that surged in his blood with every beat of his heart. He would smile and suffer and patiently wait for the payoff long overdue: Tonight he would have his woman in his arms, in his bed, at last!

As he made his way down the stairs a short while later —showered, changed, and even, painfully, reshaved—he had to smile as the familiar strains of "The Sweetheart of Sigma Chi" came floating out of the living room. Kitty must already be there and those asses were serenading her, thinking it would flatter and please her. He knew differently, and sure enough, when he reached the entrance hall and looked in, she was seated on the piano top, delicate in a pale gray silken creation that was crossed by laces under each firm round breast, falling in tissue-thin shimmering folds around her shapely hips and thighs, a statue, still, stiff, uncomfortable smile on her lips.

Jay Shulman, perspiring faintly but obviously enjoying himself, was playing the piano—as he had at every musical show during their years at Hampton. Clustered close to the instrument were seven or eight men Dan could recognize, in spite of thinning hair or paunches that hadn't been there ten years before, as Sigma Chis, singing at the top of their voices and looking quite as drunk as Courtney had said. Not that they were the only ones around the piano; more and more people drifted up every second; but at the moment they alone were singing. Then he caught sight of Benno, standing slightly apart from the rest, arms folded across his chest, looking disdainful.

His eyes inevitably went back to Kit. She really hated being the center of attention. For a split second he pondered the kind of politician's wife she might make. She was a very private person, was Kit, and quietly stubborn. She was perfectly capable of refusing to appear on the podium with him. Still, it was that private, secretive quality that made her so terribly desirable, so extraordinarily exciting. When a woman as closed off as Kitty opened herself—in all senses of the word—it was like being handed a special gift. All that hidden passion, for you alone! What mattered now was that she was his one love, his own, and the time had finally come to claim her. To hell with the stupid details. She was worth it.

He had taken only a few steps toward her when a hand grabbed roughly at his sleeve. Startled, he turned to see the face of an older man—a somewhat familiar face it took him a moment to put a name to.

"Professor O'Hara!"

There was no answering smile. "That's right, Copeland." The voice was edged with rancor and fuzzy with drink. The man's breath was heavy with liquor. "*Professor* O'Hara it is, no thanks to you!"

"I beg your pardon?"

"As well you might, but you'll never get *my* pardon, you redheaded devil!"

Dan gaped. What in hell was the man ranting about? "I'm sorry. You've lost me."

"Ah, and if Hampton could've lost you eleven years ago, it would have been better for a lot of us."

Politely, Dan said, "I think you've had a bit too much to drink," and started to move away.

O'Hara grabbed his arm again, hard. "Maybe I've had a drop or two. Just enough to loosen my tongue, boyo, not my brain. You and your damned pinko cohorts nearly ruined me—and well you know it! But you didn't succeed!"

"Professor Profiles!" Dan blurted as understanding dawned.

A very tall and willowy creature wrapped in something silvery, her large dark eyes anxious, came hurrying up.

"Bill O'Hara, what's going on? I can't leave you alone for a *minute!*" The familiar deep voice told Dan who it was, even as his eyes had difficulty believing it.

"Lee Rivers! For God's sake!"

"Dan Copeland—for the devil's!" She pressed a warm, scented cheek to his briefly—nervously? he wondered as she pulled quickly back. The big Irishman glowered at them. Lee laughed. "Put an Irishman in a room with any-one else, *anyone,* and he'll start the Irish Rebellion all over again."

"You know damn well—" O'Hara began truculently.

She put a finger on his lips and teased: "Rather fight than have fun, would you, boyo?" And his face, chame-leonlike, twisted from belligerence into open lust. Dan thought the man unbelievably gross; but when he glanced at Lee, she seemed to like it.

Putting one hand possessively on Lee's rounded bottom, O'Hara favored Dan with a leering grin. "We Irish never rebel against a woman's desires," he said, poking his tongue into his cheek and winking. "Let's go *now,* girl, dear." He steered her toward the front door.

Over her shoulder Lee gave Dan a sharp, swift look he couldn't read, and mouthed silently: "See you."

Dan gazed after her, staring at the door even when she was out of sight. Hard to believe it was the same Lee. He'd seen pictures, of course; her picture was everywhere. Still, to be confronted with the change in person—! Es-pecially since he could still vaguely recall the flamboyant curves of her 1970 body. She was quite the glamour girl! The only thing he couldn't figure out was what in hell she was doing with that tired-out rogue O'Hara. After all these years, hadn't she learned better? And then he had to laugh at himself: And what about *you,* Dan Copeland?

From his place behind the baby grand, Benno watched the brief tableau in the foyer with interest. When O'Hara had first reached out to grab Dan's arm, Ben had been tensed to run, to fight. But nothing more had happened, so he had stayed where he was, willing his heartbeat to slow back down to normal.

And then it had begun to thump again when he saw Lee Rivers appear. Funny. They were old enemies, he and Lee. He hadn't found her particularly attractive in school—had he? Well, not attractive, exactly, more like challenging. He'd never liked her, he didn't like wise-cracking girls, they made him nervous. Still, he had heard the stories: Lee Rivers had round heels. And he had been a virgin, right up to his senior year. A dim memory floated by him, of walking down a darkened street with her, carrying her guitar or something, on their way to a rally; and fantasizing as they walked along that she would turn to him and say, "I dig you, Akkardijian," that she would take him and be so eager that she wouldn't notice it was his first time.

He smiled to himself as he contemplated the sophisticated vision floating across the entrance hall to give Dan Copeland a quick kiss hello. It would be fun, now that they were all grown up, to tell her about that; to let her know that all her digs at him about his innocence had been gratingly true. It was . . . satisfying to make her laugh; she was so sharp herself, and so blazingly honest. When Lee Rivers laughed at a funny line, you knew it was damn well *funny*. And then, when he saw O'Hara claim her with his hand on her butt, he felt . . . disappointed, resentful. He had been the first one to rediscover Lee Rivers tonight; he thought she had enjoyed being with him. And there she went, scampering off into the night with the number one Dirty Old Man on campus.

When Copeland came into the room, Ben went to meet him and demanded: "What's she doing with *him?*"

Dan laughed. "What do you care? But if you must know, she was his little girlfriend our senior year . . . oh, come on, Ben, you knew that! Well, actually, I guess I didn't, either, until the very end." For just a moment he had a flash of her heavy, soft body, after he'd taken her to O'Hara's place that night and found the Irishman had flown the coop. Ah, the comforting, undemanding, unquestioning warmth of her. They had both had a great deal to drink, his memory had been fogged with liquor, but he remembered it had been *nice*. It hadn't been her fault she wasn't Kitty; but unlike the aftermath with most of the others, he hadn't felt so grubby and depressed, just soothed.

He almost mentioned it to Benno and then thought, No, no, I'd better not. Instead, he said, "Everyone's reliving '70, Ben; join the stampede backward."

"Yeah."

"For instance, here I am, back ten years in time, going to rescue Kitty from the unsavory clutches of the Sigma Chis." He laughed again and moved away, not bothering to answer Ben's swift: "But she ended up with a Sigma Chi, anyway, old buddy, don't forget that."

Kitty gave Dan a look of intense gratitude when he held his arms out to her. He lifted her down and gave her a secret squeeze before relinquishing her. "Not that I want to," he murmured, "but I think we'd better hang around and pretend to sing." She smiled coolly. It was amazing, he thought, the way she was able to mask her inner feelings. To look at her, you would see only a beautiful young matron with an old friend who didn't particularly interest her. No one else, he was sure, would notice the pulse fluttering uncontrollably in her throat.

Courtney beckoned them with flamboyant gestures to stand near her. Jock stopped singing long enough to give Kit a hug. "Still the most beautiful girl in the world! Right, Copeland? Too bad you lost out, but you've got to move real fast when you're up against a Sigma Chi." He laughed, enjoying his own joke immensely.

Dan smiled and nodded and hoped that his disdain didn't show. Jock Standish didn't have to go very far emotionally to get back to *his* college days. He'd been constantly looped back then, and it looked as if nothing had changed during the intervening years.

Subtly, Dan moved a bit closer to Kit, so that their shoulders were just touching, and joined in on the chorus of "Down by the Old Mill Stream." Kitty began to sing, too, looking straight ahead as if she didn't know he was there. But in a minute he felt the back of her hand rubbing against his, sending an electric message.

They think nobody can see them, but I see everything. They think they're so smart, but I'm smarter. Just look at them, rubbing up against each other like animals in heat. Disgusting!

Serena stood alone at the back of the room, half hidden behind a window drapery. From her vantage point she could see everything going on around the piano. And nobody would ever notice her back there. Nobody had noticed her at all that evening. I'm just too smart for them

171

all, she thought. She had put on a cocktail dress and walked in with a large group, right by the tables in front, and nobody had said a word. Everyone was too busy shrieking and yapping and drinking. *She,* on the other hand, was going to stay clearheaded. She had a lot of work to do. One slug of gin before she had left the apartment and that was it . . . no matter how badly she wanted more.

Dan Copeland hadn't been out of her sight for more than ten minutes. She'd lost him when he'd gone upstairs —she'd started up, but that blond bitch had got there first.

She stared at the tall, broad-shouldered figure with the thick, carefully barbered copper hair. Oh, why couldn't he have married me? Then everything would have been fine! That stupid man! Why couldn't he have seen that? Why hadn't he listened?

Because he's evil, she answered herself. He turned my father against me and he killed my sister and her baby. If that wasn't proof of evil, she didn't know what was!

Serena heaved a great sigh, her eyes still fixed unwaveringly on him. He was really such a good-looking man . . . It was a shame he had to be punished.

CHAPTER NINE

Reunion, Lee and O'Hara

THE QUADRANGLE WAS awash with the last red-gold rays of the sinking sun, the old limestone buildings burnished with a glowing pink light, while beyond them the bands of clouds turned mauve and purple and burnt orange, like tattered banners in the darkening sky. Herringbone-brick pathways angled through the lush lawns, recently mowed. Birds clustered in the huge old maples, singing farewell to the dying day. The air was soft with just a hint of autumn's tang.

Lee and O'Hara walked slowly, arms wrapped around each other's waists. The peace of the evening had erased his belligerent mood and he was quietly reciting poetry . . . and she was content to lean her head against his shoulder and listen idly while she sniffed the fragrant air of sweet memory.

"'. . . hide thy heart and hoard thy lip/Wed no man. Remember me,'" O'Hara finished, and twisted his head to place his lips on her temple.

"Nice stuff," Lee said languorously. "What's it called?"

"It's a translation from the Gaelic," he told her. "Seventeenth century."

"Never mind the lecture. What is it?"

O'Hara cleared his throat a little. "As a matter of fact, it's 'Death's Warning to Beauty.'"

Lee laughed. "Oh, great! Of course it's Irish! Trust the Irish to write something that sounds like love poetry and is really a dirge!"

"Well, if it's *typical* love poetry you want, what about 'Loud will her heart be in her side/And white the excitement on her face/And song and wing shall fill the place . . .' Well?" he demanded, sliding one hand up her side to curl around her breast. "Is that better? I can feel that your heart is loud in your side, and my song and wing shall surely fill the place just as soon as we're alone."

"I don't think that's exactly what the poet had in mind."

"Ah, no, perhaps not. But you and I . . . we're a different story, now, aren't we?" He stopped and turned her to face him, pulling her hips in close to his. "Aren't we, girl?" he murmured, leaning over to bite softly at her earlobe.

A shudder went down her spine. "Why are we wasting our time *here*, O'Hara?"

He chuckled richly. "I knew it!" he chortled. "Still as hot-blooded as ever!"

"Wrong, O'Hara." She had to laugh at the look of sudden consternation on his face. She patted his cheek. "*More* than ever."

"Jesus, Mary, and Joseph, it's all coming true." His voice rang with the overtones of triumph.

For a second she felt cold. "What's all coming true? Is this all part of some master plan?"

He flung an arm around her shoulder, urging her forward. "Of course it is, girl, dear. I've been able to think of nothing else but making love to you again since I saw you tonight." His voice dropped intimately. "Did you think I could've forgotten my gypsy sweetheart?"

"I've certainly never forgotten *you*."

"A wonderful woman, a wonderful goddamn woman." He tucked her arm tightly beneath his and she nestled closer into him as they strolled on.

Suddenly the air was filled with the pulsating music of bells as the carillon in the bell tower of Hawthorne Chapel began its nightly concert.

Together, O'Hara and Lee exclaimed: "Seven-thirty!" and then looked at each other with the delight of memory shared.

"First it'll be 'The Bells of St. Mary,' " Lee recalled, "followed immediately by Bach's Fugue in D minor . . ."

"And then it's 'A Stranger in Paradise,' then 'Some Enchanted Evening' . . ."

"And then 'Jingle Bells,' " Lee added triumphantly, "ending, of course, with 'The Hallowed Halls of Hampton.' "

They laughed gleefully, hugging each other, and Lee thought, It's all right . . . it's better than all right . . . it's perfect. Over his shoulder, the sun was just sinking behind the distant hills, and several stars were poking through the lacy-leafed silhouettes of the trees. "Oh, Bill," she cried, "it's—"

"Hush," he hissed, lifting her hands from his shoulders and stepping back from her.

"What—?"

"Hush, for the love of heaven. Just keep walking." He began to stride away, suddenly very businesslike, leaving her with no choice other than to trot along behind him or be left standing like an idiot in the middle of the path. She went. And then, as she came abreast of him, she saw the reason for his strange behavior.

Three girls were coming toward them, giggling and talking. It took Lee only a moment to see that the two on the outside were teasing the tall, rather heavyset girl in the middle—a pale-skinned girl with thick glossy hair cut in a Prince Valiant style. They were nudging her and poking her, but their eyes were directed at O'Hara.

The girl in the middle was plainly uncomfortable; her eyes slid to O'Hara and away again nervously. In a minute they had passed, without a word being exchanged. But as they walked away, an agonized whisper sounded clearly through the dark: ". . . could die! You're not supposed to know!"

O'Hara kept going as if nothing had been heard. Keeping step with him, Lee felt an icy grip clutch at her heart. "Let me guess," she said smoothly. "The chubby one in the middle is your Coed of the Year."

"Nonsense!" he blustered, not looking at her. "What makes you think I'd be interested in a homely mutt like that?"

"Come off it, O'Hara. I wasn't such a raving beauty the year you took *me* on."

"You were different," he said, still staring straight ahead. "You were older, more sophisticated, more . . . knowing. Why, that infant had never been to bed with a man before—" He stopped, swallowing audibly.

"Yes, O'Hara?" Her insides had turned totally to stone; heavy, rigid, and lifeless. Why did he lie so much? "Before you taught her?"

"She has a crush on me, girl, dear. You remember how it is. How could I hurt her? I've been good for her . . . brought out her self-confidence. I've—listen here, my dear, you didn't expect that I'd lived like a monk these past ten years, did you?"

"You're shouting, O'Hara." She was astounded at her own control. "I expect nothing. All I did was remark that she must be the one you're sleeping with these days."

He stopped, burying his head in his hands like a naughty, small boy. "It was so beautiful," he said, his voice muffled into his palms, "so perfect—you, the evening, the sunset, the bells. I didn't want anything tawdry to spoil our magic. Say you forgive your errant, erring O'Hara!"

Lee regarded him, smiling a little. What blatant histrionics. But the beauty of it was that he really believed every word he uttered, no matter how insincere. And it *had* been everything he said: beautiful and magical. Maybe it could still be recaptured.

"Well," she said, as much to herself as to him, "we're just a block away, anyhow." And was rewarded with a big grin and his outstretched arms gathering her in once more.

It was so strange, going in that door again after so long. It all was so familiar, even though the room was much smaller than she had remembered, and it seemed to her that the leather couch used to be sideways to the fireplace rather than facing it. But the shabby Oriental rug was the same . . . there was that tear in the corner. And he still had a bar under the window and a fur rug thrown carelessly in front of the hearth. One small lamp burned softly on the desk, just as it always had.

No sooner had he locked the door behind them than his arms were roughly around her. His mouth came down hungrily, the tongue eagerly searching and probing, while his loins ground relentlessly into hers. She felt herself melting inside, like taffy in the sun, and she was grateful for the iron pressure of his arms supporting her.

Still caressing her, he led her to the fireplace, where he tenderly settled her onto the fur, drawing the tunic down so that he could kiss the soft flesh of her shoulder and breast. She kept her eyes half closed, reveling in the sensations he so expertly aroused. Right about now, she thought lazily, he would take off first his own shirt and then hers.

O'Hara leaned back on his heels, shrugged off his jacket, and swiftly stripped the fisherman's sweater over his head, tossing it carelessly behind him. Then he bent to her. She lifted up her arms in anticipation, waiting for him to undress her.

But he didn't. She opened one eye. What had happened to him? With a grunt, he pushed himself to his feet and headed across the room.

"O'Hara, where are you going?"

"I forgot the wine. It's right here, cooling."

"Wine!" Why do we need wine? she wondered. Why was he stopping right in the middle of everything to get a dumb glass of wine? It was as if he had a script for this evening that he must follow to the letter. Which of his caresses, she wondered, were a response to her, and which, part of his act? A little chill ran through her. She sat up, hugging herself a little, as he returned with a filled glass in either hand.

"Ah, Lee," he said softly, "lovely lady with breast more white than a branch heavy-laden with snow."

"Your timing's off, O'Hara. You usually wait with that line until the girl's shirt is off."

"Lee! Darlin' girl! Whatever do you mean?" He held out a glass to her. She ignored it.

"I mean," she said, scrambling to her feet, "that there's something overpracticed about this scenario. I feel as if I've just walked into the first act of a play that was supposed to have closed ten years ago." She marched over to the record player—a new, more expensive model, she noted, than the one he used to play gypsy music on all those years ago.

There was a record on the turntable, ready to be played. She bent to see what it was, and it was what she had half expected: the same old record of Theo Bikel singing Russian gypsy songs, the same old jagged scratch across the first band.

"Who's the gypsy music for?" Lee asked tightly. "Your old gypsy sweetheart . . . or whoever else you managed to find?"

He was still clutching the wine glasses, as if they were support. "Of course it's for you, girl, dear. No one else has ever been my dark gypsy. I put it on especially for you. Come, take your glass—it's the Chablis you always liked—and sit here by the hearth. I'll turn the music on and we'll make love to it just as we used to."

"Oh, really? Then you were expecting me?"

"Well, I—I hoped—when I saw your name on the list—"

She put her hands on her hips and eyed him pugnaciously. "Oh, really. How interesting. Since you pretended to be *so* surprised to see me at Enders. And it seems to me that you couldn't quite place me at first, isn't that right? Come off it, O'Hara. I'm being featured in the window of the Hampton record store and in the Student Union and in the bookstore. My face has been plastered all over campus for two weeks."

His mouth moved, but nothing would come out. He stared at her, his face reddening, and then in a kind of panic, he looked from one wineglass to the other, as if consulting them for advice. It was ludicrous.

"What's the problem, O'Hara? Have I made you forget your lines?" It occurred to her that he looked a lot like a grounded fish gasping for air . . . a grounded Irish fish. And the thought of a special Hibernian species of fish tickled her so, she began to laugh, quite out of control.

Something splashed onto her face and went dripping down her neck and shoulders. It was wine. She could smell it. Stunned and spluttering, she wiped at it with her hand. The stupid jerk had thrown a glass of wine at her!

"Of all the childish—" she began, but he interrupted, his voice cracking with fury.

"Laugh at me, will you! You're the one who's laughable. Acting the big star when you're really just a Spic bitch from the Bronx slums!"

For a minute she just stared at him. Then anger rose like bile from her stomach. "Spic, am I? Well, at least I really am who I am—and not a phony copy of someone's idea of an Irishman. You and your hint of a brogue! I happen to know you took your very first trip to Ireland when you ran away from me that spring!"

"That's a lie!"

She smiled calmly at him. "No, it's not. I know. You didn't think I'd just forget all about being stood up, did you? I made it a point to find out a few things about you. Such as the wife in Missouri you've never divorced."

"You rotten bitch! You vindictive little tramp!" He was purple with rage, shaking with temper.

"Oh. And I thought I was lovelier by far than any rose that bloomed in old Tralee," she said sardonically. She longed to leave, but she was afraid. To get to the door she would have to walk right by him, and he looked murderous.

"Never you mind who or what I am. I know damn well why your first gold record was 'Bill.' I know why you sang it with such feeling. You were crazy in love with me then. And, as a matter of fact, you were ready to jump right into bed with me tonight." His lip curled. "As a matter of fact, Miss Superstar, I was a little afraid you might want to go at it right on the floor there in Enders."

"You're so in love with yourself, you think every woman's ready for you all the time!"

His voice took on a caressing, singsong quality. "Oh, they are, girl, dear, they are. Shall I tell you about my latest? You were right, it's that Rubensesque child we saw on the path . . . She reminds me of you, big hips and big breasts and always hot to trot, that one . . . I remember, you know, I remember the homely, overweight girl, so grateful to get it regularly. It took you only six minutes to get here from your sorority house, and that's a record. Never had to take *your* clothes off, you were half undressed before I even got the door open . . ."

Lee stared at him, her body as cold as ice, unable to move or to take her eyes away from his soft, rubbery mouth. There was a buzzing sound in her head. Was this the reality? That her great love affair was only the tale of a homely, overweight girl who had been grateful to get sex regularly?

He was going on and on. Lee blinked back the tears of disappointment and forced herself to turn away. She was no longer listening to the stream of ugly words that poured from him. She wanted only to get away, far away, so that she could not hear the sound of his voice. Quickly, almost frantically, she pushed past him to the apartment door.

O'Hara was right behind her, still ranting. When she got to the door, he leaned on it with one hand, trapping her.

"Wait, wait. Don't go, Lee. You mustn't leave."

She swallowed. "Move!" she grated.

"Ah, Lee, you know I didn't mean any of that. You know me—the more I care, the crueler I become when I'm rejected. *You* remember. You don't want to go, not really. Ah, we were feeling so close, our feelings have been so strong."

Lee took a deep breath. When she spoke, her voice was husky. "If you don't move and let me out of here," she said, measuring her words out carefully, "I'll scream rape. At the top of my very well trained voice. I mean it!"

"Lee . . . darlin' gypsy . . . come back by the fire and let me kiss the frown from your lovely brow . . ."

"You make me sick. Now *move!*"

She could feel his ragged breath on the back of her neck. "I'll move, I'll move, whatever the Queen of Tarts wants! But you needn't go, thinking you were ever very much in bed. You were easy and you were available. And I was adding sums in my head the whole time. I never felt a thing, not a goddamn thing. You were my own personal little whore, that's what you were—and you're still playing the part to perfection! All I had to do tonight was say, 'Come here,' and you were there, hot as a pistol, all ready to take up right where we'd left off. That's what's bothering you, your own groveling sluttiness—"

Blindly, she turned and pushed at him as hard as she could. He stumbled backward, grabbing at a lamp for balance and sending it crashing to the floor.

"Go to hell!" she yelled, pulling frantically at the doorknob.

As she went running out, he shouted after her: "Slut! Slut of sluts!"

Lee ran down the street, not knowing or caring where it took her. She had successfully fought off tears while he could see them; now they flowed unchecked down her cheeks. After a few minutes, she slowed to a walk, mopping at the wetness with her sleeve. Her heart was thumping painfully. Oh, God, the horrible things he'd said!

It had begun like a dream coming true: the soft twilight campus, her arm linked with his, the familiar smell and feel of him, the caressing sound of his voice. What was I doing with him? she asked herself, agonized. What dream did I think I was going to fulfill? But she knew. She was going to rewrite her personal history. O'Hara had been the man she felt she would have died for, and it had ended badly, brutally. So she was going to make it all come out right this time.

Grimly, she laughed aloud. Oh, sure, she was going to put a happy ending on it. On what? On a cheap, sick affair between a naive college girl and a narcissistic, infantile egomaniac. And she had been taken in by his act, yes, she had. He was right, he was right, damn him, she *had* been ready to fall into bed with him. If he hadn't overplayed his hand so clumsily, she would be there now. She shuddered. The thought of him, cold and calculating, arousing her, fondling her, mouthing his poetry, pretending passion—all so that she would once more become besotted with him. "And I would have!" she moaned aloud. "God help me, I would have! I'd have taken him back to London with me!" She groaned.

Without thinking about it, she had made her way back to Enders. The building loomed out of the darkness, all the ground-floor windows blazing with warm, welcoming light.

Oh, God! all those people! Everyone had seen her leave with him, smiling and happy, and here she was, returning, half of her soaked with wine, her mascara probably running, her lipstick smeared by his kisses. "Ugh!" She rubbed at her mouth with the back of her hand; she wanted no part of him left on her, not even in memory.

She stood for several minutes, immobile, staring at the old dormitory. Should she sneak in and scramble up the stairs to the safety of her room? No, she decided, that was not Lee Rivers' way. She'd make a quick repair here, by the light of the street lamp, and face them all with a smile on her face.

But when she got inside, the living room and entrance hall were deserted. She was puzzled for an instant, and then she heard the buzz and clatter from the dining hall. A glance at her watch told her it was eight o'clock. She almost couldn't believe it; she felt as if she'd been trapped in that scene with O'Hara forever; she wouldn't have been surprised to find it was three in the morning. Fixing another smile on her lips, she marched down the hall to the dining room, throwing her shoulders back and lifting her chin.

Yet when she looked in, it was just too much. Her clothes were a mess, the lights were glaringly bright, there was so much noise, and the place was packed. At one of the round tables directly opposite the door, she saw Kit, flanked by Benno and Dan, Courtney and Jock, too, and others . . . too many others. A chair had been left empty —it must be for her—but the thought of going in there and being assaulted by the noise and the chatter, of having to sit and make bright conversation and *eat!* when all she wanted to do was to curl up into a very small ball and disappear . . . Quietly, she turned and left. It didn't matter. Nobody had seen her.

"Hey!" Kitty cried, half standing.
"What's the matter?" Dan asked. "What did you see?"

181

"Nothing. I'm sorry, I didn't mean to upset you. But that was Lee."

"Where?"

"Out in the hallway, by the door. Just for a moment. And then she left."

"She remembers the dining-hall food," Ben quipped.

Kitty smiled. "Maybe. But I think I'd better go see if everything's okay. I'll be back in a minute." Carefully, she met Dan's eyes. "Save my place," she said lightly.

"Oh, absolutely." He grinned and gave her a little wink.

Just a little wink and her heart turned over. Feeling a little flustered, she bumped her way through the massed tables. That bastard O'Hara! She *knew* he was bound to be bad news. Look how he had made Lee run off in '70 without even attending her own graduation. She could have told Lee, long before that awful night, that he would never be straight with her. Just like him to sneak off like that, leaving Lee deserted and wounded. He was incapable of realizing that other people had feelings—or that they even existed.

She ran up the staircase, her indignation mounting. He'd done something tonight, she knew it. He'd done something slimy. Lee had been so enthralled with him, so open and eager. What had he *done?* Oh, that creep!

Their door was locked and she banged on it, calling, "Lee! It's me! Open up!"

One look at her friend's pinched face and she knew she had guessed exactly right. "That bastard!" she cried, locking the door behind her. "What did he do this time?"

"Oh, Kitty, it was horrible!" Lee slumped as if all her bones had gone limp. "It was like something out of a cheap melodrama . . . with me in the starring part." She collapsed onto one of the beds and began to laugh hysterically. "Kitty, you should have seen him—all dimples and elfin smiles and a lot of Irish blarney all but set to music—" Abruptly, the laughter changed to wild sobbing, and she turned to bury her face in the pillow.

Kitty sat on the edge of the bed, next to the shaking figure, and patted her friend's back. "But you're here now. And it's still early, so not too much could have . . ."

A muffled sound—half laugh, half sob.

"If you mean, did we screw, the answer is no." Suddenly Lee sat up, her face streaked with tears, and pushed her hair back with short, nervous gestures. "Not that I wouldn't have, Kit. *Au contraire.*" Her mouth twisted wryly. "I was—as he so succinctly put it—hot to trot."

"Oh, Lee! Don't!"

"No, no, he was right. I was trying to live out a fantasy. I thought we might discover that we were still in love—can you beat it? In *love,* that's how I thought of it. When all it was—all it *ever* was—was the beast with two backs. Oh . . . dammit, dammit, dammit!"

"Lee, for Pete's sake, stop. Ten years ago you were the original Free Spirit. Don't I remember you giving the whole sorority lectures on the pleasures of sex without guilt? My God, we all believed you! How I envied you your honesty and your freedom! I could no more have done what I felt than I could have walked naked across campus. I was in constant battle with my own emotions, and there you were, shrewd and sassy, taking exactly what you wanted from life.

"Of course," she added dryly after a moment, "why you ever wanted O'Hara I could never understand."

Lee sighed. "He was a helluva lover. What else is important when you're young? At least, *then* I thought he was good in bed. After all those dopey college boys with their secret double standards, he was heaven on earth!"

"But you knew his reputation, Lee!"

"Oh, yeah, sure. Coed of the Year. But *I* was different, see? The exception that proves the rule, whatever *that* means. And, oh, I guess I ought to face it: He was so *un-Latin.* And I was still trying to get away from my background. As if you ever can," she added in a mumble. "My first real boyfriend was one of those bony, clean-cut, Anglo types. I guess I thought O'Hara was just an older version of Val Cooper. Valentine Cooper . . . God, does that bring back memories! He was so different from the men in the barrio. Barrio means . . . oh, neighborhood, I guess. But what it really means is ghetto. I was trapped . . ."

Leonor Rivera had been tall for her age—fourteen—and lushly curved. She hated her body because it seemed to embarrass her mama and poppi so much. She hated the lively, crowded neighborhood where the sounds of Hispanic music were heard twenty-four hours around the clock. She hated her life. It was so unfair. Poppi had been a lawyer in Cuba, where she and her brothers had been born; they had had plenty of money, a big house, dinner parties, maids, private schools. And just because of Castro, they were now in a stinking slum in the Bronx, all five of them squashed into four crummy rooms, four flights up. Poppi was having difficulty with English— Mama had given up trying—and the only job he could get—he, an educated man—was as elevator operator in a department store.

Leonor was expected to behave like any proper young Cuban lady. No dates without chaperones, no neighborhood dances, straight home from school every day, no hanging around in the street. She spent long, long hours in her tiny room, playing the guitar, practicing her singing, and watching herself in the cheap, cloudy mirror.

She liked boys and secretly smiled when they made kissing sounds at her and yelled, *"Mamacita!"* and *"Bella! Bella!"* But they were strictly forbidden, *prohibidos, peligrosos*. They were no-goods and nothings, and besides, they would get her into trouble. All she had to do was look around to see the truth of that: fifteen- and sixteen-year-old girls, already pregnant or with tiny babies, looking burned out before they'd even had a chance to try life.

Not for me! Leonor decided. None of it for her. She had to get out of this lousy neighborhood, that was the first thing. Had to escape before it was too late. Because Carlos Rodriguez had taken to walking beside her every afternoon when she came home from school, and Carlos was beautiful: dark-skinned and solidly muscular, already with a thin mustache outlining his upper lip, his glistening black hair waving down to his shoulders. When he was beside her, she could barely breathe. And when he put his hand under her arm, so that the back of it rested against the roundness of her breast, as he had done several times, she thought she would faint. Staring at her reflection in the mirror, she told herself sternly, "Stay away from Carlos. You'll end up *embarazada* like the others. Get out of here." She was in the ninth grade, and already two girls from her class had dropped out, their bellies swollen.

The answer was the High School of Music and Art. She auditioned without telling her family, and then battled with Poppi to let her go after she'd been accepted.

"You really want me to stay here, in the barrio, and end up with *un cualquiera?* You keep telling me I'm better than they are, you won't let me have anything to do with them, you keep me a prisoner here in this apartment. And now you won't let me go to a decent high school where I can get some training and learn how to do something and maybe get to college? Poppi, you can't have it both ways!"

He smiled his weary smile, finally, and said, "I will tell your mama."

It was at Music and Art that she met Valentine Cooper. He was a tall, gangly kid with floppy blond hair always falling into his eyes and a thousand freckles scattered over his pleasant, open face. She noticed him at first because you rarely saw Val Cooper without his cello tucked under his arm, like a gigantic doll in a canvas bunting. Of course, he wasn't the only cellist in the school, but he was by far the tallest and skinniest. And, in fact, he was the only boy Leonor knew who was taller than she. She was already five feet eight and an embarrassment in her neighborhood of short, compact Hispanics. She had taken to slumping over, hunching her shoulders and bending her head, to look shorter.

They were assigned seats next to each other in solfeggio class, she and Val Cooper. He gave her a big friendly grin the first day and said hi; she smiled back but didn't know what to say to him.

And then he whispered, "You really ought to stand up straight, a nice-looking girl like you. What do you want to walk around all bent over for?"

At first taken aback, Lee retorted: "Well, I don't have a cello to lean on." She was amazed at how hard he laughed—she didn't think it was *that* funny—but it made them friends right from the start, even before they knew each other's names.

She'd never known anyone quite like Val. In the first place, he wasn't Spanish or Cuban or Puerto Rican or Colombian or anything she was familiar with. "I'm a hybrid," he said. "Jewish, Polish, and Scots!" And he was so relaxed with her. None of the macho bit she was so accustomed to; just nice and funny and easy to talk to. One day she remarked on this to him and he laughed. "I'm not much on the me-Tarzan-you-Jane routine," he said, and then gave a diabolical laugh, adding, "My methods are much more subtle." She was ashamed because she didn't know what the word "subtle" meant. But the nice thing about Val was that you could tell him you didn't understand what he said, and he'd explain it without coming on all superior.

"Subtle," he said, taking hold of a lock of her hair and curling it around his finger, "means sly and clever and quiet. It means that I'm hot for your body but I'm not going to come right out and say so. I'm gonna wait until you're ripe."

Leonor stared at him, not knowing if she had heard right. And when she realized that yes, she *had* heard right, she blushed scarlet and then, in spite of herself, she had to laugh.

Their relationship grew and flourished on laughter, on jokes and talk, and—after a while—on hugs and kisses in whatever doorway they could find on the way to the subway. She couldn't take him to the barrio—she'd die first—and she couldn't go with him to West 79th Street. "You don't understand, Val," she said frantically. "I'm not allowed to go anywhere. And if Poppi knew about us, he'd kill me. I'm not supposed to be alone with a boy."

"You coulda fooled me," he teased, but he didn't press her. He never did. He was just the most wonderful, cool person she had ever known. What Valentine Cooper had, she knew, was that elusive something called Class.

She couldn't understand what he saw in her, an overweight Cuban kid with a big nose and frizzy hair. "I like big women," he laughed. "You're so soft and warm and . . . yummy." He nuzzled her neck, pushing the thick hair back. "And you smell good." He kissed the tip of her nose. "And I don't have to stoop over to kiss you." Then he put his lips to hers and gave her a long, lingering kiss that made her weak in the knees. He was a bit breathless, too, and he grinned, saying: "Sex rears its tousled, curly head. You sure you don't want to come home with me? We'll be all alone until seven-thirty."

It was May and deliciously warm. They had been creeping into doorways to snuggle for months and months. She loved him dearly, his snub nose and his quick laugh and the gentle strength of his bony body. She thought of the fate that awaited her back in the neighborhood: marriage, one day, to a boy like Carlos, who wanted a *querida* who would walk five steps behind him and follow his every order unquestioningly and make babies, one after the other. No jokes; no good, serious talk; no music; no love; no life.

"Yes," she said. "Yes, Valentine, oh, yes."

"We were lovers," Lee said, sighing again, "until he graduated at the end of my second year. It was so good with him, so clean and honest and . . . and fun. He taught me that sex isn't a dirty, shameful thing that you do in the dark and then snigger about later. From him I learned that girls are allowed to have desires, just like boys, and it's okay. I'd never met anyone outside the nabe before, so I didn't know he was unusual. I thought all gringo boys were like him. You know, he was the one who started calling me Lee. It was his name for me, and I've been using it ever since." She paused, smiling a little.

"Don't stop now," Kitty urged. "What happened to him? Where is he now?"

"The Pittsburgh Symphony. Oh, I haven't been keeping track of him. He went off to the Eastman School of Music, far away in Rochester, and I got some letters from him and even spoke to him on the telephone during that Thanksgiving vacation. He told me, 'I miss you.' Oh, how I clung to those words, saying them over and over like a rosary when I was trying to fall asleep at night.

"And then, just before Christmas, I got a letter from him and it said he hated to tell me and he really cared for me a lot, but there was this violinist at college named Joan and . . . Well, he married her, so I guess it was the real thing. A few years ago I saw in the *Times* that they were giving a joint recital at Town Hall. Then they came to London to perform and I went to see them. He was the same, big and skinny, with that hair flopping into his eyes and that sense of humor . . .

"And I honestly thought O'Hara was more of the same. Funny, isn't it, when they're so opposite. But in the meantime, I'd had a taste of the Great American Double Standard. You know: Boys can like it; girls can't. It made me so mad to find that what was real and honest in me would be considered dirty or immoral or something to take advantage of or an easy lay or sleeping around. Ugh! It took me a while, but I learned that not all Anglos were like Valentine. And it just made me act more free and more fearless. They weren't going to change *me*—not after I'd finally learned! And you see what I really learned—zilch. Well, never mind—"

Lee got up and rapidly stripped off her clothes, leaving them in a silken puddle on the floor. Going to the closet, she reached in and brought out, triumphantly, a shabby chenille robe, once bright pink but now faded to a streaked pinkish white.

Kit grinned. "Your old robe! I can't believe you still have it!"

"Not have it? Don't be ridiculous! This is my security blanket! Right now," she added softly, "I *need* it."

"Oh, Lee! What in the world did he *do* tonight?"

Lee made a long business of wrapping the robe just right and tying the worn belt in a perfect square knot. Carefully looking anywhere but at her friend, she said, "Told me the truth."

"I doubt the man would know the truth if it came up to him and punched him in the jaw."

"I know the truth when it comes up to *me* and punches me in the jaw. And tonight it did. Everything I thought about him was a mirage. I thought he was another Val, open and honest. And all the time he was really a dirty old man, secretly sniggering and snickering about all the filthy things he was doing and getting away with . . . Do you know what I mean? I was sure that he loved making love to me. That he liked me for what I was, that I was free—with him, at least—to act exactly as I felt . . . Oh, hell, I don't know any more *what* I believed he thought."

"So what 'Great Truth' came bubbling up out of his grungy mind tonight?"

Lee made a face and strode nervously to the window, where she stared out at the street below. A group of students came around the corner as she watched, five or six of them on skateboards, shrieking and giggling and elbowing one another. They rode out of the thick shadows into the circle of light shed by the street lamp and quickly disappeared into the night, their voices trailing behind them.

"I wish I were twenty again, down there with the kids, having fun and not knowing what is hidden in people's heads. No, I don't." She turned abruptly. "O'Hara called me a slut, a whore."

"Oh, how horrible! He'll say anything. Don't tell me you're taking it seriously?"

"It's the truth."

"Lee! For God's sake! That's nonsense!" Rapidly, Kitty walked to her friend and put a hand on her arm. "His calling you stupid names *can't* have hurt you!"

Stubbornly: "It's the truth. That's what hurts. Look at me. Thirty-two years old and on my third lover this year. You wanna hear about him? He's nineteen and adorable, an Oxford student, a young lord. He wants to *marry* me, Kit! He wants to take me home to Mothah and Fathah. I've had it all figured out, how I'll break off with him when I get back after the reunion . . . Of course, I had a notion in my head that I might have O'Hara . . ." She wiped away the last sentence with a swipe of her hand in the air.

"And after Cheltonham—that's his name, Andrew Cheltonham—there'll be another," she said intensely. "Oh, I don't go running around London, eyeing the busboys or picking up strangers in a pub, nothing so crass. But eventually some other man will catch my eye and I'll catch his and . . . And I won't have to think I'm madly in love, because sex is *natural*."

Then she reached out and took Kitty's hand, squeezing it hard. "And so what do you call that, Kit? A woman who sleeps around? A woman who doesn't love anyone? What do you call that? What does anybody call it! A slut! A whore!" Her face was burning with agitation and she pulled her hand away, striding over to the dresser and lighting a cigarette. "I shouldn't have this," she remarked in a dead tone; "it's bad for the voice. Oh, hell! I've been going along, thinking I knew all the answers. I was so sure of myself. And that lousy, phony Irishman, who doesn't dare take on a real woman so he sticks to his little coeds, puts it to me and it's the goddamn truth! Now I see myself clearly, Kit, and it's ugly! Here I am, famous and rich—or so they keep telling me—and think, Kitty, I have *nothing!* I loved Val and he married someone else. I loved O'Hara and he thinks of me as something cheap and easy. When will I ever love a man who will love me back? Of course I'm a whore!" She stopped abruptly and took a deep drag on the cigarette, then stubbed it out and flung herself down on her bed.

Kit again sat next to her, absently rubbing her back. "I'm a worse whore than you, Lee," she said in a quiet voice.

Lee twisted her head around. "What are you talking about?"

"I sold out, that's what I'm talking about. I married for all the wrong reasons: because it would look good and because my mother would like it and because it would demand very little of me. I sold myself because I was a coward."

"Aren't you being a little hard on yourself, Kit? That sounds like the same reasons everyone used to get married for. Although it *did* surprise me when I got your cable. I thought you were getting all settled in at graduate school, preparing to conquer the world. And then, of course . . . Whit. I was . . . well, *surprised* says it."

Kit laughed ruefully. "So was I."

Lee gave her a tired, lopsided grin. "And so was Whit, I'll bet."

Kitty got up and moved restlessly about the small room. "Just look at this!" She made a sweeping gesture, taking in the bare walls, the uncurtained windows, the empty dresser tops. "We used to put pieces of ourselves everywhere, remember? Teddy bears and photos and posters and rugs. There's nothing personal in here, nothing at all. I can't believe that after we leave, two real-live freshman girls will come back in here, girls who laugh and talk and worry about dieting and whether a particular boy will call again. It's more like a motel room than a room in a college dorm. I wonder if they're good friends . . ." She drifted off, biting her lower lip.

"No," she continued after a moment. "I doubt that Whit was surprised, not really. Remember, I was always part of his life plan. If he thought anything, he probably figured that a piece of his life plan wouldn't *dare* end up doing something else. As it turns out," she added wryly, "he was one hundred percent right, wasn't he?"

"Bigger than both of you?" Lee inquired. "I can't buy that."

Kitty grimaced. "Fate, you mean? Kismet? No, nothing like that. Expediency: That's more like it. He was there, I needed him, I knew he'd have me—all I had to do was silently agree to behave and look beautiful and not bother him with anything like my inner feelings.

"And do you know what kept me going for the first couple of years? My mother's pleasure. After all those years of hating her ambitions for me, after all that vowing and swearing that I'd escape from all that . . . And, in the end, when I called her to tell her we were married and she cried and said, 'Oh, Kitty, darlin', it's just what I always hoped for you,' I was positively aglow with pride of achievement. I was being a good girl for my mama.

"Every time she came to visit and her eyes lit up because there I was, living in a mansion with servants and acres of grounds and a pretty little baby—I lit up, too. Any time Mama was around, puffed with pride, I felt certain that I was doing the right thing. I was very satisfied to be living out her dream. Maybe because it kept me from looking at my *own* dream, from realizing how far I'd gone down the wrong road . . ."

She had drifted over to the window, staring out without really seeing anything. As she watched, people began streaming out the front door, laughing and calling to one another. Their voices were shrill with holiday excitement and liquor. There were Buffy and Sparky, changed into normal clothes at last, and poor old Courtney, her hair carefully groomed and stiff with spray, one arm ever so casually around her husband's back—supporting him, Kit knew at once. Jock Standish was drunk, not yet at the falling-over stage, but close. Had she ever seen him quite sober? she wondered; and thought, Probably not. She saw Jay Shulman walking with Benno, and for a moment found herself looking for Dan's copper head. But, of course, Dan wouldn't be down there. Dan would be in his room, waiting for her. The thought made her heart leap.

"I've been living a lie for ten years, Lee!" she burst out. "I've been living the life of a whore—oh, a highly paid courtesan might be a better description, but what it

all amounts to in the end is— Talk about dishonest!
I've ruined it for four people. Oh, God, Lee, all I had to
do was *see* Dan tonight and I knew it had all been wrong,
all of it, all ten years. I love him! I don't suppose I've
ever stopped loving him. And yet, even now, we're always
at each other. Pushing and pulling. Is *that* love? I'm sure
I love him. But is it supposed to make you feel as if
you're being torn to bits, as if you're being overwhelmed
and conquered? At least with Whit, it's always been
peaceful."

She turned from the window, her eyes stinging with
tears. "Lee, listen. You've got to stop calling yourself
names. They don't apply. At least you've always done
what you wanted! Not like me, settling for safety. Look
at me. Do you really think I'm better than you? Do
you—"

She broke off. There was no doubt about it: Lee was
snoring, gently and in a thoroughly ladylike manner, but
snoring nevertheless. She had fallen fast asleep.

Kitty laughed. "Some friend *you* are. Allowing jet lag
and a rotten bastard to take precedence over my confes-
sions. Ah, it's just as well. I was about to tell you . . .
everything. I must not tell anyone, not even you, dear
Lee."

She tiptoed around the room, undressing, hanging her
clothes carefully in the closet, her lips twisting in a rueful
smile because it was Mama who had taught her, so scru-
pulously, that you took care of your good clothes and
that's how they stayed nice. My clothes have stayed nice,
always, she thought. But have I?

Wrapped in a robe, she wandered over to the dresser
and eyed herself in the mirror. "Am I a nice person,
Trudy?" she asked softly. "Do I deserve to get back the
man I love, after what I did to him? Do I tell him what
I *really* did to him?" The green eyes stared back at her,
deep and clear, telling her nothing. But the small neat head
with its smooth flaxen hair moved slowly from side to
side. "No," she murmured. "No, I don't tell him. Unless,
my dear Trudy, you're shaking your head at my continued
cowardice. Well, to hell with you, Trudy. I want advice,
not criticism." With deft fingers, she plucked out the pins
that held the coil of hair at the nape of her neck, loosening the long, thick fall with her hands, watching with ap-

proval as it slid smoothly over her shoulders, framing her face with languid waves. "Much better," she commented, and went back to the closet, reaching in for the new ecru silk gown that clung to her breasts and hips. For the first time in years, she wanted to look beautiful. Beautiful for love, beautiful for Dan. Suddenly eager, she dropped her lingerie, leaving it on the floor, and slid the gown over her head. Deliciously light and smooth, it slithered over her bare skin. She didn't need the mirror to know that it looked lovely. Hastily, she slipped her arms into the robe and began to gather a few things together.

A soft, sibilant sound made her turn. A folded piece of paper, slid under the door. *Dan* was her first thought. Dan saying not to come. Oh, no! Not after waiting all this time, not after— She opened the folded note, her heart hammering. And caught her breath.

The message was printed in neat, childlike block lettering. Stunned as she was, she noticed that straight, light lines had been ruled across the paper to guide the printing.

I SEE EVERYTHING. YOUR HANDS ALL OVER EACH OTHER. WHORE OF BABYLON, BEWARE. YOU WILL NOT HAVE DAN COPELAND, HE BELONGS TO ME. SOON, SOON. STAY AWAY FROM HIM OR YOU WILL GO, TOO.

CHAPTER TEN

Reunion, Kit and Dan

KIT STARED at the note until the letters blurred. The skin on her arms was prickling, and when she glanced down, she saw that she was covered with goose flesh. She crumpled the paper in a quick movement of disgust, prepared to throw it away; but then she changed her mind and smoothed it out, folding it carefully.

Dan, she thought. I must show this to Dan. She ran to the closet and pulled out her raincoat, belting it quickly around her waist. A pair of fluffy scuffs completed the rather odd ensemble, but she was too flustered to look for anything more suitable. If anyone saw her . . . too bad.

The corridor was deserted. She hurried, her heels clacking loudly in the quiet. Most of the doors were closed, no lights showing beneath. As she passed one room, the door opened, revealing six or seven of her classmates in their nightgowns and robes, sitting cross-legged on the floor, all talking, it seemed, at once. All the lights were on, all the pillows were on the floor, and the air was blue with the haze of cigarette smoke. A small transistor radio was playing "Saturday Night Fever," and one woman leaped up to do an impromptu dance. Kit hurried by. But the briefly glimpsed scene remained in her mind's eye: so cozy and comfortable and *normal*. A bunch of women at reunion, doing what women at reunion always did: recapturing the special joys of dormitory life.

All the men were being quartered in the East Wing. At the corner, she glanced down the east corridor, but there was no one in sight. So she turned the corner, half running, hoping that nobody would pop out of a room and kid her about being in the men's wing. She felt furtive and silly and also a bit frightened—the horrid little note had unnerved her—and kept her head down, wanting to laugh at herself. After all, she was actually running down the hall of the men's wing to keep a tryst with her lover. Lover . . . In her mind she savored the word, turning it over and tasting it. Lover. My lover, Dan Copeland. So many long years, fighting the memories. So many long, wasted, empty years—

She suddenly plowed right into another body and let out a little squeal of alarm. Even before she looked up, she heard the familiar rumble of quiet laughter.

"Oh, Dan! I've got to talk to you. Quickly!"

"You throw yourself into my arms and then you want to *talk?*"

"No, listen. Something—something happened. Something grubby and nasty. Can't we go to your room?"

He was smiling. "That's the whole idea, my darling. As a matter of fact, I was on my way to get you." He paused delicately, leading her down the hall with one strong arm across her back. "You got one, too."

Kitty gasped. "You know, then!"

He opened a door and gestured her in, then reached inside to grab a towel from the bureau top, hanging it on the outside doorknob before closing the door and locking them in.

"What was that all about?" Kitty demanded.

"An old signal, Kit, dear. It'll tell Ben that I've got a girl in my room." He laughed and strode toward her, encircling her with his arms. "At last, at last, I've got the girl in my room," he murmured, bending his lips to hers. It was a long, lingering, gentle kiss, and it sent little shivers up her spine.

But as soon as he lifted his mouth, she insisted: "Dan! We *must* talk about these notes."

He kissed her cheekbone. "No, we mustn't. It's stupid hate mail. I'm used to it. Forget it. What I want to do now . . ." He wound his fingers in the spill of her hair. "I want to wrap myself up in your hair." He kissed her nose and then her chin. "I want to be wrapped so tightly that I can't escape."

"Dan! I'm really frightened."

"It's nothing," he muttered, placing his lips at the spot on her throat where the pulse quivered.

"I'm not used to it, Dan. I'm *scared*. Please!"

He pressed his lips into her throat briefly and then, with a sigh, straightened up. She looked at him anxiously, but he was smiling. "Okay, let's discuss it. But I promise you, it's meaningless."

"No, Dan. I'm convinced it's not. This note . . . it mentions you. It says you're being watched and that he's going to get you. Read it." She handed him the piece of paper and scanned his face as he read its message.

"Pretty good style," he remarked. "No, no, don't give me that look. I've had tons of hate mail and this is pretty mild. Very vague, actually. Some of them are mighty specific."

"But, Dan!" Kit was wringing her hands in consternation. "Somebody at this reunion is watching us. Doesn't that make your flesh creep?"

195

"Well, I don't like it. But I'm sure it's just a sick joke. It's probably someone who was jealous back in the sixties, someone who never quite made it. Remember, you were the campus beauty and I . . . I was Mr. Mouth. And this is a very small campus." He crumpled the note and tossed it expertly into the wastebasket.

"But, Dan, the note—it was so *ugly!* You can't toss away the ugliness."

"Ugly, yes. But not dangerous. I learned about danger . . . I learned to watch out."

"Vietnam?" Kitty said softly.

"Yeah. Funny, when that truck backfired, there was something about the noise. Even though I knew I was at Hampton, on a quiet college campus, looking out at a couple of girls playing tennis, talking to my old roommate . . . even so, when I heard that sound, I *knew,* I was sure I was being shot at. It was immediate and instinctive. I hurled myself to the ground without thinking." He laughed shortly. "Wonderful thing, instinct."

"It's not a joking matter, Dan. I thought my heart would stop beating when I saw you lying there so white and still."

"My precious girl." He gave her a melting look that sent her heart flying and held out his arms.

Instead of running to him, Kitty backed away a few steps. "Wait," she said softly, smiling at him, and slowly unbuttoned and unbelted the raincoat, her eyes fixed on his. As the coat dropped to the floor, revealing her body outlined by the clinging, shimmering silk, he drew in a sharp breath and took a step toward her.

"Dan," she remonstrated in a faint voice, "let me." Still holding his eyes with her own, she went to him and, with trembling fingers, unbuttoned his shirt and pulled it from him. He stood very still, quivering slightly with the effort to maintain self-control, his eyes fired with passion. When Kitty ran her hands down his neck and over the tight pectoral muscles, he licked his dry lips but still did not move. But when the small, tapered hands descended to his belly and began slowly to massage the firm flesh while she tipped her head back to watch his reactions as they chased over his face, he lost all resolve.

Growling in his throat, he seized her, stripping the gown from her shoulders, pushing it impatiently to the floor. With burning lips, he began to taste of her body. Kitty, eyes gleaming with a feral light, offered herself with eager joy. As he knelt before her, his lips pressed to the gentle curve where waist melted into hip, she ran her fingers through his thick hair, forcing him to look up at her.

"Take me now, Dan. Now!" Her voice was fierce with desire, and with another sharp intake of breath, he came swiftly to his feet, lifting her easily in his arms. The long pale hair fell like a flow of satin over his shoulder and down his bare back.

"Kit . . ."

"My dearest . . . please . . . I need you . . . Take me, take me—"

Their coming together was hungry, wild, ecstatic, almost brutal. Kitty lost all sense of time and place; there was nothing in the world except his body, caressing her, surrounding her, enfolding her, pounding at her, arousing her, penetrating her, and finally, after a long, timeless time, bringing her a sense of peace and completion she had never known before. They lay on the narrow bed, still entwined and breathing hard, her head nestled into the curve of his shoulder, his lips resting on her forehead.

After several minutes, he whispered, "What are you thinking?"

She lifted her lips to his, her hand gently rubbing his lean hip. Against his mouth she murmured, "More," and his arms tightened around her.

"Yes," he answered, and once again she was lost in a world of swirling sensations.

When she was next able to focus her thoughts at all, it was to hear—muted, from the distance—the chapel carillon ringing out its good-night medley of lullabies. Kitty kept her eyes closed, snuggling into Dan's warm body, smiling at the music which she had once heard every single night at eleven-thirty. When the bells began to chime their slightly discordant rendition of "Rock-A-Bye, Baby," she and Dan both laughed with delight.

Rolling a little away from him, but with her hand firmly clasped in his, Kitty stretched languorously. "Oh, God," she said, "I feel marvelous."

Dan propped himself up on one elbow to peer into her face. "Ten years ago I waited to hear you say that."

"What do you mean? I was never . . . *cold* with you."

"Oh, Kitty, how we forget!" But he smiled at her tenderly. "Don't you remember how it always ended with you in retreat, saying, 'Don't' or 'Stop'? This is the first time I've felt you really wanted me as much as I wanted you. You were all there tonight, Kit, all of you—body, soul, and spirit." He leaned over to nuzzle her cheek. "It was marvelous for me, too. It was perfection. And to think that tonight is just the beginning of a lifetime— *You're doing it again!*"

"Doing what?"

"Withdrawing. Don't you think I can *feel* it?"

Kitty let out her breath in a sigh. "Well, *you're* doing it again. You're laying claim on me. I can't be pushed into a corner, Dan, or I begin to panic."

He cupped her chin in his big hand. "Kitty, darling girl. I love you. Of course I'm laying claim on you. You're mine. And I . . . am yours. I mean, it does work both ways. I don't know why you should feel so threatened. After the way we made love tonight, it's obvious that we belong to each other. I don't understand."

Kitty was silent for a few moments, staring at his face, partly highlighted by the moonlight streaming in the window. She could not read any expression in his eyes, dark and fathomless, lost in deep shadow. A wave of longing, piercing and sweet, shot through her. How she loved him: the craggy face; the tight, hard body; the impatient intelligence; the direct sensuality—even his overwhelming wish to remake the world. He was right: She did belong to him. He need make no claim. She belonged to him. There was no one else for her.

"If only I could explain it," she began. "I was made into a Professional Beautiful Child, Dan. I spent my whole life before Hampton being posed and dressed up and fussed over. I hated it. I hated being pretty and I hated the way so many men responded to it. Like starving animals. There was always a little pinch here or a little pat there. Or an arm stayed around me a bit longer than absolutely necessary. Or a nice uncle would always insist I sit on his lap. And I *knew*, even as a very little girl, that there was something not nice about what they were doing.

"I guess what bothered me the most was that my

mother was usually right there. She could see everything that went on, and she never, ever said a word. So I began to wonder whether *I* was the one who was not quite nice, whether all of this was somehow *my* fault."

"Oh, my poor darling."

"It's all so long ago, I know, and it seems silly to even think about it any more. But it went on constantly, Dan —you can't imagine how many contests and pageants and parades I was in. And when you're a kid, it never occurs to you to complain.

"But the worst thing of all was Mr. McIntosh. My eighth-grade science teacher. Oh, I thought he was wonderful. He was tall and skinny and had perfectly round glasses and a mop of brown hair that kept falling into his face, and he was *funny.* He kept us laughing all the time, and we learned.

"He was such a good teacher; didn't act as if you were demented or retarded if you didn't understand a point. He'd just patiently go over it with you, alone, until you understood it.

"I was having some trouble in class—couldn't get something straight. And so for a week I stayed after school for an hour and Mr. McIntosh tutored me. Oh, it was lovely. It meant I was using my brain and that I was safe there in the science room with nice Mr. Mack. Nice Mr. Mack!" Her voice changed subtly, and with a sudden movement, she sat up straight in bed, pulling her knees up and wrapping her arms around them. Dan said nothing; he watched her and waited.

"Oh, it wasn't anything much. He didn't rape me. But he might as well have. We were going down the stairwell one afternoon—it was a Thursday, I remember that— chatting away. And on the landing, he suddenly grabbed me and forced me into the corner and kissed me. He kissed me the way a man kisses a woman, his mouth open, using his tongue. I was only thirteen, and it was a horrible shock.

"I didn't know what to do, how to react. I wanted to get away, but I was frozen. It was so frightening. He was panting and squirming around and grabbing me all over. He was like a different person. When he finally pulled back, his face was distorted and flushed and his eyes looked crazy. I was pleading with him to let me go, but he didn't hear me, he didn't seem to really see me, even. He talked on and on, saying things like, 'Kathy, Kathy, you're so beautiful, I can't help myself. I'm sorry, I'm sorry, but when you look at me that way, I just can't resist. No man could. Please don't fight me, Kathy, I can't help it. I'm sorry, but you're so beautiful . . .' and stuff like that.

"I pushed at him and yelled, 'I don't look at you in any way—I don't! Stop it! I don't like this! I'll never look at you again!'

"He let me go, mumbling at me, something about being sorry, I don't know. I didn't wait to hear any more; I got out of there as fast as I could, down the stairs and out into the fresh air. My heart was racing, and every spot on my body where he had handled me felt as if it had been burned. I'd never seen anything like that before; it was as if a dirty, secret place in the adult world had yawned open in front of me. So *that's* what all those men were about with their pats and pinches! That's what I was thinking as I ran home—that, and the certain new knowledge that it had all been my fault. He said he grabbed me because I had looked at him, because I was beautiful. There was something about me, then, that I had to watch very carefully to make sure this didn't happen ever again."

Kitty laughed a little. "That's all it was. Nothing, really. When I got home I scrubbed my mouth and took a bath right away. And I stared at myself in the mirror, the way girls are supposed to do when they lose their virginity, trying to see in my eyes what it was that was so powerful that it could change even nice Mr. Mack into a . . . beast."

In the darkness, Dan reached out for her hand. "I could tell you that, my love. Those eyes get me every time. They cast a spell."

"You never take me seriously."

"Oh, but I do. I remember the first time I looked into your eyes. They're so deep, so clear, so cool on the surface. But in their depths, for anyone who searches, is a smoldering sensuality, under control but only waiting for the right touch to flare into life."

Kit smiled. "All that in one pair of eyes?"

"All that," he agreed, leaning over to kiss her lightly on

the temple, "and a great deal more. Intelligence, compassion, tenderness, humor . . . and fear."

For a moment they were both silent. "The thing was," Kit said finally, "that for days after the incident on the stairs, I found myself recalling it. Thinking about it with a queer little thrill of pleasure." She shuddered. "Even now, remembering it brings back that same perverse excitement. You see, I liked it, even as I hated it. And that only made it worse! It meant that I not only had to control whatever signal I was sending out, I also had to suppress my own responses. In the end, I guess, it was easier just to hide from my own desires.

"Stupid, isn't it?" she added in a different tone of voice. "I'm thirty-two and a mother . . . and still harking back to one little five-minute incident that happened to me when I was thirteen. You'd think I would forget it, wouldn't you?"

"Honestly? No. Obviously it was traumatic. Look, I *enlisted* in the Army. I was a gung-ho kid of eighteen who wanted to make the world safe for democracy—"

"Dan! You?"

"That's right. 'A real live nephew of my Uncle Sam,' as the song says. My father was a World War Two vet and proud of it—proud of all the Nazis he'd killed and damn proud of me for signing up instead of waiting like a coward to be called.

"And there I was, true-blue and desperate to blow away my share of the VC—gooks, they called them, as if they weren't really human. And I bought the whole package."

"I don't believe it!"

He heaved a sigh. "I don't either, now. But I remember. That was me, all right. I was so sure we belonged there, that we were doing the right thing, that we would surely win in the end because we were the Good Guys. It was so simple for me. There was us and there was The Enemy. Good and Evil.

"And then one bright October day I was heading a patrol: a cleanup operation. We had chased the VC from a little village in the jungle, and now we were going in to burn it so they couldn't use it again. It was not the most pleasant assignment—you had to look out for booby traps—but I knew I was good at it, so I didn't mind.

"We walked in, fanning out, rifles at the ready, trying to look everywhere at once. It was so quiet there, I remember, not even the sound of a bird. Almost too quiet. I got a tense feeling in my spine, warning me.

"I was just approaching an empty hut and was ducking to go in when a bullet went whizzing by. I hit the ground and the sniper got off two or three more shots. I could tell he was shooting from high up, probably hiding in a tree, and after a minute, by God, I spotted him. Something metal catching the sun and glinting. And I remember how I chortled to myself, thinking what a dumb ass, that he was a goner and it was his own stupidity.

"In a way, Kit, it was like playing a game, like grown-ups doing cowboys and Indians. That's how unreal it was to me.

"I took aim with my carbine, lying there on my stomach on the dirt, and got that metallic gleam right into the middle of my sights. And just as another bullet went thunking into the ground right near me, I squeezed off a shot and he came tumbling down, crashing through the branches.

"That brought the others over. We all crept up slowly, because he might still be alive, waiting to shoot. I crawled a ways and then walked in a crouch. The body sprawled there never moved. Even so, when I reached it, my rifle was aimed at him, because you never knew.

"But when I looked down at my would-be killer, my enemy, the gook, the Bad Guy, the dirty Commie, I suddenly saw a skinny, undernourished ten-year-old kid. I don't know . . . it was as if everything I believed in had been torn away all at once. I *saw* that kid, I really saw him. He had a scrape on one knee, the kind of scrapes that little boys always get. My mother used to say that my knees were permanently in Band-Aids—from bike riding or playing baseball. And this little boy was the fierce enemy I had so joyfully shot, so happily killed.

"I was sick to my stomach quite suddenly, right there. I thought I would never stop vomiting.

"And that was it. I was never the same again. I still dream about it—see that child clutching his rifle tightly in his hand, dead."

"Oh, Dan. How awful for you." Kitty kissed him softly.

"Not awful. The most important thing that ever happened. After all, it made me the Dan Copeland you met at Hampton."

"There's an awful lot we don't know about each other," Kit said thoughtfully.

He grabbed her fiercely. "I don't have to know everything about you to know that I love you. I *know* that I love you."

"Well, I love *you* even more than before," Kitty said, "knowing that you've had doubts, that you haven't gone through your whole life absolutely sure about *everything*."

"Tell me again," Dan demanded. "Tell me again that you love me even more than before. That's one thing I've *never* been absolutely sure about."

In answer, Kitty put one hand on either side of his face and tenderly brought his mouth down to hers. In that kiss were all the lost years of longing, and when she moved away, he let out his breath in a ragged tremor.

Softly she asked: "Now are you sure?"

He gazed deeply into her eyes, at first with solemn adoration. And then she perceived, deep in the dark depths of his, a little spark of humor.

"Not quite. I think you'd better do it again."

"Oh, Dan!" But she complied with pleasure.

This kiss left them breathless, and when Dan slid them both down on the bed so that they were lying thigh to thigh, she put her arms around him eagerly, tipping her head expectantly for his kiss.

But he did not bend to her. He stared at her, his grip tightening. And then he said abruptly: "You're going to leave him." It was a statement, not a question, and it took her by surprise. Nothing could have been farther from her mind then her husband. She had been floating in a world of *now*, a simple crystalline world with no history and no future.

"What are you talking about?"

"You *can't* stay with him, not now," Dan insisted. "It would be completely dishonest."

Kitty's laughter revealed an edge of hysteria. "Dishonest!" she gasped. "Dishonest! That's a laugh! I haven't been honest for a single moment with Whit, not in all these years!"

"Then come home with me! There's no reason on earth why you can't!"

Kitty pushed herself up again. "What are you saying! Of course there's a reason I can't, the best reason in the world. I have a child! And I'll never, never leave her."

"I'm not asking you to leave her! Of course you'll bring her—we'll be a family! She's yours, isn't she? I know I'll love her!"

Kit smiled. "You really would love her, Dan, she's such a nifty kid, she really is. So bright, so full of the devil. The two of you would probably get along famously. She's an awful lot like you." She stopped talking suddenly, putting her hands to her face. For she had finally heard herself say aloud the thoughts she had forbidden herself to think.

"But that doesn't matter," she went on in a rush. "I can't pack my toothbrush and my daughter and leave just like that. Dan, I've had a marriage for ten years, and it hasn't been entirely bad. I *owe* him . . . I owe him more than I can tell you. He was there when I needed him, he took me without question, and—I can't explain it all to you. It's so complicated. It's—I just can't leave him all of a sudden. I need some time."

Dan grabbed her harshly by the shoulders, digging his hands into the soft flesh. "Why did you do it, Kit?" he gritted. "Why did you marry him? When we made love in Florence, it was so clear that we were meant for each other! How could you have done it? Run from me to— *him! We* should have had these past ten years! You and me, together!"

"I've told you! He was secure, he was safe, he was all the things I needed then. You were a very terrifying young man, Dan Copeland, ready to take me over and eat me alive! I needed space to breathe in—"

"We're here together now. For the love of God, Kit, you *can't* run away from me again!"

She clenched her teeth and willed the tears not to spill from her eyes. "You're doing it again. You're pushing me against the wall."

She felt his body begin to unknot as he dropped his hands. "God, I'm sorry, I'm really sorry. I should play it cool, I know you well enough for that. It's the damn waste of it all: these past ten years, gone and irretrievable."

"Not irretrievable, my dearest," Kit said, melting. "Not quite." She slid down beside him, and curving her body to meet his, gently, tenderly, and sweetly began to make love to him again.

CHAPTER ELEVEN

Washington, D.C.

IT WAS ONE-THIRTY in the morning when the polished black Lincoln Mark IV limousine pulled up silently in front of the hotel's elegant canopied entrance. It had hardly come to a complete halt when Whitney Harris stepped smartly out of the back seat and gave the chauffeur a brusque salute that unmistakably said: "Go."

The automobile pulled away at once, but Whit Harris lingered for a moment, savoring the soft, almost sultry warmth of the air. As often as he came here, he was always surprised to be reminded that Washington, D.C., in spite of its bustle and busyness, was really a Southern town.

Hefting the heavy soft leather briefcase, Whit turned and set off briskly across the deserted and dimly lit lobby. The noon meeting with his own committee had been brief, terse, and to the point. The rest of the day had not. The remainder of the afternoon, and the evening and night, for that matter, had been spent in the company of Senator Bruce Crawford and had included two heavy meals, a cocktail hour, and two sets of tennis.

Whit smiled to himself. Never mind. It had been a thoroughly satisfactory day, with much accomplished. Not a wasted moment. He had kept talking even while he and Crawford had done their laps in the Senate pool. It was Whit Harris's pride that he never stopped working, not even while he was playing. Of course, play was important. Anyone beyond the age of sixteen knew that in D.C. more deals were made over the tables at Sans Souci or at the seventh hole of Burning Tree than in any office or committee room. Part of your mind always had to be on what was important.

Balance, that was the thing. You couldn't let any one part of your life overshadow any other. His work kept him very busy, but he always found time to be home for parties, to have a chat with Lily, to make sure Katherine didn't feel neglected. This morning, for instance: He hadn't had to stop by her suite more than a minute to say goodbye, but that little extra bit of attention was what a woman needed to keep her feeling wanted, keep her from feeling left out of a man's life.

Bruce Crawford, now, he hadn't yet learned about balance, even though he'd been on the Hill for ten years. Smart man, Crawford, but too easily distracted. He had a little girlfriend, an administrative assistant or something; that was all right. That was understandable. Crawford was a big, alive man, full of energy. Of course he needed a release from time to time; a man was a man, after all.

But to leave his apartment in the Watergate at one in the morning to go up to Georgetown because she had called and whispered sexy words to him over the phone— that was stupidity. "We've got a great thing going," he'd said, not the least bit sheepish. "It's like dope; it gets to the point where you've just gotta have your fix."

Whit made a face. Crawford had grinned like an idiot, *proud* of his weakness. No woman would ever get away with that with *me*, Whit thought smugly. Not with a big meeting the next morning, hell, no. To be successful, you had to know, every minute, exactly where your priorities lay . . . and then he smiled at his own unconscious pun. Crawford should be aware that his priorities tonight did not lay with a woman. Tomorrow morning the Senator would come in bleary-eyed and exhausted: an easy mark. They'd have him in the bag before lunch, a sure thing.

His own sex life, now, was just right. Making love drained a man, robbed him of his vitality. It had to be kept within bounds. And, of course, Katherine had to be considered, too. She was the perfect wife, always on an even keel, her needs and desires perfectly balanced with his. Never any sudden demands, sweetly acquiescent the once or twice a week when he came to her bed. He never had to beg or tease or talk her into it; he never had to say anything. When he climbed in next to her, she always turned immediately to face him, her body moving right into the position he preferred. And when he was finished, a kiss good night and no fussing or clinging. Not like some women. Greedy women, like pigs, always demanding more, trying to manipulate, trying to squeeze the last drop of life out of your body. But not Katherine. Of course, lately she hadn't been so sweetly acquiescent all the time; he was beginning to suspect that she was not really sleeping every time she seemed to be. But he'd soon put a stop to *that*. A little authority and she'd come right around.

He stopped by the desk, watching as the night manager reached up to the correct box for his key. They knew who he was here. Knew his name, the room he preferred, his brand of whiskey, the time he liked to be awakened. It paid to be familiar, and to tip well.

Tucked neatly under the big key was a yellow envelope. "Telegram, Mr. Harris. Came in around ten o'clock."

Whit took both, unperturbed. Something at the home office, he supposed, that only he could deal with. Well, he was nearly finished with Bruce Crawford; he'd done well today. Crawford had started out, months ago, babbling about the dangers of all these artificial chemicals. If it had been up to him, pharmacists' shelves would be empty and people would be dying all over the place. He could see only the problems. "Good Lord, Bruce," Whit had explained, "chemicals aren't artificial. Your whole body is a chemical factory. Half the babies dying in this country are *missing* chemicals. Half the research is trying to find a way to put chemicals *in*." It had been an inspiration, bringing in all the new enzyme research—Tay-Sachs and so forth. Crawford had been biting his lip this evening, a sure sign that he was really beginning to buy an idea.

At the bank of elevators, Whit ripped open the envelope and rapidly scanned the message inside. His pale eyes narrowed and his lips formed the word "no," although no sound emerged. "No!"

But the block letters did not change.

DAN COPELAND WILL STEAL YOUR WIFE AWAY UNLESS YOU HURRY. A FRIEND.

His mind skittered about wildly and he fought to focus his thoughts.

He should have known, should have guessed, should have anticipated. Know the opposition: That was a rule of life. Never underestimate the opposition. He had erred badly, underestimating the power of nostalgia and— Damn Copeland, always hanging around her at school, trying to get her, using all the force of his personality. Copeland had *lost*, damn him! You didn't go after another man's wife; it wasn't done! He'd been stupid not to figure . . . Copeland had never cared a damn for convention, for the right thing.

He forced himself to calm down. What was the reality of the situation, after all? Someone—who, he could not guess and didn't even care, really—*someone* had seen them together. So it had to be in public. Copeland was after her, that was it, sticking by her side, putting his damn hands on her. The thought made Whit grit his teeth. Like having a crook sneak into your house, drink your wine, and steal your money.

But Katherine would resist Copeland. Of course she would. She had never so much as flirted with any man since their marriage—and he watched her more carefully than she guessed. She was much too fastidious to allow anything more than a casual touch. So it was still not too late to put a stop to it before an emotional scene was created that might prove an embarrassment.

He would have to rush things a bit tomorrow morning. He would have to force some kind of commitment from Crawford, and quickly. And then—

Lips thinned to a pale line, he wheeled about and marched back to the desk.

"I want," he announced, "a reservation on the ten-thirty flight to Syracuse tomorrow morning."

Without waiting to hear the manager's undoubtedly obsequious response, he strode back to the elevators, jabbing impatiently at the button. Katherine would have done nothing. It simply wasn't like her. She wasn't your typical woman, self-centered and overemotional. And there was the child to consider. At the thought of Lily, he tightened his broad jaw grimly. Lily. Of course, Lily. *He* had forgotten to consider Lily.

Never mind. Nothing much could have happened in just one evening. Tomorrow was time enough. That his reservation would be waiting for him early tomorrow morning he didn't doubt for an instant. Those who dealt with Whitney Harris learned early on what was expected. And those who didn't learn? They were soon taught a lesson they would never forget!

CHAPTER TWELVE

Larry, the Tattooed Man

IT TOOK FOREVER to say good night. After spending the entire evening at The Pub, most of the reveling alums were bombed; Jock Standish could barely stand. But finally, everyone went his or her separate way and Benno found himself on Enders' second floor—completely unknown territory, since men had never been allowed upstairs when he was at school.

He trudged down the hallway, squinting at room numbers, not at all sure he remembered which was his and Dan's. It had been Dan's reservation, and besides, after so much vodka, his brain might be pickled. Not that he *felt* drunk—no, he wasn't even a little dizzy. Just exhilarated. High. Young. That's how he felt, like a kid again. And why not? Tonight at The Pub, everything had been like an instant replay of ten years before: Jock throwing down the booze and Courtney hovering over him, pretending it wasn't really happening. The Sigma Chis singing. The New York crowd off by themselves, talking and dancing languidly; well, they had always been so cool, he recalled. It was part of their style. A few couples who probably didn't belong together, huddled into the back booths holding hands and God only knew what else. Everyone having such a roaring good time that it made you wonder if they all weren't working just a bit hard at it.

He and Jay Shulman had sat together at the bar, making wisecracks about everything and everybody, laughing at their own wit and feeling smugly superior. He hadn't known Jay that well when they were in school—their interests hadn't coincided—and it was fun discovering they were kindred spirits.

Still, he had been sorry Dan wasn't there. But Dan had insisted that he go on with the others, saying he himself was exhausted and was going right to bed. "I'll play with the kids tomorrow, Mother," Dan had laughed. But it would have been more fun with him there tonight. Come to think of it, where were Kitty and Lee? He'd been kind of looking forward to seeing more of Lee. She'd really changed. Funny, how what had seemed so pushy in '70 had emerged as attractive self-confidence. She interested him . . . Well, maybe they'd joined another party somewhere; there must be dozens going on.

Then he saw the towel hanging on the doorknob and he began to laugh, stifling the sound with his hand. Yes, this was the right room, and how many years since he'd last seen *that* signal? Sneaky Dan. Going right to bed, was he? Well, well, well. That answered at least half of his question. He knew where Kitty was, anyway.

He let out a low whistle and shook his head. "Trouble," he muttered, "nothing but trouble . . . Oh, hell." Now, he realized wearily, he would somehow have to find himself an empty bed. But at this hour? In the semidarkness of a girls' dormitory?

He did an about-face and started down the hall. A solid wall of firmly closed doors faced him on either side. He could try them, one by one, but what if he walked in on someone? "It's the couch in Beau Parlor Number

Three for you, my lad," he said. No blankets, of course, but at least the cushions were soft.

But at the turn into the other corridor, he heard, very definitely, the sound of voices: voices and laughter and music. Life! He hurried toward the noise.

Room 27's door had been cracked open, and he could instantly see why. In the wedge of light, heavy cigarette smoke hung like a thick blue pall. He opened the door wide and called in: "Does anyone here smoke?"

There was a general shriek of female laughter at this. After a moment he could make out some half-dozen women, wrapped in blankets or robes, sitting in a loose circle on the floor, surrounded by a litter of potato chip bags, beer cans, overflowing ashtrays, and greasy pizza boxes.

"Hi, there, handsome!" a voice called out. "Come join us."

"Couldn't find my way through the fog," Ben said.

The same voice answered: "I'll even come and get you."

Benno grinned. "Ladies, I've often dreamed of a moment like this, alone in the night with a harem. But alas, I have spent the past several hours at The Pub, and all I need right now is an empty bed."

"Wouldn't you know," another voice put in. "The only man available at two in the morning, and all he's interested in is sleep."

More peals of laughter, while another woman yelled, "Reminds me of my husband!"

Benno held out his hands. "Ladies, ladies, you see before you a tired man. Tell you what: Find me a bed and you can *all* tuck me in."

The original speaker said, "You can use my room. I'm sure as hell not going to get there *tonight*."

"Bless you, my dear."

"Third door down. Just make the bed in the morning."

As he continued down the hall, Ben thought, Crazy ladies! Who could stay up all night and talk, at our age? Who, he added to himself with a laugh, would *want* to?

He lost track of the doors and paused in front of one. Was this three down, or two? Or four? She hadn't told him a number. This was Room 31. And then he thought,

Thirty-one! Why did that ring a bell? Oh, well . . . He turned the knob and opened the door.

The room was in semidarkness; even so, as he stepped across the threshold he sensed the presence of another person.

"Whatever you do," said a familiar voice from the shadows, "don't turn on the light."

"Lee!"

"Benno? What the hell are you doing here?"

"I was drawn, as if by magic, across the campus, down the corridor—"

"Cut the comedy," Lee said.

He thought her voice sounded grim and sad; and without warning, he reached over and flipped on the overhead lights.

"Damn you!" Lee snarled, but she did not stir from her position, hunched up in the corner of the bed, completely wrapped in a rough gray blanket to her neck. Without makeup, she looked more familiar, younger, more vulnerable . . . more like the girl who had so antagonized him back then. But the dark eyes were sunk deep in their sockets and looked out at him with such naked misery that he felt a surge of embarrassment, much as if he had found her stripped. Instantly he switched off the lights.

"I'm sorry, Lee." She did not answer. "I'll get out."

"No! Please. Stay. I'm sorry I yelled like that. I can't seem to get to sleep." The tone of her voice changed subtly. "Maybe if you come in and talk to me, you'll bore me to sleep."

"Oh, well, if *that's* how you feel, sure. Swell. I love an attentive audience." He felt relieved that she was able to give him the needle. Her eyes had looked . . . beyond death. Not that that had interfered with her wise mouth. Thinking he would probably regret this, Ben eased his loafers off, and carrying them, padded carefully across the room until he bumped into the other bed. Kitty's bed, he reminded himself; but, of course, Kitty was behind a locked door decorated with a white towel and wouldn't be back very soon. He wondered if Lee knew, wondered if he ought to tell her, decided no.

By this time he was stretched out on the bed, the two skimpy college pillows doubled up under his neck, his hands laced together behind his head. His head was a mite muddled, and the hard mattress under him felt just fine. Not the Ritz, but better than Beau Parlor Number Three. It was not quite pitch-dark in the room. Light from the street lamp filtered through the leafy trees and speckled the wall with faint, indistinct shadows. Lee was a shape with a halo of fuzzy hair, over on the other bed. She had uttered not a sound since the insult.

"Lee? You there?"

"No. I'm at the ball, dancing with the prince."

"One hardly expects *you* to be so silent."

"Nor you to be so solicitous. Sorry. I didn't say that. I—I'm not in such a wonderful mood. I *did* ask you to please stay, didn't I?"

"Tell you what I'm gonna do," he said lightly. "I'm gonna talk about my business. That ought to bring the sandman running. It always bored my wife."

"Wife? You—*married?*"

"Huh! Dan was surprised, too. I wonder what that says about me."

"What do you think? That we're amazed somebody could put up with you. Obviously somebody could. Apologies. Felicitations and all that stuff on your marriage."

"Well . . . actually, I'm not married, not since yesterday. She *couldn't* put up with me."

In the darkness, Lee shifted position. "I have a big mouth. Can't see your face. Glad or sad that it's over?"

"Oh, glad. Most definitely."

Silence for a moment. Then: "What was she like? What kind of girl did you pick out, anyway?"

"Neat, small, blond, pretty."

"Sounds like Kit."

He laughed. "Oh, I had my eye on Kit once upon a time. Those cool, controlled WASP types are the favorite fantasy of every Egyptian-born, half-Italian, half-Armenian, red-blooded boy! I always thought it was the physical type . . . so opposite, you know. But it suddenly occurs to me that it isn't the looks so much as the style."

"The style?"

"Yeah. All that elegant understatement, all that quiet good taste, all that carefully controlled emotion. A place for everything and everything beautifully in its place. And if it isn't, it's put in its place. To a Levantine type like myself, this would look not like repression, oh, no, but like the very epitome of high-class behavior.

"My family, now, specialized in loud shrieks of joy or loud groans of pain. Good news called for a lot of hugging and kissing and plenty of tears. Bad news meant . . . well, a lot of hugging and kissing and plenty of tears."

Benno laughed again. "The emotional climate in my family ran to hot, hotter, and hottest. What the rest of the world calls vulgar. Helena—my, er, wife—was everything opposite. She was everything I wasn't."

Lee said, "Sometimes that works out beautifully."

"Yeah, sometimes. But she wanted me to be different. Opposites may attract, but they aren't always good for each other." He paused. "Hell, give me a Mediterranean type *any* day: warm, open, quick on the draw. At least you know what you're dealing with!"

"I know, I know. Listen, I *grew up* with that problem."

"If you're a WASP, I take back everything I said."

Lee gave a cracked laugh. "WASP? Me? Hardly. I'm Hispanic, pal. *Cubana.* High-grade Cubans, escapees from Castro and his everyone-share-everything politics. Akkardijian, you ain't *seen* control and good taste until you've been in a gently bred Cuban family.

"And there I was, noisy, vulgar me with a lid clamped firmly down on all my behavior. We lived in the barrio, surrounded by Puerto Ricans. Our family disdained the P.R.'s, noisy, vulgar creatures that they were. I was not to associate with them. But I *loved* the P.R.'s. I spent my childhood longing to shout from the window down to the street, to go down and dance with them, to turn my radio up high, to fight and scream and hug and kiss. It looked so . . . alive, and our apartment seemed dead and depressed by comparison . . ."

She drifted off into silence, which Benno broke by asking, "So where does a Hispanic kid get a name like Rivers?"

"Would you believe from the Hampton College computer? Really. It changed the 'a' in Rivera to an 's' somehow. I tried to get the spelling changed back, but if there's one thing I learned, it's don't try to convince a computer. And what the hell, I was trying to run away from my background, anyway, so who cared?"

"Why run away? Hispanic's nothing to be ashamed of."

"Oh, God, I know that. But back then . . . I wasn't ashamed of it, really, just sick of it. It was stifling! I was a girl and had to be protected, while my big brothers went charging in and out of the house, free as eagles. And when I looked around, it was even worse to be a Puerto Rican woman. There's no freedom at all for a female in the Hispanic world. I was supposed to be delicate, fragile, virginal—above *all*, virginal. Well, by the time I was twelve, I was already five feet seven, and by the time I was fifteen—but never mind all that. I was a prisoner of my society. Luckily, I had this voice, and Mama and Poppi allowed me to learn to play the guitar. So I got into a professional high school and won a scholarship to Hampton, of all places! And the rest," she added acidly, "is history."

"It's true," Ben said gently. "By the time I met you, you were a far cry from being delicate or fragile."

"Or virginal, for that matter. That's okay. I was never ashamed of it—" Her voice broke for an instant, but when she spoke again, it was normal. "Kitty got me into the sorority; she *insisted*. But they were damn glad to have me later on." She laughed briefly. "Half of them found out about sex from me. And the rest? They lived vicariously through my . . . adventures. And all that time, of course, I secretly envied them all the things I'd spit at: the cool, the control, the air of knowing precisely the right thing to do."

Benno stretched and sat up straighter. "That's how they've got the whole world bulldozed, Lee. They seem to have all the answers, and all us warm, passionate, wonderful people believe the propaganda. Hell, it should be the other way around!"

"Right!"

"We're always letting the world tsk-tsk at us and tell us how loud and childish we are. Yet now all the cool, controlled types have to go to group therapy to learn how to touch each other and look into each other's eyes and make contact. Whereas we, Lee—you and I—we already know how." He shook a clenched fist into the darkness, feeling lighthearted and excited.

After a moment she said, "Still feel like second fiddle around Dan Copeland?"

It took him a minute or two to recall that casual conversation downstairs earlier. "Oh—that. That's when I was a mere, pimple-faced youth. But let's be honest, Lee, Dan's a natural-born leader; hundreds of kids followed him, not me. I happened to be his roommate and a stranger in a strange land. And he happened to be older and handsomer and very sure of what he was doing."

"Too sure, sometimes."

"What does *that* mean?"

"I don't know . . . just that sometimes I get the feeling that he uses people, uses the way they feel about him— oh, it's not worth going into. Just something that happened once, a long, long time ago."

He laid her once, Ben thought instantly, and then told her, very sweetly, to get lost. Ben knew the whole routine; he'd watched it often enough. There had always been enough devoted groupies hanging around Dan, and Kitty Cameron hadn't allowed any sex in her life. But Lee? She'd never made herself available, she'd always been too busy. So when—? But she was right, of course. It wasn't worth going into. And what was that quote?

" 'It was another time and another place, and besides, the wench is dead,' " he muttered.

"What?"

"Nothing. Wandering mind . . . the thoughts of a brand-new bachelor."

They lay side by side on their separate beds in companionable silence. Then Benno turned his head to find that she, too, had turned to face him.

"Ben?"

"Mmmm?"

"Guess we're sort of alike."

He cleared his throat, suddenly filled with a nervous anticipation. "Yes, aren't we?"

There was a long silence. Benno strained to see Lee's face, but it was no more than a white blot against the shadowed wall. Then she said thoughtfully, "That's probably why we tangled so much back then."

"But—" Benno began, and quickly added, "Agh, what's the use of talking about the past? *This* is the moment . . . and at this moment, I'm feeling completely wide awake. How about you?"

"You didn't manage to bore me, after all. What good are you?"

"I'm the guy with all the great ideas. What do you say we pick ourselves up and go take a walk around campus?"

"A *walk*. At this hour?"

Ben checked his wristwatch's glowing green numerals. "What are you talking about? It's the shank of the morning: three-oh-seven, to be exact. Isn't that when a popular singer is usually partying it up with crowds of admirers? It seems to me that I read in *People* magazine that Lee Rivers never gets to bed before five."

He heard her bare feet hit the floor. "Enough with your lousy issue of *People* magazine! I'll *go* for your lousy walk across the campus. Although what you hope to do at three-oh-seven in the morning . . ."

Benno got up and walked to the window, peering out. "We'll see plenty," he remarked. "C'mere."

The deserted street was flooded with a blue-white light that frosted the leaves with silver. The night was utterly quiet and windless; not a single leaf stirred. High in the inky sky, a full moon floated serenely.

"Oh, perfect," Lee breathed. "Just let me get dressed and we'll go."

When they emerged from Enders, they both began to tiptoe and to talk in whispers, as if they might wake the sleeping world. Stifling giggles like a pair of guilty teenagers, they scooted quickly across the empty street. Not until they were behind the main library, on the quad, did they both burst into laughter.

Benno now could see her face clearly in the bright moonlight. She looked quite different from the distraught, haggard woman he'd had a glimpse of earlier. There was a flush of excitement across her prominent cheekbones, and her large dark eyes looked bright and alive. She's really a beauty, he thought, somewhat surprised.

"No wonder the cosmetic industry makes billions," he said lightly. "You're a changed woman."

Lee put her hands on her hip. "I'll have you know, wise guy, that I'm not wearing any makeup. None. Zero. Zilch."

"You look so different."

Lee laughed and began to stroll down one of the brick pathways. "My claim to fame. That's why they love me; my face reflects everything I feel." She laughed again. "If

you think I looked bad before, when I was only depressed, you should see me when I'm hungry!" She bared
her white, even teeth and growled.

They swung along down the path, their steps matching.

"So tell me, Lee, now that I have you alone . . . how
does it feel to be a celeb? Really."

"Really? Okay, let me think. When I'm working, a
walk in the moonlight, like this, is an impossibility. A
weekend like this, with just friends, is another impossibility." She paused. "In fact, almost everything normal and
natural and nice is an impossibility. God, it sounds awful,
doesn't it? It's not. But there *is* a shortage of privacy.
There's my agent and my business manager and the hair-
dresser and the costume designer and the music arranger
and the boys in the band and my secretary. Everyone has
business with me. Everyone. All the time. That's what it's
like to be a celeb. Oh—and the fans. Bless them and
curse them."

"And you love it all," Ben said.

She touched him lightly on his arm. "Yes . . . and no.
Mostly yes, of course. I'm not going to play coy and pretend I hate fame and fortune. But, especially with the
fans, there's a love-hate thing. I've had them banging on
all the windows of a closed car, and their faces looked
predatory and hungry. And yet I know they would call it
love. They have a way sometimes of pressing in on you
. . . sometimes you wonder if they're ever going to let you
go. And sometimes you tense up, because you have a
creepy feeling that at any moment these adoring people
will turn into a mob, pulling your clothes to shreds and
tearing your hair . . ." She shivered a little. "It's happened, you know. They do love me and admire me, but
they don't seem to realize I'm a living person, and they're
ready to rip pieces from my body."

Benno reached out to touch her but drew back—for
what reason, he didn't know and didn't want to think
about. Instead, he gave her a light punch on the arm.
"Shucks, Rivers," he said with a grin, "who could blame
them, with a body like yours?"

"Agh!" She slanted a look at him, smiling her funny
half smile. "You asked, Akkardijian. I'm sorry if you
didn't like my answer."

"Who said I didn't like your answer?"

"It's an old trick of yours. When you want to change the subject, you make a joke."

Benno stopped walking, eyeing her closely. "Jesus, you're right. That *is* what I do, isn't it? Poor Helena." They began to stroll again, in silence, but his mind was in a whirl. Yes, he had changed the subject; had tried to lighten an emotional mood. But not for the reasons Lee thought. No. More and more as the night progressed, he felt close to her, protective somehow. Two or three times he had had to fight off the urge to put his arm around her.

For God's sake, he scolded himself. What do you think you're doing? She doesn't need you. She's surrounded by people who are paid to protect her. What the hell *is* this, anyway? You flatter yourself, my man. If you did reach out, she'd probably laugh in your face. Up to an hour ago, you were still antagonists, remember? And besides, there is bound to be a man in her life; there always has been.

By this time they had crossed the quad and were on the other side of the campus, on Simmons Avenue.

"Which way?" Benno asked.

"Any way but left." A block away was O'Hara's apartment house.

For five minutes they walked without speaking or feeling the need to. Ben was aware that they were avoiding O'Hara's place, and he wished he knew what had gone on earlier in the evening. What that horse's ass had pulled on her to make her weep alone in the night. That guy deserved to be punched out, he thought. Here I go again, thinking I'm a knight in shining armor. Wouldn't it give her a big laugh if she knew what I was thinking?

"What are you thinking about?"

"If you only knew," he said, and laughed. "No, no, only kidding. I was thinking about . . . reunions, I guess, and what they do to people. Take us. We meet after ten years and everything is different, while Dan and Kit, on the other hand . . . ."

Lee smiled. "Yes, Kitty and Dan. After ten years, everything is the same."

"Not quite."

"What do you mean?"

"Ten years ago she wasn't married. She sure made a mess of things! You should have seen Dan when he found out she had married Whit. The man was a ghost for months. He expected Kitty to marry *him*. I think she played a dirty trick on him."

"Well, I happen to know that he never asked her to marry him! He never even told her he loved her!"

"That's bull!"

"That's what you think. The trouble with you men is you think women are going to fall all over you—without your doing a thing to deserve it! You all think you're doing us a great big favor! Well, let me tell you—!" She broke off and began to giggle. "You look so *ferocious*. And here I am, yelling like a fishwife. It's *their* fight, let *them* battle it out. I don't want to break our truce." She gave him a lopsided grin, and once again Benno fought the impulse to reach out and pull her into his arms.

"You're right, Rivers," was all he said.

It was after four when they spotted the brightly lighted diner. A neon sign almost as big as the building flashed in florid script: GOOD EATS.

Together, they burst out: "Good Eats! It's still here!" and broke into a babble of remembered all-night study sessions and late-night breakfasts under the watchful eye of Archie, the cook/baker/owner/father confessor.

As they hurried down the hill, Lee asked excitedly, "Do you think he's still there? Remember how he used to sober up Jock Standish every year for finals?"

"And he could time to the minute exactly when a demonstration would run out of steam. He'd actually have the coffee all poured when we got there."

"Oh, Lord," Lee muttered as they pushed the diner door open, "I do hope he's still here!"

The place was nearly empty; the radio played quiet jazz. The vacant booths were washed and neatly set up for breakfast with bottles of maple syrup, pots of jelly, coffee mugs turned upside down. The paper place mats featured a map of Jefferson City, Missouri. Obviously Archie was still getting his odd lots of place mats from the same printer. "Remember the World War Two ones that said, 'Loose Lips Sink Ships'?" Lee recalled. "He said they'd been lost in a warehouse in Rochester for twenty years."

But Benno wasn't listening; he was looking around, a fond smile playing on his lips. This little coffee shop was packed with memories. The leadership of the Students' League had used it for headquarters whenever the apartment got too messy and crowded. Many and many were the nights they had jammed in here, spending hours over a few cups of coffee while arguing about tactics.

And there was Archie, behind the counter, looking a bit grizzled but essentially unchanged. He was an ex-merchant marine, big and burly, with thick-fingered hands that were surprisingly deft when flipping an omelet or rolling out pie crust. He still wore the crew-cut style they had given him in the service during World War II—"I'm used to it; it keeps my head cool," he used to say—and what looked like the same gaudily studded cowboy shirt. He was busy at the grill, not even turning his head as he said, "Be with ya in a minute."

But in less than half a minute he had turned from his cooking, a mischievous grin splitting his broad, pug-nosed face, offering a plate balanced on each big hand.

"Morning, folks. Here you are."

For a moment both Benno and Lee were unable to take it in. They hadn't ordered, he had made a mistake . . . And then Lee saw what was on one of the plates.

"Archie!" she cried. "You really remembered! After all these years!"

"Sure, kid. Toasted corn, lots of butter, hold the jelly, a side of sausage. And for you, sport, the usual: lots of bacon, period."

Ben shook his head. "Remarkable. After ten years! How do you do it, Archie?"

"The eyes. I always go by the eyes because the eyes never change. Of course, for a big-timer like the kid here, all I gotta do is look at the cash register."

Lee frowned. "The cash register?" She looked at it and then laughed. For hanging neatly framed over the register was one of her more ubiquitous publicity stills: back-lit, full of dramatic shadows, and showing a lot of skin. "Oh, Archie, that's sweet! Would you like me to sign it?"

"Hey! Wouldja? Thanks a million!" After plunking the two plates down on the counter, he got the picture, extricated it from the frame, and presented her with a pen. "Yeah," he remarked as she scribbled *To my old friend*

Archie, with love and kisses, Lee Rivers, "you're the most famous graduate of Hampton that I know of. I been following your career for years."

Lee looked up, an impish gleam in her eyes. "Following my career? Say, Archie, you haven't been sending me red roses all over the world, by any chance?"

He looked puzzled. "Gee, no, kid. Roses ain't my style exactly."

"Never mind. Somebody's been sending me flowers, and I was just hoping it'd be someone nice like you."

"Aw . . ." Archie colored and then quickly pushed the plates toward them. "Hey, your breakfasts are getting cold. And here's the coffee." Two thick mugs emitting clouds of pungent steam came sliding across the counter. "I gotta get back to work."

They carefully carried everything to one of the booths and settled in, facing each other; by unspoken agreement, they both dug in. Finally, Ben stuffed the last crisp piece of bacon into his mouth and looked up. "God, I needed that."

Lee smiled and licked butter from her fingers. "Me, too." She craned her neck. "Still the usual night people here, I see."

Two booths away, six sleepy-eyed kids were wolfing down triple hamburgers, one of Archie's specialties, as they blue-penciled long galley sheets for tomorrow morning's *Daily Hamptonian.* Near the door sat Hampton's best-known insomniac, a retired professor of indeterminate age, sipping tea and nibbling cinnamon toast while he read from a battered copy of the *Iliad* propped against the sugar bowl. Two town cops lounged against the counter in unconsciously identical postures, each one with a hand resting casually on the shiny leather holster at his hip, discussing the merits of grass seed versus zoysia plugs.

The only other customer sat crouched into the farthest corner booth, crumbling a saltine into a hill of fine powder on the table top. She was a painfully thin woman who glowered at her soup, her lips moving. Lee glanced at her and then couldn't look away. She appeared young and unlined—probably, Lee thought, about my age—but she was a parody of a little old lady, her hair skinned back so tightly that it slanted her eyes, her nails bitten down short. Her colorless eyes seemed pushed deep into her skull. Lee kept staring at her; she had a feeling of déjà vu, as if she had seen her somewhere before. The woman suddenly banged her fist angrily on the table, folded a dollar bill compulsively until the corners matched perfectly, and marched out, still muttering, tightly hugging against her chest a zippered briefcase with orange vinyl trim.

"Pathetic," Benno said.

Lee made a face. "Craziness . . . There, but for the grace of God—"

"Oh, come off it. You've never been anywhere *near* that!"

"Oh, you think so? Much *you* know. There were times when I thought I was in Psycho City. Larry, the Tattooed Man, for instance. Wanna hear about Larry, the Tattooed Man?"

"Are you kidding? Of *course* I want to hear about Larry, the Tattooed Man."

"Well, it started in Chicago . . ."

Chicago had been melting in the midst of an enervating heat wave when Lee arrived, cramped and grimy after two days on a bus. She had hoped to leave her hurt and disappointment far behind her in Hampton, but O'Hara still haunted her. Each time she thought of him, she had to fight off a wave of heavy depression that poured over her. He had abandoned her and she would never see him again, never have his arms around her, never again feel his instantaneous arousal when she touched him, nevermore see his eyes grow wild above her. Hurt twisted in her heart like a hot knife.

She *had* to forget him. More important, she had to find a job. She had $13.42, a duffel bag full of clothes, and her guitar. And that was all. And your voice, kiddo, she reminded herself. Yes, and no job. She looked around. Why did I come here? I should have gone to New York. But here she was, and there wasn't enough money to take her anywhere. She had to find a job.

Well, as long as she was starting from scratch, she figured, she might just as well look for a singing job as anything else. She got a room at the YWCA, dumped her duffel on the bed, took a shower, changed her jeans, asked the desk clerk where she might find nightclubs, got a funny look, ignored it, and began to walk.

It was pure dumb luck, after three days of trudging around and being laughed at, to come upon The Grotto. It was a cellar club, reached by a winding flight of metal stairs, and if she hadn't been looking so hard and so desperately, she would've missed it. The little neon sign, all in blue, was hardly noticeable—especially in the glaring sunlight.

She was feeling really low and thinking that after this try, she'd just go and get a job waiting on tables somewhere. A bright college girl could always get a job as a waitress.

The polished wooden door at the bottom of the stairs was wide open, and, grateful for the dimly lit, cool feel of the place, she walked right in and plumped herself down on a bar stool.

The place seemed completely deserted. Chairs were neatly stacked on top of the tables, the bar's varnished wood was wiped clean, and the club had the air of being abandoned. You knew there had recently been life here, but now it was gone. She said, "Hello?" softly and the word seemed to echo. There was no answer, no sound at all.

She slumped over the bar, letting her head fall onto her folded arms. The polished wood felt smooth and cool and comforting after the steamy heat of the pavements.

Suddenly, from behind her, a gruff voice demanded: "What d'ya think you're doing here, sister? Sleep it off somewheres else."

Her head came up with a snap and she whirled around to see a broad, pouchy face with a nose that had been squashed flat. Deep-set eyes glared out at her from under bushy eyebrows, and a long-dead cigar was clamped between large yellow teeth. The man was short and squat and muscular, standing as if planted on his short legs. He looked like the killer in any grade B movie, and when she spoke, her voice squeaked:

"I'm sorry. I wasn't sleeping. I'm not drunk, just hot. I've been walking around all morning, and it's so nice and cool . . ." Her voice faded as he continued to stare at her without blinking and without changing his expression. Lee cleared her throat nervously and added, "I'm looking for a job."

To her surprise, the man immediately said, "Oh, yeah? Doing what?"

"Actually . . . singing?" She waited for him to hoot, like all the others.

"So sing for me," was all he said. And gesturing to the guitar on her back: "And play that thing if you wanna."

She did. She played and sang a couple of intimate Burt Bacharach numbers, "San Jose" and "I'll Never Fall in Love Again," keeping her voice as soft as she could. It was a small place and she knew if she let it all out, she'd have the bottles behind the bar quivering. She finished—it sounded pretty good, she thought—and then rested the guitar on her lap and waited for him to say something.

What he said, after a moment or two, was: "Okay, honey. I see you can sing sweet and soft. Now, why don't you sing like you usually sing? Belt one out."

She grinned at him; she couldn't help it. How in the world could he tell? "Hey, sister," he said, "I've been in show biz for a long time. I know a belter when I see one. Let's have one of them old torch songs; that's what my customers go for. 'Stormy Weather,' you know that? 'Can't Help Lovin' That Man,' or 'Bill'? Like that."

"Sure. I can sing anything." She chose "Bill," because she knew she could put real feeling into the words. This time, she used her whole range and all the power she had and the bottles behind the bar tinkled against each other.

When she had finished, he chewed thoughtfully on the cigar stub, and then all of a sudden he grinned. "Oh, yeah? Nice. You own a dress?"

"I—well—" she stammered, and then grinned back at him. "The truth?"

He nodded. "You don't own a dress. I didn't think so. Well . . ." He reached into a pocket and came out with a thick wad of folded bills, peeled a few off, and stuffed them into her hand. "Go buy one. You're on tonight. Be here by seven." He squinted at her with amusement. "So? You're hired, understand? But you gotta have a dress—the customers expect it—and make it, you know . . ." He made a gesture that indicated a plunging neckline.

It took her a few minutes to realize that her weary foot-aching slogging was really over. She had a job. She wasn't going to wait tables. This man was going to pay her to sing. She stammered her thanks, slung the instrument back over her shoulder, and started out into the glare of midday when he called: "Hey! Wait a minute!"

Oh, hell! He was changing his mind. She turned. "Yes?"

"What's your name, sister?"

"Oh. Lee. Lee Rivers."

"Lee Rivers . . . not bad. I'm Babe Skyriatos."

"Thanks a lot, Mr. Skyriatos."

He laughed hugely. "You call me Babe. Everyone does."

She did call him Babe. In spite of his formidable appearance, the name suited him. He was a teddy bear. He always had the kitchen bring her a hot meal after the first set, and if any male patrons hung around, he was sure to be somewhere nearby, keeping an eye on things.

Too bad, she had thought much later, that he had been stuck behind the bar, busy mixing drinks, the night Larry Peterson had drifted in and settled himself at a table directly in front of her.

There was no missing him, even if he hadn't been six foot five. Larry always wore Levi's, high-heeled cowboy boots, and an immaculate white Stetson. He had a wide, clear-skinned face, pale blue, deep-set eyes, and rather long and lank light brown hair. Yummy . . . nice-looking, she decided that first night, glancing over at him. She thought the outfit a bit self-conscious, but it suited him.

And then she noticed his hands and nearly missed a beat in "Stormy Weather." They were large, beautifully kept hands with short-clipped nails. But on the back of each was a life-sized tattoo in garish colors. On one hand, the head of a king cobra, and on the other, its tail.

She could not, after that, keep her eyes from those bizarre tattoos. By the time she had ended the set, she was looking at him, openly curious. Did he have an entire life-sized snake tattooed across his back and shoulders? *Why*, for God's sake? It was repulsive, but at the same time fascinating.

As she finished the last number, she glanced up and suddenly met his eyes. He was frankly eyeing her up and down, smiling suggestively. She could feel herself turning red, but she just grinned back. To hell with it. Anyone who walked around tattooed with snakes, dressed like a

Hollywood cowboy, had to expect to be stared at. It didn't surprise her when he gestured with his head that she should join him. There was a message in his eyes, a message as clearly stated as if he had spoken. It said, "I want *you*," and she wasn't inclined to argue. He was quite a hunk, and she had been all alone for weeks now.

She sat down across from him and said, "So what's a cowboy doing in Chicago?"

"Lookin' for a job."

"Here?"

"Why not? I do a little of everything." He gave her a slow wink. "Just so long as it's at night. I'm a night person."

"What do you really do?"

He glanced around lazily. "Oh, *I* sing some, too. You're good, you know that? And—uh—I can tend bar, bounce the drunks . . . you name it."

She smiled at him. "You may be in luck, cowboy. Our bartender left town in a hurry. That's the boss filling in. Shall I introduce you?"

"That'd be nice." Again that slow, meaningful look. "And I'd be mighty grateful."

Five minutes later he was behind the bar, deftly pouring, mixing, and serving, his jacket off. Under the sheer shirt he wore, his entire chest and back glowed with colorful swirls and curlicues, zodiac symbols, slogans, harem girls, griffins, dragons, a six-masted schooner in full sail, and, of course, the snake. As Lee had thought, it did indeed slither up one arm, drape itself across his shoulders, and coil in many-hued splendor down the other arm, tó end in the fierce, fanged, striking head.

Babe hooted when he saw this fantastic sight. "By God," he announced, "you're gonna save me money, because I'm turning off the TV over the bar permanently. You're a better sight than the fights any day of the week."

Larry had a room nearby, and that's where they went, he and Lee, after The Grotto had closed. It was nice, feeling his arm around her back; nice to lean a little into him; nice to smell his shaving lotion again. It was also nice, she discovered, having him kiss her and hold her and tell her how sexy she was. "Knew the minute I laid eyes on you. That's for me, I told myself." When they were in bed together, she was surprised at her own eagerness and hunger. He was not a bit like O'Hara—for one thing, he never said a word while making love—but he was practiced and tireless; and she was finally able to drown those recurring memories in a flood of overwhelming physical sensation.

After their first night together, Larry took it for granted that she would come home with him when the bar closed. She didn't argue. It was pleasant enough, and she was grateful to find O'Hara rapidly fading into the dim past, where he belonged. But after six weeks, she didn't know the man she was living with any better than she had the night she'd met him. He was vague about his past, liked to gossip about the frequenters of The Grotto, and took her to honky-tonks on their time off where conversation was an impossibility. He was very physical, leading her straight to bed the minute they walked in the door, ready to make love even after hours of strenuous dancing. He drank, not a lot, but continuously, and she found it simpler to go along and drink along and dance along. It was fairly mindless, but in a strange way soothing. She was singing. She was saving her money. What she would do after this, where she was heading, she had no idea. She was content to drift. It felt good to belong with someone, to be part of a pair. And when they were making love, he would whisper, "How would you like it if another guy came in right now?" or "Wouldn't it be fun if there were a couple more girls here?" and she would shake off her uneasy feelings and say, "My, my, what a fantasy life *you* must have." After all, he was just *asking;* he never really suggested any such thing.

It came as a shock when, one payday at the end of July, Larry announced: "Pack up, sugar, we're leaving."

"Leaving! What for? What are you talking about?"

"I'm not one for staying put. Not enough action around here. Time to push on. We've got enough bread." He stuffed his money into an already bulging money clip. "All we gotta do now is pack, so that's what we're gonna do."

"Listen, Larry, I've got a job singing—*singing*. I'm not going to get another one so easily."

"Hey, with your voice? And your looks? Hell, sugar, I'll get you lots of jobs. I know people in the business." He tucked the money clip neatly into his back pocket and reached out a lazy hand to caress her neck. "But before you start packing, let's play a little." With his other hand, he expertly loosened his belt buckle and began to strip. "Here comes my snake, to bite you . . ."

That night he didn't let her go until dawn was breaking. Several times he murmured that she should imagine an audience watching them, and when she said, "Oh, sick!" he laughed and laughed. "Oh, sugar, do *you* have a lot to learn!"

She awakened, groggy, at two o'clock the next afternoon. He was not in bed, and the entire room had been stripped of his possessions. For a moment she felt panic flood through her. He had left without her. It couldn't be happening again! What awful thing was there about her that made the men she was involved with leave her so easily? She sat up in bed, clammy with sweat. So that when he opened the door just then, dressed for traveling in a leather jacket, two crash helmets dangling from his hand, she leaped up from the bed and hugged him tightly in relief.

"Not now, sugar. Tonight."

"It's not that! I'm just . . . glad to see you."

He patted her rear end absently. "Hell, you're gonna be seeing me just about every minute from now on."

". . . in ten minutes flat, I was dressed and packed and had called Babe to tell him I was leaving. That made me feel bad." Lee gave a sigh and took a gulp of cold coffee.

"What did he say?"

"What could he say? That it wouldn't last a month."

"And did it?"

"Oh, God. I stayed with Larry for over two years. By the time we had left, I had really learned to hit the bottle . . . time was blurred, in a way. Life was blurred, too, and a good thing." She shuddered slightly. "Oh, yes, I stuck by the Tattooed Man with his show-biz contacts.

"Show biz. We worked freak shows in carnivals. I did a hootchy-kootchy while he stripped down to a fancy jock strap and rippled his tattoos. For a while we moved in with a commune in West Virginia that believed in Great Earth Mother and in a lot of group sex. And then he played in . . . a sex club, a grubby little hideaway filled with sweating men—ugh! I did everything he asked me to do, usually half drunk, but the sex-club thing I escaped. I refused to be tattooed. Seems the tattoos made it kinkier, better. But he found a stoned, skinny little thing named Velda, who was willing. They did . . . a dance, completely naked except for the tattoos, while the drums beat faster and faster, and in the end they . . . Well, I watched it only once, and then I went to our room and drank myself to sleep. And when he brought little Velda home with him, all ready to have a party, the door was locked.

"Wait. That was the end of that. We left and finally got to Nashville, and he did find me jobs, singing. In Nashville, he seemed suddenly to go almost straight. He didn't work, of course, although he said he was busy managing me. And he would often disappear for hours at a time while I was working, and I guess he was with other women. I found him in our bed one night with two teenyboppers, he didn't invite me to join them, and he hustled them right out of there. I thought maybe then it would be okay. I wasn't doing badly, even though I was singing Country and Western, which isn't exactly my style . . ."

Benno waited for her to continue, but she was staring sightlessly out the big window of Good Eats, her eyes focused somewhere in the past. "Well, obviously you left him at *some* point. What did he finally do?"

Lee gave him a crooked, sad smile. "Yeah, you'd think he'd done just about everything possible, wouldn't you? Well, he made me over, changed my name to Honey Doll —don't look like that, it's done all the time. Come to think of it, Akkardijian, this is the first time in the whole story that I've seen you look at all dismayed. You've got a funny idea of what's shocking. Well, okay, I was Honey Doll Dalton, and I'd cut a record with 'Losin' at the Rodeo of Love' on one side, and on the other? 'When I Lay Down to Die, Let It Be in Your Arms.' She paused to laugh shortly.

"Larry, the Tattooed Man, put on a real suit and took me on a plane and brought me to New York. He had contacts, he said; he had promises. We were going to hit the big time. He took every single cent we had and set up a big press party. And nobody came."

"Nobody?"

"Well, almost nobody. Just one fat d.j. from a rock station who looked around nervously and started to walk right out again. Larry jumped up and ran after this guy, sweating bullets, jabbering a mile a minute. At first I didn't even hear—I was so embarrassed. And then, suddenly, I did hear. That rat was offering me to the d.j.— offering my services. I can still hear him today, in my nightmares: 'Just look at those tits, man, look at that ass. Wouldn't you like a little action with that? She's terrific, I can promise you that; she really knows her stuff. She'll do anything you want, she knows it all. Just play the goddamn record once—just once, man—and she's yours for a week.'

"That tore it for me. I was finished. I looked over at Larry, my lover for two years, and realized that I wanted to kill him. I had been nipping at the bottle before the damn press party, but my head was clear enough to know I was finished being a slave.

"So while Larry went into lurid detail about what I'd do and how I'd do it, I very quietly let myself out the door and walked away. I got very drunk in a bar—that was the last time I was ever drunk in my life—and I ran to Kitty."

"Kitty?"

"Oh, I had written her every once in a while, a postcard that told her nothing. But I knew she was on Long Island; I knew the address. And I knew I had to do something very fast or I'd end up sitting in diners and muttering to myself in the middle of the night. So . . ." Lee took a deep, shuddering breath and let it out. "Now you know. Not a pretty story, right? I've never told anyone. You sorry I told you?"

Ben stared at her for several seconds, looking intently into the huge, dark, defiant eyes. "Not sorry. Honored, that you trust me enough to tell me."

Lee's eyes glistened, blinked, flickered away. Abruptly, she slid out of the booth. "Listen, can we go now? I need some fresh air."

They went out into a dawning so still and quiet that the street looked like painted scenery. For a moment there were no sounds at all, and nothing moved. In the east, a faint pink light streaked the paling sky.

"God, it's gorgeous," Benno said. "People really ought to get up at"—he consulted his wristwatch—"five in the morning all the time. It's the best time of the day."

"Usually bedtime for me," Lee remarked.

"And at five o'clock every morning, I'm running."

"And what are you doing when I start work at nine in the evening?"

He laughed. "Sacking out! Guess we're just not fated to cross paths."

Why did those words make her heart sink? She fought the feeling. This was just Benno Akkardijian, good old Ben from the old days. And this was just a reunion weekend, over in two days. Benno? Ridiculous!

They walked on, heading back up the hill toward the campus. As the familiar buildings came into view, Lee found herself dragging her feet. As tired as she was, she was unwilling to let this interlude end. She had told him so much, so many unsavory things, and yet she did not feel uncomfortable. She felt light and free. Strange, that the feisty little so-and-so of '70 had turned into this strong, accepting man. She stole a look at him as they passed under a street lamp. His was the face of a powerful, self-confident man, secure in his own strength.

As she contemplated him, his eyes slid sideways and met hers, and he winked. Warmth flooded through Lee. What a genuinely nice guy he was! He had listened to her with interest and compassion, with never a shocked look. No stupid questions, either. He had a nice way of seeing the funny side of things. As she did, she supposed. Which one of them had noted, earlier, that they were really very much alike?

They were crossing University Avenue when it happened. He took her hand in a most casual way, and it was exactly as if a current of electricity had been turned on. Her palm tingled, heat rose in her cheeks, and her heart began to beat erratically.

Oh, no, you don't! she thought. No, no. I won't have this. But inside, she was all a-tremble. She looked quickly over at his remote and impassive profile, the strong hawk-like nose jutting out, the eyes straight ahead. Not a glance in her direction, not a falter in the rhythm of *his* walk.

The stroll across the wide boulevard seemed to take forever, and when they reached the other side, she swiftly pulled her hand from his, only to have it just as swiftly recaptured. His hand was warm, slightly callused, firm.

"Lee," he said softly. She met his eyes reluctantly, willing her turbulent feelings not to show, and then had to look away. His deep-set dark eyes under their heavy brows were blazing with unspoken emotion. Then he felt it, too. Well, she simply could not deal with it. She wanted no part of it. It was silly, stupid, an illusion. They were both overtired, that's all, both a bit high on strong coffee, memories, and fatigue.

"Lee," he repeated.

Timidly, she looked at him again. Licking her lips nervously, she whispered, "You—"

"Yes," Benno said, his hand tightening on hers. "It's happening to me, too."

CHAPTER THIRTEEN

Linda Goodman Barrone

THE SKY WAS HAZY with dawn light when Kit quietly and cautiously let herself out of Dan's room. The sight of the towel draped over the doorknob made her smile, and she removed it, tossing it in onto the empty bed. In the bed she had left just a few minutes ago, Dan lay spread-eagled, his legs tangled in the top sheet and his thick hair tousled like a little boy's. Against the pillow, the strong profile made a sharp silhouette. Love welled up in her. How beautiful he was, how powerful and exciting and tender and loving. She fought off the impulse to run back to him, to nestle again into the warmth of his arms; and turning away, she shut the door firmly behind her.

She must go back, back to her real room and her real bed and her real life. The night had been glorious. Her whole body felt charged, as if all the blood in her veins had been electrified. The silence of the sleeping dormitory was heavy with hidden meaning; the sheen of the polished wooden floor was a golden glow; her silk gown was a kiss on her skin. Hoping nobody would see her at this hour, hurrying from the men's section in her nightclothes, she also wanted to shout her joy. I am in love, I am in love. The thought churned around and around in her head, like a magical incantation.

She must stop this. Whit would be here soon. A few hours, that's all the time they had left, she and Dan. Just a few more hours and then— And then? She did not know, did not want to think about it. Why had she left his room so early—what had been her hurry? She had felt so loved there, so complete, so safe. In Dan's arms there were no bothersome questions, only answers. And all the answers were the same: love. It had all seemed supremely simple an hour ago, watching his ecstatic face, lost in the pounding beat of passion.

Now, alone in the echoing corridor, she was back in reality. There was nothing simple about being in love with Dan Copeland. There never had been. He thought she had only to leave. Ah, but whoever said that leaving a marriage was easy? Marriage had been invented to bind people together, and it did, it did. All the little everyday patterns wound around you, creating a single life out of two—or, in her case, three. So much was involved: family; a child's feelings; job; career; money and belongings, even; a whole way of life. There were pride and love and hatred and disappointment and hope. There were friends and business associates and servants. There was a house, a stable, a school. As soon as she began to think about extricating herself from her marriage, she was forced to realize that she would be leaving her whole life behind, a life made up of thousands and thousands of tiny pieces. What was the one factor, *love*, against the pressure of a whole life? Her heart sank, contemplating the problems, the terrible wounds.

And yet . . . and yet. And yet there was a person hidden within all those pieces and patterns, and her name was Kit.

Kit was the wild, eager, unashamed wanton who had writhed and moaned under the power of Dan Copeland's body. And it was Kit who wrote Trudy's column; Kit who had borne the beautiful child, Lily; Kit who longed to be free, to be herself.

Katherine Cameron Harris, the beautiful, calm, controlled wife of Whitney Harris III, was a sham and a pretense. And a liar. How could she, Kit, continue to pretend and continue to lie? If she was not true to herself now, when would she ever be? Ten years had floated by, almost unnoticed. Would she let another ten smother her, and then another and another, until her life was at its end, never really *lived?*

She laughed a little to herself at her own dramatics, thinking, I ought to write to Trudy, like the other suburban matrons do. Trudy always knows what to do.

What *would* Trudy advise? she wondered. "Get to it, lady! Sounds to me as if you've wasted enough years already. Delay only makes it all the harder. The time for action is *now*."

Kit shook her head. Oh, no, you don't, Trudy, she thought. Not so fast. That's not the right way to deal with Whit Harris, uh-uh. Hit him with something suddenly and he's likely to get stubborn and hard-nosed. You have to ease Whit into an idea, let him get the notion it was his in the first place.

And besides, to be fair about it, Whit had a presentation to make this evening. He'd be tired; Washington always wore him down. She couldn't just dump this on him all of a sudden, especially when Dan was around. The trouble with their marriage wasn't just Dan—maybe it wasn't even Dan at all—but Whit would never, *never* see that. If she dared take Whit off balance, he'd be sure to lash out. He was not a very subtle man, nor a very forgiving one. She knew he was capable of just about anything if aroused. No . . . best to wait . . . when they were back in the house, in familiar surroundings, comfortable and at ease, his ancestors in their gilded frames guarding the decorum of the Harris name, a reminder that the Harrises had prevailed through all the family feuds and broken marriages.

She must concentrate on making sure that, for the weekend, Whit guessed nothing, that she didn't give out signals that told him something was amiss. She sighed. It shouldn't be too difficult; she'd been playing a part with him right from the very beginning. But before, she'd also

been sure that Dan Copeland was not part of her life.
People said it showed when you were in love. Lee had always insisted that these invisible signals existed. She called
them antennae. "As soon as some man is making you
happy," she used to say, "those antennae go up, sending
out the message that you're sexually desirable. Yes, they
do; it really happens. As soon as I'm involved with some
guy, I find thirty others who are suddenly interested.
They're getting the message. But when I'm blue and
lonely and really *need* somebody—no antennae, no messages, no men."

That's all I'd need in my life right now, Kitty thought,
amused. Thirty other men. The two I know are *more* than
enough. And rounding the corner, deep in her own turmoil, she nearly collided with a figure huddled tightly in
the corner.

"Why . . . Linda." She felt flustered, as though she'd
been caught out in a crime. "What . . . what are you doing here at this hour?" Only when she calmed down did
she notice the abject misery implicit in the bowed shoulders and the wide, frightened eyes. "Linda! What's the
matter?"

"I can't stand it! Honestly, I can't take another minute
with him!"

"Jess? What's he done? No, never mind, don't tell me
here, we'll wake everyone. Come on."

She half pulled the other woman down the hallway,
glancing at the pinched, miserable face. Did it look swollen, or was that just from tears?

The door to the smoker was open; the room was empty.
She flicked the light switch and almost laughed aloud. The
shabby old smoker hadn't changed. There were the battered easy chairs and scarred bridge tables she remembered so well. Still as ugly as ever. In contrast with the
attempt at elegance downstairs in the public rooms, the
smokers had traditionally been the receptacles for all
the old stuff that was too horrible to be seen but too
good to be thrown out. "And plenty good enough for
freshman women," the girls used to say.

Kit settled Linda into one of the chairs and drew another over to face her. Linda had been crying and her
eyes were red and puffy. Other than that, she seemed
okay, just very pale and weary-looking.

"Now," Kit said, "do you want to talk about it?"

"What a ghastly mistake! And we're fools enough to call it love." Linda dug into her bathrobe pocket and dragged out a smashed pack of cigarettes, prying at it with shaking fingers. Kit deftly took the pack and removed one of the cigarettes, offering it and then lighting it for her. "Love!" Linda repeated in a strangled voice, drawing harshly on the cigarette. "That's what I thought it was. That's what he used to tell me all the time. 'You love me,' he'd say, and I'd think, Oh, God, how masterful and masculine. Remember, Kitty? You remember when I was dating him, don't you?"

Lightly, Kit replied, "Handsomest guy at Upstate Med." And added silently, And the most arrogant.

"Oh, God! He was, wasn't he? I remember. Tonight, seeing you all, seeing Enders and the campus, it all just came flooding back. That's what's getting me! What *was!*"

"I know what you mean. We're all reliving the past a little."

"No, no. That's not it. I mean, suddenly I remembered who I'm supposed to be. Do you understand? I kept seeing the girl I was and comparing her with the ghost of a woman I am now. Ghost. Yes, that's a good word for it.

"I used to sing in the morning, remember? Everyone *hated* it. There you all were, grumping around, hardly able to get a word out. And I used to wake up at six, glad to be alive, looking forward to the day, singing on my way to the shower . . ."

"Do I remember!" Kitty smiled. "None of us will ever forget. We always said it was a crime against nature to be so happy so early." She laughed, looking anxiously at the other woman, but only a wan, tentative smile quivered on Linda's pale lips.

Linda took another drag, exhaled the smoke shakily, and stubbed out the cigarette. "Kitty, I haven't sung in the morning since I got married." She lifted her head for the first time and looked Kit straight in the eye. Her pale eyes were flooded with deep sorrow. "He—oh, I just can't take it any more!"

"Linda, what is it? What has he done?"

"What he's always done: as he pleases. He hadn't been to bed all night—at least not in *our* room."

"Oh, he's probably out with the guys. Everyone's drinking a bit too much. Second childhood."

Linda Barrone shook her head. Unconsciously, she began to wring her hands, and she studied her feet in their pink satin slippers. "I used to be so happy, so *up*. Life was full of promise, and was going to keep all those promises to Linda Goodman. To *Dr.* Linda Goodman . . . remember that? I was going to be a doctor—a *good* doctor. I would've been a good doctor, Kitty."

Kit reached over and patted Linda's hands. "Yes, you certainly would have. Why—?"

"Why? Yes, why, Kitty? Why aren't I a doctor? Why am I a nothing? I've been lying there in that bed alone, all night long, just thinking . . . remembering . . . adding up my life. In Buffalo, they think we're the perfect pair. We go to all the right parties and we entertain all the right people. We work in the same hospital, and everybody thinks Jess is just . . . *wonderful*." She sobbed on the last word.

"He hits me," she said after a moment, in a completely dead voice.

"Linda!"

"Oh, not all the time. I think I'd mind it less if it were all the time. At least then I'd know what to expect. I'd leave, probably. But you never know with him. I've gotten afraid to get near him. He might reach out and give me a hug, or he might shove me across the room. When he puts a hand out to me, it's gotten so I wince . . . Will he pat my cheek or smack it? And he despises my fear, despises it and loves it. Sometimes he taunts me, asks me why I don't just pack up and leave him.

"And, Kit, the real horror of it is: *I don't know!* Why don't I leave? Why don't I tell everyone that brilliant Dr. Barrone is a monster? I *wanted* him, Kitty. I thought I'd die if he didn't ask me to marry him. I used to pray for it. What kind of woman am I, to pick a man like that? He must have sensed a slave mentality in me, because that's what I've become . . . a scared little slave who does his bidding and covers up for him." She laughed bitterly. "They must wonder at the hospital, sometimes, how it is that I'm such an efficient nurse, and yet, at home, I seem to bump into everything . . . all those bruises I'm always turning up with . . ." The laughter quickly dissolved into large gasping sobs that tore at her thin frame.

Frowning, Kit waited for Linda to calm herself a bit, and then, reaching over to take her hands, she declared firmly: "You can't go on this way."

"I know, I know. But I'm helpless."

"No, I know you better than that. You're Linda, bright and resourceful. You *know* you mustn't stay if things are so bad. You know you deserve better than that."

There was a long pause. The room was suddenly so quiet that Kit became aware of birdsong outside in the streets. Then, almost in a whisper, Linda said, "I . . . oh, I'm so ashamed. The fact is, I don't have any money. Not a cent. Jess . . . he keeps me without money. I have charge accounts everywhere, even at the grocery store."

Kit asked none of the questions that crowded into her head. She simply asked, "If you had the money, Linda, where would you go?"

"Home. I mean, to my mother's. No, I mean *home*. It's the only home I've got! She's got the kids this weekend. They love her and—oh, God, Kit, I think Jess and I are destroying them! I long to get them away. But he'll come after us! He'll have me declared mentally incompetent! He's told me he'll do it!"

Kit kept her voice quiet but firm. "No, Linda, I don't think he'll do that. Everyone who knows you will know it isn't true. And from what you've told me, I don't really think he'd like to spoil his image by starting a scandal."

"N-no. Oh, Kit, do you think I *could* just go back home and start my life over?"

"You *must*."

Linda Barrone stood up and pulled back her thin shoulders. Her hands flew instinctively to her uncombed hair, trying to arrange it, and she took a deep breath. "I'll do it," she announced. "Somehow, I'll do it. The next paycheck . . . I just won't give it to him. I'll leave then."

"When is that?"

"In two weeks."

"Listen, Linda," Kit said after a second or two, "maybe you ought not to wait those two weeks. Maybe you ought to move now, while you're feeling strong. You don't have to do anything really *final*—just go away somewhere so you can look at it all objectively. Who knows, maybe that's all Jess needs to shock him into the realization of what he's doing."

A brief and bitter laugh. "Him? Not a chance. He's *got* all the answers already. You should hear his apologies after he's gone just a bit too far! Oh, how he loves and needs me, and oh, how I've misunderstood, and oh, what pressures he's under."

"Well, then, do it for yourself. For the children. Surely you owe yourself a few days to *think*. Your children are already at your mother's, you say? Well, you can simply join them. Does she know?"

"Good God, no! I *couldn't*. She's so proud of him, so proud that I'm the wife of a doctor. I think it would destroy her."

And I'm sure it wouldn't, Kit thought. Aloud, she said, "But she is your mother. She'll take care of you. You can think of a story to tell her—and it's only for a day or two."

"But— Oh, no, I couldn't. He'd make such a *fuss*."

Quietly, Kit said, "Still covering up for him?"

Linda bit her lips, her shoulders sagging once more. "Oh, I can't. I should . . . I must." She looked into Kit's eyes. "If I don't, Kitty, I think I *will* go mad. I—it's like living in a nightmare. We do our work, we attend social functions, we chat with our friends. And all the time it's false. And . . . *only I know it*." She shivered. "After a while, you know, you begin to wonder if you've just imagined it . . . I've never talked about it before. Not to anyone," she added after a moment. "I'm so sorry, Kitty. I mean, we don't even know each other any more."

"It's always much easier to talk to a relative stranger. For everyone. And I don't mind, really I don't." Kit smiled.

Linda Barrone stared sightlessly ahead, still twisting her hands. "It's become a lot more real, now that I've put it into words. You're right; I must go, and I must go now. If I don't . . . But—how can I?"

The answer was swift. "I'll give you the money. I have plenty. Don't worry. You'll repay me when you can. It's fine. You just go get dressed and pack and I'll get some cash. We'll meet back here."

For several moments Linda remained irresolute. Then she braced herself and tried a twisted smile. "Can you believe," she asked of nobody in particular, "that I still love him?" Without waiting for a response, she half ran out of the smoker.

Kitty entered her room on tiptoe and moved around as quietly as possible, hardly breathing, until she finally looked at Lee's bed and saw that no one was there. "Oh, dear," she murmured aloud. "What now?" She found herself irritated with her old friend; stupid, silly Lee, had she gone running back to O'Hara for some more punishment? What in the world was wrong with all of them? "All of *us*," she amended, staring unhappily at the empty bed.

All those smiling, laughing, joking, singing, drinking people downstairs before: Were *any* of them really what they seemed? Was everyone's life just a collection of façades, false faces put on merely to keep going? Even the biggest success story of the class, Lee Rivers, was riddled with old insecurities. Jess Barrone, the handsomest, smartest med student of all, was a sick man who had just about destroyed his wife. And what of Linda? Was she right that she half wanted her mistreatment, that deep inside she had known what she was getting into?

And what was Dan Copeland hiding? Kit shuddered a little and thrust the thought aside. Dan was . . . Dan. He hadn't really changed in ten years. She loved him. But Linda said she still loved Barrone. No, no, I won't think about that. Not Dan.

She would have to look at herself first: the hardest of all. What would Dan think when he discovered the truth, the whole truth, about her marriage to Whit Harris? "Too many lies," she whispered, clutching the thick wad of bills meant for Linda Barrone. "Too many lies." Maybe —the thought chilled her—maybe it was too late to change anything.

Ah, but it was not too late to help Linda. With a sense of deliverance, Kitty reminded herself that Linda would probably be waiting right now. Here was something real, immediate, substantive, to be done. Something that took no thought at all. She quickly left the room.

A few minutes later she was back, looking out the window, breathing in the fresh, slightly crisp morning air. As she watched, an old-fashioned square Checker cab pulled up in front of the dorm; and then there was Linda, her whole body taut with tension, scuttling down the front walk, nearly diving into the cab's open door. If it hadn't been so pathetic, it would have been comical.

As soon as the cab pulled away from the curb, Kitty felt her fatigue, like a heavy blanket threatening to smother her. Back and forth between the past and the present, she thought. No wonder I'm so exhausted. Her eyes positively arched with the need to close, and she yawned hugely.

A moment later her jaw snapped shut with amazement. Right down there, sauntering along hand in hand as if they had all the time in the world, were Lee and Benno. Lee and Ben! Now, how—? she asked herself, and then shook her head. She was just too tired to try to figure out how, in the course of the night, those two had found each other.

Sleepily, she raised the window higher and heard, from the street below, Lee's penetrating voice: "Wasn't that Linda what's-her-name-now, Barrone? Wonder what devil is after *her*, to send her racing off like that so early in the morning."

Kitty couldn't hear Ben's answer, just the murmur of his voice. But she had an answer for Lee: The same devil that's after all of us, my dear: love, true love.

CHAPTER FOURTEEN

Runner's World

THIS TIME the towel was gone, and the door opened when Ben turned the knob. He looked at the sprawled sleeping body and without hesitation walked over and began to bounce the bed.

"Up, up, up!" he caroled, heedless of the other's groans of protestation. "It's morning. Rise and whine!"

Without opening his eyes, Dan Copeland let out a stream of curses and vituperations.

"Oho, then you're awake. Come on, my man, and greet the dawn. It's a beautiful day!"

Yawning and stretching, Dan asked, "What time is it?"

"Not quite six."

"Not quite six! You lousy sonofa—!" Then he sat up, squinting at Ben. "What the hell's gotten into you? What is this greet-the-dawn crapola? Your nose used to bleed before noon."

Ben leaped off the bed, stripping off his clothes as he crossed the room. Almost naked, he leaned over his suitcase and went through it, throwing items to the left and the right. There they were: his Nikes. Holding the shoes aloft, he commented, "I'm a changed man, old buddy. Me for the great outdoors. See? My running shoes." He pulled on a pair of shorts and a T-shirt. "Come with me. Give you a whole new outlook on life."

Dan grinned and flopped back against the pillows. "I already have a whole new outlook on life. You run, I'll sleep."

Ben paused in the lacing of his shoes. "What do you plan for this morning?"

Another yawn. "I don't know . . . something. Maybe I'll walk Kit over to the dean's brunch." Dan's tone was completely casual, as if Ben had never seen the signal that said, "Stay out. Woman in here."

"What are you going to do about Kitty?"

The eyes flew open. "Do? I'm going to marry her, that's what I'm going to do."

"Ahem, my man, you may not have heard, but the lady is previously engaged in that activity."

"She can't stay with him now. She *can't.*"

"There's a child."

"I know. I'll marry her, too."

"You sound determined, Daniel."

"Indeed I am, Benno. This time she's not getting away." The mellifluous voice sounded as hard as iron. Funny, that love should make Dan grim and heavy. Ben felt quite the opposite.

Ten minutes later, running slowly and easily next to the tennis courts, heading out to the open road, he knew this would be a good run. In spite of the lack of sleep, his body felt in tune, the muscles all moving smoothly, without aches or cramps or twinges. He was as light as air, his feet bounding from the roadway as if made of rubber. He was breathing deeply, easily, taking in the sweet smells of early morning with pleasure.

Around the next curve there was nothing but open country, softly green, dotted with blazing scarlet and gold maples. Birds were singing everywhere, and the light was soft and hazy with promise.

A golden day, a golden day. He was surrounded by sweet silence and the smell of drying grass. He could hear his own steady breathing and the steady slap-slap of his feet hitting the roadway. He speeded up, feeling the warmth spread through his body. He was beginning to sweat now, he was into his second wind, in which he could barely feel his legs at all, the road was a best-loved friend, and if he wanted, he could go on forever.

A solitary house on the right; a small dog that scampered up to the fence and barked ferociously at him until he had passed the dog's turf. Brave little dog. But no mere dog could catch him this morning.

Somewhere along the country road he realized the sun was climbing high, that it was shining right into his eyes. He wheeled around and headed back, not even breathing hard, pushing his pace, stretching his legs, creating a wake of breeze. A car came along behind him, slowed, and the driver—a doughy middle-aged man, pipe clenched firmly in his teeth—gaped openly. Benno grinned at him, gave him a wave, and put on speed, passing him. A moment later, with an angry growl of the motor, the car went racing by, and Ben laughed. If he wanted, he could beat that car, any car. He was floating above the ground, he was strong, he was invincible.

The world fled behind him, a green and gold blur, and, sooner than he had expected, there were the tennis courts again, and Enders, and the campus. What a beautiful place this was! He sensed all the young and eager and wondering people, sleeping in this place, waking up about now to a new day, their lives stretching ahead of them like a gray fog. The unknown. How good it was to be beyond all that, to know the future, to see it shining before you.

Go back again? Not he. How futile and piddling even

to try. The answer was in today, in the perfect here and now.

There was a tree in front of Enders, an old thick-trunked maple. Nine feet above the ground, its first main branch stuck out. Slowing down a little, enjoying the swift response of his muscles to his brain, Ben smiled. If I can jump up to that branch, he told himself, she'll love me.

Nearing the tree, he flung himself into the air. And, like air, he floated up, his arms outstretched, and grasped the branch, his feet off the ground, his heart thumping wildly. He swung back and forth, laughing.

Lightly, he dropped down, landing perfectly on both feet, and started for Enders' front door, where he found half a dozen coeds clustered, applauding. He wanted to kiss them all.

CHAPTER FIFTEEN

Gladiators and Wariorrs

CLOUDS FLOATED like puffs of cotton in a cerulean sky and sent their shadows slowly and lazily over Hampton Hill. Below the bronzed and scarlet maples, between the stone and brick buildings, crowding the herringbone paths and spilling onto the clipped lawns, dark lines inched their way from every direction, all moving toward a large grassy oval surrounded by ramparts of old, rosy brick. The dark surging lines were in reality brightly dressed, noisy football fans, pennanted and pomponed, in such numbers that the automobile traffic was slowed to a creeping pace and the sounds of impatient horns mixed with the shouting and laughter and singing that filled the air.

Homecoming weekend. The traditional game. Seneca versus Hampton, a rivalry over half a century old. Signs held aloft by patriotic students said, "GO, HAMPTON! GO!" and "DOWN, SENECA, DOWN!" and "HAMPTON GLADIATORS SLAUGHTER SENECA BRAVES!" and "ROMANS CONQUER INDIANS!" and sometimes exactly the opposite. Hampton's colors of scarlet and gray mingled with Seneca's more flamboyant gold and purple as the throngs slowed to view the huge posters on the front lawn of every fraternity and sorority house and every dormitory. Some of them were better than twenty feet high, painted during laborious all-night sessions in four-foot squares and later assembled, in the dark of night, on a frame. The Sigma Chi poster, one of the largest, featured a very bosomy Indian maiden swooning into the arms of a spectacularly muscular Roman in full armor. WHEN DEFEAT IS INEVITABLE, RELAX AND ENJOY IT, was the message; around the base of the poster, fraternity boys dressed as gladiators bearing black plastic swords chased girls in Indian regalia with a great deal of shrieking and suggestive horseplay.

Slowly, slowly, the stream of humanity moved toward the stadium, past Fraternity Row, past the Science Building and the women's gymnasium and the chapel. Then, suddenly, reared Wentworth Stadium's solid stone walls. As people trickled in through the arched entrances, the huge Hampton marching band was already on the field, tootling and riffing as they warmed up for their opening number, the national anthem, followed immediately by the Hampton fight song.

At a quarter to one in the afternoon, several hundred spectators were scattered throughout the bleachers, eating bag lunches and waving their team pennants; but among the vast cavern of seats, they looked tiny and insignificant. Hot dog carts and popcorn and beer stands were set up, and soda vendors shouted their wares in loud voices. At each of the eight entrances, clusters of fans peered at the signs that sent FROSH TO SECTION C . . . PLACARD CHEERING, SECTION H, CHECK WITH YOUR LEADER . . . CLASS OF 1970, SECTION A, AND WELCOME BACK.

Earliest to arrive in any numbers were the '70 reunionites and the freshmen placard-cheering sections, dressed in red sweaters and gray pants or skirts. They all wore the little scarlet beanie known as the Frosh Lid, and they all held thick sheaves of instructions and a colored cardboard square, red on one side, silver on the other. They would sit together in a block and, at a signal from their leader, would each hold up a colored square. From a distance the red and silver squares would combine to form a simple message picture. This was a Hampton tradition from the mid-fifties and was clung to fiercely.

The class of '70 made its way, in groups and in couples, halfway up the bleachers overlooking the fifty-yard line to Section A. There, they stood talking, drinking beer, shouting to one another, preening themselves in the brilliant sunshine, and recapturing memories of scents and sounds and sights.

The hands of the big old-fashioned clock, gift of the class of '09, moved jerkily closer and closer to the hour of one, and each lurch of the big hand seemed to bring another wave of spectators into the stadium. Soon the warm-up of the marching band could hardly be heard above a babble of shouts, orders, vendors' cries, laughter, and some scattered impromptu cheers. On the Hampton side of the stadium it was becoming almost too crowded for comfort, as people mobbed in from different entrances, shoving and occasionally tripping over each other's feet.

A ripple of applause broke out as the cheerleading squad cartwheeled down the sidelines, white legs flashing amid a whirl of bright scarlet skirts; followed by a surge of cheers as the Hampton mascot, a gladiator, came onto the field, standing astride the back of a pickup truck artfully disguised as a chariot. Waving his silver sword with abandon, he circled the field several times.

Jock Standish pulled the hip flask from his jacket pocket—it had been his father's and he was proud of it —and took a long swallow. He looked for a minute at the tight young thighs and calves of the cheerleaders, at the flash of red panties, and licked his lips. Cute. Too bad they'd all go to flab a few years from now. He turned and shouted to nobody in particular, "Say, if all the virgins in Hampton were laid end to end . . ." and guffawed with delight when the quip was completed by several voices shouting back: "It wouldn't surprise me!" He took another, smaller swig from the flask. Better go slow, it didn't hold much. Better sit down, too, he decided as the familiar dizziness swept behind his eyes. He plopped down, then turned around and bellowed: "Say, if all the virgins in Hampton were laid end to end . . ." and then realized he'd just said that, so he finished it himself: "I wouldn't be surprised!" Maybe he'd better shut up.

Down on the field, the cheering squad was starting one of the old familiar cheers, warming up the crowd. Without really thinking, Jock joined in. He liked joining in, liked crowds, liked sports, liked teams, everybody pulling together. Sports taught you how to be a real man. "Give me an H!" yelled the head cheerleader, and Jock gave her an H with all of his might. Everyone in the whole damn stadium was yelling "H"; it gave him a nice, warm feeling.

The noise level throughout the huge amphitheater was steadily rising as the crowd thickened. It was a movie set of a day: bright blue sky; shouting, leaping cheerleaders; sun glinting off the brass horns of the marching band; elegantly dressed alums drinking and shouting and laughing; everyone revving up for the wonderful moment when the boys in scarlet and gray would come pounding out onto the field, powerful and padded, hearts thumping with the will to win.

As Lee and Ben came into the class of '70's section, they were surrounded. Lee had to laugh. In a minute, they couldn't move an inch. Fans! even here, even her old classmates, who ought to know better! It was wonderful. All she had to do was stand right where she was, and they kept pushing programs and napkins and autograph books and train schedules—whatever came to hand— onto her. She signed her name and signed her name and signed her name again, flashing her smile broadcast, not caring where it landed.

She felt floaty, buoyant. Something was happening to her, something wonderful, something so unexpected and delightful that she refused to put a name to it; refused, really, to think about it at all. It was enough for now to be totally aware of Ben standing just behind her, his hand idly rubbing her left wrist; to smell his shaving lotion; to know that he was there. They had not even kissed yet, and she was afraid to. But she needed to know that he was near.

What a day! What a perfect day! It made her remember her first football game at Hampton, when she had signed up for placard cheering in her freshman year.

How carefully she had dressed, in borrowed finery, her Frosh Lid sitting precariously atop her thick, unruly hair. She had emerged from the tunnel-like entrance into the dazzle of the open stadium, blinking and breathless. It had been so big, so full of color and sound. For a moment she had marveled at the twists of fate that had brought Leonor Rivera all the way from the Bronx to this. She had looked around, mouth open, thinking, Holy Mother, and every single person here is a *college* person. It had flooded her heart with warmth to realize that she was in a place with only collegians, which had meant to her that everyone was smart: no pregnant, ignorant girls, no pimps, no numbers runners, no welfare idlers, no crazy old people. Just smart people, college people. It had been the most wonderful moment of her life.

She had always thrived on noise and crowds, but in the barrio she had learned that the excited sounds were not always happy and that the busy crowds were filled with dangers. But not here, not in this place, not in a college. Here, it was all it had seemed to be. No dirty surprises lurking underneath. It looked perfect and it was. That was what she had thought that day, her heart flooded with a happiness so intense it had made her dizzy.

Sitting with the other placard cheerers, her eyes fixed firmly on the leader standing near the bottom row, she had concentrated on her card, a square of cardboard crudely painted red on one side and silver on the other. She had half sat on the purple-ink-printed instruction sheets. The leader had held up two fingers. Cheer Number Two. Lee had been number eleven, row K. On cheer Number Two, K-11 had held up silver. Silently, proudly, she had turned the card and held its silver side up over her head. With a thrill, she'd watched as the whole row, the whole section, just as quietly had held its cards up. From across the stadium had come cheers and whistles. Her heart had swelled with the wonder and joy of it all.

Lee signed her name again and yet again, and sighed inwardly for the happiness she had known that day. She would never experience it again, of course not. She had soon discovered that all college people were not smart and that football games bored her to tears. Ah, well . . .

Her eyes raked the little crowd still waiting for autographs, measuring their numbers. And she found Courtney's frantic face, tense with eagerness.

Everybody was pushing and shoving, and Courtney didn't like it a bit. After all, Lee was her sorority sister, and these other people, acting as if they owned her, hadn't even known her . . . well, almost all of them. For just a second Lee's eyes met hers, and Courtney sent out a silent signal. But Lee hadn't really been focusing on her, she was just looking around. Oh, *shoot*. Well, *she* wasn't going to demean herself one minute more by milling around like a silly sheep. She'd just go back and sit down. She had places saved for Lee and Kit, and she'd get the autograph then, after they'd all sat down.

It was nearly as difficult to turn around and get away from Lee Rivers as it was to get near her. Had Jock remembered to save all three seats? He was so hung over this morning, it was hard to tell if he understood how important it was.

As soon as she was out of the crowd surrounding Lee, Courtney shot a glance over to row F and her lips tightened. Jock was nipping from the flask already. He'd *promised*. She stopped where she was, leaning on the railing, and studied him. He looked like . . . like some kind of animal, gulping at the flask, as if he were starving, darting his eyes around and probably wondering if anyone was watching him. Well, *she* was watching him, and it was disgusting. It was just as if he weren't her husband at all and she were looking at a bum, a drunken bum. For the first time, Courtney wondered why in the world she had married him; at this moment, she couldn't remember.

On the concrete stairs leading to Section A, the air was slightly cool and damp and rather soothing. Kit and Dan walked together, carefully not touching, but she was totally aware of him next to her, of his rough tweed jacket, his scent, his taut, muscular body. When she was near him, everything else seemed to disappear. The physical need for him was so strong, it almost sickened her. It claimed her, took her over. The more she was with him today, the more uneasy she became.

They both stepped aside quickly to avoid crashing into the group of six chattering, hurrying figures clattering down the steps, and her hand accidentally touched his. It instantly brought images of him looming above her last night, the rock-hard feel of him . . . She shook herself mentally and said in a bright social tone: "Where do you suppose the New York crowd is going in such a rush?"

Dan gave her a swift, warm smile. "To New York?"

"Oh, they couldn't be. The weekend's just begun!" The moment she said it, a cold lump formed in her throat. Not for them. For them, the weekend was coming to its end. The thought clutched at her, and her heart began to race. Why had he insisted upon coming to the game? He had never liked football games. This was their only time left; they should be together, alone. They should be discussing things. Soon Whit would be here, probably right after the game, and then . . .

They emerged into the sunlit stands. The stadium was blazing with light and color and noise, and Kitty blinked, uncomfortable. This was *not* what she wanted. This was *not* where she wanted to be. Directly in her line of vision, Jen Gladstone bulked, a heavy silhouette against the bright blue sky, shifting from foot to foot and looking around, trying to appear casual. Poor Jen, was Kit's immediate thought. Waiting and waiting—for what? Just waiting for something to happen in her life?

And then she pulled herself up short. Who was she, after all, to pity a woman who waited? Kitty Cameron Harris was exactly the same: a woman who waited for things to happen to her. Who allowed others to put form to her life. Only once had she made an attempt to shape her own destiny—she had asked Whit Harris to marry her.

Some independent decision *that* was! she chided herself. Why, she had just been repeating her life with Mama: smiling, allowing herself to be dressed and primped, following all the rules and regulations. At this point you smile. Now you say thank you very much. Here you give a pretty little sigh. Always be polite to the Important People: the congressman, the minister, the president of the trustees. Behave properly and you will get your reward: a tinsel crown and adoration.

From Mama's grand scheme to Whit's. And now?

Now, befuddled by passion, she was all set to fit herself into Dan's life. This sudden insight so stunned her that she stopped all at once, causing three people behind to stumble into her.

This morning, for example, Dan and Benno had awakened both Lee and her at eight-thirty, hustling them good-naturedly but peremptorily into an itinerary already planned out. The dean's breakfast! Who in the world, except those in academia, ever bothered with that? Well, Dan Copeland did. He had looked at her with tender exasperation when she'd asked, "But *why?*"

"I'm giving a speech tonight, remember?" he had replied. "I really have to show up. I'm a politician, and politicians are always ... well, politic."

Yes, Kitty thought with growing anger, squinting off into the distance but not seeing anything of the colorful spectacle around her. Yes, all very well, but I'm not a politician, Daniel, darling, *you* are. *You* go to the dean's breakfast! I don't have to! And then she had to laugh at herself. Too late now; she had already sat through the entire boring morning, half asleep. How could he have! Had it been *that* important for him to give up his last few hours with her? I would have given up *anything,* anything at all, to be alone with him. Well, not Lily, of course—

"What?" she said, a bit stupidly.

"Where *are* you?" Dan laughed and snapped his fingers. "Come back, come back, wherever you are. We'd better go find seats before they're all gone. What a mob!"

"No."

"No? What, no?"

"Dan, we must talk. No, don't give me that look; I mean *really* talk."

"We'll talk, don't worry."

"No, there's no time left. I have ... something very important to tell you."

He grinned at her. "Darling Kit, everything you say is important to me."

"Don't condescend to me!"

"Kit! What's the matter?"

"Please, Dan, let's get out of here and go somewhere quiet."

"What, and miss a Great Tradition?"

Kit frowned at him. "Since when are you so big on tradition, Dan Copeland?"

Again he laughed. "All part of a politician's life. You'll get used to it." He wasn't looking at her, but searching out empty seats, his hand lightly but possessively on her arm.

I can't leave, Kit thought. Those are his rules. She pulled away from him.

"Kitty, please. Don't start battling me, not here, not now. Everyone is at the game. If we don't show, there's bound to be gossip. Not very discreet, to disappear together."

"Is this the same man," Kit said tightly, "who suggested I just pack up a few things when I get home and leave my husband? That wouldn't be very . . . discreet."

"Oh, Jesus! Kitty, I just don't want any gossip before we've talked with Whit. We can do that tonight."

"No, no!" she said swiftly. "I'll talk to Whit. This is first and foremost between Whit and me. You're not to say a word. Promise me."

He threw his hands up in surrender. "I promise, I promise. But I wish you'd leave the dirty work to me. I know what I'm doing."

That's right, she thought with growing bitterness. You always know what you're doing, you always take charge.

She must tell him the whole story before anything further happened. As soon as she thought about it, she knew it was the right decision. Enough of her being pulled along on the force of his feelings, his strength, his personality, his wants and wishes and desires, his, his, his.

She kept her voice down—oh, she could be as discreet as anyone—but it shook with intensity. "I have something to discuss with you. It is very important. Will you leave? Now?"

"Come on, Kitty!" he protested. She could see that he was amused more than anything else. "We can't leave at this point. It would be too obvious, and too many people have already seen us." His voice sank. "I'm just as eager as you are, my darling. Every time I look at you, I remember you last night, and it . . . I know how you're feeling. I'd like to be alone with you, God knows how much."

"That's *not* what I meant! Everything important isn't spelled S-E-X. I said *talk*, and that's exactly what I meant! And if you aren't willing to listen to what I have to say, then I'll see you at the twenty-fifth reunion!" She whirled, walking rapidly away, hardly believing she'd really said that. But, she realized, she meant it.

He called her name, low and urgently. The sound swung her around, belligerent and proud, to meet his soft and pleading gaze. He laid the palm of his hand over the curve of her cheek, and she could feel the blood rush and rise to meet it. She closed her eyes momentarily, willing her heart to slow its pounding, but it was no use. She could feel her whole body swaying, without volition, almost imperceptibly closer to his.

Like quicksilver, Dan thought, half bewildered and half annoyed. Just when I think I have her, she slips away. He was aware of a kind of power his nearness to her gave him, and he watched the blazing anger in her eyes melt away, but he felt no surge of triumph. He was more tired than he cared to admit. He loved her, he wanted her, but oh, God, how he wished she would quit fighting him. Last night he had dreamed of 'Nam. Why last night, after so many months? Why, in the wake of tumultuous love, when he should have been at peace, why was he once again at war?

That backfire and his crazy reaction must have affected him more than he'd thought. It had unnerved him, that was for sure. After so many years, in this place of peace, he was beset once again with that ice-cold feeling of danger—like a blade across his back. He had an itch to look over his shoulder.

If only she could read his mind. He didn't want to be here in the middle of a mob, either. His skin was crawling with a mixture of danger and erotic tension. If she only knew how much he needed her right now.

He had decided to tell her, had opened his mouth to speak, when a shrill, crazed voice screamed out his name from somewhere above in the bleachers.

"Dan Copeland! It's your turn!"

He knew. This was it. *Enemy,* his mind registered, and without any thought at all, he reached out to shelter Kitty.

Whit Harris had taken the stairs two at a time. Not that he was truly worried, but he could faintly hear the band warming up for the national anthem. It must be almost game time, and he was beset by the feeling, however unrealistic, that if he didn't find Katherine before the game started, he might not find her at all. That crazy telegram. Of course it was crazy, it sounded crazy, only crazy people sent telegrams of that nature. Still, where there's smoke . . .

At the top of the stadium he blinked into the sudden bright sunshine, then squinted into the crowd. Right away he spotted Lee Rivers. You couldn't miss that frizzy head towering over just about everybody. She was signing autographs, it looked like, surrounded by a bunch of squealing fans. Katherine wouldn't be there, but she was probably close by. All she had talked about was seeing Lee again. Unless that had been a cover-up for other plans . . . but no, of course not. He was letting that wire get to him, he who always operated on facts. He looked around, edging into the walkway above the stands. God, what a mob. Reunion weekend was always a mess; the cab had taken twice as long as it should have to get to the campus—

He saw her, but he had to look twice to be sure it was she. Her hair flowed down her back; she hadn't worn it like that since college, except in the privacy of the bedroom. He was so overcome by surprise that it took another second to realize that Dan Copeland was with her, standing close to her. As he watched, Copeland put his hand on her face in a gesture of unmistakable intimacy. A grunt of pain rose in Whit's throat. Ten years—ten years, and the redheaded bastard was still pulling his old tricks! It was too much, too much!

And then he saw her face, Katherine's face, the face of his wife, as it softened, yearned, tilted toward Copeland with a look of complete surrender that *he*, her husband, had never seen.

So. It was true, then. He had miscalculated badly. Some things, apparently, were never completely finished. All right, he had made an error. Now he would rectify it. He would—

He heard Copeland's name, shrieked out in a kind of frenzied rage, and instantly he knew that the voice and the hand that had written that telegram belonged to the same person.

She was standing, swaying slightly from side to side,

255

in the bleachers just above Section A: a woman, thin to the point of emaciation, dressed inappropriately for this hot, festive day in a long-sleeved black dress buttoned to the throat. Dark blue shadows looked like dirty smudges beneath eyes pale and glittering. She pointed one finger at Copeland and Katherine, chanting loudly, tonelessly:

"Beware, sinners, and hear your sins! Murderer! The slaughter of the innocents . . . my poor lambs. Your doing, Dan Copeland! Your doing! You and your whores! The name of the wicked shall rot. You will rot in hell, Dan Copeland!"

A pool of silence rippled out from her. Everyone had gone very still. The scene was almost surrealistic as all heads turned to stare at the masklike face with its stiff lips and fevered eyes; at the accusatory finger.

But beyond the hushed circle, the large noisy crowd was intent upon enjoying itself. And down on the field it was business as usual. At the very moment that the hands of the old clock pointed to the hour of two, the marching band broke into a blaring rendition of the national anthem, amplified over dozens of speakers. The crowd rose as one, everywhere but in this small circle, to sing "The Star-Spangled Banner."

The sudden blast of music took the crazy woman off balance and she paused, looking about wildly. Then she screamed—she couldn't be heard, but her mouth gaped wide with it. All through "The Star-Spangled Banner" her chest and shoulders heaved with the efforts of her drowned screams.

At the far end of Section A, Joe Rugowsky, looking as if he had been catapulted, hurtled the railing and then disappeared, Indian-fashion, into the crowd. His fringe of red hair bobbed through the bleachers, heading silently for the woman, who still ranted, unheard. At the anthem's ending, in a pool of sudden hush, her voice suddenly blared out. "Kitty Cameron! Whore of Babylon!"

Katherine! Whit's head snapped around. Copeland was one thing, but if she dared attack his wife! His wife, who, he noted, was pale but composed, standing very straight in the shelter of Dan Copeland's arms, her hand over his. How dare she advertise her indiscretions, her . . . her romantic follies in front of the whole of Hampton! No!

it was unthinkable! But even as he started toward them, Copeland released her, vaulted the rail, and made his way toward the crazy woman.

"Hussy!" she was shrieking. "That man is married. He should have married me, but Daddy wanted . . . Daddy, Daddy, where are you . . . ?"

Quite suddenly, she stopped mid-syllable, looking first to the left, then to the right. "Get away from me!" she shrieked. "Both of you! I've done nothing wrong! I've broken no laws! I've only spoken the truth, and the truth shall set ye free! Somebody? Seize *him*, take that murderer, Dan Copeland, take *him!*" But she did not move, and closed her eyes as if in surrender.

When the men each grabbed an arm, she went limp for a moment but suddenly shrieked and began to struggle savagely. Dan was amazed at the strength it took to hold her, and he was glad that Rugowsky had her other arm. He felt dizzy with relief; he was *not* crazy. His intimations of danger were not just nightmares left over from Vietnam. This woman must have been following them.

He and Joe managed to force her, a step at a time, toward the entrance. Halfway down, she went limp again. On either side of them, people backed off, staring, and a wave of agitated whispers followed them. At the bottom of the bleachers, their prisoner turned and spat at Dan, "I should have got you, Copeland! It's your turn. Murderer! Killer of innocents!"

For a shocked moment he saw Vietnam once again, the blasted earth, the ruined forests, the burned bodies; and he thought, It wasn't my fault. I didn't want to. I was just a kid! And then something in the cracked voice brought back a different memory. He looked at the drawn, skull-like face, the mouth edged with spittle, the eyes narrowed with manic rage, and suddenly, with shock, he recognized her.

"Serena!"

She did not respond. Although she glared at him, Dan realized that she was not really seeing him. She was looking inward, at some private horror.

"You killed her, Dan Copeland!" she howled, her eyes rolling. "Killed her, killed her, killed her! My baby, my baby!"

"All right, lady, take it easy," Rugowsky growled. "It's

all over now. We'll take good care of you." Over her head he raised his eyebrows at Dan.

"My wife's . . . my dead wife's sister. Her name is Serena Malverne. I—I haven't seen her for years. She disappeared. I wouldn't have known her." Dan paused, gazing at the ravaged face, the sunken sockets, the sharply jutting bones. "She's changed." But the eyes and the heavy brows were unmistakable; they were copies of Big Jim's.

"Changed? I can imagine," Rugowsky muttered. "Well, let's get her where she'll be safe. Come on, Serena, that's a good girl. Nobody's gonna hurt you."

"Murderer! Murderer! You will feed on wormwood and have but gall to drink! Murderer! Where is the retribution for the dead babies? Repent, Dan Copeland. Repent!"

Rugowsky flashed Dan an understanding look and shook his head sadly. "Off the deep end . . . too bad."

A hand touched Dan's shoulder and a deep voice said, "Okay, Mac, I'll take it from here. Thanks for your help." It was a trooper in full regalia.

"Hanley," Rugowsky said, "good. Where were you five minutes ago?"

"I was where I was supposed to be, on the other side of the stadium. Off duty, Joe?"

"Supposedly."

"It's always that way. Well, anyway, I called the ambulance from St. Claire's."

"Good." Rugowsky turned to Dan. "She got family nearby?"

Dan made a face. "Besides me, you mean? No, there's just her father. And he's in Wisconsin. I think I'd better call him. But in the meantime . . . should I come along?"

"Nah. You get in touch with her father. I'll get back to you later. Where you staying? Enders? Okay. Meantime, you go back to your seat and enjoy the game." He laughed. "If you *can*."

Indeed. If he could. Dan's eyes swept around, looking for his beacon: that pale and shining head. Then he saw her, her face parchment white. And then saw the arm behind her back, the hand curled around her shoulder, the manicured nails, the short blunt fingers, the heavy gold wristwatch that caught the sun. When the hell had Whit arrived—and why so suddenly? Whit's eyes met his, straight on, expressionless, yet somehow gloating. Dan nodded a greeting, let his gaze move on to Kit. He tried to meet her eyes. She looked at him, but her eyes were wiped clear of any emotion. He might have been looking at a stranger instead of the woman who only a few hours earlier had come again and again to him with avid demands for love.

He hesitated, then, jaw clenched, headed straight toward them.

"Fast work, Copeland," Whit said smoothly. His large, pale hand caressed Kit's shoulder. "Who was the other fellow? He looked familiar."

Looking at Kitty, Dan replied, "Joe Rugowsky."

"Huh! No wonder. He was always pretty fast for a big fellow. Won't they want you at the police station?"

Not a word about Serena. Not even a flicker of curiosity. Most people would want to know what the hell was going on. But not Whitney Harris III. He was a cool one. And as for Kitty . . . her expression hadn't changed. She looked frozen. Was this what it was like for her as Whit's wife? Was this what the bastard did to her?

Answering Whit's question, Dan said, "No. They're not arresting her. She's . . . disturbed. Obviously. They'll take her to St. Claire's."

"Typical bleeding-heart bullshit. The hospital! The woman should be put away permanently. But you'll see, they'll look her over and cluck a little and she'll be back on the streets by dinnertime tonight." Color had climbed in his face, and the meaty hand tightened perceptibly on Kit's shoulder.

"Things are not always what they seem, Harris." After a beat, Dan added, "She's Jim Malverne's daughter."

One eyebrow raised swiftly, then dropped. "Ah. Yes. And that would make her . . . your sister-in-law, I believe?"

"Yes." With tightened lips. If the bastard wanted to know any more, let him ask, damn him. But Harris was content to smile his smug smile. "Now, if you'll excuse me, I must call her father." Dan stared at Kitty, trying to give her a silent message.

Wait for me, he told her silently. Don't let him get to you. I'll come back and fight for you.

But there was no answering love, no desire, no melting softness in the green depths of her eyes. Just a warning.

CHAPTER SIXTEEN

Dan and Whit

DAN TURNED AWAY from Kitty and Whit and walked swiftly down the steps and into the dim, tunnel-like passage that led to the street beyond the stadium. It was cool and he was alone. The cheers of the crowd were muffled and far away. He stopped suddenly and stood breathing heavily, fists clenched at his sides.

Serena! The call to Jim would be hell. And what could Jim do for her? Serena. That tortured skeletal face! He tried in vain to see her as she had been in Madison, a blue-jeaned teenager, a bit bulky, a bit shy. Only Polly's vacant, pretty face appeared to him. Serena had disappeared right after the funeral. Jim had never mentioned her, had never mentioned either of them. Now Serena had stalked Dan to scream her crazed accusations of murder . . . maybe Jim considered him a killer. But no, of course not, Jim had been behind him all the way.

But Serena knew. She had screamed, "The murderer! He killed them! He killed them!" I didn't kill them, he thought in agony. I never *wanted* to kill anyone, not really. I was a kid, brought up knowing that we were the Good Guys, that our side was the side of Right. I didn't realize that they would actually *die*. That *I* might actually die. Not for a long time. Then there was the day when that child had died . . . by *his hand!* And then it became unendurable and the only way to bear it, to keep going, was to drink. You started as soon as you woke up in the morning, and you learned how much you needed —just a nice, thin haze of alcohol and a little dope to make everything bearable. Better to be off in dreamland

260

than to face the terrible shape of Death: an adorable little child or a pregnant woman or a wizened old man stooping under a load. The enemy could be anyone, anyone at all. But he had never *wanted* to kill anyone.

He walked on, his footsteps echoing. No! He suddenly realized that of course Serena hadn't meant Vietnam. She had meant Polly . . . and the baby . . .

The plane crash: the serene open field with its small lump of smoking wreckage, the bright sunshine spilling over the scene. Only Serena had wept, screamed, and raved into the deadly quiet. Polly, her mouth a trifle open, had looked asleep, unmarked, so pretty even in death. And all he had been capable of feeling was a vast relief that it had been taken care of so simply and so finally. Now he would not have to deal with his guilt. Because she could still arouse him, even after he'd realized something was terribly wrong with her. She'd liked playing little games, dressing up, painting her breasts like flowers—the nipples bright red—behaving like a whore. A few times he'd had meetings at home, important meetings. And she would call to him from the bedroom and he would go in and see the lights dimmed, incense burning, and her sprawled naked on the bed, caressing herself, looking at him feverishly, murmuring invitations in language he hadn't known she had learned. He should have been horrified, nauseated, repelled. Instead . . . she would look at his growing excitement and laugh, and he would flee, back to his waiting colleagues. But later, ah, later . . .

Kitty, Kitty, he thought, I never loved Polly. I never loved Polly, not at all. Then why did you marry her? he asked himself. Why did you follow her up the stairs to that little-girl's room? It had been so easy, and Big Jim had wanted . . . what, exactly, had Big Jim wanted? A son, perhaps. The invisible tiny fetus curled up in Polly's belly, had it been a boy? A son? He could no longer recall how he had felt about the pregnancy, except that he hadn't been able to leave her. Had she wanted that child? Kitty had a child. He tried to imagine them, Kit and the unknown daughter . . . His head was whirling. He groaned aloud.

Half an hour ago he had been up there in the sunshine, prepared to chat pleasantly with his old classmates, to cheer his team, to behave as politicians have always behaved at public events since the beginning of time. But it seemed a lifetime ago since he had walked into the stadium, holding his body carefully away from Kit's, his senses filled with her, the smell of her perfume bringing memories of the night before—the satiny smoothness of her skin, the look of her smooth, pale belly as the muscles tautened, her soft murmurings of delight . . .

Ah, the past was gone. He could not bring it back and change it. Vietnam was over and Polly was dead. The flick of Fortune's wheel, all of it. But for the rest of it—his life, his election, his love for Kitty—that was all up to him. He paused, tucked his shirt in tightly, pulled a comb through his hair, straightened his shoulders, and emerged from the quiet of the corridor into the warmth and confusion of Stadium Street.

He headed for the nearest phone booth, a three-sided shelter. He would have preferred something more private, but what the hell, it was there. Mechanically, he dialed Jim's office, looking out into the street. Above the clicks and hums and buzzes from the receiver he suddenly heard Serena's hoarse, strident voice. Craning, he saw the ambulance coming quietly up the street, its roof light flashing blue into the hot, sparkling afternoon air. And there were Rugowsky and his buddy, marching her professionally and as unobtrusively as possible over to the vehicle.

"Killed her . . . meant for *me* . . . No, Daddy, I don't want to any more, I can't, she's too fast . . . Don't make me pretend she's okay, I can't, can't, the kids all know, please, Daddy, let me kill him . . ." A spate of senseless words came pouring out of her mouth. Dan thought he had heard something important and was trying to think back, to catch it, when the phone was picked up in Wisconsin, the familiar voice growled, "Yeah?" and he had to start talking.

It was one of the most difficult things he had ever had to do. And he had to shout to be heard over the street noises.

"Who?" Big Jim yelled, unbelieving. "Serena? She *what—?*" And after a long silence: "Okay. I'm on my way." He hung up abruptly.

Dan stood holding the phone, hearing once more Serena's sing-song plaints in his mind. Wait a minute, he thought, slow down, let me get this straight. What had she been saying? She had been saying something quite important. "Don't make me pretend." Wasn't that what she'd said? She'd been talking about Polly, of course. Thoughtfully, he stared as the three of them piled into the ambulance, the big door banging shut. In a moment, it had pulled away and was gone from view.

What could she have meant? Was she completely crazy, or was it possible . . . could it be . . . that Jim had known *all the time* about Polly? If he had, then he had trapped Dan, had deliberately set him up . . . No! That was unacceptable. Not Jim, his mentor, his manager, his trusted friend! But a sense of dread was growing in him.

Ugly truths were coming to the surface, after years of careful deception and masquerade. And there were more to come; he felt it in his gut. Truth, truth, truth, he thought. We all insist that's what we want. But when it stares us in the face, it often looks like a death's head. The truth of what Serena had in mind . . . the truth about his marriage to Polly . . . about Jim . . . about what there was between Kit and himself, or Kit and her husband. If what was true all came out, all at once, it could destroy everything, everything!

He looked down at his hand, surprised to find himself hanging on to the frantically beeping phone receiver. He replaced it on the cradle and turned, wondering if Kit was sitting with her husband up there in Section A, nipping from a flask and cheering on the team. But no, of course not, that was not Kit's style, not now and not back then. She had never really liked football . . . never really liked crowds.

He stepped out of the phone booth and found himself face to face with Whit Harris. "You don't look so hot, Copeland. Did the lady get to you?"

Which lady? Dan wanted to ask; but he didn't want to start anything. Not now. Kit had asked him not to.

"I'm fine," he said.

"Did you get hold of Malverne?"

Dan squinted at the big bland face. It was hard to read. "Why do you want to know?"

"Come, come, Copeland. Surely you know that American Health has evinced an interest in your . . . election. It cannot be strange that I might want to talk to your manager."

"He'll be here later . . . on the governor's jet." What the hell did Harris want, really? he wondered.

"You going back there?" With a shrug to the stadium.

Dan looked up. Cheers and trumpet calls and a general roar seemed to emanate from the very stones of the high wall. The thought of climbing back up all those stairs, of climbing back to the old days, really . . . it made him tired, but he supposed he would, in the end, make an appearance. "In a while," he said. "I thought I might drop by The Pub for a beer first . . . some place quiet."

"I'll give you a lift," Harris offered.

"No, thanks."

"What the hell. The car's right there." He gestured, and the big silver Mercedes rolled up silently, as if on cue. "Maybe you'd like a ride in the country? It's quiet there."

Dan stared at the bland face for a moment. After all, why not? If he was going to take the man's wife, why niggle at taking a ride in his car? And in spite of Kit's warning, he couldn't help but feel that this was first and foremost a matter to be settled between Whit and him. Just as it had been back in college, just as it had always been. So he nodded curtly, and within five minutes they were settled into the soft, leather back seat, rolling smoothly over the patched country road, past fields stretching away on either side.

Both men sat in the far corners of the seat, as if putting as much space as possible between them. Dan was very aware of Whit Harris's bulk, of his air of authority. Damn the man. Would he, Dan wondered, lose his presence if they had been riding, say, on a bus? Or in a beat-up old Chevy? And he decided, No. Whit Harris probably always had that air of owning the world, ass that he was. None of the events of the day had so much as touched him.

And here *I* sit, Dan thought, drowning in old memories and old guilts. That crazy Serena! Why did she have to pop up *now*, when he had so many other things happening? Polly had been only a vague memory for many years. He stared out of the car window, watching the cow pastures and the corn fields, now sere and brown, skim by. At the end of this day, would he find his future as flat and bleak as that landscape of empty fields?

Damn it, he needed to do something, to *act*. Why did Kit demand the impossible of him? He had always, always, tried to play it her way, he was so afraid of scaring her off. All those years of holding her, kissing her, wanting her, only to be denied. How many girls had got the benefit of Kitty Cameron's "Noes"? he wondered. They had all responded to him like normal women, warm and passionate. And he couldn't remember a single one of them.

He was a one-woman man—and that one woman had always kept him at arm's length. Damn it, after last night he had thought all that was in the past. She had been wonderful, real, all there, all for him—the way it was meant to be. Yet today she was up to all her old tricks: pulling back, withdrawing, ordering him to wait. To wait for *what*?

Anger began to swell in him and he welcomed it. It was definite and powerful, and it was replacing all those other feelings, ambiguous feelings he did not really want to face. The question of Kitty: Yes, that could be faced. It was clear enough: Whom did she belong to? He knew the answer, and she knew it damn well, too. The only thing left was to let poor old Whit know.

"Scotch? Or do you prefer bourbon? Or perhaps a cocktail?"

"Huh?" He turned, wrenching himself from his thoughts. The Harris car—as of course it would—held a mahogany bar, completely outfitted with silver tools, bar glasses, and a selection of whiskeys. But why sneer at wealth? He could use a drink right now, in fact.

"Do you have Jack Daniels?"

"Of course."

Yes, it *would* be "of course." Dan took a large gulp of the drink. It spread, warm and soothing, through his chest, seeming to seep even into the taut muscles across his belly. He relaxed and yawned hugely.

"Didn't get much sleep last night?" Whit drawled. Dan looked sharply at him; the big face was as bland as ever. He'd known Whit Harris as a college boy and now he was seeing him as a man—a powerful and respected corporation president—and there was no difference. As a young Sigma Chi, Whit Harris had already known exactly where he was going and what his place in the world would be. Harris Pharmaceuticals would be his.

Such certainty had deadened the man to all other possibilities. His face was not etched with lines of sorrow or disappointment, indecision or self-doubt. No new knowledge sharpened the light in his pale blue eyes. Nothing had happened in the past ten years to interfere with his image of himself, shaped at birth, waiting only for him to grow into the outline and fill it out. It was frightening to look at a man who had never questioned himself, or, indeed, anything.

Dan found it hard to imagine Kitty living with this caricature of a human being, buttering his toast, asking his advice, turning to him in bed—no, the imagination boggled. Maybe Whit *liked* the cool, contained surface she displayed; maybe he never demanded anything different. Dan felt a surge of delight: All that warmth, all that passion, all that life, were for him *alone*.

"You'll never have her, you know. Never." Harris's unwavering stare was a challenge.

Good, Dan thought. Now the battle lines were drawn. He was ready. "You've never had her!" he countered.

The thin lips tightened a trifle. "She's *my* wife."

A shrug. "Nevertheless . . ."

There was a choked silence. Then Whit leaned forward and snapped, "Martin! Stop here!" The car instantly pulled to the side of the road and came to a halt.

Dan grinned. "Kicking me out? When we obviously have so much to talk about? Shame, shame, Harris." He drained his glass with a dramatic gulp.

"I'm getting out, too, Copeland. We'll walk back from here. And talk."

As soon as they were outside the car, Whit began to stride down the middle of the narrow road, not even casting a glance at the silver Mercedes as it passed them and sped silently away, dwindling quickly into the distance. Dan fell into step beside him, easily matching his pace; and for a moment or two they marched grimly along in unison, their feet hitting the ground at precisely the same instant, their faces set in identical stoic masks.

The afternoon sun was low in the sky, casting long blue shadows onto the road in front of them.

"What happened to *your* wife?" Whit asked abruptly.

"Died in a plane crash."

"Oh. Sorry."

How simple the world was for people like Whit Harris, Dan thought. Everything was diminished to a social gesture. Oh, your wife is dead? Sorry. You nearly got killed in 'Nam? Lucky you didn't. You've been making passionate love to my wife? Well, she's mine. But there must be some way to reach him, shake him.

"This can't be easy for Jim Malverne," Whit was going on in the same conversational tone. "One daughter dead and the other a crazy. She'll spend the rest of her life in an institution, no doubt." He shook his head. "A pity. One has such high hopes for one's children. Do you have any?"

"Isn't this all quite beside the point, Harris?"

But the inexorable voice continued. "Katherine and I have a daughter, did you know that?" His pale eyes slid sideways to catch Dan's puzzled nod. "Beautiful child. Reddish hair." There was a pause. What does he expect me to say? Dan wondered. But again, he simply kept talking.

"There's nothing like the joy of seeing a child grow up strong and intelligent and competent. Lily's athletic—she's as good as any boy, better than lots of them—you should see the way she sits a horse! I gave her her own, and she's grown up caring for it. Great character builder, that sort of responsibility. She's a wonderful girl. Katherine is very attached to her; they have an unusually close relationship." Again the delicate pause, the swift, darting glance from under the lids, as if to gauge Dan's reaction to all this.

"Speaking of Kitty—" Dan began, but the other man's voice rose over his.

"The Harrises can be traced in a continuing line from the days of Charles the Third of England. So, you see, Lily is very important to us."

"Yes, I can see that." Dan waved an impatient hand. "But let's get back to—"

"Too bad you haven't known that particular joy."

Irritated, Dan snapped: "I've never particularly wanted a child. Not in this lousy world."

"Oh, indeed?" There was something subtly different in Whit's tone, and Dan turned to look at him. The man was smirking, there was no other word for it. Just what in the hell did he think he had over Dan? His goddamn fatherhood? Was that supposed to make him sacrosanct—safe from a marauding lover?

"When Kitty's with me, Harris, I'll give her a dozen kids if she wants them." He enunciated each word carefully, as if to make sure that Whit had no chance to misunderstand even one syllable.

Blood surged into Whit's face, reddening the careful tan. He lengthened his stride suddenly, his fists clenching. Dan kept up with him, smiling to himself. He'd got to him. Finally!

"You bastard!" Whit exploded. "You haven't changed! You've always tried to corrupt her! Ever since the very beginning—you never let her alone, never let her be. After her, after her! She didn't want your filthy attentions. She hated it, hated it!" As he spoke, he walked faster and faster, flinging the words out before him like a spray of bullets.

Dan lengthened his own stride. "The hell you say," he shouted. "She's always loved me!"

"Never! Don't ever say that! She never loved you. She told me, don't think I don't know, how you pushed at her and tried to force her, all the way through school."

"I was good for her! She was all tied up in knots, afraid of her own feelings! I never had to trap her or force her! I set her *free!*"

To Dan's surprise, Whit began to laugh—a high-pitched, strangled sound. "Oh, Copeland, if you only knew what an utter fool you are! You set her free! Oh, my God, that's rich! You don't even know *what* you did! You sent her straight to me—to *me! She* proposed to me, did you know that? No, I see by your stupefied look that you didn't. Well, she proposed. She came after *me*. She wanted freedom, all right—from *you!*"

"That's a lie! She loved me, she loves me now. She doesn't need your—"

Harris stopped suddenly, whirling around, so that Dan

nearly walked into him. They were nose to nose, both breathing heavily.

"When I first met her," Whit said in a very different voice, so calm it sounded almost dead, "she was pure and perfect. I remember it just as if it were yesterday. We had elected her Sweetheart of Sigma Chi, and she came down to the living room at Enders. She looked like an angel, so serene and pale and ethereal . . ." He took a deep breath. "You cheapened her. With me she was always at peace, above anything tawdry—"

"*Sex*, you mean. Above sex."

"Keep your filthy thoughts to yourself. Katherine is a born lady."

Dan stared at him. "I don't believe this," he said. "You're not kidding, are you? A real lady, who won't demean herself to feel passion? Is that what you're trying to tell me?"

"I know her." Stubbornly. "I've lived with her for ten years."

Dan shook his head. "You've never really known her at all. You may have been married to her for ten years, but with your attitude, God only knows how the two of you managed to create a child!" He began to laugh.

The fist came flying at him so swiftly, he hardly had time to note it, much less duck. But Whit was so enraged that the blow glanced off the side of his head, making his ear ring. Whit made no further move but stood very still, rigidly controlling himself.

"Holy Jesus, and I thought I'd seen *everything*. Whose virtue are you protecting—Kit's? After she's been married for ten years, the mother of a child? Save the heroics, will you? She's no alabaster saint. And that's exactly why she's going to leave you, Harris—because this weekend she's had a taste of being treated like a flesh-and-blood woman. She loves it, Harris. And that's why she's coming with *me!*"

Whit rubbed automatically at the knuckles of his hand. "No. She won't go with you."

"Oh, yes, she will. I know her. I know what she wants." They both began to walk again.

"I won't let her go," Whit warned.

"You can't stop her."

"I can, and what's more, I'll stop *you* as well."

Keeping his voice even, Dan asked, "Just what is that supposed to mean?"

"I mean I have the power to ruin you, to end your career. Just like that—" He snapped his fingers.

Dan laughed. "You mean that lousy hundred thou? You can take that money and shove it! You think that'll end my career? You can't be that naive!"

They were already on the far boundary of the campus, at the very edge of the farmlands, and the top of Enders could be seen through a screen of trees, gilded by the low-ering sun. Suddenly, from the distance, came the thunder of a cannon's roar, followed by the clangor of the chapel bells pealing out the alma mater. And a swelling rumble.

Whit stopped in his tracks and smiled. "Hey! We won the game!"

Dan could only stare at him. Perhaps this was the core of Whitney Harris, that everything—wife, marriage, blackmail of another man, a winning touchdown in a col-lege football game—was of equal importance. No wonder he was always so calm. Nothing mattered enough!

Yet his voice, when he spoke again to Dan, was harsh with threat. "Remember Muskie? Top contender. Very popular. But he was finished, destroyed forever, by just one letter, one newspaper, and one press conference. Fin-ished, Copeland, by a story that wasn't even true.

"It's all so fantastically simple, you know, to plant a rumor, write a letter . . . to do anything, really, anything at all . . ." His voice had become dreamy, its very gen-tleness tinged with such menace that Dan felt a shudder between his shoulder blades. "I can do it, you know, Copeland. I have the contacts, the money, the power. Everything I need."

"You're forgetting one important fact, Harris." Dan made his voice sound certain, confident. "Hurt me and you'll hurt Kit, too, since she'll be living with me by elec-tion time."

Whit laughed, a short bark. "No, *you're* forgetting one important fact. Katherine will never go with you. I'm sim-ply warning you to stop bothering her, to leave her alone."

"And if I agree? How do I know you won't play dirty tricks, anyway?"

"Aha. You *don't* know. But . . . I *am* a Harris."

So saying, Whit quickened his pace just a trifle. So did Dan. He found this whole scene incredible. It was straight out of the nineteenth century; at any minute, he expected to be challenged to a duel. However, there was one real element in this farce: Whit Harris could do what he threatened—and very easily.

The politic thing to do right now, the Jim Malverne thing, would be to play up to Whit. Apologize like a gentleman, promise to behave, grovel a little—in a very masculine manner, naturally. Whit had all the aces, and it was a stacked deck, anyway. Dan was vulnerable; Whit wasn't. It was as simple as that. And she *was* his wife. Dan could almost hear Jim now, saying, "Hell, boy, go along. Take his advice and take his money now. Then, after you're elected, take his wife!"

The quiet streets were filling with people who had hurried from the game at the winning touchdown. Knots of kids were hurtling along, singing and screaming, on their way to the fraternity houses for the victory beer blast. And what looked like a solid phalanx of alums was crowding down the walks, heading for Enders, now just around the corner. It was now or never. Soon they'd be swallowed up in sociability.

Dan had a flash of himself thirteen years ago, fresh from Vietnam, his anger new and young, standing on the steps of the Poli Sci Building, shouting: "This generation will never sell out! By the power of our voices, raised together, we will *end* this war! And we'll go on and end the rest of the crap!" Oh, the roar of approval, the wild cheering, the clenched fists raised like clubs.

He'd meant every word, too. Copeland, the campus radical, the campus agitator, the campus firebrand, not far from becoming the Daring D.A. And now here he was, considering how best to save his own neck, steal a man's wife, and get applause while doing both. Figuring which lies he ought to tell, and in what tone of voice. When had he lost his courage, his convictions? On the first date with Polly, guaranteed to please Big Jim? Or even before, when he hadn't actively discouraged the lovesick look in Serena's eyes? When had he first begun to lie a little, cheat slightly, bend the truth to get ahead? Had it become a habit?

"No, Harris," he grated out. "I won't play. I won't be

271

blackmailed. I love Kit and she loves me. The cute little games are over. Do your worst. I'll beat you, anyway. And if this is the only way you can keep your wife, you don't deserve her in the first place!"

To his surprise, Harris laughed in genuine amusement. "You're not only a bastard, Copeland," he said, "you're a stupid bastard. I don't have to do a thing to keep her. She'll stay with me and it'll be her own choice. I guarantee it. You wait and see." And with a nasty little smile, he turned away, striding rapidly up the path.

A minute later Dan was after him, half running. The arrogance of the man! Kit would never willingly do any man's bidding. Only by force . . . He had to get to her first! Shoving impatiently past clusters of people, he took the stairs three at a time. If Whit so much as put a finger on her—!

Her door was closed. And locked, he discovered. He knocked as softly as possible, not wanting to call out her name. It would only attract attention. Their classmates were filtering upstairs; the sounds of footsteps, chatter, and laughter were everywhere. But she was there. He knew it. She was there, and so was Whit. He paused, listening, sure he could hear breathing, maybe whispering, beyond the door. Then he banged with his fist and called her name. No answer.

He wasn't going to let Whit Harris get away with this. He thought, I'll kick the goddamn door in if I have to. But then a call came floating down from the stairway, strident and familiar: "Oh, yoo-hoo! Dan Copeland! What's the trouble?"

Dan clenched his teeth, glaring at the solid door, at the silence behind it. Courtney—damn the woman! He pasted a smile on his face and reluctantly turned away. No need to make a federal case out of this, not in front of the class's chief gossip. He'd pretend to leave. But he'd come right back. What could happen, anyway, in ten minutes?

CHAPTER SEVENTEEN

Whit Harris and His Wife

KITTY STARED at Whit, who was leaning heavily against the door, his eyes darting about, his whole body rigid with tension. "What—?" she mumbled, her voice thick with sleep. She had been napping on the bed when he came bulling in, slamming and locking the door behind him.

He shook his head fiercely, warningly, a finger on his lips. From the hall outside there was the sound of running footsteps. Then the doorknob rattled and fists banged furiously on the door.

"Whit," she whsipered, "open the door!" He glowered at her, shaking his head. "It might be Lee!" Again no answer but that impatient shake of the head. The knocking and banging became more insistent, and she pushed herself up. It was her room, after all! Hers and Lee's. What in the world had got into her stolid, imperturbable husband? But when she approached him, his hand shot out and clamped on her arm, holding her immobile. Then came the unmistakable sound of Dan's voice calling her name. Kitty struggled in Whit's grasp and opened her mouth to protest. Instantly his other hand clamped over her lips. Frozen, she could do nothing but stare at him.

The banging ceased and it was suddenly very quiet. Then came the normal everyday sounds of people drifting upstairs, calling to each other, opening and closing doors.

When he took his hand from her mouth, she licked at her lips. "That was Dan!"

"I know who it was."

"What happened? Why did you lock the door? What's been going on between you two?"

The grip on her arm tightened. "Mr. Copeland and I have been discussing items of . . . mutual concern."

"Whit, you're hurting me!" He glanced down and released her, staring at his hand as though he'd never seen it before. Quickly she moved away, feeling suddenly chilled, and drew the silk robe more tightly, wrapping her arms around herself.

He gritted out: "You can stop barricading yourself against me."

"What are you talking about?"

"I'm talking about the fact that you are my wife. I've already reminded . . . *him;* now I'm reminding you. You belong to me, Katherine—no, don't turn away, it won't do you the least bit of good. There'll be no more turning away from now on."

Kitty stared at him. Her heart was thumping so hard she was sure he could see it shaking her body. She had been so positive she knew every facet of Whit Harris, that there were no surprises left. But the man who faced her— livid, quivering with rage, the hard muscles in his shoulders bunched for attack—was a stranger. And the smug way he looked at her—she longed to slap that look of divine right off his face, but he frightened her. She stared at him and felt a surge of disgust rise, like nausea, in her throat. Why, oh, why, she wondered, had she been so sure that marrying him was the only way out? Anything would have been better than their cold union of two strangers. But, of course, ten years ago anything else had seemed incredibly complicated. Impossible. Oh, God—her eyes stung with tears—if only she had had more courage!

The rain had been coming straight down in thick gray sheets, splashing as it struck the sidewalk on Columbus Avenue. Thunder rumbled off in the distance, but still loud enough to be heard over the New York City traffic.

Kitty ducked her head and walked doggedly, heading downtown. She was wearing a rain poncho with a hood, but it was short, and in just a few minutes her bare legs, still tanned from the Italian sun, and the pretty leather sandals were soaked. The omnipresent nausea was beginning to churn in her stomach. She had purposely set out on foot so as not to be forced into an airless bus or, worse, the dank confines of the subway system. But the sick feeling persisted, even in the fresh air. The mornings were bad enough, but it always got worse late in the afternoon. By dinnertime every day, she felt as if death were preferable to the gagging that threatened to choke her.

It was close to six right now, and here she was, getting sicker right on schedule. Under the rubber poncho, sweat began to trickle down her sides and between her breasts. Only the thought, reiterated silently again and again in her head, that all this would soon be over kept her walking. Soon, soon, she promised herself. But clamminess enveloped her, and her head began to spin. Afraid that she might faint, she looked wildly around for some place to rest. And found herself in front of an antique shop, its curved windows dimly lit from within. Its front door stood wide open.

Gratefully, she slipped through the door and leaned against the jamb, her eyes half closed, swallowing repeatedly.

"Miss? Miss? Are you all right?" A huge woman loomed up next to her, billowy curves swathed in what looked like a hundred yards of brightly colored cotton. Her face, almost lost in folds of rouged flesh, was kind, concerned, and Kit almost burst into tears.

"I . . . I'm feeling faint, that's all."

"Oh, you poor thing, and it raining like all hell just broke loose—except, of course, it doesn't get wet in hell, does it? Well, never mind, just come on over here, let me take your raincoat—no, it's all right if it drips. The floor's not an antique." She laughed.

The flood of talk was as soothing as a warm comforter. Kit allowed herself to be led and seated and hovered over, She breathed deeply of the dusty-smelling air.

"There, now. That's better, isn't it? No, no, don't thank me. There won't be any customers, not on an afternoon like this. Funny, isn't it, how rain keeps people from going out? You'd think they were made of sugar and are afraid of melting. Here, let me get you a little sip of sherry—it's good for what ails you."

Kit thought bitterly: Not for what ails *me*. But she leaned back in the overstuffed chair, unwilling to open her eyes, grateful for this moment's respite. She had to be at the doctor's office at six-thirty. That was after his regular hours. She had been told to ring three times. He was expecting her—that is, Kitty thought with brief rancor, he was expecting "Mrs. Smith." So Mrs. Smith she would be, with her dime-store wedding band, her soaked shoes, and a face she knew was paper-pale and slick with sweat.

A large glass was pressed into her hand, and she sipped gratefully. She opened her eyes and managed a smile at the woman, who grinned back at her with a flash of gold teeth and said, "Better, eh? I thought so. Now, you just sit there and drink your nice wine. Don't bother about me, I'll just be puttering around. When you own a place like this, it's dusting, dusting, dusting all the time. Well, then—" And abruptly she moved away, humming a little.

The wine went swimming straight to Kit's head. It was a nice sensation, numbing her and making everything— her nausea, her fear, her jumbled thoughts—seem very far away. Dr. Burns, with his after-hours special services, also seemed very far away. She took a larger gulp of the sherry, thinking, Good, I'll get sloshed and then it won't really be happening. She wanted Mama so badly, needed her so much! But her mother would be absolutely useless in this situation; her mother would recoil from the entire thing.

Well, who could blame her? I'd like to back off from the whole thing myself, Kitty thought. It was hard to believe now that she had found those hours in Florence so magical, that she had been so eager, so full of hunger. It had all led to nothing but trouble, just as she had always thought it would. She had always had the feeling that Dan was a dangerous man to get too close to. But now he was out of her life forever.

She studied her refuge, a large, high-ceilinged room jammed and crammed with huge old pieces of furniture. Breakfronts and armoires towered over her on every side, cheek by jowl with highboys and lowboys, chests and trunks, étagères and bakers' racks. And everything that contained a shelf had objects crowded onto that shelf: bits of brass and iron, Dresden figurines, bells, old picture frames, boxes by the dozen. There was something ordered about this disorder, perhaps because everything looked clean and cared for, washed and polished and waxed. The wonder, to Kitty, was that the proprietress was able to maneuver her large bulk through the narrow spaces. Did she go sideways . . . or just point the way to a customer . . . or perhaps, like Peter Pan, fly overhead? Oh, dear, the sherry was really making her muddle-headed!

Kitty sighed deeply and wondered how late it was getting. She really had to be going. She sat up straight, pretending to be organized, and prepared herself to leave. And there, directly in her line of vision, was the little angel, obviously a garden ornament. It was a fat cherub, its head cocked to one side, smiling and dimpling—she could see the carved dimple even from where she sat—beating on a tiny drum, all made of gray stone and yet so lifelike, so impish, so endearing, so . . . *alive.* The dear little baby, she thought, and then stood up as if levitated by her sudden, irrevocable decision.

"I can't do it," she said aloud. She reached out one hand to gently touch a chubby stone arm. It was smooth and warm, and for one instant she had the sensation of touching flesh. I'm going to have this baby, she thought, no matter what. I just can't . . . kill it.

Looking around for the owner, she called out, "How much for this?"

The woman peered out from behind a sideboard, squinted, and said, "The cherub? Well, it's kinda old. Two hundred is what I'd planned on, but I'll *take* a hundred and eighty in cash." She waddled over, smiling broadly, and remarked: "So. I was right, what I figured."

"About what?"

"You're pregnant. I knew right away. More than the sickness, there's a look you can't miss. Yup, I knew, all right, and this is a celebration present, is it? Awfully cute, isn't it? Those Italians, they know how to do babies."

"I'll take it." For the first time in weeks, she was absolutely sure of a decision. That cherub was *hers.* "That is," she added hastily, "I'll pay you for it. But I can't take it with me. I'll have to let you know when I can take it."

"Not to worry, not to worry." For several minutes there was a great deal of hustle and bustle as the bill of sale was filled out and a sticker put on the statue and phone numbers exchanged; and then it was done. The money meant for Dr. Burns ("pay in advance") was gone, and Kitty was outside, where the storm had subsided into a misty drizzle through which street lamps sent out phantom halos of light. She took several deep breaths of the damp, faintly cool air and started to walk downtown once more.

She came to a dead halt at the edge of Columbus Circle. Wait a minute, where exactly do I think I'm going? she thought. She couldn't go back uptown and face that empty room. She watched the heavy traffic circle around and around, and laughed at herself. It was all very well to disdain the idea of an abortion. But reality must be faced also. She had to her name right now one scholarship to Stanford which she couldn't use; one little statue worth a hundred and eighty dollars which she had no place for; thirty-five dollars in traveler's checks; a baby on the way; and a dime-store wedding ring. What was she going to do? Go home to Mama? That was no good. Go to Dan? Out of the question. He scared her.

And then it came to her. She had the obvious solution. There was a phone booth on the corner of 59th Street and Eighth Avenue, and she headed for it without another moment's hesitation, dropping the cheap ring in the middle of the street and putting a hand to her belly to reassure herself that it was really still flat.

He was still in his office. "Hello, Whit?" Her mouth was dry. "It's me, Kitty."

"Katherine! Where are you?"

"Columbus Circle. I'd like to see you . . . Could you—?"

"Could I! I'm a block and a half away! Do you . . . can we . . . ?" He cleared his throat. "May I take you to dinner?" he asked in a more formal tone.

Alone in the phone booth, she smiled. Good old predictable, solid, substantial Whit. He hadn't forgotten her; he hadn't changed. Now everything would be just fine.

"I'd love to have dinner with you," she replied in her best sweet-girl voice, the voice she knew he always responded to. "Where shall we meet?"

"I'll pick you up, of course." Of course. "You just stay right where you are and I'll—where *are* you, by the way?"

Kit smiled again. He was flustered. Good. Then he was still smitten; he hadn't found someone else. She closed her eyes in a silent thank you and told him precisely where she was. After he had rung off, she shut the telephone-booth door firmly and fixed her makeup as best she could in its feeble light.

Afterward, she never could remember the name of the little French restaurant, where they sat side by side on a plush corner banquette. She only remembered that it was dimly lit by tiny pink-shaded lamps, one on each table, lamps that gave so little illumination that the waiter, who materialized instantly at the table, was almost completely in shadow . . . and the only things she could see in detail were the bouquet of marguerites on the table and Whit's blunt-fingered, pale, meaty hands with their manicured nails and the heavy gold signet ring.

He was so pleased to see her. It made her feel relaxed and safe. And grateful. As a matter of fact, looking at his face, which was flushed with pleasure and more animated than usual, she felt a surge of affection. She reached out and took his hand, managing to startle him considerably.

"Katherine?"

She laughed, very aware of his lovelorn look, and very aware that she was acting in a way he had long hoped for. She wrinkled her nose at him, leaned forward, and gave him a light kiss on his lips, hearing his sharp intake of breath with an excitement growing inside her. It was going to work out! "I'm glad to see you, that's all. Aren't you glad to see me?"

"Glad to see you! I thought—that is, it was my understanding on graduation day that you would be in California at least for the next two years. This is . . . completely unexpected, you must realize that. And to find you so . . . so . . ."

"So *what*, Whit?" She looked at him from beneath her lashes.

"So . . . affectionate."

"After all those long good nights all the way through school . . . didn't you consider them affectionate?"

"This is different."

She had to look down. "Ah, well, I haven't seen you in so long. And . . . and . . . I missed you." She held on to his hand tightly and took a deep breath. "Whit . . . Whit, listen. I'm ready to marry you now. If you still want me."

She could not resist glancing at him and then almost wished she hadn't. Across the bland, broad face, several emotions chased: first a slight frown of puzzlement, followed by a flash of triumph, smug and gloating; then everything wiped away, to be replaced by his standard I-love-you-aren't-you-lucky look. For one infuriating moment she was tempted to pull her hand away and run out of the restaurant. In her mind's eye she could see the whole scene: she, pushing by the table, the glasses all trembling and clinking together at her rush; Whit, dumbfounded, unable to move for the shock; and she, out in the dark, neon-lit street, free, her own person once more, running . . .

Ah, yes, but running *where?* She dropped her eyes, studying the starched white napkin lying in her lap, examining the way it cast crisp blue shadows in neat patterns.

"You'll never regret this," Whit was saying, and she looked up at him, coming back from her fantasy flight. He was, she realized, completely oblivious to anything she felt. He was capable only of seeing what was directly on the surface. "I'll always take care of you," he went on, and she nodded at him, smiling her good-girl smile. But inwardly she was shouting: Fool! Don't you even want to know *why?* Don't you even wonder why I've suddenly changed all my plans? Don't you *care?*

She watched his face as he talked. He was always so clean-shaven, it was difficult to believe his beard ever grew. His skin looked . . . polished, well padded. He was a handsome man, she decided, but his eyes were like mirrors, reflecting what he thought appropriate to the occasion. Whereas Dan's were windows, giving you a glimpse into his soul. When he had made love to her, they had been smoky with desire . . .

She must not think of him, she must *never* think of him again. She had made her choice and here it was, smiling at her in the proper manner, calling for champagne in the proper manner.

"When shall it be?" he was asking. "Christmas? Or perhaps New Year's Eve. Unless, of course—" Properly tender, he leaned toward her just a bare inch more to show intimacy. "Unless you've always wanted to be a June bride?"

"June! Oh, no! That's much too long to wait!" Panic squeezed her. This baby would be born in May! But she must be cautious, she must be very careful with him, or it would all be ruined. She gave him a brilliant smile and took a large gulp of her champagne. "We've been dating since our freshman year . . . dear. Why wait so long?" And was rewarded with a tender look.

"Very well, then, what do you think of New Year's Eve? It would be ideal in many ways. The whole family's always together over the holidays, and we could have the wedding in the Long Island house. I think we'll live there, Katherine; you don't want to crowd into my apartment in town, do you? And we'll have a lot of entertaining to do —there's a staff at the house. It hasn't been redecorated since Mother did it ages ago . . . you'll have a *wonderful* time. Just call McMillan and they'll send someone." He paused and smiled at her. "I'm babbling on, aren't I? It's just that I'm so happy . . . dearest Katherine."

Kit took another drink. Secretly, it was her toast to their first cautious endearments. Was it her imagination, or did the words come out somewhat strangled from both of them?

"New Year's Eve?" She pretended to think it over. "How about . . . next week?" She laughed gaily. "How about City Hall?" He was half scowling, trying to hide his distaste. She spoke quickly. "Oh, Whit . . . *darling* . . . you know how I hate crowds, how I hate being the center of attention. Remember the Sweetheart of Sigma Chi event? Remember how you rescued me the first time we met?" She inched over on the soft seat, closer to him, letting her voice drift off.

Whit licked his lips, flushing a bit. "Of course I remember," he said. His voice had softened. She was going to win. Then he added tenderly: "But don't *you* remember? I convinced you it would all be just fine, and it was. You were the most perfect Sweetheart our chapter ever had . . . New Year's Eve, I think. Now, you'll probably want to use the bridal department at Bendel's—Mother always said they're top drawer." He put a finger over her lips, which were opening to protest. "Don't worry about a thing. Just go in and arrange everything and charge it to me."

Oh, great! Just great! Kitty thought. She felt as if a soft, doughy bulldozer were pushing her, ever so gently but ever so inexorably, right against the wall. I wonder, she ruminated, what Bendel's has in the way of all-white maternity numbers. She had to stop this, but looking at him, knew she would be powerless against his assumption of control. She thought quickly, desperately. She had to do *something,* and she had to do it *now.*

She sidled over until her thigh touched his. "Oh, darling, don't let's talk about dresses," she murmured. "Let's talk about *us.*" And she held her glass to his lips, offering him a sip. "That's right, where my lips touched the glass." Then she turned the goblet and took another sip herself, looking at him through her lashes. Color climbed in his cheeks and he pulled in a ragged breath. Snuggling against him, she put one hand on his cheek, very lightly, stroking his skin with the tips of her fingers. He grabbed her hand, bringing it to his lips, which were dry and very hot. She smiled at him wistfully, whispering, "Darling . . ." Gently, she drew her hand from his, letting it linger over his lips, then passing it slowly along his jaw and throat, until it was resting on his chest, where she could feel the loud thumping of his heart.

"Katherine," he protested, "I really don't think . . ." but she shushed him, leaning over to refill both glasses with one hand while she ever so casually slid the other hand down his torso—she could hear him gasp quietly—and finally letting it rest, fingers splayed possessively, on his hard thigh.

Kit stared at him, scrutinizing every change in his eyes. She dared not move too fast or he might recoil. For a dreadful moment she thought she saw something uneasy in his eyes, but she must have been mistaken, for immediately after, he moved even closer, hip to her hip, and curved an arm around her shoulder with his fingertips hovering just above her breast.

At that moment, more than anything else, she longed to lean into his solid strength, to be surrounded by it, enveloped by it, to find her own strength in it. She wanted to cry, to let go. She was so weary, so sick of the struggle. She looked up at Whit, her eyes swimming, and he said huskily, "You know what you're doing to me, don't you, Katherine?" His hand brushed her breast. "You know what I'd like to do right now? Take you to my place, where we could be alone . . . but—"

"No buts," Kitty interrupted softly. "Let's."

She would never forget the look on his face: a blend of

shock and delight as she rose from the table, daring him with her eyes to follow.

The look was still in his eyes as, once in his bedroom, he undressed her with faltering hands: the look of a man who cannot believe his success and cannot quite handle it. He gazed at her naked body lingeringly, biting his lower lip, and then turned out the one dim lamp by the bed.

They made love in a smothering darkness. He was a silent lover who entered her eagerly, and eagerly pounded at her in a regular, almost mechanical rhythm. Her memories of that night were of his sobbing breath against her ear and the relentless weight of him as he drove into her. She held on to him for dear life, doing her best to seem responsive.

When he had finished, he rolled immediately off her and lay panting next to her in the darkness. He had said not one word. She groped for his hand. Suddenly he spoke. "Good. Now you're mine." And she answered, "Yes." And so they were married within the week, just as she had wanted.

That was why she had married him: for his utter certainty that she belonged to him, and for her certainty that this meant safety.

The trouble was, he had never changed. He always came to her in darkness, always claimed her body without preliminaries, always took her with the same remorseless rhythm as the pounding of a drum, always withdrew from her with the same announcement: "Good." And, always, she could hear the silent words that followed: "Now you're mine." It had been a fantasy, thinking she could gather strength from him. Whitney Harris III never gave anything away, not even on loan. Any strength she had gained had come from within herself. Their whole life followed that pattern. He lived his life essentially separate from her, making contact only occasionally to ensure that she hadn't forgotten whom she belonged to.

Quietly, she said to him now, "You've never let me forget whose wife I am."

"And this weekend . . . ?"

"What about this weekend?" Her fists clenched reflexively and she saw his eyes flick to her hands, amusement quirking the corners of his mouth.

"I don't think it's necessary to discuss it . . . ever."

Her voice rose. "And what if *I* think it's necessary?"

"What you think, my dear, matters not. I have settled it, and the subject is closed. You will never speak to . . . him again, is that clear?"

She stared at Whit through a haze of anger. Those two, behind her back, had discussed the whole thing, and between them had worked out her fate. It was as if she were the spoils of combat! She didn't know where to direct her fury: at the absent Dan, who had broken his promise to her, or at the self-satisfied man who so calmly faced her now, giving orders.

In a voice she hardly recognized as her own, she gasped, "You—can't—tell—me—what—to—do! You can't make rules for me, not any more! This is *it!* I'm leaving you!" She whirled, heading for the closet to get something to wear, the breath sobbing in her throat with fury.

He came after her. "You try it. You'll never see Lily again!"

"Don't threaten me with Lily, you smug, pompous, self-satisfied ass! How dare you—*how dare you!*" Red splotches danced before her eyes. "You can't threaten me with Lily. She's not even yours!"

The silence that followed was so absolute, she could hear echoes of her own words ringing in her ears like the cries of dead dreams.

There was no joy at having deflated him at last, only dread as the silence dragged on. She could not breathe . . . and then she could, but it hurt her chest and there was a thin, high ringing in her ears.

I never said it, she thought, I didn't, I never said it! It was like a prayer.

She did not want to look at him, but she knew she must. Sweat broke out on her upper lip as she forced her eyes up, up, up to the horrible, the inevitable, confrontation.

But what she saw in those pale eyes was neither shock nor consternation, nor even the total rejection she had expected. No, it was the feral gleam of victory, a look she had seen all too often when he had got the best of someone—a look she had always hated. She opened her mouth to speak, but nothing would come out.

"That's right, Katherine." He smiled. "I've always known."

Again her mouth moved.

He went on. "I can't father a child, Katherine. I am sterile. Oh, yes, it's quite, quite certain. Let's just say that I was . . . ah . . . *amused* when you told me we were expecting a little bundle from heaven so soon after we were married. Where could it have come from, this happy surprise? I asked myself . . ."

Kit's hand flew out. "Oh, Whit! I'm—"

He gestured her to silence. "I knew you had remained faithful to your lawfully wedded husband. I cannot fault you there. It was a question of . . ." He paused delicately. ". . . *before* the fact, as it were. It had to have happened in Italy. I wondered for a while if I'd be presented with a little wop baby—"

"Whit! Please—God!"

"No, not God, Katherine. Dan Copeland." He gave a mirthless grin. "I only had to take one look at her the day she was born."

Kit buried her face in her hands, barely breathing. In one moment he had turned her world upside down, and yet he stood there, perfectly calm, perfectly composed, completely in charge. She looked up and blurted out: "I don't believe you!"

"Don't talk nonsense, Katherine. I'm in no mood for stupid denials or other lies."

"I mean, I can't believe you'd—you'd *keep* us all those years, if you knew! Why did you do it? Why did you pretend for all these years?"

"Why did *you*?"

She could no longer stand to look into his eyes. At once she hid her face in her hands.

"I kept you and Lily," Whit said in a remote tone, almost as if he were telling a story about someone else, "because it suited my plans. I wanted you; you were the ideal wife for me. I'd known *that* since the first time I saw you. I couldn't believe my luck when you called that rainy day and told me you were ready to marry me.

"I should have known . . . And when you announced your pregnancy, then, of course, I was certain you were just using me. But, as it happened, I could use *you*. A workable basis for a marriage, don't you think? I had been wondering how to keep my . . . problem a secret from my family. It would have infuriated Father to learn that the Harris line had ended. This way, with a child, he never had to know. It seemed a reasonable solution . . ."

Her voice muffled through her fingers, Kit said: "Why didn't you tell me? Don't you think you should have told me?"

A harsh laugh. "You're a fine one to complain, Katherine. We were even. Of course, I watched you very carefully—what man wouldn't, under those circumstances?—but it seemed you weren't interested in other men . . . I have never had cause for complaint. Until now, you have been an exemplary wife, and I have been very pleased with you. Until now. And I have come to cherish Lily as if she were my own child." Again that bark of a laugh. "She *is* my child. Everyone sees a lot of me in her, isn't that true?"

She heard his heavy footsteps approaching, felt him standing very close to her. And then he took her hands in his and forced them down from her face, remaining silent until she raised her head to look him in the eyes.

"Now, then. Listen to me carefully, because I'm going to say this only once. Lily is yours only as long as you remain in my house, as my wife. No, don't wiggle; I'm not letting you go until I've finished. If you leave me, I will take her away from you."

Mesmerized, she stared into his narrowed eyes, hard as stones. "You can't do that!"

"On the contrary. I *can* do that. I *will* do that. I'll tell you exactly what I will do. I will start court proceedings for custody. I will tell the whole story . . . everything. I will explain why I was willing to bring up your bastard as my own child. I will—"

"No! You can't do that! It would destroy her! You can't do that to Lily!" She struggled, but he had her hands fast in his grip. "I'll kill you! You hurt Lily, and I swear I'll see you dead!"

"Oh, Katherine." His smile was a rictus. "I'd hate for a judge to hear you quoted. I should think that my case would be that you are emotionally unstable . . . which you have certainly acted these past two days, haven't you?"

"You're hateful—horrible!"

"Am I? And you haven't really had more than a hint of what I can do."

"You're a monster!"

"Not a monster, Katherine, just a loving husband who had let things slide a bit too long and has decided to save his home and his marriage."

Kit sighed. The room was airless and he was too close. In a moment he would smother her. She squirmed in his grasp again, without hope, and said dully: "*What* marriage? We've never *had* a marriage! It's all been phony, from beginning to end! All of it!"

"Phony, has it? It's been phony? All right, the pretense is over! Now I'll show you something real!"

With a sudden, violent push, he shoved her backward to the bare floor. She gasped for air as he flung himself onto her, bearing down heavily. He yanked off her robe and tore at the flimsy silk of her underclothes. She fought wildly, kicking at him, pulling his hair, pushing against the bulk of his chest. "Stop this! Stop!" she hissed, even now aware of the thin walls, but he was panting heavily with rage or lust or both, and seemed not to hear her at all. The weight of his body pressed down on her; his hands seemed to be everywhere at once, and then his mouth, wet and greedy. She writhed and wriggled frantically, twisting and turning, trying to escape the avid lips, the probing fingers, the massive erection that throbbed through his clothing against her thigh. She sobbed with her efforts, her eyes wide open and staring at this strange, wild creature who growled in his throat and leaned on her with one powerful arm while he stripped rapidly, flinging his clothes across the room.

He entered her with a jolt that drove the breath from her body, covering her mouth with his, molding his hands around her hips to lift them, lunging into her so deeply that she felt each stroke as a pulsating electric shock. It was impossible to breathe; she was suffocating. She bit his lower lip viciously and tasted the salt of his blood on her tongue; but he did not pause, only groaned and thrust harder, nibbling at her lips, then lowering his head to suck and bite hungrily at the flesh of her neck and her breasts.

Shivers began to run over her spine, little thrills that moved lower and lower, then swiftly became deep, deep

shudders. In her head she was screaming, No! No! No!
but she no longer had a voice, she no longer had a will,
she was nobody, she was only a mass of sensations, one
piled on the other, shock after shock, shudder after shudder, and all of it centered on his flesh that stroked and
pounded, making her feel . . . making her want . . .
making her move with urgent thrusts of her hips, frantically pushing into his—

And then he stopped. He came to a sudden halt and
reared back, grinning down at her, licking the sweat
around his mouth. To her horror, she heard herself beg-
ging, "Don't stop, don't stop!" His answer was to swoop
down on her with an open-mouthed kiss so avid, she
thought he would suck her completely into him; and then,
drawing back and laughing, he rolled them both over so
that she lay, her heart hammering, astride him.

"Now!" he ordered. "You! You want it, *you* work!"
His face was flushed and gleeful, hateful . . . and yet
she was unable to stop herself from moving faster and
faster, from arching her back in pleasure, from trembling
with anger and loathing, and yes, with lust. And she
gloried in it. Her hair, damp with sweat, flew around her
shoulders and swept over his gloating face. Rivulets of
sweat ran down her back and between her breasts. Her
identity was gone, lost. On the floor, male and female
moved together, mindless, frenzied, caught up in a whirl-
wind of sensual demands, mounting together to a huge,
pulsating explosion. Somewhere, she heard her own voice
and his, both grunting like satisfied beasts. Somewhere,
she felt her own body, beset by tremors, fall limply across
his; felt the dizziness of desire flow out of her.

And then, abruptly, she was back in reality, lying
sprawled belly-down over Whit's heaving chest, sobbing
wordlessly. Then she lay quietly. She could see balls of
dust gathered under the nearby bed, a crumpled wrapper,
one of Lee's shoes. She thought of herself as she'd been
just a moment ago, riding Whit like some bitch in heat,
and felt a wave of burning shame sweep over her body.
She wanted to die, to disappear, and most of all, to make
time go backward, to undo what he had done . . . what
she—oh, God, it was really true—had done.

Shakily, she pushed herself off his motionless body and
got to her feet. The room was a shambles: the rag rug

pushed around a chair leg, clothes lying everywhere. The spread from her bed had been pulled halfway off and lay, twisted and patched with damp splotches, near his outflung arm. She quickly averted her eyes; she did not want to look at the big, powerful body, did not want to be reminded of what it had aroused in her. Her mind flicked to Dan, to their moans of love and delight, to their entranced joy in each other's responses. And what did it all mean in the end? Nothing! Nothing at all! What she had done last night, certain it was love, the love of a lifetime, she had just repeated with a man she loathed! She looked around wildly for her robe. It was lying, crumpled and soggy, under his shoulder, and the thought of touching him—! She shivered. How *could* she have? He had threatened her, blackmailed her, spoken to her as if she were dirt under his feet, and then had thrown her to the floor and taken her against her will. She should have frozen into ice; what decent, sensitive woman would not? Instead, though, she had . . . ugh! She tried to turn her thoughts away from it; they would not go. She had loved it, that loveless rolling around on the dingy floor. She had reveled in it, had even—she shivered again, feeling slightly sick—laughed aloud at the pleasure it had given her!

He stirred, and the movement reminded her that she was still naked. She must cover herself. He must not . . . not again. She grabbed a raincoat of Lee's hanging on a hook and wrapped it around her.

Whit lazily propped himself up on one elbow, making no move to rise from the floor. He licked his lips, catlike, his eyes as blank and slitted as a cat's. Why did her heart begin to race? She stared at him, half afraid and half something she did not want to examine, while he looked her over.

"So," he said finally. "Now I see. Now I understand. Inside the lady lurks the whore. Very"—he stretched—"revealing." He paused, as if waiting for a response. "I've known of women like you, but I never thought . . . Women who long to be raped. Was that how it happened ten years ago, Katherine? Did Copeland get tired of waiting and finally rape you? And did you beg *him* for more?"

"You *are* a monster!"

His lips twitched in a tiny smile. "Ah, but you didn't

feel that way a few minutes ago. A few minutes ago you were—"

"Forget that! It meant nothing!" And maybe someday, some year, she would be able to believe that.

He did not answer her, but pushed himself up from the floor and began to pick up his clothes without haste, brushing them off carefully. He walked by her, where she stood absolutely still, feeling rooted to the floor, and paused.

"Don't—don't—don't touch me!" Kitty stammered.

He laughed shortly and moved on, dressing himself in his usual methodical way, brushing the thick straight hair carefully until it was perfectly smooth, peeking at his reflection in the dresser mirror. She might not have existed.

Kitty huddled into the too-large coat, feeling like an abandoned child. She should get dressed, she knew that, but the idea of putting on a cocktail dress, of walking into the big, Saturday night dinner on his arm—No! She could not do it. And then, to have to meet Dan's eyes—! How could she face him? How could she ever again in this world lift her lips to his, offer her body to him, without writhing inwardly with shame? How could she ever speak words of love to him without choking on them? Whit might be right: Did she secretly long to be ravaged, to be taken by force? She suddenly remembered Mr. Mack, backing her against the wall at school, kissing and squeezing her in a kind of frenzy. She had been frightened, yes, but—admit it, admit it—excited, too, hadn't she?

What kind of woman *am* I? she wondered angrily. Maybe she was just an old joke: the repressed girl who, once awakened to the joys of the flesh, will take it anywhere, with anyone. And the ten years of carefully suppressed longing, the ten long years of waiting, the eagerly awaited reunion with her one true love—maybe all that was just a joke, too. The fantasy of a professional virgin.

Whit, still ignoring her, moved away from the dresser, and she took his place, gazing at her image in the glass. The face that looked back at her with unhappy eyes was flushed, the hair a pale matted tangle. Down her throat to the collarbone were bite marks and large, dark bruises, and she knew without opening the coat that there were others, many, many others. No, she could not face Dan now—perhaps never. Momentarily, she closed her eyes against the flash of anguish that clutched at her. When she opened them, Whit's face was in the mirror, behind hers. He was fully dressed now, as impeccable as always. Except for a slightly puffy lower lip, he looked untouched, either physically or mentally, his face a smooth, tanned mask. It gave Kit a small nudge of satisfaction to know that under the expensive, only slightly rumpled clothes were the marks of her nails in his skin. She hoped they hurt. He ducked down slightly, readjusting the knot of his tie a micromillimeter to the left, and allowed his eyes to meet hers briefly in the glass.

"You know, Katherine, I think you might want to pack and go home now."

It was an order, in spite of the casual, almost questioning tone. Kit stiffened a little; her immediate response was to let him know he did not own her, not even after . . . that.

But he continued smoothly. "And you can forget any thoughts of Copeland coming to rescue you. We've already had a nice, long talk about your . . . ah . . . situation, and he now understands that I will wreck his political career if he ever comes near you again. Oh, dear, I *am* sorry, but you know how politicians are. And I'm sure you wouldn't *want* to be the cause of his—ah—disappearance from the scene, now, would you?"

She only half heard him. Betrayed, betrayed, betrayed. She had warned Dan, had *begged* him to leave it to her. Apparently his ambitions were stronger than his—than whatever he felt for her. She had been betrayed by Whit, betrayed by Dan, betrayed by her own body. A great emptiness spread through her. The only thing left for her now was to make sure Lily stayed safe from all this. Her shoulders drooped a little, and Whit said with satisfaction, "Good," as if he had been listening in on her thoughts.

She stared at his reflection, trying to glean some understanding of him—what he was thinking, what he might be feeling. Nothing showed, nothing but his usual expression of absolute certitude and absolute control. It was all she really knew of him, and it added up to nothing. Nothing—wasn't that how she had thought of him all these years, she and Dan both, as a square, stolid, rather bumbling nothing? Yet in the end he had beaten them both. He had beaten them *all*. Winner take all, and Whitney Harris III had won.

CHAPTER EIGHTEEN

Big Jim

"WHOOPS! Sorry!" Dan stood in the open doorway, his key in the lock, feeling foolish. Lee and Benno, who were locked in a steamy embrace on the bed, sprang apart at the sound of his voice like a pair of adolescents discovered *in flagrante delicto*, Lee clutching at the open front of her shirt. For half a beat the three of them stared at one another uncomfortably, and then, in unison, they all began to laugh.

"Where the hell did you disappear to?" Ben demanded. "Who the hell *was* she? What the hell was going on, anyway?"

Dan cleared his throat and returned wryly, "Where the hell did *you* disappear to? Who the hell is *she*? And what the hell is going on *here*?"

When they had stopped laughing, Ben said, "The lady attacked me at half time, sir. And after that, it's all a blur."

Dan smiled, but his mind was elsewhere. He checked his watch, figuring. Courtney and all the rest of them should be safely tucked away in their rooms by now, sleeping off the effects of drinking throughout an entire football game before the big dinner. It was close to six; Jim should be arriving at the airfield about now. The dinner started at eight, his speech was scheduled for nine—

thirty, but he'd have to be there from the start. That didn't leave him a whole lot of time. And he had to settle things with Kit, reassure her, make sure she understood he was ready to give it all up for her. Not that he thought he'd *have* to give it all up. If he couldn't have television, he'd just go on the road, show his face everywhere, at every shopping center, every square dance, every Grange meeting, every public forum. Big Jim wouldn't like it, he wouldn't like it one bit, but he'd be able to live with it. He'd dealt with worse. As for the rest of Whit's threats . . . well, Dan would confront *them* as they came along. But he had to convince Kit, pour some of his resolve into her. Once again, he glanced at the wristwatch.

"What's your hurry?" Ben complained. "You just got here. I won't let Lee start that lovey-dovey stuff again. Grab a chair and fill us in. What happened after the smoke cleared?"

"Huh! You know what happened," Lee commented, straightening one of the pillows behind his head. "They caught her. Dan and good old Joe Rugowsky. Our Heroes!" She grinned at Dan.

"Yeah," Ben said, "but I wanna know all the other details, sweetie pie. Come on, Dan, divulge. Who was she and what did she have on her mind—besides mayhem?"

Dan inhaled deeply. Then he said, "Remember Serena?"

"Serena? Serena . . . ?"

"Polly's sister." As Ben's jaw dropped in comprehension, Dan turned to Lee. "Polly was my . . . wife. She died in a plane crash."

"Ohmygawd. Then this lady is—was—your sister-in-law! But where the hell did she come from? What was she doing here?"

"Apparently she lives here . . . in town. According to the police, she's been working in the Alumni Office for the past six months or so."

"Jesus Christ!" Ben exclaimed.

"But . . . *why?*" That was Lee.

"Why? Because she's crazy, that's why."

"But all those things she was screaming in the stadium . . . what was she trying to do? What made her think—?"

"Sweetheart," Ben interrupted in a very firm voice,

"why don't you run downstairs and get some ice for our drinks?"

"Ice! But we don't need— Oh. I get it. Okay. You want me to leave? I'll go, but not quietly."

"No, no," Dan said. He looked again at his watch. "I've got to run, anyway. I have some things to do. Before Jim Malverne gets here." He turned to Ben. "He was supposed to get a plane out of Madison right away." He began to pace back and forth at the foot of the bed. "I don't really know what to say to him. I'll just have to play it by ear . . . first things first . . .'

Lee gave him a shrewd look. *"First* things? Where *is* Kit, anyway?"

"Christ, Lee, I haven't seen her since the game. I don't understand that woman—she blows hot and cold all the time. I can't keep up with her moods.

"Of course," he went on after a pause, "since then, Whit and I have had it all out. He's threatened me and I've told him to go to hell." He reached over to Lee, who had just lit a cigarette, and took it from her hand. "Thanks." He puffed nervously and handed it back to her. "But now, goddamn it, he's *with* her. I'm sure of it. He's got her locked up in the room with him . . . I don't know what he's doing or saying, but one thing's for sure. I'm going back there and find out just what the hell's going on! If I have to kick in the goddamn door!"

He had gone halfway to the door when Lee's voice stopped him. "Dummy. You don't have to play Gangbusters. I have a key, remember? And furthermore, you're making a mistake! I know her—probably better than you do." Unwillingly, he turned around. "You've always pushed her too hard. That only makes her dig her heels in all the more. Your trouble is, you rely too much on sheer force. It's scary, Dan. Especially to someone . . . private, like Kitty."

"I'm getting a bit tired of everyone telling me what my trouble is!" Dan's jaw thrust out aggressively and he drew in a deep breath, as if to say more. The phone shrilled. He jumped a little, then made a lunge for it. "That must be—"

At the sound of the voice on the other end, his whole face seemed to sag for a moment. "Oh . . . hi, Dinah. What a surprise . . . You are *here,* aren't you? Okay. I'll be right down." Staring into space, he let the receiver fall into the cradle, then pulled his shoulders back and turned to the others with an unreadable expression on his face. "You want to know what my trouble really is? My trouble is that it's *all* catching up with me."

He left, pulling the door closed behind him, and ran swiftly down the stairs. Take it as it comes, he repeated silently, take it as it comes. When he rounded the last landing, he saw her immediately, pacing up and down, her boots clacking on the glossy lobby floor. Heads turned to eye her voluptuous form, clad in tight pants and a sweater, her dark mane of curls tumbling over her shoulders. She was a real eye-catcher. This time, though, he couldn't appreciate it. He hadn't been looking forward to dealing with Jim, but far better Jim with all the tensions, both political and personal, than Dinah, now that everything had changed.

She spotted him when she turned back to pace toward the stairway. With a dazzling smile, she ran, arms outstretched, and flung herself at him, hugging him enthusiastically. "Dan! Jim said . . . Oh, I'm so *glad* to see you!" And tilting her head back, she kissed him full on the mouth with soft, half-parted lips.

He tried, he really tried, to kiss her back. Affection mingled with regret as he held her familiar softness in his arms. It would have been nice . . . if things had been different, if Kit hadn't come back into his life. He hugged her mechanically, wondering just how he would tell her.

She backed away from him, a frown creasing her forehead, her eyes bright with apprehension. "You okay?"

"Considering everything that's gone on today . . . I'm fine."

"That's not what I meant and you know it. What's happened?" she insisted.

"Dinah, dear, can we discuss it later?"

"Uh-oh," she said. "I knew it. Who is she, Dan?"

"Please, Di. Not now. We'll talk later, I promise. But I have to speak to Jim first. Where is he?"

She shut her eyes briefly, turning her head away. "On the phone. To the hospital. We came straight here from the airport . . . to make sure you were really all right." The last words were tinged with sarcasm. "But I can see—" Her voice caught.

"Di," he began, reaching out for her. And then, behind him, he heard the unmistakable sound of Whit Harris giving orders. He whirled around, every muscle tensed. But it was not Harris he saw. Instead, he found himself looking straight into the bottomless green eyes he knew so well. He was so shocked to see her right there, right then, that he gave an involuntary gasp. But her eyes dropped instantly, shifting away from his, and she hurried down the last few steps, hugging her suede coat close to her body, shrinking as far from him as possible.

"Kit!" But she scurried away from him, out the front door, pretending she had not heard. Dan stood, his arm outstretched, the color climbing in his face. She would *not* run away from him again!

He had taken no more than three strides when a hand gripped his shoulder and that smooth voice said, "How nice of you to want to say goodbye, Copeland. But I'm afraid Katherine simply doesn't wish to have anything to do with you. No, it's no use. She won't speak to you."

"Get your hand off me, Harris. She'll talk to me . . . if I have to punch you out to get to her."

Surprisingly, Whit released his arm and murmured, "No, not now she won't." As he spoke, Dan caught a glimpse of the big silver Mercedes silently pulling away from the curb. "You see? Katherine has decided to go home, where she belongs."

Dan clenched both fists. Harris stood easily, relaxed, looking slightly amused.

"Forget it, Copeland," he said. "I've won."

Without a thought, Dan lashed out with a fist. But Whit only laughed and ducked, saying, "And now we're even, I believe."

"Dan! Dan, don't! Everyone's staring!" Dinah was tugging on his arm. "Cool it. Jim'll be here any minute. Don't let him see you like this."

She was right, of course. And anyway, brawling had never been his answer to difficulties. Nevertheless, it took a great effort to turn away from the smirking Harris and allow Dinah to lead him away.

Dinah planted herself directly in front of him and in a businesslike way began to brush him off. She spoke lightly, almost casually. "So. That's how it is. I see. I wondered why you were so set on this reunion; it just didn't make sense. But now, of course, it does. She's very beautiful, I'll say that. But a *married woman*, Dan? *His* wife?" Her eyes rolled heavenward. "And with him right here? I don't believe you."

He looked at her with misery. "She and I go back a long time. I knew I'd see her here, sure, but I didn't know— Hell, Dinah, I didn't *plan* this, you should know that!"

"I know, I know. It was bigger than both of you. And I'm supposed to smile and be a good sport about it all."

"Aw, Di. You're not making it easy for me!"

"I don't intend to!" she said tartly. "Why in hell should I? You think it's easy for *me* to stand here calmly, pretending nothing has happened, when I'm longing to throw myself on the floor and kick and scream?" She shrugged. "Well, at least now I know whose ghost has always been in bed with us."

"I never—" he began, and then winced. Two nights ago he'd been in bed with this woman, enjoying every minute of it, glad of her. What in the world could he say to her now that wouldn't make him feel cheap, that wouldn't make *her* feel cheap? "Oh, Dinah, if only—"

Her ripe mouth twisted wryly. "Sure. *If only.* That's the title of my autobiography."

"Come on, now. What we had was real, Di. It was good. It just wasn't . . ."

"Just wasn't good enough. I get it. Don't worry about it, Dan. I'm *not* going to lie down on the floor and kick and scream."

"Oh, Christ, Dinah, if only I could—"

Her expression suddenly changed as she put on a false and glittering smile, talking through her teeth. "Watch it. Here's Jim."

Dan turned from her with relief and walked briskly to meet his manager, hand outstretched. "God, Jim, what a mess. Have they let you talk to her?"

Jim looked gray with fatigue, and his deeply set eyes were empty. He clasped Dan's hand, though, with his usual firmness, looking him over carefully. "As long as it doesn't hit the papers, that's the main thing. No, I haven't seen Serena. Some doctor's looking at her right now. I'll go over in a while and see what I can do." He sighed loudly, patting his breast pocket for one of the omnipresent cigars. "Out! Wouldn't you know it! I need *something*, that's for sure. Is there a place around here where a man can get a drink?" His eyes roved the room, agitated.

"The campus bar is just a few blocks away. That okay with you?"

Jim immediately headed for the front door. "Jesus Harold H. Christ, what a day!" he grumbled. "Anyway, for sure nothing much *worse* can go wrong." He stopped in his tracks, staring at Whit Harris, who had been slouching quietly against the wall, watching them. "For the love of —Harris! Hey, good to see you! What do you say?" His voice was suddenly animated.

"What do I say? I say you'd better keep your boy Copeland in line, Malverne. Otherwise . . ." Whit smiled coldly at the older man's stupefaction and drew a meaningful finger across his own throat.

Big Jim frowned. "What the hell are you talking about? Speak plainly, man."

"Ask your boy; it's his doing. I'm just warning you in a friendly way." Sketching a bow in Dinah's direction, he turned abruptly and walked away.

Still puzzled, Jim turned to Dan. "What's he *talking* about? Can you make any sense out of it?"

"Let's talk at The Pub, Jim."

"And what about Dinah?"

They both turned to look at her. Dinah fluffed her hair out with her fingers and smiled. "What *about* me? I'll grab a cab or something out to the motel. Maybe I'll take a nap. You want me with you when you go to see her, Jim?" Her glittering eyes carefully avoided Dan.

"For the big family reunion? No, no, I don't know how long it'll take. Anyway, I want you at that dinner tonight to catch the reactions, see how the speech goes with the class of '70. You can get her in, Dan."

"Sure," Dinah said. "I'll do my usual number."

"Dinah—" Dan began.

Another bright smile. "Yes?"

He grimaced. "Nothing. Nothing. I'll pick you up at seven."

"You're the boss . . . Boss." She stood in the lobby long after the two men had gone from view, staring outside, her eyes thoughtful.

*   *   *

The Pub was half empty—it was the dinner hour for most of the kids on campus—and the huge neon-lighted jukebox was silent. With the ease of familiarity, Dan led Big Jim through the large room to a scarred booth in the back corner. "My table," he explained, pointing to the initials "D.C." and the year "1968" carved carefully into the surface. As soon as they had slid in on opposite sides, a young girl appeared out of the gloom and took their orders.

When she brought the drinks, Big Jim swallowed his bourbon in one gulp and held the glass up for another. Then he let out a gusty sigh and leaned forward, his hands clasped together on the table top.

"Okay, Danny boy, let's have it. What the hell was Harris talking about? What did you manage to do to him in just twenty-four hours?"

"Nothing . . . something. Something personal. It's not important."

The thick brows drew together. "What do you mean, not important! Remember who you're talking to, my boy. I'm no lousy reporter out to get a story. Not important! Jesus Harold H. Christ on a pogo stick! Without that money, we got no TV, you realize that? You can't go around antagonizing people like Harris!"

Dan eyed his mentor. Business as usual, as usual. Feeling a bit chilled, he watched Jim dispatch the second drink with gusto. But he forced himself to smile. "Come on, Jim. This is no time to think about television. My God, here you are, reunited with your lost daughter after so many years—and all you can think about is the election? I find that incredible!"

"Ha! Lost daughter! Shit! She hasn't been *lost*, although there've been times when I might've wished— But hell, I always knew exactly where she was—I've been sending her money all the time. She didn't want to have anything to do with me, and believe me, the feeling was mutual. She was always a moaner and a whiner, not ever willing to take care of her poor little sister. Then, wouldn't you know it, when Polly died, she went off the deep end, accusing *me!* I did the best I could. I—"

"Hold on, there, Jim. Backtrack for a minute. What do you mean, *poor Polly?* Why was Serena supposed to take care of her?"

Jim slumped back on the seat, his eyes hooded. "Get that little girl again, wouldja? I could use some more of good old Jack Daniels." And when Dan just looked at him steadily, he shrugged. "Oh, you know . . . their mother died when she was just a little thing. I mean, Serena *was* the big sister. The way I was brought up, you took care of your little sisters and brothers, and none of this alibiing and talking about dependence and all that garbage."

"No, no." Dan waved a hand impatiently. "Not that. You meant something altogether different, didn't you?"

"Jesus Harold H. Christ! Are you going to get me another drink or aren't you? It's all over and done with; way back in the past. What does any of it matter now?"

Dan spoke with a deadly calm. "You knew all along, didn't you? You knew exactly what Polly was."

"What she *was*? She was a sweet, adorable little girl . . . a bit headstrong, maybe . . ."

"You *did* know. Goddamn it, Jim, you knew everything, all the time! You knew perfectly well she was sleeping with every male within a twenty-mile radius! You *knew!*" Jim was sitting bolt upright, his face purple. "Yeah, you knew, all right," Dan went on. "As a matter of fact, you knew what would probably happen the night you maneuvered me into taking her to the movies . . . I can't believe it! I'm sitting here and looking at you, and I can see on your face that it's all true, and I still can't believe it!"

"Ah, Dan, listen. I loved that little girl. She was the sweetest, best little baby you ever saw. There wasn't a prettier little thing in the entire county. And good? You could leave her alone in her crib for hours, and she'd just goo and smile and play with her toes. God, you hardly knew she was there. And then you'd go into her nursery and she'd smile. Smile, all over her face. You never saw such a sweet smile . . ." His voice drifted off. "You think I *liked* it, Dan? Watching her carry on the way she did? It just about broke my heart. But, Jesus, I couldn't be watching her every *minute*—I had things to do, a living to make! And her sister . . . her sister wasn't *willing* to share a room with her, oh, no, it didn't suit Miss High and Mighty—" Jim leaned across the table, his eyes filled with old memories, old pain. "You can't blame me for wanting her safe, Dan. I just wanted her safe, and happy. And she *was*. She loved you, she was so happy with you. It was the perfect answer . . . now, wasn't it? Wasn't she a good little wife, never giving any trouble? Wasn't she—"

Dan pounded a fist on the table. His voice was edged with steel. "You set me up! You set me up, you son of a bitch! You dangled a political career in front of me for bait and you set me up good!"

Jim shook his shaggy head. "You don't understand. Backing you wasn't a *payment* for loving her. Christ, no. I already had plans for you. Then, when she said how much she liked you, I thought, How perfect. For everyone."

Between clenched teeth, Dan gritted, "For everyone, sure, everyone but *me*. I never *loved* Polly, and you knew it, Jim, you must have known it. She blackmailed me. I thought you'd throw me out for seducing your pretty little teenager. I thought it'd kill you if you found out she was lying down with every boy she saw. I thought you'd be outraged! Hurt! Yes, and I also thought it would be the end of me in Wisconsin politics . . . and it would've been, am I right, Jim?"

Jim's heavy face was mottled with emotion. "No, no. It wasn't like that. Listen, son—"

"Don't you 'son' me. You were just using me all the time, using me for your own purposes. Pretending she was sweet and innocent, pretending I wanted to marry her, pretending she was normal. Yeah, that's what I said, Jim—pretending she was *normal*, when you knew damn well—"

The big man half rose from his seat, bulking over Dan. "Don't say another word, boy, not another word. I had to slap Serena down for talking that way once, and I'll do the same to you!"

"So that's why she never wanted to see you again! Well, I don't blame her! You bastard, hiding it when you *knew* Polly was retarded!"

"Not retarded! Not retarded!" Jim sat back down heavily and sagged as if the words had been blows. "Don't say 'retarded.' Maybe a little . . . childish in some ways. But not retarded." His voice was loaded with panic. "Why, by the time she was two, she could already count to twenty! And she loved her books. She was a *bright* little thing. She was! It was later—" He stopped, swallowed, then scowled. "And anyway, who are *you* to judge me? Nobody held a shotgun to your head. Nobody forced you into her bed. You were a big boy, Daniel, with a mind of your own. My feeling is, she turned you on. My feeling is, she got you where you *live.* No, never mind scowling at me that way. I don't want to fight, and if I did, I could still beat you, old as I am. My feeling is, you got something out of it, all right. You weren't as cheated as you're making out . . ."

They were both silent for several minutes, avoiding eye contact. Jim snapped his fingers loudly, and a moment later the barmaid slid another drink onto the table. This one he sipped at, gazing at Dan now, waiting.

Dan ran one hand through his hair, balled a fist, and then let his arm drop lightly to the table. He opened the first with great care, finger by finger. "You've been using me all along," he said quietly. "All these years I've been haunted by what I did to you. That's a joke, isn't it? And all the time . . . What was it, Jim? You needed your own man in Washington to make sure of the patronage? You getting old, Jim? Losing your grip on the clubhouse?"

"Don't you worry about me, boy! I don't need anyone. And don't you forget who made you—" He stopped, shook his head, and tried a smile. "Come on, what the hell are we doing, raking up the dead past? What does any of it matter now? We are where we are, and that's number one, right? Come on, Danny boy, we've come this far together, it's a helluva time to screw things up. And what the hell, the worst fights are in the closest families, aren't they? Have a drink with me and we'll toast your victory—and to hell with Whit Harris and the TV, if that's what you want!"

Dan's lips quirked. "Kiss and make up, huh, Jim? Just like that. Sorry. I can't turn myself around that fast. I've found out a few home truths today, and I have to tell you, they bother me. They bother me a whole lot. To pander your daughter—! And come to think of it, Jim, wasn't it you who found Dinah? The perfect assistant, isn't that what you said? Tell me, just out of curiosity, have you known all along that Dinah and I were lovers?"

"Sure. Of course I knew. Why? You're a man like any other man. You'd been a long time solitary. She was good for you . . . Aw, come *on*, boy, you can't mean you're angry about *Dinah!* Hell, I didn't *hire* her to sleep with you. I never said one word. But she's one helluva good-looking woman, and if it happened, I figured, all to the good. But I never— Say, what kind of a person do you think I *am?*"

Dan rested his head on one hand. "I'm not sure any more," he muttered. "I'm not sure about anything." When Jim whistled up another drink for him, he did not protest, but gulped it thirstily. They did not look at each other. Dan emptied the glass, put it down with a bang, and said, in a tone of voice that denied the whole previous conversation: "You really ought to see about Serena, Jim. She's in real trouble. You won't recognize her. I didn't."

"Yeah, I guess I ought to. Yeah, I will, I will. I wish I could understand why she did it. You never hurt her. You never had anything much to do with her."

Dan sighed. "Maybe that's exactly it, Jim."

Jim made a face. "Don't get started on any of that psychology stuff. I don't go for it—a lot of malarkey, if you ask me. She was always a problem, plain and simple. I was never able to handle her." He let out a loud breath between his lips. "I don't suppose you'd come along with me, would you?"

"What! Jim, for the love of God, think! Serena wishes I was dead. What makes you think that my presence would *help?*"

"I—oh, the plain truth is, I don't want to see her. The plain truth is—for the first time in my life, I don't know *what* the hell to do." He swirled the dregs of the drink and the ice cube in his glass and poured the liquid down. Then his face changed completely. "But you'll give your speech, won't you? I mean, none of this"—a vague gesture with his hand—"is gonna make any difference . . . ?"

Dan snorted. "Oh, Jim. You really are incredible! Tell you what. When I find out whether any of . . . *this* makes a difference, you'll be the first to know." And slapping a five-dollar bill onto the table, he got up and left.

CHAPTER NINETEEN

Dinah Franklin

FROM THE OUTSIDE, the Colonie Country Club might have been deserted. The wide sloping lawns and artfully curved gravel paths lay sedately empty under discreet outdoor lights.

But once you went through the front door, Dinah discovered, lights blazed, glasses clinked, voices shouted, music blared. Across one wall, a large hand-lettered banner proclaimed this the scene of "The Well-Kum-Back Klass of '70 Dinner Dance and Decennial Blast."

She looked around uneasily. She did not belong here. That word, for instance: "decennial." What the hell *was* that, anyway? She'd never heard it. But then, she'd never had a chance to go to college, like all these people. She glanced at the chattering, laughing groups—with their shared memories, their air of knowing it all, their absolute self-assurance—and felt awkward and overdressed. She knew darn well she looked fine. Her velvet suit came from Marshall Field, and her shoes were identical to those worn by a smashing redhead across the room. She knew her feelings of inferiority were stupid. Huh! she thought, while *you* were playing at being students, running around in your convertibles, and planning the next prom, *I* was working at two jobs, sending money home to my parents, and putting that bastard Jerry Franklin through college. Sure, and when he'd finished and had his damned degree, he'd said, "Sorry, kiddo, it won't work any more. The fact is, you haven't kept up. I need another kind of woman now, one who can help me in my career."

Well, that was his mistake. His second wife, by all reports, was now one hundred pounds overweight and spent every day playing bridge. While *she* had hoisted herself up by sheer determination and hard work, college diploma or no college diploma. It didn't bother her much any more, not after all these years, but every once in a while something would come along that reminded her of what she had missed . . . like this stupid reunion dinner. And that damn fancy word. Next to her, Dan snorted. "What idiot thought of *that?*"

"Of what?"

"*Decennial.* How affected can you get? What's wrong with saying tenth anniversary?"

So that's what it means. "Maybe it's a joke," she said.

"Agh! This whole weekend's been a joke—a not very funny joke. Let me get you a drink. The usual?" And without waiting for an answer, he escaped into the smoky, low-lit bar.

The usual. Didn't we know how that hurt her? *The usual* meant not only the brand of whiskey she preferred, nor that she took her coffee black with sugar. It wasn't just the intimate little details he knew about her. It was everything: eight to six in the office, dinner, then drinks, then bed. *The usual* meant every day, day after day, becoming closer and closer, working together better and better, falling more and more deeply in love.

She shook her head, impatient with herself. Not him, though. What she had taken for love was apparently just convenience for him. Because no man in love could, overnight, fall for someone else. Overnight!

Yesterday morning she had kissed him goodbye in front of his building. And tonight, suddenly, it was all finished. Done. Over. Ended. Each word pierced her like another knife in her heart. She still couldn't accept it. If she hadn't seen that blonde vision this afternoon with her own eyes, if she hadn't watched that whole scene being played out, she'd think she was imagining his disinterest.

Oh, God. She hadn't pushed him, she hadn't pressured him. She didn't even want to marry him; once had been more than enough of that particular experience. But they were so good together! It had happened without games and without fuss, completely natural all the way. They worked well together, they fed each other ideas. As a matter of fact, they often thought of the same thing at the same time. That was the way they'd first gone to bed together. During a late-night supper after work at a bar down the street, she had looked across the table at him and suddenly thought: I'd love to be in bed with him right now. She'd been working for him for three months and hadn't really thought of him that way. But that night she hadn't been able to *stop* thinking of him that way. And instead of dropping her off in front of her building, Dan had turned off the ignition and, without a word, taken her into his arms. Natural, easy. It had hit them both at the same moment.

How had this terrible thing happened? How could this woman come along and change everything in just one night?

Dinah blinked back angry tears. It wouldn't do to smear the eye makeup. Not at her age. A tear-streaked face, so appealing on a twenty-five-year-old, simply looked grotesque on a woman who was forty-one. She stole a look at herself in the mirrored wall opposite the entrance. From a distance, she'd do. She straightened her back, noting with relief that the extra ten pounds only made her look more voluptuous. But she'd have to watch it. Not an ounce more.

I'm right for him, I'm perfect for him, she thought. Everyone who knew them told her Dan had never been so relaxed and happy with a woman. He could be himself with her. She knew him, warts and all, and she loved him, warts and all. There had always been the comforting warmth of total acceptance between them. What had that skinny blonde done to him?

He was coming back with their drinks, and when she caught his eye, he gave her an embarrassed smile that made her cringe inside. It made no difference how perfect she was for him if he didn't realize it. No difference that she loved him, when he didn't care at all. Oh, it hurt. It hurt like hell. But it was the truth and "the truth shall make you free." Free! Who wanted to be free at her age?

She sipped her drink and followed him into the big banquet hall. It was hung with bunting, jammed with tables dressed in blue and yellow cloths, and already thick with the mind-jarring din of hundreds of voices all trying to make themselves heard at once.

"Now, let me see," Dan said. "You can't sit with me, because I'm at the head table. But let's find a place nearby, okay?"

"Sure, Boss." He gave her a sharp look, which she refused to acknowledge. "I forgot. I got this together for you on the plane. Alumni stuff. If you can sneak in a few of these facts, it won't hurt." She reached into her bag for the folded papers and handed them to him.

"On the plane! Woman, you constantly amaze me. No wonder I can't get along without you!"

She made herself smile, keep the voice light. "Well, Boss, you're going to have to."

"Don't you walk out on me, too!" he blurted, and then colored painfully, avoiding her eyes. "Oh, Christ. Dinah, we've really got to talk this over. But—"

"I know. Not here, not now. I hate to tell you this, Boss, but it's going to be *never*. Because the minute I get back to Madison, I'm packing my bags and moving on."

"Dinah! Please! Reconsider! If nothing else, think of your career!"

She smiled blandly at him. "Why? Won't you give me a good reference? I mean, I've really been the all-around assistant, haven't I? Good at this, good at that, and especially good at the other thing."

He rounded on her. "Don't! Don't put yourself down! I can't explain what's happened in two simple sentences, because it's not a simple situation, goddamn it. As a matter of fact, it's even more complicated than I *thought* it was."

"Simple. Complicated. What difference?" She shrugged. "It all adds up the same way, Dan. Goodbye to us."

He grabbed her shoulders. "Yes. No. I don't know what it adds up to, Di. My feelings are . . . I don't know. Right now"—his voice lowered—"I want to put my arms around you and make you feel better. I do. I care for you. But—"

"Don't *do* that!" Her voice came out sharp with pain. "Don't tell me you 'care' for me in that condescending tone of voice, you son of a bitch! I can't stand it. It makes me sick!"

"Dinah, listen. It was never my intention to hurt you. I had no idea—I'm ambivalent."

"Ambivalent! That disgusting word—I hate it! Half a

307

promise, half a truth. No, thanks! You can take your . . .
your *ambivalence* and lay it on your little blond friend!
I'm not going to hang around and wait to see if it works
out for you—oh, no! I'm going to take care of number
one!"

She didn't know where to run to—away from Dan was
all she could think of. She turned from him and the next
thought just came sliding in: the bar. What she needed
now was another drink.

It was lovely and dusky in the bar. She asked for a
whiskey sour. No more of "the usual." She'd never drink
Jack Daniels again as long as she lived. When a stool became empty, she slid onto it, sipping slowly, looking
around at the crowd. In the back a large, rowdy group
had pulled four or five tables together and was noisily
toasting each other, chug-a-lugging. From the looks of
them, no more than half would make it to the dinner table. What was the sense of making a special trip to see all
your old friends if you just got loaded right out of your
mind?

The men who were alone appeared in better shape.
There were half a dozen of them at the bar. If they were
getting crocked, at least they were quiet about it. Given
her choice, which one would she pick? *There* was a good-
looking man—big and rugged—and she liked red hair.
Nope, he was with a woman. The dark one with the lean
face, he was interesting-looking. The tan said Florida, or
maybe California. He was looking at her . . . or was he?
She turned her head; she really ought not to stare so bla-
tantly. But another moment and another drink later, she
was eyeing the lineup again, leaning one elbow on the bar.
Of course, they all were probably a lot younger than she;
if she had gone to college, she'd have been the class of
'61. But what the hell, if the girls nowadays could size up
men, so could Dinah Franklin.

He was four stools away: big, broad-shouldered, and
expensively dressed, fondling the stem of his martini glass
and appearing neither lonely nor self-conscious. Of all
these cocksure, well-dressed men, he looked by far the
most successful. Well, he ought to. Whit Harris could
probably buy and sell all these guys without even thinking
about it. She gazed thoughtfully at his neat, all-American
profile. Mr. Super-WASP: short nose, thin lips, blond, and

blue-eyed, just like in all the movies. Was he handsome? She squinted a bit and decided, Yes, he was. A bit predictable, perhaps, but definitely nice. Too nice, maybe. Those WASP types tended to be boring in bed. The redhead would probably be more primitive, and the dark-haired guy . . . well, he had the smell of show biz somehow, he'd probably think of a few new twists on the old game.

A pang shot through her as she realized all over again how horribly free she was. Free to line 'em up and pick 'em out . . . and feel like a dirty old woman. She swiveled the stool, turning away from the wall, and when she swiveled back, there he was, on the stool next to her.

"Hello, Mr. Harris."

One eyebrow shot up. "You know me?"

"Doesn't everyone?"

He frowned a little. "You have the advantage, I'm afraid, uh—"

"Dinah Franklin."

"I know that name. I've seen it . . . on reports sent by Jim Malverne, isn't that right?"

"Probably." She wanted to steer clear of any talk of Dan, so she hastily asked, "Is this your reunion? I mean —was this *your* class?"

He smiled and cocked a thumb at the jumble of tables in the rear. "Yes, indeed. And that jolly crew fast drinking itself into disrepute is, I'm afraid, my old fraternity. I never could keep up with them, so I don't even bother to try." He lifted a casual hand, and magically, another whiskey sour and another martini appeared on the counter. "I gather you're here to listen to his speech."

"His?" Her head was getting just a trifle muzzy and it felt wonderful. "Oh. Dan. Yes, you gather correctly. But I don't work for him any more, so I'll be an interested observer."

"Not working for him? Might I ask why? Er—have you *heard* anything?"

Dinah took a sip of her drink and smiled demurely at Whit over the rim of the glass, thinking, Not very subtle. "Heard anything?" she said. "D'you have anything particular in mind?" She wanted to laugh out loud. She'd heard something, all right. Orders from Big Jim, half whispered over the telephone from the hospital. "I'm in a

terrible hurry, Di," he had said, "but listen. Whit Harris
is pissed at our boy. I don't know why; couldn't get a
straight word from Dan. But it's bad. You turn the charm
on Harris at that dinner, you hear? You know how. See
if you can find out why, and maybe you can turn him
around. I *know* you can do it." And when she had asked
ingenuously, "Just how far do you want me to go . . . with
the charm?" he'd spluttered and blustered. "Now, Dinah,
you know damn well I didn't mean—! Well, *you* know."
Well, she did know, and he damn well *did* mean— The
old faker! Politicians! She wondered what Whit Harris
would say and do if she told him right now, "Yes, I heard
something. I heard you're against Dan, and I'm supposed
to make you change your mind—in bed, if necessary."

"I haven't heard anything in particular," he was saying, his eyes radiating truth and honesty as he fibbed.
"It's just . . . there are rumors around that Copeland's not
doing as well as everyone thought he would."

"He's doing all right. He's very popular, you know. I
think he'll make it."

"And yet . . . you've quit your job with him? Don't you
like a winner?"

She pushed her empty glass away and he signaled immediately for a refill. She was getting high, but what the
hell . . . the more she drank, the dimmer became the
pain. She raised her glass and said, "You're more my
type of winner, Mr. Harris." The moment she said it,
she was sorry; he was a bit of a stick. But to her surprise,
he looked pleased, unconsciously straightening his shoulders and lifting his big square chin a little.

Then he leaned in closer to her. "What type of winner
am I . . . Dinah?"

"The born type."

He laughed. "A born winner! I like that!" Very carefully, almost unnoticeably, his hand shifted to rest lightly
on her arm. "I believe you're the same type. I think
you're quite wise to get off the Copeland bandwagon. Before it crashes. Don't repeat that." He laughed again,
nervously. "I seem to be talking too much. Too many
martinis." His fingers tightened just a trifle.

Thinking, Two can play *this* game, Dinah shifted
closer, so that her shoulder was barely nestling into the
curve of his, and noted that his eyes brightened and he

310

licked at his rather thin lips. "As someone once said," she cooed, " 'One martini is too many and two aren't nearly enough.' " She waited for his laugh and then added, "A big man like you can hold a lot of liquor."

"I like you, Dinah. You're terrific. Wasted with a small-timer like Dan, who's about to . . . never mind." His eyes flicked over her. "You should be in D.C. with the big boys. Perhaps with—well, we can discuss that later." His hand moved to cover hers and he squeezed lightly. "What do you say we continue our conversation after the dinner? A nightcap, perhaps? There's a quiet little bar in my hotel . . ."

Their shoulders were now just touching. She felt no electricity, no tautening of her sexual responses. But there was something solid and comforting about the sheer bulk of him. She felt like leaning against him, to rest, to feel some human warmth. He was gazing at her, his face calm and noncommittal. This was no eager boy. This was a man who weighed and measured everything. Would that satisfy her, accustomed as she was to Dan's responsive, almost feverish lovemaking?

Sliding her eyes away from his, she saw them both in the mirror: he, large, broad, substantial in his dark suit, the fair hair sleek and shining; she, intense, curvaceous, color flaming on her cheekbones. Her eyes seemed to glitter, and the curling hair, loose and cloudy, looked primitive, and yes, admit it, sexy. No wonder he kept creeping closer and closer. Even she could see, in the blurred reflection, that she was a living invitation. Dan's rejection seemed to suit her. Her mouth twisted in a sour smile.

The little lines around the eyes and mouth didn't show in the soft bar lighting. The years of knocking around weren't perceptible to a man who'd had a few too many, a man whose wife had cheated on him. Two of the walking wounded, softening life with too much to drink and a few minutes of passion? She met his eyes again and saw, faintly, a bit of anxiety. Maybe he wasn't totally the imperturbable WASP. Maybe. And besides, at her age, how many more rich, attractive men were going to come down the pike? How many men, *period*?

So she gave him a flashing smile and tossed her head a trifle to make the thick hair ripple. "That sounds wonderful," she said.

Satisfaction softened his face briefly, and then he was all business once more. "Good." A glance at the heavy gold wristwatch. "We should go in to the dinner now. You find yourself a seat and I'll meet you afterward. Here." He swiftly scribbled a name and address on a bar napkin and slipped it and a folded bill into her palm. "Take a cab to this hotel and I'll meet you in the bar. You'll find it quite . . . discreet."

He did not wait for her acquiescence; that was taken for granted. A final pat on her arm and he was gone. It was obvious he did not want her to follow him or to be seen with him. Dinah sighed inwardly and fingered the crisp, folded money. Maybe she'd meet him and maybe she wouldn't. Slithering around "discreetly" to meet a married man wasn't her style; and now that he was gone and the ghost of Dan was creeping back, he didn't seem half so appealing.

She tried her sexiest smile on the bartender, a good-looking boy in his twenties, but his eyes just slid right over her. Too old, that's what I am. Old, she realized suddenly, didn't mean getting ugly, necessarily. She was still damned attractive. No, it just meant a narrowing of choices. Pretty soon there might be no choices left at all, and she'd be forced to join the ranks of lonely middle-aged women who bought series tickets to everything to convince themselves that they were busy, busy, busy. She'd seen them eating together, drinking together, at the theater together, their eyes feverishly roving, looking for the last chance. She shivered and drained the rest of the drink in one gulp. She'd sit through the damn dinner, and sometime during this horrible evening she'd make up her mind about Whit Harris.

The banquet hall was stuffed with people, couples threading through, looking for two seats together. A woman alone had no trouble, and she took the first empty chair she saw.

The people sitting at the table were obviously a closed group and were so engaged in trading "Do you remember's" that they didn't notice her. In any case, she didn't have to make conversation. She had hardly settled herself when a Dixieland band started to play so loudly that nobody could be heard, anyway. She nibbled at her food as it was pushed in front of her, ordered another drink from a sweating and harassed waitress, and tried very hard not to yawn at the succession of speakers who introduced each other at great, great length. Both Whit Harris and Dan were seated at the long head table, up on a dais, draped with class banners and school colors; and for a while she amused herself by comparing them. Whit, she decided, was like one of those smooth, highly polished stones: a piece of jade or agate that glowed without ever shooting off sparks of light; whereas Dan seemed full of planes and hollows, changing as he moved, radiating an underlying sparkle, like a half-cut gem. She had to smile at herself. So that's what they meant by a diamond in the rough!

Whit Harris's suit seemed impervious to wrinkles. What would it be like to make love with a man who didn't wrinkle? Sex was usually so magnificently messy. She very carefully kept herself from remembering Dan in bed. It was too agonizing, and that elegant little blonde she'd seen so briefly on the stairs at the dormitory kept intruding. He'd been with *her!* While she had done her nails and watched TV in Madison, smiling to herself and planning what she'd cook for him the night he got back—if she'd ever be able to get out of the bedroom and into the kitchen—while she had so blithely looked forward to his return, he'd been—oh, the bastard! His strong arms around *her,* his hand patting *her* rump and ruffling *her* hair, biting his lower lip when he was ready to—the bastard! Letting her sit there in her ignorance being *happy* while he poured his ecstasy into that skinny little body! The blonde was a poor, pale little thing. Gorgeous clothes and a beautiful face, that had been obvious even in one quick look. But a frail, almost childlike body. That wasn't Dan's type, not at all! A woman like that wouldn't ever be any good to him! So closed in, so private. That was no good for a politician! What did he *see* in her?

Dinah closed her eyes momentarily against the sudden thrust of pain. When she opened them, Dan was standing at the podium adjusting the mike, grinning, relaxed, his eyes taking in the room. She'd listen to him and she'd report to Jim, but that was the very last job she'd do for them. Whit Harris would be her *own* private project.

Dan was good, as usual. He was awfully good with crowds. They always laughed at his throwaway jokes.

They always hushed when he furrowed his brow, leaned forward, and grew serious. And when he leaned back, so did they all, loosening right up with him. He might just make it, even without the American Health money, even without the television spots. People were ripe for a change. And most voters didn't realize how the system worked. If they elected Dan, they'd have a freshman congressman instead of the Good Old Boy they were blessed with now, who'd been twelve years in Congress and held the chairmanship of an important committee, plenty of jobs and plenty of pull. Dan Copeland was bright and honest and smart, but it was anyone's guess how much he'd actually be able to accomplish. Congress was a big club and most members moved slowly, carefully, cautiously, because seniority counted.

Oh, hell. She wasn't working for him any more. She applauded with everyone and thought for a moment of leaving. But then Whit Harris caught her eye across the huge room and gave her a nod—a "discreet" nod. Dan wasn't even aware she was in the room! Let him go to his flaxen-haired madonna, his pale lady. They'd soon be miserable. What did *she* know of the life she'd be leading? Never seeing him. Always coming second to the great electorate. Her life full of his cronies, most of whom she would hate . . . hell, most of whom *he* didn't even care for! A life marked in two-year segments, with preparations for the campaign and then the campaign and then recovery from the campaign. And then preparations for the *next* campaign. Phone calls at all hours. Political dinner after political dinner. Late-night trains and late-night planes. A life that was mostly male, that mostly excluded women, kept them separate, only turning to them in bed—and sometimes not even then. Did the blonde beauty know how exhausted he could get, for weeks at a time? Was she prepared to wake from a deep sleep and fix sandwiches for fourteen people? Was she prepared to sit constantly by his side and smile and smile and smile? Was she prepared for loneliness? For no life of her own? For making do with good works?

He should have stuck with me, Dinah thought. I know what it is and I could do it, easy!

"What?" she said. The woman across the table was tapping her hand.

314

"There's Judy Slavin. Remember Judy?"

"I . . . I'm not sure." It was just too much trouble to say she wasn't a returning classmate.

"President of Pan-Hell our senior year, silly! Still full of beans! Just look at her!"

Dinah focused on the head table. An overweight woman, looking immense in a fluttering, many-colored caftan that billowed about her shapeless body, was clutching at the microphone and waving at the crowd. Her frosted hair had been teased and lacquered into an elaborate puff, and when she tossed her head, which she did often, it sat without a ripple, like a dead thing, not a hair stirring.

"Hi, everyone!" The girlish voice came stridently over the speakers. "Isn't it wonderful to see each other again?" There was some scattered applause and a few weak cheers. "I just want to say: Will the girl whose left ear I pierced in 1970 please step forward and I'll do the right one!" The whole room erupted into loud laughter and the woman's large, round face beamed with pleasure. Off in the back of the room someone shouted, and when Dinah turned, she saw a woman standing in the midst of the dessert plates on her table, waving both arms. "Sue Babcock!" the amplified voice squeaked. "For goodness' sake! I'll be right over!" And, to a great deal of applause, the former president of Pan-Hellenic gave the microphone over to a slender, balding man who apparently had been class president.

Prizes were given: the most children . . . the most successful . . . Here, Dinah was somewhat startled to see the dark man she'd noticed at the bar come up to take a bow. Jay Shulman, his name was, and he was apparently a movie producer of some renown. ". . . and I'd like you all to meet," he said, after giving thanks for his prize —a gigantic class banner, "one of Hollywood's newest starlets . . . Miss Gigi Vaughn. Stand up, darling." Again there was an outburst of applause; and Dinah, amused, wasn't quite sure whether the applause was for Miss Vaughn's up-and-coming career or for her up-and-coming breasts, barely covered by a sequin-embroidered halter which slid breathtakingly from side to side as she bowed to the room. Dinah herself caught sight of one large pink nipple for just a second, and she noted that the men at her table looked as if they had collectively stopped breathing.

The girl was very young and very tall—how tall became apparent as Jay Shulman joined her, one arm curving around her hip, his dark head on a line with that splendid bosom. Shulman was smiling away and the girl seemed not to mind the audience's reaction; her pretty, rather vacant face never changed. Dinah's stomach muscles tightened. Didn't that girl see how she was being used? I wonder, Dinah thought, if every woman here feels flat-chested and inadequate. They shouldn't. She's nothing but a Barbie Doll, and *he* ought to be ashamed of himself.

"Can you picture *that* on a mattress?" one of the men at her table said loudly. "Oh, man! Oh, man!"

"Something like that'd keep me busy for ten days," another remarked.

To which his wife retorted: "For ten seconds, more likely! You wouldn't even know where to start!"

Dreamily, her husband said, still staring: "I'd know where to start." Which elicited uproarious laughter from the rest of the group.

I've had enough, Dinah thought, and got up. She inched her way through the crowded tables, only half hearing the next prize: the most famous—Lee Rivers. At the entrance to the room, she turned for a last look, feeling rather superior to these overgrown babies. From all the way across the room Whit Harris's eyes met hers, and he gave a shrug that seemed to echo her distaste. Yes, she decided, she'd meet him and have a drink or two. And then she'd make up her mind.

He came at her the moment the door had closed behind them, urging her toward the bed, shedding his clothes as he went. Buck-naked, ecstatically erect, he stood impatiently, waiting for her to get undressed. No playtime, Dinah thought, and it was the last chance she had to think anything. He took her, eager as a teenaged boy and just as self-centered. Nothing subtle, nothing practiced; yet she could not help enjoying it. He was big and strong and lusty, and he made her feel fragile and small and very young.

At the end, he collapsed over her, murmuring, "Good,

good," then rolled away and in a moment was fast asleep. She could hear his deep, regular breathing as she lay, still on her back, staring into the gloom of the plush, over-done room. She was more alone than ever, swamped with sadness, lost in the darkness of a strange room with a stranger sleeping beside her.

This is how it is, she told herself. Now do you remember? The casual encounter: the sure road to nowhere. She moved restlessly, hoping it would rouse him. Damn him for the illusion of intimacy! And then just to go to sleep! Tears of self-pity stung at her eyes. This would be her fate through those long years stretching ahead. One one-night stand after the other. Good old Dinah Franklin, always available to a man who made the right moves. What was it she'd overheard Big Jim say about a widow he knew in Madison? "So she's not so young and pretty any more. So what? Throw a flag over her face and screw for Old Glory!" How he had roared; how the roomful of men had laughed. The bastards!

She blinked frantically at the tears building up. When Whit Harris woke up, she dared not let him see a ravaged old broad lying next to him. Oh, yeah? What was she say-ing, she *dared* not? She still had options. Some options: stay or leave. Well, okay, then, she'd leave. To hell with him and to hell with all of them. And to hell with Dan Copeland—it was all his fault, anyway!

She stirred and sat up, and instantly a hand shot out to curve around her hip. "Where do you think you're going?" The voice sounded awake.

"Home. To my own room."

"Wait." He shifted to lie on his side, facing her. "Don't go. I want to talk to you." He laughed self-consciously. "Remember? I said at the dinner that we'd talk later."

"Yeah, well, I guess this is *later*, all right."

He ran his hand gently over her hip and into the curve of her waist. "Was it . . . good for you?"

"It was . . . well, you make love as if you'd never done it before. Very enthusiastic."

After a pause, he said solemnly: "In a way, I never have. At least not with a woman like you."

She longed to ask him what that madonna was like; longed to hear how cold and sexless she was. But Whit Harris was not the kind of man you peeled like an orange.

The warmth she felt from him now was very tentative. She felt that one wrong question would turn him off; and, she realized, she did not want to turn him off. She asked: "What was it you wanted to talk about?"

After a pause: "There's a job for you at the American Health lobby office in D.C. Thirty-seven five and a nice expense account."

"Thirty-seven five! For doing *what?*"

"It's not what you think, Dinah! I'd have offered it to you even if we hadn't . . . well, even if we hadn't. It just slipped my mind downstairs." His voice grew husky as he leaned closer to her. "I just couldn't think of anything else right then." Then, all business again: "Public relations director is what it is. A lot of press contact and a lot of writing. The girl doing it now has given notice: she's got a job with the *Post*. You'd do a great job. The pharmaceutical lobby represents millions of dollars and impacts the health of everyone in the country. Dan Copeland is small potatoes. Believe me, I've known him for thirteen years, and he's always been the same self-serving bastard. You'd be doing the same sort of thing you did for him, only with more clout."

Dinah began to laugh. She could hear that it sounded hysterical, but she couldn't stop. The same sort of thing she did for Copeland, indeed! So true, so horribly true!

"Whatever you're thinking," Whit said severely, shaking her, "forget it. I'm not interested in knowing what sort of . . . relationship you may have had with him, and I'm certainly not talking about that. I'm discussing a *job*. Are you interested—in a job? Or not?"

She stretched to snap on the bedside lamp and turned to look him in the eye. Did he mean it, really? He blinked at the light once or twice and then regarded her steadily. Without his expensive clothes and with his hair rumpled, he looked very different—younger, more vulnerable.

"I'm interested, of course I'm interested," she answered. "That's very nice money and I love Washington. But . . ."

"But you're wondering what else you have to do to earn your salary. Nothing. Just your job." He pulled himself up to a sitting position and reached out for her hand. "Of course, I'd be lying if I said I don't hope . . . I do find myself in D.C. quite often, several times a week in fact, and . . ."

"Yes?" She stiffened. *"And?"*

"I'm doing this very badly. The job is yours if you want it. You don't have to go out with me if you don't want to. It's not part of the deal. But this . . . tonight was wonderful. *You* were wonderful. I look forward . . . Dinah, I *like* you. I'd like to see you again. But if you have qualms . . ."

He left off, obviously in distress. Uncomfortable color was climbing up his face. To her surprise, Dinah felt maternal. Hell, she was actually *sorry* for the poor guy.

"Never mind, Whit. I understand. I get the job even if I never go to bed with you again. Right?"

He flushed even deeper and licked at his lips. "That's putting it bluntly. But yes, I suppose that's what I mean."

She regarded him carefully. "I'm forty-one."

He leaned over and ran a slow hand down the curve of her breast. "You don't look it. And frankly, I don't care."

Well. She had her options, all right. Hang on in Madison and hope for the hopeless, or take a chance on Washington and Whit Harris.

"Okay, then. You have a deal." She swung her legs over the side of the bed. "See you in two weeks."

"Wait!" She turned to look at him over her shoulder. "Where are you going at this hour?"

"We had our talk."

"Yes, but . . . Look, Dinah, can't you stay all night? I—I'd like you to." He ran a hand down her back. "You're so soft and warm," he murmured, and then added in almost a whisper, "Please."

She sat very still on the edge of the bed, leaning into the stroking of his big hand. To go to her room now, to cold sheets and empty walls, with no company but her own bitter thoughts . . . No. At least here there would be someone in the night beside her, the weight of his body warm against her. And when she woke tomorrow, he would be there. Maybe they wouldn't be able to look each other in the eye, but at least tonight she would not be alone.

CHAPTER TWENTY

Klass of '70 Kum-Back Komments

JANUARY 15, 1981

Hi, there, Klassmates! This is ye olde editor
COURTNEY WILLS STANDISH, reporting on our
glorious Well-Kum-Back Reunion.

Wasn't it fun? Wasn't it just the best ever? JOCK
and I certainly think so and hope you all agree.

I'm sure all of you have heard about our great excitement the day of the big football game, when that
woman had that fit at DAN COPELAND and he and
JOE RUGOWSKY had to carry her out of the stadium!
Would you believe she even attended Hampton for a
while? Although, of course, she never graduated! And
my guess is that's where she heard of DAN, who was
definitely a BMOC in those days.

Former State Trooper JOE RUGOWSKY tells me
that the lady has been committed to an institution in
New Hampshire. Yes, I said "former." JOE recently
left the state police, even though he was promoted to
sergeant, to take over a big dairy farm. Says he wants
to spend more time with Elaine and the kids. Good luck
to JOE!

Hey! And good for us, '70ers! Together, we all
pledged $56,872.57 to the scholarship fund. A whopping
72 percent of our class made their pledges. And the
dean would like to know who is the cheapskate who
pledged that $2.57! Ha-ha.

All the questionnaires I could wait for are in.
Shame, shame on the twenty-six alums who enjoyed

the reunion but did *not* do their homework. Haven't changed since college days, have ya? To all you others, thanks a million. Now it can be told: Eighty-nine percent of us are married. We have an average of 1.6 children each. We've traveled everywhere from China to Alaska. We live in 22 states and 3 foreign countries. We have 34 lawyers, 16 doctors, 4 farmers, 3 veterinarians, 27 schoolteachers, 54 businessmen, 2 politicians, 3 judges, and a Sumo wrestler. (Wasn't it wonderful, seeing old DICK MERWYN again at reunion in his funny Sumo get-up? He won the prize for coming the longest distance, all the way from Tokyo!) Thirty-eight percent of us are gay divorcées (not really gay, ha-ha!), and that includes the latest, LINDA BARRONE, who will soon be attending med school at Downstate. Sorry your marriage didn't work out, but good luck, anyway, LINDA.

Now, here's some nice news: JENNIFER GLADSTONE, for those of you who remember her, has just been appointed a Family Court judge. Isn't that terrific? And she never said a word for the whole reunion weekend. Don't be shy, JEN! We always want to know all about our famous classmates.

Speaking of famous, our own JAY SHULMAN, the renowned Hollywood and Broadway producer, is deep into a revival of *Gypsy*. The word is that it'll cost him *three million dollars* and guess who's gonna have the lead? None other than our famous and popular LEE RIVERS. It can't miss with a Hampton team like that! Right gang?

And listen to this, people: JAY courted his leading lady by sending her anonymous roses all over the world. LEE spoke to me about it at reunion, and she didn't have a *clue!* Then, at the Well-Kum-Back Dinner and Decennial Blast, didn't he present her with a dozen roses and an offer to do *Gypsy*, right in front of everyone! LEE looked absolutely astonished!

So see what you missed, all you pikers who didn't come. Read it and weep! She sang a number for us, too. Some of us got her autograph (I was one of them, lucky me!) and, believe me, it's really going to be worth something one of these days!

And wedding bells will be ringing soon, in London,

for LEE and BENNO AKKARDIJIAN. This is the romance of the year, gang, and it all happened at— guess where? Right here at Hampton, the weekend of the reunion! That's right, LEE and BEN hadn't even seen each other since graduation. It was love at first sight, thanks to the Well-Kum-Back Kommittee, who dug up everyone's address. They'll be married in February.

And here's another famous person: DAN COPELAND (former chief of the Students' League, back when it was so active on campus. Sad to say, there's no more S.L. at Hampton) is now a United States congressman from all the way out there in Wisconsin. He won his election by a narrow margin, just 257 votes, but so what? He's still a big winner in my book, and we all wish him well at his new job in Washington, D.C. DAN gave a rousing speech at our dinner. See what you missed?

DAVID HABER has been named an assistant vice-president of Burke & Knowls, one of the really big-time advertising agencies in New York City. LYLA HABER has been a top exec at Flair Designer Fashions forever. Keep up the good work, DAVID. You'll catch up with your wife pretty soon . . . maybe. Ha-ha.

WHITNEY HARRIS III, who presented Hampton with a beautiful new lab in honor of his father, WHITNEY HARRIS II ('36), at the dinner, has just been elected a director of the Nassau County Trust Co. Congratulations, WHIT! How about a nice mortgage for a bunch of old classmates? Seriously, though, Hampton's Chemistry Department is extremely grateful to WHIT for a most generous gift. (And it was swell seeing our Sweetheart of Sigma Chi, WHIT's wife, KITTY, too!)

And here's my exciting news! JOCK and YOURS TRULY, along with SPARKY and BUFFY MORTON, have bought a perfectly adorable old inn right outside Geneva, just seventeen miles from the thruway. It's kinda falling apart, but we're going to fix it all up ourselves and invite you all to come by and have a meal, any time after July of this year. Yes, it's a lot of hard work, but those of you who live near Hampton know how famous BUFFY's bran muffins are and the Junior League usually gobbles up my Quiche Lorraine, so we

shouldn't have too much trouble setting a good table.
The house is a quaint Victorian, and we plan to paint
it pink and call it The Pink Gables, isn't that cute?
Look for our brochure, which will be coming to you
in the U.S. mail sometime this spring. And do come
visit The Pink Gables. We'll need all the business we
can get. Ha-ha.

Well, JOCK and I just can't believe it's already
after New Year's and three months since the Well-
Kum-Back Weekend. How time flies! And already
many of the Klassmates are writing me to say they just
can't wait until the twentieth reunion. Should we have
a fifteenth? What do *you* think? I think it's a neat idea.
Let's have votes from all of you out there. Send a postcard to me, COURTNEY WILLS STANDISH, c/o
The Pink Gables, RFD #4, Millfield, N.Y. 11872.

Well, it's time to say goodbye for now. Don't forget,
send all your news to me.

Hamptonly yours—

COURTNEY WILLS STANDISH
Klass Sekretary

CHAPTER TWENTY-ONE

The Harris Family

KIT LET THE MIMEOGRAPHED SHEETS slide from
her fingers. Good old Courtney, she thought, always in
there trying so hard. Sorry, Courtney, but you missed
some good stuff. How about this one? "WHIT HARRIS,
dynamic prez of Harris Pharmaceuticals and board mem-

ber of organizations too numerous to list, has not slept
with his wife, KIT, since he threw her on the floor of
Room 31, Enders Hall, Saturday evening of the Well-
Kum-Back Weekend, and had his way with her." Oh, and
there's more: "This delightful expression of love and devotion took place just hours after KIT had sneaked away
from the room of well-known politician DAN COPE-
LAND, where she had spent the night. Who would've
guessed it of little KITTY CAMERON, the Zeta Phi Offi-
cial Virgin? Well, good luck to you all, KITTY and
WHIT and DAN!"

She could just picture the look of genteel disgust on
Courtney's face, and the actual lip-licking delight she
would take in such a wonderful tidbit. The thought made
her smile a little.

"What's so funny?" asked Lily. "The thing you got
from Hampton? Lemme see it . . . oh, goody, gossip. I
love gossip." She bellied herself across the breakfast table
to grab the newsletter.

"You won't find it interesting, honey," Kit warned.
"And I don't think this glass was meant to hold sixty-five
pounds."

"But I have to read it," Lily said, sliding off and plop-
ping back onto her seat. "It's all about your ree-*yoon*-yun
. . . oh, they tell about Daddy . . . and here's a thing
about Auntie Lee . . . oh, it's only about her getting married, and we already know *that*. Oh, wow! Here's all
about that crazy lady. Did you know Dan Copeland,
Ma?"

"Yes." Kit held her breath, waiting for the next inevitable question, but Lily only read on in a quick mumble.

"Huh!" she snorted. "The best ever! *You* didn't think it
was the best reunion ever!"

"What makes you say that? I thought it was lovely."

"Well, my God, you came home early! A whole day
early! So how good could it be?"

Kit picked up her coffee cup and stared at the child
opposite, who was wolfing a blueberry muffin. "Imagine
you remembering that, Lily."

Lily's face went immediately blank and bland. "I generally remember things," she said smoothly. "I'm not exactly dumb, you know." Her lips curved into a smug little
smile.

Kit quickly looked away from her. How like Whit she looked and sounded at this moment! The same smug certainty, the same silken tone smoothed over iron. Lily was changing. Kit had noted the physical changes for some time: the tiny budding breasts, the shadows in the cheeks where the baby plumpness used to be. Lily had lengthened out during the past couple of months and had taken to tossing her long hair in a certain pseudosophisticated manner. And did Lily come less and less often to her to be snuggled and cuddled, or was it just her imagination?

Kitty sighed. But this . . . this *toughness* was something new. Or perhaps she simply had not noticed it before. She had been very preoccupied since her return, very much into her own problems, very conscious of the need to keep Whit placated. It seemed to her sometimes that she spent most of her time reminding herself why she could *not* leave, however desperately she wanted to. The thought of Lily's sitting hour after hour in a courtroom, hearing herself labeled illegitimate: a bastard; hearing the man she called Daddy deny her; seeing her mother suddenly as a liar, a cheat, a fraud— No! Kitty could not allow it. A child of almost ten just couldn't handle all that. Lily would never be the same.

But it bothered her to see her candid, unaffected daughter mimicking Whit's worst qualities. That bland tone of voice with its hidden messages . . . was that something she wanted her daughter to emulate? Yet the longer they stayed here, in his house, the worse it would get.

"And anyway, Ma, how did that crazy person get into the game? Couldn't they *tell?*"

"Lily, darling, anyone with the price of a ticket can get into a football game." She sipped at her coffee.

"Even at *Hampton?*"

"What do you mean, *even* at Hampton? What's so special about Hampton?"

Lily grabbed a pear and spoke with her mouth full. "Well . . . you know . . . Daddy's always talking about how special Hampton is. Only the cream of the crop, he says. I mean, gee, isn't that why the Harrises have always gone there? *I'm* going there."

"Cream of the crop! Is *that* what he's told you? It's a very good school, yes, a very old one. But all *kinds* of people go there, Lily. Even people who aren't Harrises.

Even people who are . . . very different from the people you know around here."

Lily pondered this for a moment. Then: "We're rich, aren't we?"

"Yes, you could say that."

"I like it. I don't ever want to be poor and live in a slum and not have my horse and be dumb."

"Lily! For heaven's sake! *I* was poor. Do you think I'm dumb?"

"But . . . you're different, Mommy!" With a shrug, Lily dismissed the subject. "And besides, you married Daddy."

So I did, Kit thought, so I did. Strange, how she hadn't realized that day by day, over all these years, Whit would surely be influencing Lily. Why had she been under the impression—the illusion, actually—that she was raising Lily all by herself? Because he was absent so frequently? Because of the cool distance that permeated all his relationships? But to a little girl, he was *Daddy*. Of course, she'd been stupid not to have seen it, not to have expected it. And here was her little Lily, almost ten years old, on the verge of preadolescence, modeling herself after him. Was a candid, outgoing child destined to become a typical Harris? Kit shivered. Not if she could help it!

She despised him. She supposed she had never really loved him, but there had been gratitude and perhaps a kind of affection. No more. Their . . . confrontation at the dormitory had destroyed the façade. He hadn't come after her to win her over, not at all. He had been intent upon her humiliation—and, she thought bitterly, it had worked. Since then, it seemed he could not bear to be near her. He had lowered her to a position where he could disdain her, yet he still claimed ownership.

He'd made his feelings very clear these past few months, reminding her of what he had threatened if she dared think of divorce. And how proudly he had smirked when he'd brought her the Madison newspapers. He'd had letters sent to the editor, hinting that the Students' League at Hampton had been Communist-backed. And a large mailing to the voters, postmarked Washington, D.C., claiming that Dan Copeland had taken illegal funds; that the plane in which his young wife had died had been tampered with; that he was a well-known womanizer; all kinds of nasty innuendoes.

The last offering he had brought her, she had crumpled up after a glance, saying, "You are disgusting!"

And he had laughed with real pleasure. "I can remember at least one occasion," he'd said slyly, "when you didn't feel that way, my dear Katherine."

Oh, he was horrible, horrible! But at least where Dan was concerned, all his conniving hadn't done him any good. In spite of everything, Dan had won his election—barely squeaking by, but he *had* won. He was Congressman Daniel Copeland of Wisconsin now.

He had taken office only two weeks ago. She couldn't help thinking about him, wondering what he was doing, what he was thinking, whether he thought about her. *Personality* magazine had done a short piece on him, with a picture. He was moving into his new office, shirt sleeves rolled up, a big grin on his face, the dimple flashing; surrounded by three pretty girls, members of his staff.

"At thirty-five," it read, "Congressman Copeland is not only one of the younger, handsomer new faces around, he is also that rarity of rarities on Capitol Hill: a bachelor. Rumor has it that women were lined up three deep to get a job on his staff. It is a fact that he has the prettiest staff around. (See above) And in a city where women outnumber men two to one, he is already on the top of many social lists. Administrative assistant Margie Gordon (the blonde at the far left) says: 'If we accepted every invitation he gets, he wouldn't have a minute for his real work.' What Congressman Copeland's real work will be remains, of course, to be seen."

She knew it by heart. She knew the picture by heart. Margie Gordon was small and fair—like herself, she thought with a pang. In the picture, her piquant little face was turned adoringly to him and her body seemed to yearn toward him. One little white hand touched him on the arm. How long would it be before little Margie Gordon was in bed with him? It hurt horribly. In some of her wildest fantasies—usually late at night, trying to fall asleep—Kit imagined herself writing a letter to the director: "Congressman Copeland loves *me*." It was crazy, of course. But that should have been *she* in the picture, on his arm, part of his life. Oh, sure, and what would the caption have read? "Congressman Copeland with his great and good friend Mrs. Whitney Harris III, whose husband is suing her as an unfit mother."

Maybe she *should* have gone with Dan that morning he had come out there to get her—just picked up and packed up and *gone*. But how *could* she have? To have left Lily behind would have been impossible. And if she had taken her along . . . ? No, of course it was crazy. She'd done the right thing, the only thing possible. If only she could have explained. But that would've been impossible, too. She should never have gone to the reunion. She knew now that she had gone *wanting* him to love her still, wanting to be with him again, wanting the old magic to work its spell. Oh, what a mess she had made of things!

And now she dreamed of him often . . . but it was a chilling dream, recurring night after night. It would begin sweetly enough with Dan making love to her. And then his face would melt and change and it would be Whit above her, a gloating, greedy Whit. It was always the same, and always she awakened sweating, her heart pounding painfully. It was so real, it would take hours to shake off her feelings of guilt and shame.

She had to stop thinking this way . . . but what if her body knew no difference between them? It could not be that; it *must* not be. That time with Whit, her animal responses, that had been an accident. Meaningless. It had just . . . happened. Such things happened to lots of women; she knew that from Trudy's mail. But she seemed unable to believe, herself, all the reasonable words she used to advise her readers. They wrote her gushing little notes of gratitude, while she sat and wallowed in guilt. It was getting harder and harder to pretend to be strong, wise, and sharp-witted. She had already warned her editor that she might not be able to write the column much longer.

Kit smothered a sigh and pushed herself up from the chair to refill her coffee cup. Lily had drifted into the kitchen, where Kit could hear her badgering Cook to make her a Boston cream pie. *"Immediately,"* she was insisting. "I *have* to have one." The time had come to put a stop to this sort of thing. When she was a tiny child, it had been cute and amusing to hear that piping little voice giving orders. Now it sounded obnoxious. "But it will only take you five minutes, my *God*, what a fuss!" Lily was saying, her voice loud with imperious annoyance. She sounded like a spoiled brat. Her Lily!

With a thump, Kit banged the coffee cup down on the table. Whit, Lily, the article about Dan, her own guilty feelings, everything swirled together. It was *all* spoiled and rotting! To hell with Whit's threats and Dan's good-looking staff of unmarried women. To hell with all of them. In the end, it all came down to herself and her child. She had to get them both away from here!

It wasn't as if she'd be ruining a working marriage or breaking her husband's heart. There was nothing left. Whit had hardly been home since the reunion weekend, spending more and more time in his office in Washington or off on one of his interminable business junkets. The only time she was sure he would be in the house was when they were entertaining for business purposes—and even then he kept his distance. Several times, at night, she heard his footsteps out in the hallway and thought he paused by her door. But he always went on, leaving her with thumping pulse and dry mouth.

He seemed to make a point of walking in, appearing in his soundless way, while she was in the tub or toweling herself. Always when she was nakedly defenseless. He never came close, never approached her, just stood leaning against the doorway, smiling his tight little smile, looking her over as if she were an inanimate object he might or might not be interested in buying, and making small talk all the time.

It made her flesh creep, waiting to see whether he would come closer, whether he would touch her or try to handle her. But all he ever did was to stand there scrutinizing her, his arms folded across his chest, the blunt fingers stroking endlessly at his sleeves, while he discussed banalities: the bad air service in Cincinnati, the menu for a coming cocktail party, a tree that had to be removed from the front lawn, Lily's school grades. Banalities, while she waited with every muscle tensed for him to . . . what? As soon as he had gone, she would begin to shake. But, horribly, she could never be certain, was it because she had been dreading his touch . . . or, in some sick way, anticipating it.

She was sure he knew the effect he had on her and that he enjoyed it. Yesterday morning he had materialized at the doorway while she had still been immersed in the steaming water. As he had chatted on and on about something or other, the water had cooled. But she had been unwilling, that time, to get out of the tub, to stand naked, exposed to his watchful gaze. She could have leaped out and quickly grabbed her robe, but she had not wanted to give him that satisfaction.

At last he had gone away, leaving her once again to face the strange mixture of feelings these visits evoked. She had stepped from the tub, letting herself drip, luxuri- ating in her privacy. She had arched her back and stretched the muscles gratefully, both her hands resting on the curve just above her buttocks, her legs slightly apart, her head tilted back.

Idly, she had looked through the glass doors at the snow-drifted little garden. And had met the lazy, laughing dark eyes of Raymond, the young gardener. He had been leaning on his snow shovel, unabashedly admiring her and smiling a little. She had stared at him, frozen with shock, unable to shift her eyes from him, noting the mat of dark hair showing in the V of his thick sweater, noting the skin-tight faded jeans, noting how slowly his breath had plumed up in the still, cold air.

In a moment, she remembered thinking, he will move, he will put down the shovel, he will slide open the door, he will come inside, he will come to me, and I will not re- sist, I will . . .

And then he had stepped forward—or she'd thought he had—and she had run frantically, slamming the door of her bedroom behind her and bursting into wild sobs.

Whit, on his cat's feet, was suddenly there in the break- fast room, startling her as usual, pulling a chair back, and leaning over to get a croissant from the covered basket on the table.

"Why aren't these hot? Cook! Fresh croissants, please!"

It was not Cook who ran in with a fresh batch of the buttery rolls, but Lily, who delivered them with a kiss on his smooth, freshly shaved cheek.

"Well, haven't got time for an egg this morning. I'm off in fifteen minutes."

"Off! Oh, *Daddy!*"

"Now, Lily, don't carry on. I have to be in Washington for a very—"

"Washington *again,* Daddy? My *God,* what's so wonderful about Washington all of a sudden?"

"Watch your tongue, young lady."

"Well, sor-*ree!*"

"Lily!" Warningly. "What do we say when we've offended someone?"

"I *said,* 'Sorry.' "

"But not in the way *I* taught you."

In a subdued and honeyed voice, Lily said, "Sorry, Daddy," and quickly added in a more normal tone, "But I still don't know what I said that was so bad."

Indeed, Kit thought, watching them, what *had* the child said? Something about wonderful Washington? And then she smiled inwardly, thinking, Oho. Could it be the old story that out of the mouths of babes . . . ? She eyed Whit more closely. Was *that* why he looked at her as if he were hiding a secret? Why he made a point of looking but not touching? Could it be? Stiff, conservative Whitney Harris III with a girlfriend? Of course. That had to be it. Whit had a lady friend in Washington. And, as usual, he was operating on two sets of rules: one for himself and another for the rest of humanity. She was to toe the line and behave to his credit—while he went running off at every opportunity to be with his mistress!

Two sets of rules. Her set said she belonged to him no matter what. And now she was positive: He *had* been having her watched. Ever since her return from the reunion weekend, she'd had the feeling that the staff was asking rather more questions of her than usual. "Where will Madame be—in case needed?" "At what hour will Madame return?" "Where is Madame planning to shop? Yes, and after Bergdorf's?" Come to think of it, every time she'd planned to call a cab in the past few months, Martin had seemed to pop up out of the woodwork. The unutterable gall of Whit, to set spies on her while he blithely did precisely what he was punishing her for!

Her attention was drawn back to Whit and Lily by a whining tone in her daughter's voice. "And Mommy says *no,*" Lily was complaining.

"Why?" It was both demand and accusation.

"She says I don't *need* a new saddle, that the old one is big enough. But—"

"The old one is fine," Kit interrupted. "My God, Lily,

you just got your new boots and jodhpurs—a whole outfit
—for Christmas. There's no reason to spend four-hundred
dollars just because—"

Whit waved her to silence. "Let me hear the child out,
Katherine."

"Well, gee, Daddy, all the girls in the Pony Club are
getting new ones, and I can't be the *only* kid—"

Whit turned to face Kitty. "If she wants a new saddle,
get it for her."

"But, Whit, there's no reason—"

"She *wants* it. That's reason enough for me. Get . . . it
. . . for . . . her."

Lily hurled herself at her father, hugging and kissing
him noisily. Half laughing and half irritated, he removed
her, holding her at arm's length. "What do we say when
we've been given a present?"

Sweetly: "Thank you, Daddy." They smiled identical
smiles at each other.

Kitty observed all this without the anger she had expected. She felt remote, in fact. He had, of course, always
overridden her—or anyone else, for that matter—but usually with a little more finesse. Now, apparently, he was
ready to make it quite plain that he was in sole command, that she counted for exactly nothing. And to do
it so that the message came over so clearly to Lily—! This
was obviously not a matter for discussion. There was to
be no other way but his.

There was no changing Whit, in any case. He was fixed
in place—probably had been since childhood. And her
only influence over him was gone now—gone to Washington, she thought wryly.

He had pushed his chair back, was patting Lily on the
head. His goodbye, always, to his daughter. To Kitty he
said, almost as an afterthought: "Oh, and, Katherine,
when Judy and Louisa come for lunch, please have them
park their cars in back of the garage instead of on the
drive."

He left then, with Lily tagging along, chattering at
him, asking for something or other. Kit only half heard,
only half saw the snowy landscape outside. How could he
have known that Louisa and Judy were coming for lunch,
when she had just called them this morning on her private
line? *So. I have proof. I am being watched. Cook? But*

she had told Cook only that there would be three for lunch; she had never said *who*. And that had to mean that her phone calls were somehow being monitored. Anne-Marie. Oh, no, not Anne-Marie. But who else was as intimately involved with her comings and goings?

When Lily came back, to announce that she was leaving for the Pony Club, Kit kissed her absent-mindedly, her thoughts elsewhere. Upstairs, actually, in her own supposedly private suite. Where, even now, Anne-Marie was busily going about her business. And what was Anne-Marie doing? Taking care of her things or going *through* her things? And how many times had those clever Gallic fingers handled the page torn from *Personality* magazine, and what had that clever Gallic mind deduced from it? Whit must be paying Anne-Marie well for such disloyalty. But after all, was it disloyalty? They were *his* staff, paid to be loyal to *him*. What was she, anyway, but an appendage. Was she, she wondered, more or less valuable to Whit than the Mercedes? It, at least, had been custombuilt to his specifications; whereas he had taken her *as is:* pregnant with another man's child.

His rage must be incredible, she thought. All those years he must have been seething. And hiding it, pushing it down, pretending it wasn't there. She saw now that what he had done to her on the floor of that room in Enders Hall had not been making love. He had been making *hate*. And it was out of hate, not love, that he was determined to keep her here, captive to his blackmail. Not because he wanted her any more, but because he wanted a flawless picture of his marriage to show to the rest of the world.

Oh, no. Not her. Not any more. It was time to stop allowing herself to be pushed passively along life's road. She saw her life clearly at last, and she didn't like what she saw: a pallid, placid woman who bent with every breeze. Who was still just going along, pretending, denying her *own* anger, showing a false face of cool composure.

She remembered very well when she had decided how to present herself to the world, to keep the world at bay. A real live girl had boarded the bus in Virginia that September. But the Kit Cameron who had got off in Hampton was a careful creation: the cool, distant, untouchable beauty. And it was this creation who had made her entrance into Enders Hall that bright and sunny afternoon, very aware of heads turning to follow her every carefully planned step. Even her voice, modulated and never allowed to rise above its soft level, had been part of that creation.

I've been playing that role so long, she thought, covering her face with her hands, that I forgot who I really am! All just so I would be left alone! Just to keep men, their eager eyes, their clutching hands, at a safe distance. It was ironic: So sick of being treated like a beautiful toy, she had turned herself into one. Kit Cameron—the Virgin Goddess, Sweetheart of Sigma Chi.

Dan had been right all along. She had been herself— alive, emotional, involved—only with him. And, like a fool, she had *fought* it. Fought *him*.

Oh, what a fool I've been! She laughed aloud at the triteness of the thought. But it was true. And it was time to change all that. She ran from the breakfast room, went leaping up the stairs two at a time, and burst into her room, making sure the door was locked behind her.

She picked up the phone, her heart thumping with excitement. She'd make it all come out right! He had begged her to go with him—now she *would!* One phone call, one word to Dan—"Yes"—and a new life would begin—for her, for Dan, for Lily. She wanted to laugh out loud; it was so easy, wasn't it, once you made up your mind to move. To the devil with Whit; they'd take him on gladly! Dan would never give in to Whit's tactics, never! He was too strong, too smart.

She dialed the Washington area code and then 555-1212, hoping she could hear the operator's voice above the wild pounding in her ears. "Congressman Daniel Copeland," she said, enunciating very carefully. "No, the office, please . . . C-O-P-E-L-A-N-D . . . yes, that's right . . ." But she did not write the number down. She sat, suddenly very still, her hand poised above the paper as if frozen. She hung up on the operator's cheery "Have a good day." Quickly she lifted the receiver again, listening. With great, gentle care, someone else was cradling an extension somewhere in the house.

She smiled—a grim twitch of the lips. Too bad, Whit, she thought. That's not where I'm going. Because she *couldn't* go to Dan! It was *not* a simple matter to wipe away years of mistakes. How could she even have considered it? Dan was just beginning *his* new life. How could she involve him in the kind of dirty, messy court battle Whit had promised? How could she endanger his career that way? Surely Whit would name names and give *all* the intimate details. The Washington papers would go crazy. How selfish of her! How stupid! She had no right to drag him through her personal mud . . . to wreck his career, maybe ruin his life. Not if she really loved him.

And I do, I do! She looked at her reflection in the mirror with despair. All her golden fantasies of the three of them—Dan, Lily, herself, a family at last—faded rapidly into nothingness.

Dan didn't know about Lily. This realization gave her an odd, hollow feeling in the pit of her stomach. Dan had no idea he was Lily's father. She couldn't just spring the truth on him. What if he was repelled? There was no way to take back the act of cowardice that had sent her running from him . . . running straight to the man he despised most. There was no way to make up for ten lost years, she could see that now. What was done was done. There was no running to Dan now. She would have to do it on her own.

She gazed at herself thoughtfully. What did she see? A small, thin woman, undeniably good-looking, but was she strong? Was she strong enough to break away and start afresh? The clear green eyes were sad, but the mouth was firm with determination. What's more, there was a good brain behind that porcelain brow. She could do it. And Lily? Could she imbue Lily with the strength necessary to leave this easy, money-cushioned existence, her friends, her school, the Pony Club and her horse, all the things she believed to be immutable and forever? Well, she'd just have to, that's all.

Kit stood up slowly and began automatically to get dressed. Funny, how suddenly it was so definite. She was leaving. Yesterday she would have waffled and wavered. Even an hour ago she would have put off thinking about it. Yet right now she knew exactly when she would go, and where, and how. It was so simple, suddenly. She and Lily would go to Lee's wedding and would not return. She considered this decision as calmly as if she had planned it for months. She would leave and face the other problems later. Unless . . . but no, there wasn't a chance that anything could be saved from her marriage.

She began to pace the room, walking back and forth, twisting her diamond wedding band around and around her finger. The next time he came in to stare at her, playing his little game, she would not cower like a cornered mouse waiting for the cat to pounce. She'd *do* something. What? She didn't know. Something. Maybe they could talk about a trial separation. Maybe . . . She shook her head. She'd figure out what to do when it happened. But first there was the matter of Anne-Marie. Anne-Marie had to go, or her every move would be reported. And then . . .

With a sudden smile, Kit stopped the nervous pacing. She stripped the rings from her finger, putting them carefully away in the little wall safe. A childish gesture, perhaps, she told herself, but she felt better, anyway. Lighter, freer. The first step on her way to a new existence. For just a moment Dan's face flashed in front of her. She clamped down on it, hard. Maybe, after Whit had vent his spleen on her . . . But now, now, for the first time, she was proving her love for Dan. She was doing, not what was best for her, but what was best for him. He might never know it. So what? *She* knew it. She was strong, she was free. And soon, soon, she would be on her own.

CHAPTER TWENTY-TWO

Whit and Kitty Reprise

SHE WAS AS BEAUTIFUL AS EVER, he thought. He stood in the doorway, watching as Katherine stepped gracefully from the tub, unaware of his presence. Her back was to him and he admired the delicate curve of waist into rounded buttock, the sheen of lemony winter light on her glistening skin. She was so fair, she might have been made of marble, except that the morning sunshine, streaming in the windows, lit the downy hair on her body with sparks of living gold. He followed one pearly drop of water as it tracked its way down the slender backbone, hesitated, then curved over her hip to drop invisibly to the floor. She stretched for the towel. Graceful, yes. And lovely—extraordinarily so, considering she had borne a child. Not a mark on her, not a sag. She half turned, the profile of her body silhouetted in sharp relief against the glass doors. Belly flat, breasts still high, smooth line from hip to thigh: so perfect, really, and he felt nothing at all. It made him want to laugh.

Because who would believe that he could be looking at this gorgeous creature in all her nakedness, knowing that he need only say the word and she would submit, and he did not even want her! He could hardly believe it himself. Katherine, he knew, was a woman most men fantasized about. He had seen plenty of them, here in his own house, at dinners or parties, using any excuse to put a hand on her. He had watched them, over the years, staring at her, fawning over her, yearning after her, wishing to God that they could be Whit Harris, if only for one night. He had often felt particular pleasure as he took her, imagining them looking on with lust and envy.

He licked his lips, remembering. The envy of other men was something he reveled in. He enjoyed all his beautiful possessions and was glad to put them on display. He disdained other men in his position who acted as if they were ashamed of their wealth: driving cheap cars, wearing their clothes to shabbiness. He knew they felt superior, keeping their riches secret, but he thought them simple-minded. It was the duty of men like himself to set an example, to show the world how things were done by a man of substance.

"Oh! My God! You frightened me!" Katherine had turned and was looking right at him, her eyes wide and her body trembling a little. It irritated him these days, her doelike supersensitivity. The least little thing startled her. In the past he had found it pleasurable, even stimulating on certain occasions. But in the past, of course, he had found his possession of her pleasurable in *all* ways. Things have changed, he thought with satisfaction.

She colored and hastily wrapped herself in the towel. This only amused him. Don't worry, he told her silently. I won't come anywhere near you. I'm no longer interested. And what do you think of *that?* Not even the thought of her pinned helplessly under him on the dormitory floor had the power to arouse him. Not even the memory of her own unexpected lust. No, on the contrary, he found that rather distasteful. It was not at all the sort of behavior he had ever wanted from his *wife*.

"Next time," she was saying, "a knock on the door—?"

"Oh, come, now, Katherine. You *are* my wife. Surely I needn't knock. Surely I have a right to be here whenever I wish?"

"Yes, it's *your* house, isn't it?" she said acidly. "So I suppose, yes, you have a right to be here. But I don't like finding you here all of a sudden. Please say hello or something, would you?" She turned away and began to dress, just as if he were not there. But he knew she was keenly aware of him. Her body was held very tensely and her movements were studied.

And all for nothing. Because he felt no desire whatsoever. It was really gone. Since Dinah, Katherine seemed to his eye almost birdlike, overly frail, skinny, even. Dinah, now . . . Dinah was soft everywhere, everywhere curved and cushiony, her breasts firm, her legs a vise around his back. No sharp bones in Dinah. When he took her in his arms, he simply sank in.

Katherine raised her arms to get her shirt, and the small, sharp bones of her ribs pushed against the white skin. Too thin, too delicate. A man might well fear ripping that narrow body apart. Whereas Dinah . . . it was like plunging into velvet. His loins tightened and the flesh stirred. Not again! He shifted slightly to hide the sudden bulge. Ever since that first night with her, it had been like this. Three times he had taken her, and each time had been better than the last. Even in the morning, half asleep and very tired. He had not known a woman could make you feel like that. It was disturbing that a man like himself should be so out of control. He kept promising himself to stay away. But he couldn't seem to stop. His thoughts had only to drift to her for a moment, and—like this time —he would find himself rigid with desire.

Bare-breasted, still holding her shirt in one hand, Katherine was coming toward him, a little half smile on her lips. She must have seen! She must be thinking—!

She stopped, mere inches away from him, almost touching him, and lifted knowing eyes to his. "Whit?" And she stood there, waiting. He cleared his throat and smoothed his hair with one hand. Perhaps he should take her quickly. Otherwise, she might wonder . . . and he was keeping Dinah a secret. No one knew; he was sure no one even suspected.

But Katherine's smell of herbs and soap was astringent. And it was not the musky scent that lived in Dinah's skin. He gazed down at his wife and thought, Others may dream of you, but no one can have you. Nobody. He wanted to laugh in her face, a poor thing with nothing left but her sterile beauty.

"What is it?" he said.

"It's been three months since . . ."

She knew about Dinah! But how?

"Yes . . . ?" he said, his voice wary. "Three months since—?"

"Since the reunion. Since we came back. Since you started avoiding me."

He relaxed. "Not at all. I'm perfectly satisfied with things as they are."

"Whit, don't *do* that. Don't evade the issue."

"I don't know what you're talking about."

"Whit, for God's sake, you're never home! We never speak! We haven't slept together! We don't have a marriage any more! That's what I'm talking about!"

What did the woman expect of him? She'd cheated him from the very start, tricked him, lied to him. But she was lucky. She happened to have all the qualities he needed in a wife: She was beautiful, socially adept, but essentially cold. Let them all long after her—and they did, they did!—she was above that sort of thing. Perfect. Many a deal had gone through because she had enchanted some executive or other.

She was an *asset*. His asset. Why should he give up an asset that paid off in such handsome dividends? There were far worse marriages than theirs; he saw them all the time. Most of the men he knew didn't sleep with their wives. Who cared? Didn't she know how lucky she was that he hadn't sent them both packing ten years ago? She and Lily would never lack for anything. What else could she want, for the love of heaven?

"Really, now, Katherine. I don't have the time to discuss trivialities. As a matter of fact, I'm on my way out."

"Indeed." Again that strange little smile. And what was so amusing? Did she or did she not know something? She had moved even closer; she was crowding him. He backed away from her. Strange, how insensitive the female of the species could be; didn't even know when she wasn't wanted.

Katherine smiled at him. "Thank you, Whit," she said. "You've just answered all my . . . *trivial* questions, anyway. We needn't talk any more. You're free to go."

So she was *allowing* him to go, was she? Who did she think she was? After all he had done for her? So calm and controlled. He clenched and unclenched his fists. Ungrateful bitch, making a mockery of her marriage vows—from the very moment she had uttered them! Calmly, still smiling at him, she shrugged her shirt on and began to button it.

His hands darted out, grasping her breasts, squeezing. She gave a sharp gasp and the smile dropped from her lips. "That's right, Katherine," he grated. "You're my wife. Mine. Until *I* say otherwise." She stared at him, all the color draining from her face. He squeezed harder and watched with pleasure as she winced. "That's right, my dear. I could take you right now. But I'm not going to. Do you want to know why? Because I don't *want* you."

He let his hands drop from her breasts, seeing with satisfaction how she stumbled a bit backward, how she clutched the shirt together in front of her chest, her breathing ragged. "Good," he said, feeling his urgent flesh begin to stiffen once more.

"I'll be in Washington," he added, already moving away, his thoughts spinning ahead to Dinah's succulent body. To hell with tomorrow's meeting; he knew what everyone would say, anyway. "And I don't know when I'll be back!" he shot over his shoulder.

He was half running and almost to the stairs, so he couldn't be sure if he was imagining it. But later, thinking about it on the plane, he believed he might have heard the sound of her laughter.

CHAPTER TWENTY-THREE

Kit Harris's File Marked "Trivia"

LONDON, JANUARY 26, in a rush.
Darling Kit,
How marvelous! You were the one I really wanted to witness my delicious folly. Can you believe—me, getting *married*? I can't. I pinch myself every day to make sure I'm not dreaming. I love him, I love him, I love him. I love the whole *world*, that's how much I love

him. Kitty, was he always so terrific? He's funny and charming and smart and stubborn and strong and sexy, and he's always there when I need him. He knows me so well! How I do gush on. I hope I don't embarrass you when you're here. Ben found a lovely little flat off Sloane Square for you and Lily (I'm so happy she's coming)! Not far from us, you'll love it. Someone will pick you up at Heathrow. Please don't mind if it isn't us; my schedule is packed. We'll call soonest. Yes, a long dress, if you please. Wait till you see my gown! All satin and lace and embroidered pearls! It's a giggle. Oh, I can't wait to see you.
Love, Lee

January 20
Anne-Marie:
Enjoy your vacation. Here's a little something extra to thank you for all your special attention. Give my best to La Belle France.
Mrs. Harris

Dear Mommy,
I hate it when you and Daddy don't talk to each other, it skares me. If you want a divorse its okay. I know all about divorse from my friends. I'll cry but I can take it.
Love, Lily Cameron Harris

To: Bosley Stanworth, Headmaster
SEABROOK COUNTRY DAY SCHOOL
This is to inform you that Lily Harris will be absent from school for the first two weeks in February. She will be visiting relatives abroad. May we have her assignments for those weeks so she can keep up with her class? Many thanks.
Katherine C. Harris

Dear Mrs. Harris:
Attached are two 1st-class tickets to London, departing Flight #206, February 1, Kennedy Airport, 11 A.M. Arriving Heathrow, 10:40 P.M. Return Flight #733, departing Heathrow, February 17, 12 noon. Arriving Kennedy 2:35 P.M.

Please remember to reconfirm your return flight in London. Let me know if there is anything else I can do for you.
Sincerely,
Lionel Williams

27 January
TO: K.H.
FROM: Marvin
RE: New Series
It's all set. You send us four pages every week. To be called LETTER FROM LONDON. Human interest, your usual good stuff. Contract enclosed. Sign three copies, keep one. "Trudy" lives on! Ron Arnold says he'll give it his best. But between you and me, it just won't be the same. Hurry back.
Best, M.
P.S. Last "Trudy" from you running 1 Feb. per your request.

Dear Trudy,
My husband doesn't love me any longer, and I know he is having an affair in another city. As a matter of fact, Trudy, I don't love him, either. Yet he will not let me go. I'd like at least a separation, but he won't hear of it. He's told me over and over that if I even try to leave, he'll involve me and our child in a messy custody battle.

I have already consulted an attorney without his knowledge and have been told that there are ways to protect my child. The marriage is over; even our child knows it and has told me so. I feel the time has come to leave and give us all a chance at happiness. I can't understand why he hangs on in spite of everything.

I've made my plans (secretly, because secrecy is necessary) to leave soon. After ten years of a loveless marriage, do you think I owe him anything? Is he crazy, or am I? Am I right to end this dead-end relationship? What should I do?
Sincerely,
Puzzled

Dear Puzzled:

What do you mean, what should you do? You don't sound very puzzled to me. It seems to me you've already made up your mind; seeing an attorney shows that.

But if you're asking me what I think about loveless marriages, well, perhaps I'm romantic, but I believe that love is what makes the world go round. If love is missing from your marriage, I'd say there's no marriage at all.

If a small child can see there's bad trouble, my advice is, get that child out of the line of fire. Kids know more than you think they do. My mailbox has often seen letters from kids who ask me, "Why don't my folks just go and get divorced instead of making each other miserable?" The plain fact, Puzzled, is that a Mom and Dad at daggers drawn wound the innocent bystanders—their kids.

You seem to be doing the only possible thing. Make a clean break now, while you have the courage. Too many couples hang on and on to something that's already dead.

Your husband only *thinks* he needs this marriage. He sounds desperate to me. Is he perhaps thinking of what others might say? Or is he just so possessive that he can't let *anything* out of his grasp? Either way, it bodes no good for you *or* your child. My guess is, you'll all be healthier apart. Go to it, lady. Set yourself free. By freeing yourself, you'll be freeing *him*, too. In his heart, he'll thank you for it.

Yours truly,
Trudy

On February first, Kitty neatly folded the newspaper open to page 8, to show the "Tell It to Trudy" column, and left it on Whit Harris's night table.

CHAPTER TWENTY-FOUR

London, England

DAN WALKED SLOWLY, savoring the intimate, human scale of the London scene. His head felt slightly fuzzy from the hours on the plane, doubly so since it was now eleven in the morning and he had left Dulles at eleven last night. Still, jet lag or no, London was an eternally fascinating and comfortable city. He was skirting the edges of Sloane Square, where the grass was bright, dewy green and the fountain, even in February, bubbled gaily. What a change from D.C., where only yesterday they had been trying to dig themselves out of an unexpected ten inches of snow!

Here it was cold, but not bitter, and a white mist hung in the air, softening the edges of the buildings and creating halos around the street lamps.

Typical London. As if they ordered a romantic fog especially for the tourists. He drew in a deep breath and exhaled with pleasure. It was good to be away from the hurly-burly of Washington. It was good, especially, to be here, in this most civilized of cities. He was glad he'd let the cab go early.

Now he checked again with the cable folded into his coat pocket.

TAKE CAB 9 SLOANE SQUARE SECOND FLOOR REAR STOP KEY UNDER FLOWERPOT STOP SORRY CAN'T MEET STOP SEE YOU BREAKFAST BEN

He looked around. Number nine should be across the square. Some friend! Invites you to be his best man and

345

can't even meet you at the plane. Maybe it was better this way. He'd let himself in, it would be nice and quiet, and he'd run himself a bath and have a drink and sack out. No ringing phones, no last-minute crises, no sudden meetings.

He crossed the square, anticipating the luxury of soaking in a hot tub and feeling the ache of tension seep away. There'd be enough excitement at the wedding, that was for sure. He laughed to himself. What had Ben told him? Lee's entire, large, noisy Cuban family was being flown over en masse from New York, while Ben's entire, large, noisy Armenian/Italian family was being flown over from Rome, Paris, Zurich, Salonika, and Rio de Janeiro.

Kit might be there. He hoped Kit would be there. He hoped it so much that he hadn't dared ask. To be told "no" would have meant the end of his fantasies. She was a constant ache in his heart. Even when he was at his busiest, the thought of her nagged at the edge of his mind. He had to forget her. But the fact was, he couldn't forget her. Couldn't. Couldn't let her go.

He had been fool enough, back in October, to drive seven hours through the dark to the Harris estate, all the way from Hampton, chasing after her.

It had been a misty day, very much like this one in London, when he had finally arrived at the locked gate spanning the wide drive, with the chauffeur standing watchfully on the inside. He had been fuzzy with exhaustion then, too. His eyes were smarting from the effort of night driving on unfamiliar roads, and he stumbled a bit getting out of the car.

He had thought of her all the way down, filled with righteous anger. He was the white knight in shining armor, come to rescue his lady from the tower, with Whit the evil black knight, of course. It stood to reason, he thought, leaning against the iron gate, that the picture was complete, even down to the dragon guarding the locked castle.

"I want to see Mrs. Harris."

The man was stone-faced. "I'm sorry, sir, nobody is allowed past the gate until Mr. Harris returns."

"Mrs. Harris will want to see me."

"I'm sorry, sir."

"Goddammit, I insist that you tell Mrs. Harris I'm here!"

"I'm sorry, sir, but I have my orders."

Dan sucked in air and gripped the iron curlicues tightly. "Goddammit—!" Then he told himself to stay calm. "Listen, er—Martin, isn't it?—I've been on the road for nearly seven hours . . ."

"I'm sorry, sir. My orders . . ."

Damn Whit Harris for anticipating everything! He allowed a note of pleading to edge his voice. "At least tell her I'm here. See what *she* says." He noticed a gray metal telephone box attached to the stone pillar. "Does that phone connect with the house?"

"Yes, sir."

He marched over, picked up the receiver, and pushed every button on the thing, holding them down. Without another word, Martin turned and trotted toward the house. After a few minutes a cranky, high-pitched female voice crackled: "Yes? What is it?"

"Let me speak to Mrs. Harris . . . please."

"Do you know what *time* it is? Mrs. Harris is still asleep and—"

Kit's voice, blurred and indistinct, broke in: "It's all right, Mrs. Decker. I'll take it . . . oh, and you can go now."

"Kitty!" His voice was hoarse with relief.

"You shouldn't have come here."

He was shouting into the mouthpiece. "I had to come! Why did you run away from me? Kitty! What happened? Let me in!"

There was a long, static-filled pause. "No," she said. "I can't. You must go, Dan. Please."

"I'm not going! Let me in! At least *talk* to me! At least let me *see* you! It's—" He looked around wildly at the solidly locked gate, the avenue of scarlet trees hung with morning mist, and, beyond the curve of the drive, nothing. She was back there, warm and real. And all he had was her distorted, disembodied voice. "How can we talk when we can't see each other? Christ, it doesn't even *sound* like you! Are you still there?"

More static. Then, "I'm still here. Dan, please go. It's no use."

He was shivering in his dinner jacket. "Kitty, don't *do*

this to us. He can't keep you a *prisoner*, for God's sake. Let me *in!*"

"I can't, Dan. I can't explain . . . now. It's just too . . . complicated. Please, Dan, don't make trouble. *Please.* I'm sorry."

"That's not enough!" He pounded on the huge implacable stones with his fist. "Why? At least tell me that, tell me why!"

"I can't, Dan. Don't ask why. Just go and leave me alone." Her voice broke off abruptly and he heard strangled, echoing sobs, then, suddenly, silence. No static, no sound whatever. She had been cut off. He pushed his fist against the row of neatly labeled buttons and leaned on them. A pale sun was struggling against the wall of mist. What time was it? He didn't know. He didn't care. Where was she, goddammit? Where had she gone? What the hell was happening in there, anyway?

The chauffeur's voice suddenly came through. "I'm sorry, sir, but you must leave now."

"The hell you say, Martin!"

"I'm sorry, sir. Mr. Harris has instructed me to call the police if you refuse to go."

"Where is he? Send the bastard out here. Let him tell me face to face!"

"I'm sorry, sir, Mr. Harris is out of town . . ."

"Then put *Mrs.* Harris back on."

"I'm sorry, sir, but—"

"Put . . . her . . . on, I said!"

"I'm sorry, sir, but Mrs. Harris refuses to speak to you. I think, sir, it would be best if you left now."

The click was loud, final, definite. The air was quiet suddenly, just birds twittering in the trees. Dan backed away from the gray metal box, looking around. It was almost unbelievable that this was just an ordinary autumn morning in the Long Island countryside, trees lining a gravel drive, a stone wall, fat squirrels chittering. Her voice was gone, even her voice, and he had no way, no way at all, of getting to her. No way! Fury and frustration rose in his throat, threatening to strangle him. With a snarl, he grabbed at the metal box and pulled. It wrenched free, trailing colored wires. He pulled it out completely and flung it into the woods as hard as he could. And then, suddenly weary, he got back into the rental car and left.

Time had gone by and he had tried to forget her. With Margie Gordon, he had thought there just might be something. Margie reminded him of Kit, small and neat and fair. But after three dates it was obvious there was nothing. Nothing to say to each other. No chemistry. When he touched her, nothing happened. When they talked, he would find his thoughts wandering. Three dates were the end of it.

And what about Kushalata, who had pursued him so relentlessly? An Indian princess, gorgeous, exotic, determined to enact the whole of the Kamasutra within the next month. At first she had been diverting, to say the least. But in the end, he found he couldn't both keep on seeing her and do his job. And when he wasn't seeing her, he found he didn't care.

To his eternal shame, he had even thought of trying again with Dinah. When he spotted her at a cocktail party in Chevy Chase, he couldn't believe his eyes. She had left Madison without a word; her landlady said, "No forwarding address." And there she was, big as life and twice as beautiful, looking a bit heavier than he remembered, but oh, God, it was so good to see her there across the room full of strangers and he the new boy in town. By the time he had pressed himself through the crowd to her, she was gone. He looked everywhere; she had left. And then, when he got her telephone number from information and called her, she laughed at the sound of his voice. "Forget it, Dan," she said. "I don't want to see you." And hung up.

Dammit, there would always be women available to him. But none of them was Kit. That's what it all came down to in the end. Kit might be indecisive, selfish, cowardly, secretive, changeable, maddening—but *she* was the woman he loved.

Love. Elusive concept. Everyone talked about it, went searching for it, wrote songs in its praise. And yet, didn't most people walk right by, not even recognizing it? How many people in a man's life could he count on for love? Dan himself had cast off too many . . . out of stupid pride.

He began to dream about his father, seeing him young again, smiling at him, the hair still amber, untouched by silver, the body lean and straight. Not at all like the stooped and disappointed man who had roared: "Traitor! My son, a traitor and a pinko! Get out of my house! I can't stand the sight of you!"

It had started differently, the day he had returned from the war. His father and mother had met him at the station, teary-eyed and smiling. It had all been fine at first. He'd even been able to forget his rage, his disgust, at Vietnam. And then to come into the house and find the hall and the living room strung with balloons and crepe paper streamers, all set for a big party. He had felt so depressed, but willing to go along. Until he had seen the banner stretched full-length across one wall: WELCOME HOME OUR HERO.

Hero! He had turned, half choking, to his father. "Get that thing off the wall!"

The proud smile had been wiped off the lean face. "What do you mean?" his father had said.

"I'm not a hero! It's a goddamn lie! None of us are heroes—we're all patsies! Killing little kids! Burning down villages! Destroying every goddamn living thing in sight!" And he had stopped, breathing hard, the familiar cold sweat breaking out all over his body.

His father had tried to smile. "I know it was real bad, son. But that's war."

"That's *shit!*" He hadn't cared that he was hurting his father. He hadn't cared at all about anything. All his rage and disgust had come pouring out as he had stood in the gaily decorated living room and screamed his anguish. At the end of his tirade, his father had been pale with shock and anger. It was through clenched teeth that Dan had hurled the epithets, while his mother had wept behind him, pulling at him and making incoherent noises, trying to halt their inevitable breach.

He had left angry and had stayed angry for a long time, in spite of his mother's pleas. He had never seen his father again. The older Copeland had died of a sudden heart attack the year before law school graduation. Dan missed his father. Once they had been close, and because of his self-centered fury, he had cast his father out of his life, refusing to apologize. He had been too busy insisting upon his own moral purity to feel any compassion for the old man.

At least with Big Jim he had been more generous. He

had not arrived back in Madison from the reunion weekend until late Monday afternoon, when he fell into bed, weary and heartsick. Only an hour later he was dragged out of a deep sleep by the ringing phone. It was Jim—a strangely cautious, soft-voiced Jim—who said: "Well, at least *you're* back. Or are you?"

"What? What are you talking about?" Dan shook his head to clear it.

"Well, hell, boy, I haven't been able to find you all day! For a while I was thinking you'd quit on me, too."

"Too? Talk sense, will you, Jim? You just woke me up."

"Dinah's gone, Dan. Flew back, packed her bags, and just took off. I don't know what got into her." There was a long pause and then, very casually: "Do *you* know what happened?"

"Oh, Christ. I can guess, Jim. I don't know where she's gone, but I can guarantee one thing: She won't be back."

"Jesus Harold H. Christ on a pogo stick! What's the matter with these women, anyway, Dan?" There was another rather long silence. "I put Serena . . . away this weekend. And when I looked for you, up there on the campus, you weren't anywhere to be found. And then . . . you weren't here, either! I was beginning to think I'd lost *everybody* . . ." He tried for a laugh, but only a strangled sound came out.

It was that pale imitation of a laugh that did it. Dan's resolution—that he was finished with Jim—so carefully thought out on the long drive back from Long Island and again on the plane to Madison, burst like a soap bubble. Jim sounded lonely, almost afraid. That garrulous, forceful extrovert! Jim's anguish wrung at him. He had done it to his father. He couldn't do it again! To be so sure of his essential rightness that other people became expendable. How bereft his father must have felt . . . and that thought had never even entered his mind!

And so, instead of telling Jim goodbye, he said, making his voice hearty, "Well, you haven't lost *me*, Jim. Your favorite bad penny is about to get up, get dressed, and get back to work. We've got an election to win!"

Now the laugh was full and genuine. "That's my boy!"

Well, Jim's boy had done it. If he couldn't win the

woman he loved, he had to win *this*. That's what he had told himself. And he had won.

And there was number nine; he had almost walked right past it. A four-story modest building, its ground floor a Mexican crafts shop. The small door off to the side opened easily, and he was faced by a steep flight of stairs. Somewhere up there was the sound of a typewriter. But as he reached the first landing, the sound stopped.

Sure enough, there was a large Mexican flowerpot next to the door of the second-floor rear apartment. Big, brightly colored paper flowers overflowed from the earthenware vessel. And under it was a key.

He unlocked the door. He could almost feel that hot bath right now, could almost taste the smoky tang of Scotch on his tongue. He was in the tiniest foyer he had ever seen, barely room to turn around. No furniture, just an umbrella stand and three hooks on the wall. He slipped out of his raincoat and jacket and hung them up. Carrying the small case, he went into the sitting room, noting with surprise that a fire was burning in the fireplace. Ben's work? And then he sniffed; there was the aroma of coffee in the air. No, not Ben. A maid, perhaps? He made a face; he had been counting on being completely alone.

"Hello?" he called.

A door at the far end of the room swung open. Damn! It was a maid. He'd give her the rest of the day off. She stood by the door, small and blond, blue-jeaned and barefoot . . . *barefoot?*

Then he really looked at her.

"Kitty!" He stood rooted to the spot, still gripping his bag, gaping at her. It was like having a dream and waking up to find yourself still dreaming. But the Kitty who faced him looked very different. A pencil behind one ear, an oversized velour shirt drooping over the faded jeans, and . . .

"Your hair!" he blurted. It was short, cropped into a cap of pale shining curls, and from her ears hung large hoops of hammered copper.

"Is that a way to say hello?" She smiled at him.

"What are you doing here?"

Kit walked toward him. "I *live* here. What're *you* doing here?"

There was something unreal about all this. He had fantasized seeing her again, and now here she was, but she was different. The last time he had spoken to her, she had begged him, sobbing and distraught, to leave her alone. And now she was coming straight toward him, completely at ease, amused, even.

"I—I—Ben gave me this address—I have a cable somewhere. He left a key. I—I'm sorry—" Why was he stammering like a schoolboy?

She came toward him in the most natural way, reached over, took the suitcase from his nerveless hand, and put it gently on the floor. "Oh, those two! They think the whole world should be in love." She looked up at him through her lashes, laughing. "They even took Lily away with them. And I was so dumb, I didn't even guess why they insisted I should stay home and work!"

He gawked at her, feeling more than ever at a loss, thinking, Christ, how I love her. And then he stopped thinking. She was locked in his arms and he was kissing her, her hair, her nose, her neck, her mouth; hungry, greedy; crushing her tightly, reveling in the feel of her slender body molded against him. He would never stop kissing her, he would never let her go. Her mouth was warm and avid under his, her body pressed pliantly into him. The taste and smell of her were delicious. He pulled her even closer, aware of the urgent thrust of his own demanding flesh, the heat from her delicate loins. This was what it was all about!

When he lifted his lips for a moment, she started to pull away and he tightened his grip. She laughed softly. "I'm not running away this time, darling. I'm trying to take you to bed."

"Where?" The sound of his voice, ragged and rasping, surprised him. And when she pointed, wordlessly, to the open door, he scooped her up in his arms and all but ran, the blood beating in his temples.

This time it was slow and tender, sweet and searching. Kitty's eyes never left his. She gazed at him, watching his face, moving in response to what she saw there. She murmured to him, told him what she felt. "Is this good for you?" she would ask. "Is *this?*" She laughed a lot, a throaty, lusty sound he had never heard from her before. He wanted it to last forever, but suddenly he felt as if he were exploding, and then exhaustion dropped over him like a dark warm blanket.

"It's still the same," he slurred. Sleep was rolling over him; he could not keep his eyes open. "Isn't it, Kitty?"

He vaguely heard her answer: "This . . . this is always wonderful." And then, swiftly, sleep took him.

He opened his eyes slowly, heavily, The room, filled with deep shadows, was unfamiliar, and he struggled to place himself. And then the memory of her came flooding back and he was filled with a happiness so intense he thought he would burst with it. This was a love he must not lose.

He searched the bed with his hand. She was gone. And it was late, it was dark. He hadn't dreamed Kit! He called her name, then again, louder, feeling weak with relief when she appeared in the doorway.

"It's about time you got up. You almost missed tea." She leaned over to turn on the bed lamp. Dan pulled her down, his arms tight around her, nuzzling into the sweet warmth of her neck.

"Never mind tea," he murmured. "You're all I need."

After a while he drew back to gaze at her, smoothing the short mop of curls with his hand. "I just can't get used to your hair . . . No, no, don't pull away, I like it. I love it. I love you. And besides, I think I do want my tea, after all."

She laughed and gave him a swift kiss. "Well, come and get it, then. We'll sit by the fire and be very English."

"In that case, I'd better put some clothes on."

"Not necessarily," she said, and then, winking, backed out of his reach. "In the sitting room, if you please." And she disappeared, blowing him a kiss.

Dan lounged on the bed for a moment, stretching his legs and smiling. He felt . . . he felt something he couldn't quite put a name to, something light and floating. As he pulled on his clothes, it came to him, making him laugh aloud. He was happy!

There was a large silver tray on the sitting-room rug, near the fireplace, laden with sandwiches and slices of cake, a bowl of fruit, two cups and saucers, and a fat, steaming teapot. Big, puffy cushions were piled invitingly on the floor; a cheerful blaze hissed and crackled in the grate. Kit stood looking out the oversized front windows, whose heavy draperies were pulled aside to reveal a sea of white, swirling fog.

"I'm awfully glad Lee and Ben decided to make Stonehenge an overnight trip," she remarked as he came into the room. "I wouldn't like Lily traveling back in the car now, especially if Ben's driving. He's a maniac!"

Dan sat down near the tray, grabbed the nearest sandwich, and wolfed it hungrily. Licking his fingers, he said, "Gone all night? Isn't *that* nice. Come over here, woman, and let's play house." He patted the cushions.

She smiled at him. "Okay. But I want to *talk,* Dan."

"Sure, of course." He felt irritated. If she pulled away from him—*again!* He did not speak until she had sunk to the floor—not very close to him, he noted—and begun nibbling on an apple. Abruptly, he asked: "What did you do with Whit, by the way?"

Kitty turned to look directly at Dan. "I've left him." But when he reached out for her, grinning broadly, she held up a hand. "Wait a minute. It's not so simple, Dan. We didn't agree to separate. I did this on my own, and he won't even be sure I've really gone until after the wedding —when I don't come back home. And then? I don't know *what* will happen. Nothing good, that's for sure."

"What are you worried about? You've got *me!*"

She appeared uncomfortable. "Dan, I can't . . ."

"Don't tell me you can't come with me *this* time!" he protested angrily. "You're *free!* I'll make sure he can't hurt you—you or the kid. I'll—"

Kitty bit her lower lip and sighed heavily. "Dan Copeland, are you capable of listening to me? I mean *listening* instead of taking over and telling me what's going to happen? Can you?"

"I—yes. Of course. I'm listening." He grabbed another sandwich, taking large bites.

"Whit has threatened . . . No. Let me start again. Since the reunion weekend, it's been obvious that the marriage is over. But Whit won't let go—no, it's no use asking why. You know him. What's his is his forever. Even if he no longer wants it, no one else can have it. He's told me, in no uncertain terms, what he'll do if I leave him." She stopped talking and glanced away, clearly thinking about what next to say.

Finally she went on: "He's promised me a battle royal for custody of Lily, including dragging her into the thick of it. If I'm with you, he'll drag you in, too, and . . . I . . . I have to handle this alone."

"Why? Why must you do it alone? I love you!"

"Dan, please. You're . . . part of it, don't you see that? He knows I was with you at the reunion weekend. He hates you! You mustn't get involved!"

"I *am* involved, goddammit, Kitty! There's no way he can get to me! He tried with the election. He couldn't do it!"

"No, Dan." Her tone was final. "Absolutely no. There are other factors . . . things I simply can't tell you right now. You'll have to trust me."

Swiftly, he moved to her, enfolding her in his arms. She was rigid, unyielding. "I trust you, Kit. Why can't you let me take care of you just a little? Why are you shutting me out?" Still her body remained stiff. He dropped his arms and looked searchingly into her face. She stared back at him, calm, and shook her head.

"I have to do it alone."

"Alone! Alone!" he shouted. "I'm sick of that word from you. You're always insisting on being alone—even when it's something that involves the two of us!"

"Dan, that's unfair!"

"Oh, is it? Why wouldn't you let me in the gate that morning? Whit wasn't even there! All I wanted was to *see* you, to see your face while you told me to go away!"

"I told you: I couldn't!"

"Bull, Kitty!"

"Dan, I told you Whit made . . . certain threats. He had me watched by the staff. Martin was standing there the whole time. Oh, what's the use? I can't make you understand!"

"You don't love me," he blurted.

"I love you, Dan, more than I can say. No, please don't hold me now, this is serious. Please believe me when I say that I'm doing things this way *because* I love you."

"That's bull, too!"

She sighed. "I'm sorry you feel that way. But I *do* love you. And you can't trust me. So there we are."

He leaned forward, sweating a bit. "What's happened to you, Kit? You're different. You were never like this before, not with me. All this cool calculation—that was for the rest of them. Even in bed before, you were . . . different somehow."

"I thought it was heaven!"

"Oh, Christ, it was, it was! Still . . ."

"Still . . . yes. No hysteria, that's what you missed. My poor darling." She laughed suddenly, her face changing completely, and edged herself close to him. "I feel free now, don't you see? Free to take my time, free to let myself enjoy you, free to study your face and watch you move. Do you know what I'm saying? All those years I was so busy keeping my defenses intact—don't you *dare* laugh, that's not what I meant and you know it! I was always in a frenzy. And later, when I would try to recapture some of it, to remember what you had done and said, I couldn't. It was all blurred. I wanted to keep it all clear. I wanted to really *see* you, to *know* you . . ."

Breathless, she let the words drift off and leaned her head on his chest. Dan absently played with the curly tendrils on the nape of her neck. He wanted to feel happy again, as he had earlier. Instead, he was bothered. It had all been so easy and natural at reunion. Now, unanswered questions haunted the back of his mind. Something was askew. Everything she had said made sense, was fine. And yet . . . it bothered him.

"I always thought," he said, "it was enough just to love each other."

"Dan. Darling. It's never enough just to be in love. You know that. We've never been together long enough; we've always been so frantic . . ."

"You say frantic. I say crazy in love. I don't like analyzing feelings half to death. It's all a crock!" Why was she making him so angry, when all he wanted was to love her for the rest of her life? With a sudden movement, he shifted her around, grabbing her by the shoulders and bringing her face close to his.

"From the first moment I saw you," he said in a low, intense voice, "I knew you were the girl for me. And it's never changed. That's love. Isn't that enough for you?"

She looked at him tenderly and said, "No, Dan, that's not enough. Because I'm no longer the girl you saw all those years ago. How can you be sure you love me?"

In answer, he bent his head and began to kiss her.

Within moments they were locked together on the rug, all tangled up in their clothes and the pillows. When they paused to draw breath, he murmured in her ear, "There's my answer. That's how I can be sure. What other proof do you *need,* in the name of God? Now, let's just forget all this 'alone' stuff. You're coming back with me and everything's going to be just fine!"

She went very still in his arms, and pulling herself back slightly, regarded him carefully. "You're always so . . . certain," she said. "It's one of the things I love about you. But you tend to use it as a weapon, Dan. You're bulldozing me again, in the name of love."

"Because love is all that counts between a man and a woman."

"Oh, *really?*" She looked into his eyes for a long time. Then, with a quick tightening of her lips, she said: "Let's see, Dan, shall we? Look over there."

He followed her gesture. All he could see was the mantel above the fireplace. Nothing unusual there: an old brass clock, a jug of russet flowers, two ornate candlesticks, and a framed color photograph.

"I'm looking. What am I supposed to see?"

She struggled to her feet, straightening her rumpled clothes in silence, and, also in silence, held out a hand to him. He stood with her at the mantel and, uncomprehending, took the photograph she extended to him.

"Lily," she said.

He looked down at the picture, waiting for her to say more. She said nothing. It was a studio portrait of a pretty, laughing little girl with masses of long red-gold hair and even white teeth. How like Kit she looked, he thought. It would be easy to like her once they were all living together as a family. She had a lively, sparkling air about her; there was mischief in those clear hazel eyes.

"She's beautiful, Kit. Beautiful. Just like you. Except the coloring. You know, my father had that titian hair."

"That's not surprising."

Startled, he glanced away from the photograph to find her regarding him steadily, unblinkingly. "What? What do you mean?"

"She'll be ten in April. She has reddish-blond hair. And one dimple in her left cheek, right next to her mouth."

For a long time he stared at her, his mind refusing to

work. He knew what she was telling him, but he could not take it in. He felt stunned, unable to speak or react. Somehow he forced himself to look again at the photo. The little girl laughed out at him and suddenly he could see it: in the shape of the smile, in the little crinkles at the corners of her eyes. And yes, in the hair and the familiar single dimple. He stared at the unchanging picture, unwilling to look up at Kit, while pain, unlike anything he had experienced before, rose in his chest, strangling him. Gently, he replaced the picture, adjusting its position. He still had not looked at Kitty; he was afraid to.

My child. *My child.* The words echoed and re-echoed in his head. She had taken his child from him, had given his daughter to someone else! Bits and pieces of thoughts struggled with each other: the kids in Vietnam, his friends' babies, his conversation with Ben, pregnant Polly, his father. Dad . . . he had been a grandfather and had died without knowing it! Hadn't Whit said, "Family is very important to the Harrises"? Yes, and he had said a good deal more—all those sly questions and sidelong glances. "Have you any children, Copeland?" With that amused twitch of his lips.

Dan turned on Kitty and she shrank from him. He felt as if he were choking; he couldn't speak. As if she could read his mind, she whispered, "Yes. Whit knows. He always knew, but I didn't—"

A great wave of nausea surged up from his stomach to the back of his throat. Her face was a white blur. He had thought her lovely. She was the worst kind of cheat! *Whit always knew,* he told himself, *but not me!* Words crowded to his lips and would not come out. There were no words, nothing that could describe his desolation, his rage, his grief.

He didn't even think. His arm swung back, swung out, connected. The crack of his hand on her face was like a pistol shot. She fell to the floor in a heap and lay very still.

He stood over her a moment, gasping for breath, wanting to destroy her. But a remnant of sanity in the corner of his mind said, Go now. Go. And he went, half blind, out the door, down the stairs, into the hushed, fogbound street.

CHAPTER TWENTY-FIVE

Kit and Dan Reprise

KIT LAY VERY STILL on the floor, huddled into herself. She heard him race out, heard him pounding down the stairs, heard the outer door slam shut. Only then did she pick herself up, her head spinning. She felt stunned by the violence and the suddenness of his attack. Yes, attack. There was no other word for it. Dan Copeland, who said he loved her, had actually hit her! She found it incredible, and only the heavy throbbing of her cheek made it real.

He hit me, she thought. How dare he! And then, immediately, she was swept with remorse. I deserved it. I deserve more! What made me tell him that way? So coldly, so crudely . . . so cruelly!

She couldn't blame him at all. What a way to break the news: "Oh, and by the way, Dan, you're the father of my child—sorry I didn't tell you sooner." Standing in the middle of the room, swaying a little, she cringed as if she had been struck again. Surely she could have waited for the right moment. Now it was too late. He had gone. He was somewhere out there in the fog, hating her.

Snatching her raincoat from its hook, she stumbled from the apartment, fairly flying down the stairs and out into the thick grayness that spread heavily everywhere, smothering all normal sounds. She heard car tires whispering in slow motion, and their hiss seemed to come from all sides. The roadway was invisible. The whole world was hidden from view!

"Dan! Dan!" she called. She had to find him, to make him understand! Let him hate her forever if he chose, let him reject her completely. She *must* make him understand how it had been for her!

He had to be nearby. Nobody, not even a man crazed with hurt and rage, could venture far in this weather. Like a blind person, she took tentative steps, her hands outstretched before her, feeling her way, half expecting to crash into an unseen obstacle. Things, huge and shapeless, seemed to loom before her, just out of sight. Finally she stopped, afraid to move in any direction. "Dan! I know you're there!"

"Go away, Kit. Get back inside." He was very close, and she turned to the sound, picking her way toward it.

"Dan, where are you?"

"Go back inside." His voice sounded hollow.

"No. I have to talk to you."

"There's been too much talk already. Go back."

Her eyes had adjusted, and now she saw the outline of a body, straight ahead. It was he; she could smell his spicy shaving lotion as she came near. She put a hand on his arm. He was silent, unresponsive. She might not have been there at all. Then, in a tone of flat calm, he said, "Whit Harris is a prince, do you realize that? A prince. He knew you were pregnant by me, he *knew* it! And he kept you, anyway. All these years. He's given you everything you could possibly want—you and . . . the child. He even *loves* you!" Dan shuddered.

"Not love! It's not love, Dan!"

He went on as if she hadn't spoken. "He's always taken care of you in spite of . . . And *you,* you repay him by running away. Your usual trick." She strained to see his eyes, but only a vague outline of his features was visible. "No, Kit," he said, "I think you're making a big mistake. I think you ought to turn around and go right back to him before he realizes. You'll never get a better deal."

Hurt grabbed at her chest and brought frustrated tears to her eyes. "Don't say that! You don't know anything about it!"

"I know you proposed to him . . . he told me. Don't you think you owe him some loyalty? I do. It seems to me that old Witless got the short end of the stick this time."

"Don't! Don't say those things! You have no right! No right! You don't know how it was!" She gripped his arms with both hands, as hard as she could. She *must* get through to him!

"So tell me, Kit. How *was* it? How could you do it? You knew I loved you!"

"I knew you *wanted* me. Yes, sure . . . just like all the others, my whole life. Men were always wanting me, panting over me, trying to touch me—secretly, so that nobody would see . . ." She was beginning to cry in spite of her intentions. "Yes, it was different with you. Because I wanted *you*. But . . . love? How was I supposed to know it was love?"

He gave a bitter little laugh. "Oh, Kitty. When that poor struggling vet paid the freight all the way across the ocean to chase after you, what did you think it was for? To get laid? Christ, I could get laid six days a week and three times on Sunday right there in Hampton! And sometimes did!"

"I was an impossible prig I know," she said in a low voice.

"But I was in love with that impossible prig. I told you in Florence that I wanted us to be together forever. Why wasn't that enough for you?"

"Enough? When I knew you as a man who boasted that he lived for the moment? Come on, Dan. That Dan Copeland was not about to make any long-term commitment."

"I told you I wanted to marry you!"

"No, you didn't. You said a lot of things, but marriage was never one of them. Think about it for a minute . . . honestly. You had three years of law school ahead of you. No money. You weren't even sure what you were going to do with your life—but you were ambitious—you were always ambitious. Always busy, always involved, up until all hours—" Her voice kept breaking. It made her furious. She wanted him to *listen* to her, not pity her. "So don't tell me you wanted to get married! And a *baby*! Don't try to tell me you'd have welcomed a baby!" She stopped, out of breath.

Now he looked down at her. "Maybe not. But you should have *told* me. If only you had trusted me!"

Dan clenched his teeth against the bitter words that kept crowding up. If he went on, he would just get enraged again. And he was tired of his anger. He was weary of this whole business. Her voice was insistent, nagging. She was bringing up things better left in the past. He had been ready to marry her. Hadn't he? Yes, of course. He had planned on it. He'd wanted her more than anything . . . why the hell else had he gone three thousand miles after her? As for her being pregnant, that wouldn't have made any difference.

And then into his head flashed the face of Frank Jacobs. Frank had been in his study group at law school, a top student, a shoo-in for *Law Review*. And his wife, Toni, had been a perky little thing with a ready laugh and a joke for every disaster. And then they had had a baby and everything had fallen apart. Frank couldn't study at home and she had turned into a frenzied harridan, always tracking him down, whining about her lonely lot in life. Once or twice, the study group had attempted to work in the Jacobses' tiny apartment. It had been a nightmare, the bathroom strung with dripping baby clothes, the constant squalling and wailing from the curtained-off corner, the looks of resentment that had flashed between Toni and Frank. In the end, Frank hadn't made *Review*, and the marriage hadn't made it, either.

"*We'd* have made it," Dan said. But even as the words were spoken, he wondered. "It's senseless to discuss this now, Kit. What's done is done." She was pressing against him, shivering a little. He wished it were possible to go back and live this day over again, unsay all the harsh truths, erase the anger. Then he could put his arms around her and make her warm. And maybe he would be warm again, too.

"I was going to have an abortion," she was saying. "It was all planned. I was on my way. But . . . I couldn't. I just couldn't. I don't know why. Maybe because it was . . . yours, a part of you, I don't know. And then I panicked. I had made my decision and there I was, in limbo, feeling that I had to do something right away, something I could be sure of. Of course, if it happened to me today, I'd handle it differently. But then . . . ? All that occurred to me was that I had to find someone I knew would take care of it all. I was cowardly and I was stupid. But you can't imagine how it was!"

"Maybe not," he admitted. "It really doesn't matter now."

"It does! It does! I want you to understand!"

"No, Kit. You don't want my understanding, you want my forgiveness. And I'm not sure I can give you that." Absently, he patted her back. She was shuddering with the cold. "Come on," he said. "You'd better get inside."

The fog had thinned out enough to make visible the glimmer of the Mexican shop's display window. He guided her to the doorway and they climbed the stairs in silence. She had left the door open. Dan stood aside, impersonally polite, to let her by, then let himself in and walked wearily around, collecting his gear.

Kit stood in the middle of the sitting room, following him with her eyes. When he got his jacket and coat, she thought, almost like a prayer, Now he'll take me in his arms. And when he moved off, returning with his shaving stuff, she thought, Now. And when everything had been neatly packed in the suitcase and he was shrugging into his coat, she thought, Now. Surely now.

But he only turned sad eyes on her, saying, "It all seemed so simple when I saw you at reunion. There you were, and there I was, and it was all still the same." He gave a harsh little laugh. "That was pretty naive, wasn't it? Thinking anything could really stay the same. Hell, I didn't even know everything about myself. I didn't know I was a father, for instance."

He saw her wince. "I've explained . . ." she began, but he waved her down.

"That doesn't make it any easier to take in, you know." He found his eyes drawn to the photo on the mantel. My child. He tried the thought on for size. It felt so strange. He wanted to see her face again. He went to the fireplace and picked up the picture, staring at it. "This is my daughter," he murmured. "My daughter. Yours and mine. Ours. All those years, with you on my mind, and all the time . . ." It was an open face, innocent, expecting happiness. He thought, I fathered her: a living, breathing person, who thinks and laughs and . . . yes, Whit, and rides her horse. Who feels joy and sorrow and disappointment. Who is alive.

After all the years of being haunted by the specter of death. After all the nightmares of the blasted earth and smoldering villages of Vietnam from which he awakened in a cold, fearful sweat. And the child he had killed. That young boy, his enemy, that child, probably not much older than his daughter was right now. She, his daughter. He looked down at the flat, laughing image. She was a stranger to him; he had never even seen her. Still, looking at her face, he felt joy. Not just a child-killer. No, he was a life-giver, too.

"Now do you see?" Kit cried. "That's why I couldn't just pick up and leave with you! I wanted to, I really did! But Whit said he'd drag us both through a long, drawn-out custody battle. He said he'd tell the whole story. The whole thing, Dan! Your so-called prince would have had Lily suddenly find out . . . My God, Whit is Daddy to her! She trusts him! But what did he care? He'd do anything just to hurt you and me, and to hell with what might happen to Lily! He has no real human feelings, Dan. As long as Lily behaves to his credit, as long as he can point to her with pride and say, 'My daughter,' then he's pleased with her. But every time she dares voice an opinion of her own, he walks all over her. All he cares about is his image, and he's even willing to sacrifice some of that, if he must, in order to get at me! At us! I had to protect her. I *have* to protect her, you can see that!"

He frowned a little. "Then why did you leave him now?"

"I had to. I had to stop being afraid. I didn't like what was happening to her. I spoke with a lawyer. There are ways I can try to protect her . . ." She sighed. "And besides, I realized where his anger was directed. He wanted to make sure I never went to you. It's *you* he hates, you and me. As long as I didn't go to you . . . How could I burden you with this mess when you had just been elected? When you were just beginning the life you always wanted? Can't you imagine the newspaper stories he could generate? Now do you see? Now do you understand?"

He nodded, wishing only that she would stop talking. Sorrow for those lost years, for his child forever lost to him, seeped through him into his bones. But it was too late even for anger. Even now she couldn't seem to trust his strength, his ability to handle a tough situation, to take care of them all. And maybe she was right. He had lost all control before, knocking her down. What kind of a father would he make? He didn't know. It was too late to claim this child as his own. Too late. And if she—Lily

—ever learned the truth, she might hate him. Was he strong enough for *that?*

He steeled himself. "You're right," he said. "Of course you're right. The child . . . she comes first." He strode quickly to his bag and picked it up. "I'll leave now." He turned at the door, paused, and then said quietly, "I love you, Kit. I want you to know that."

Kitty nodded, fighting back tears. She mouthed the words, "I love you," afraid that if she spoke aloud, she would break down completely. Long after he had gone, she still stared at the door. She held herself tightly, forcing herself to turn around, thinking that she would go into the kitchen, brew some tea, perhaps work a little. Anything but think of him. She must purge him from her heart. It's all for the best, it's best for all of us, she repeated silently. And then the mantel caught her attention. Something had changed. She saw that he had taken his daughter's picture with him.

And the tears came.

CHAPTER TWENTY-SIX

Lee and Ben

"AND THEN I figure we can go to Majorca for a few days. And after that—"

"Ben, my love. You've now managed to plan a honeymoon that will last until late next year."

"What are you talking about, woman? A month and a half at most is all it is. Hand me those brochures over there . . . Ummmmm. That was nice."

"Nicer than brochures?"

"Much nicer. C'mere."

"Ben . . . ? I wonder how I was stupid enough to over-look you back in school. Those lips, those hands, those marvelous pectorals, that . . . yum."

"I had acne, and nobody loves a boy with acne . . . no, don't stop that. On second thought, do stop that. We have work to do."

"When you come on masterful, darling Ben, it just turns me on."

"Woman! In two days is the wedding. And if we don't tell Martha where we want to go and when, we ain't goin' nowhere!"

"And after I gave up three concerts. Okay. You're right . . . Ben?"

"Umm?"

"Has Dan said anything to you?"

"My Lord, woman, we've spent the past three days doing nothing *but* talk. The housing bill he's working on is really controversial. The man's got guts, I give him that."

"Ben! Don't be obtuse! You know I'm talking about him and Kit. That dinner Wednesday night was grim. Both of them perfectly correct, but . . . brrr! Hasn't he said *anything?*"

"Nope. Not a *mot,* either *bon* or *mauvais.*"

"Kit neither. And God knows I've tried. She just tight-ens her lips and looks distant. Says she'll tell me all about it after the divorce is over. D'you think Whit will really fight it?"

"Are you kidding, woman? The reason the Harrises have old money, my darling Lee, is because they have never given up a single thing, ever, without a fight. Yes, I think he'll probably make it just about as difficult as he can. And he *can.*"

"Oh, Lord. That's what I thought. Poor Kit. Poor Lily."

"Have a look at this schedule and see if it looks right . . . Poor Kit? I don't know about that. Kit seems to be in pretty goddamn good shape, if you ask me. Stronger. More with it. Not so remote and removed, if you know what I mean."

"Ummm . . . yes, this is fine. But I think Majorca is out, darling. Do you mind? I have to start rehearsing for the Palladium by—"

"Okay. Okay. Listen, I feel for both of them, Kit *and* Dan. Something happened between them while we were gallivanting about Stonehenge—at dawn, for the love of Pete! It wasn't good, whatever it was."

"Ben, I just *know* they're still in love. What do you suppose—?"

"Ah, you think everyone's in love because *we* are. C'mere . . . yes, that's just right . . ."

"Ben . . ."

"Um?"

"We have to get them together."

"Mind your own business. We already tried playing Cupid and it backfired."

"Yes, but—"

"But nothing. Butt out."

"No cozy little dinner? No lovely little restaurant with soft music playing? No—"

"No! Whatever it is, they have to work it out. Themselves."

"But what if they *don't?* Oh, Ben, that would be awful!"

"Come back here . . . that's better. Don't worry. If it's meant to be, they'll work it out. Maybe seeing the wedding, in all its pomp and panoply . . . maybe seeing us exchange our vows in voices low with emotion . . . maybe watching all your relatives stuffing their Cuban faces with goodies—ouch!"

"They're my people! Don't make fun!"

"Just joshing, my dear . . . ummmmm. Let's stop working. We've worked long enough. Let's do something that's fun."

"You're on, my man . . . don't push! You're worse than a teenager, Benno! Ummm, I *love* it . . . yes, maybe you're right. The wedding might make them realize . . . the wedding just might do the trick . . . Oh! I do love you, my Armenian-Italian prince."

"And I love you, my raunchy Cuban beauty."

"For always?"

"For always, forever, time without end, ceaselessly, continuously, and in perpetuity . . ."

"Shut up and kiss me, my fool."

CHAPTER TWENTY-SEVEN

Whit and Dinah

WHIT FLOPPED OVER on his back, groaning happily. Next to him in the bed, Dinah stirred, stretched, and reached out a lazy hand, laying it on his chest.

"Your heart's still thumping away like crazy," she said.

"Of course."

"Yes, well . . . well, *yes,* I suppose there's a very good reason for it. That was pretty terrific. You've been outdoing yourself lately." She laughed softly.

"I've never known anyone like you, Dinah. It's never been like this for me. I—I—"

Now she laughed heartily. "I know, sweetie pie, you have mixed feelings. You don't really *like* liking it. No, don't protest, I know it makes you very nervous. But I don't care. *I* like it." She turned onto her side, resting her cheek on one hand and smiling at him, her eyes tender. With her free hand, she traced the shape of his mouth. "To the rest of the world," she remarked, "you're a straight-arrow WASP. Only *I* know what you're really like . . . how wild and wonderful you can be."

"You make me this way. And yes, I guess it scares me a little. I'm . . . I'm besotted with you, Dinah." He grabbed her hand and held it to his lips. "I've never felt this way about anybody, ever."

In answer, she leaned over to give him a soft, lingering kiss. A few moments later, snuggling her into his shoulder, Whit cleared his throat and said, "Dinah, I have to talk to you."

"Uh-oh. That's your office voice."

"My wife has left me."

She squirmed around to face him, smiling broadly. "Good!"

"Well . . . er . . . not exactly. She ran off with Lily. I warned her, but she did it, anyway. And do you know how she gave me the news? Through that sob-sister column of hers! I'll show it to you later. Not a proper letter, not even a message from her attorney. Well, she won't get away with it! I've put George onto it and she'll soon see— Well, never mind. It needn't concern you."

"What do you *mean* it needn't concern me! You say your wife has left you, that you're a free man, and I'm not supposed to be concerned?"

He frowned. "I . . . well, the fact is, I don't intend to let her go so easily."

Dinah sat bolt upright. "Why not?"

"Because. Because she's my *wife*. Harris wives don't pull this kind of stunt. I'll be a laughingstock!" Dinah eyed him without speaking. "I have a position to maintain. She can't do that to me! I told her she'd better not try and—"

"And she dared to go against you," Dinah finished. "Well, big deal! Is that what's bothering you? Or do you still love her?"

"Love her! Ha! I'll drag her name through the mud— and I have the facts to do it! I'll get custody in the end. And incidentally"—he laughed briefly—"I'm going to finish off Copeland, too. They'll *all* regret crossing me!" He paused when he saw a look of distaste cross her face. "Dinah! Don't look at me like that! You don't understand; this is *war!* I've been shafted! Nobody does that to me!"

"I don't like you when you're like this . . . I don't like you at all."

"Dinah, Dinah. I'm counting on you. I'm counting on you to be here, waiting, when it's all over."

Her voice became hard. "What does *that* mean: *waiting?*"

Whit sighed gustily. "George says it would be best if . . . if I weren't with other women. It's important, if I'm to get custody of Lily . . . Where are you going?"

She slid away from his grasping hand and off the bed, picking up a robe and knotting it about her. "Okay,

Whit. As it happens, it works out just fine. Because, as it happens, I had something to say to *you* tonight."

"What?"

She tossed her long hair back off her face and turned to him, hands on hips. "I was going to tell you that I'm tired of being your secret passion, darling. I was going to tell you that I hate sneaking around. I was going to tell you to put up or shut up—see me openly or forget about it. In short, I was going to say, 'It's either me or your wife, Whit. *Choose.*'"

She paused as a look of stupefaction settled on his features, and then plunged on. "So you tell me she's left you and I think, Hooray, I don't have to say a word! But I'm wrong . . . ho, ho, am I ever wrong! Because you don't intend to do *anything* about me. Hell, no. I'm to sit here and wait around while you involve yourself in lawsuits with her. And why? Because"—her voice was heavy with sarcasm—"Harris wives don't step out of line. Well, it's obvious that she's more important to you than I am. And all that pretty talk about how it's different with me and wonderful with me and special with me and it's never happened to you before—that's all garbage!"

"Dinah! You've got it all wrong!"

"Oh, no, I haven't. You've made it very plain. You've already made your choice. Hey, don't sweat it, Whit. It's all right. I made up my mind that I'd go along with whatever decision you made. But for me, it's very simple: all or nothing."

He kicked at the sheets and leaped from the bed, coming for her. Dinah began to laugh. "You look rather ludicrous, Whit, charging around without any clothes on!"

"I don't care! You must listen to me!" He wrapped his arms around her unyielding body. "I'm only asking you to wait a while. Surely you can wait just a *little* while," he wheedled.

"All. Or nothing. Now. Tonight."

"Dinah . . ." He pressed his lips into her cloudy hair and pushed his hips close into her. "Dinah . . . baby . . ."

Dinah pushed at him. "You've already made your choice. You'd rather get even than get me." She wriggled out of his embrace and moved quickly to the other side of the room, lighting a cigarette, holding it defiantly in her lips, like a weapon of defense. She gazed at him, studying the big fair-skinned body with its thickly padded muscles, the thighs as sturdy as tree trunks. Only she knew how agile and athletic that body could be. Only she . . . She blew out a plume of smoke and said lightly: "I'll miss you."

"Dinah! Be reasonable!"

"I think you'd better get dressed and go. Now!"

He glared at her, opened his mouth, then closed it tightly and began to collect his clothes, putting each thing on with slow, deliberate movements.

She watched him, lighting another cigarette from the smoldering butt of the first one. "What are you planning to do with Lily once you have her?"

"*Do* with her? Why . . . be a father to her, what else?"

"Think, Whit. You're more often away than you're home. How are you going to father her, long distance? You have some kind of fantasy of the two of you being pals. But we both know what'll *really* happen. She'll be in the care of the housekeeper, she'll be lonesome, she'll cry for her mother, she'll start acting depressed. And you'll end up sending her off to boarding school, because the truth is, you *can't* take care of her. You haven't got the time! You're a busy, important executive. What are you going to do, do you think, quit your job so you can be a full-time father?"

He spluttered at her and then stopped, shrugging into his suit coat. "I—I guess I haven't really thought it through."

"And how do you think a messy custody case is going to make your daughter feel about you? Have you thought *that* one through? No, I figured you hadn't. How old is she? Nine? Ten? You'd put a little kid like that through the wringer? I can't believe it!"

"Christ, Dinah. Will you shut up?"

"Not on your life, mister! You're too important for me to let you go off half-cocked! And you needn't give me that famous Whit Harris drop-dead look, either. This is Dinah talking, and I'm not scared of you!" She turned her back on him and lit another cigarette. "Oh, skip it." Her voice was suddenly weary. "Just leave, will you?"

"No. Not now. You had some more to say to me. Go ahead and say it."

"You wouldn't listen."

He took a few steps toward her, his hands out-stretched. "I will. I'll listen. I'm listening."

"Okay." Dinah whirled around. "Your daughter be-longs with her mother, and you damn well know it. If you make it rough on her, she'll only end up hating you, and you know *that,* too. Come on, Whit, use your head. The smartest move you can make is to have an amicable di-vorce, one where you and your wife smile at each other through gritted teeth if necessary. The kid is happy, you don't have to worry about her, you get full visitation rights, she loves and adores you, you don't waste a year and God knows how many thousands of dollars on George and his associates, and——" She sucked in a deep, whistling breath of air, letting it out slowly. Then she butted her cigarette and walked slowly toward him. "And," she continued, "you get to keep me." She did not touch him, only tipped her head up to look him in the eye. Her gaze was direct and steady.

"I can't think when you're so close to me."

"You haven't heard a word I said!"

"Yes, I have. You're right. Of course you're right." He shook his head, frowning. "But I can't let her get away with it!"

Dinah's lips curled in a slow smile. She moved closer to him and slid her arms around his neck. "Yes, you can," she murmured. "You're not vindictive, you're big-ger than that. And really, Whit, wouldn't you rather have . . . ?" She stood on tiptoe, bringing her full lips up to his, curving her loins close.

With a groan, he gathered her in his arms, grinding his mouth into hers with a kind of desperation, pulling her hips hard against him. It was a long and fervent kiss, leaving them both gasping for breath.

"I can't give you up," Whit said. "It's crazy . . . but I can't." As he spoke, she curved her body more snugly into his, resting her head on his chest, her hands busy.

"If you do it my way, Whit, you get the best of both worlds . . ."

"Oh, Christ . . . Dinah . . . how can I talk when you're doing that? No, don't stop . . . oh, Christ . . ."

Dinah pulled away, retying her robe. "Later," she said. "Right now we have things to do."

"What things? Come over here. We'll do *those* things later."

"No, Whit. Listen to me. Where did she run to?"

"Oh, Christ, all right. To London. She and Lily are going to Lee Rivers' wedding. Katherine's a witness."

Dinah whistled softly. "Lee Rivers! That's right, she's an old classmate of yours, isn't she? All right, *call* her. Your wife. Call her in London."

"I don't know where she is. She never checked into the hotel where I made reservations. She's . . . in hiding, I suppose."

"Then call Lee Rivers."

"I tried. Her number's unlisted."

Dinah put her fists on her hips and heaved a sigh, shaking her head sadly. "I can't believe you're really so helpless, Whitney. Not *you*. Maybe you really still want her . . ."

"Not that way! And at any rate, that was never . . . I don't wish to discuss my wife with you! Marriage is a sacrament, a contract. It's not easy for me to . . . dismiss it just like that. But, of course, you wouldn't know anything about that sort of thing. No, I didn't mean that— I'm sorry!"

She moved restlessly over to the night table, where an opened bottle of wine stood, and poured herself a drink. "Up to you," she said coolly, sipping delicately.

He stared at her for a moment, then threw his hands out. "What do you suggest I *do?* Now? Tonight? When I don't even know where she is? I'll put someone on it tomorrow; I know a private detective who has overseas connections . . . No? Then *what?*"

"Where and when is the wedding?"

"The wedding? At the Ritz. Valentine's Day." He made a grimace. "Lee Rivers' idea of something cute."

"That's tomorrow. Perfect. Wire her, in care of the wedding reception. It'll reach her. I'll write it for you. Short, succinct, sure: my usual style. I'll begin with 'Lawyer drawing up separation agreement prior to divorce.' How's that?"

He stood looking at her, a scowl between his brows, his hands curling and uncurling. She returned his gaze for a moment, then shrugged and turned toward the other room, swinging one hip so that the velvet robe parted, revealing the soft, curved flesh of thigh, hip, and rounded belly for an instant before she pulled the garment around her.

Whit closed his eyes briefly, then cleared his throat. "God help me, I've got to have you. That's how it is. I just can't . . . All right. I'll send the cable and I'll do it tonight. But first I have to tell George."

Halfway out of the room, Dinah came to a halt and stood perfectly still. With her back to him, she said: "You know where the phone is." Only when she heard him dialing did she turn, her eyes brilliant and her cheeks flushed.

She seated herself at her desk, grabbed a pen and paper, and began writing quickly in neat block letters. "Mrs. Katherine Harris, Ritz Hotel, c/o Lee Rivers' wedding reception. Lawyer drawing up separation agreement prior to divorce. Have decided not to fight you on this for Lily's sake. Agree . . ." She paused, biting the tip of the pen, her eyes narrowed in thought, then nodded to herself and went on: "Agree marriage is over. Call me at my office, any hour. Leave number if necessary. Tell Lily I love her and hope to see her soon. Whit."

She read the message over, satisfaction warming her whole body. She could feel it tingling in the tips of her fingers and pumping in her heartbeat. The long, long battle to survive was over, and she could begin to relax. The paper trembled a little in her hands. The sending and the receiving of this short cable, she reflected, was going to make an awful lot of people very happy. Especially Whit. He was just beginning to loosen up a bit; he didn't have *any idea* of the delights that lay in store for him. He was such a baby. So inexperienced. He needed her . . . as much as she needed him.

She wasn't being selfish, she told herself, only half listening to his conversation with the harried lawyer. He was finding it difficult to explain to George why he had suddenly done a complete about-face. He couldn't mention *her* name, of course not. She was a secret—or so he, in his ignorance, chose to believe. Well, all that would soon change, too. She wouldn't rush it; she'd wait for him to get used to the idea. But she'd need new clothes, a *lot* of new clothes. And—she glanced down at her body—a masseuse. The voluptuous curves he found so enticing were fine for bed, but in clothes . . . She found she was smiling and that Whit had finished his conversation and was gazing at her, smiling in return.

She got up immediately, allowing the robe to fall apart as she walked toward him, and slid into the edge of the bed, close to him. When his hand moved over to caress her, she put the piece of paper into it, leaning over to nuzzle his cheek.

"Soon, darling," she murmured into his ear, letting her hand rest lightly on his thigh. "But first . . ."

Yes, she thought, listening to his voice catch just a little as he read the cable over the phone, that little piece of paper was going to change the lives of a *lot* of people.

CHAPTER TWENTY-EIGHT

Lily Harris and Her New Friend

IT WAS EXTREMELY CONFUSING. The room was huge—it was the grand ballroom of the hotel, in fact— with very high ceilings. There were one hundred fifty people there; Lily knew that for sure because Auntie Lee had told her that's how many were invited to the wedding, but they were making enough noise for three million. There was a band at the far end of the room, playing loud all the time. And those people who weren't dancing were shrieking and shouting and hugging and kissing and singing and laughing. As far as Lily was concerned, this wedding was too crowded, too hot, and too noisy.

She looked down at the plate she was carrying, heaped with twenty different delicacies by Uncle Ben's aunt or cousin or something, and made a face. All this wonderful food and she just wasn't hungry. She'd have to put it down somewhere . . . maybe at that little round table over there in the corner, behind a palm tree. And there was that jerk again: Angelo, looking for her. Yuck! He kept following her, rolling his eyes around like an idiot, and winking, and saying things to her in Italian when he knew darn well she couldn't understand a word of Italian!

She quickly trotted over to the little table, which looked kind of lost over there in the corner, its one little rose in a vase already wilting, and sat down gratefully. She took a deep breath and let it out again noisily. Weddings were supposed to be fun. Mommy kept looking over at her to make sure she was having a good time. Well, she wasn't, and she couldn't help it. But, hidden over here, she wouldn't be so noticeable; and anyway, Mommy was dancing with Uncle Ben's father and they were very busy laughing. She wouldn't be looking for Lily for a little while, anyway. Uncle Ben's father was nice; they were all nice. But they were so loud and they pinched your cheek a zillion times and she had never seen so many big black mustachios before in her life! They were very friendly and very nice, but she just didn't feel like it right now . . .

That morning, when she and Mommy had been getting ready, she had promised herself that the wedding would make her feel better. She had felt sad since Mommy had explained on the plane about how there was going to be a divorce and that they weren't going back to Long Island right away but would stay for a while in London. "I know it's going to be hard for you, Lily Dilly," she said. "It's going to be hard for all of us. But it's going to be exciting, too. Imagine: we'll be living in another country, in one of the world's greatest cities! And you know, sweetie, that Daddy and I . . . we both love *you* very much. You do understand that?" And Lily nodded, but she couldn't help crying. And Mommy cried, too. But all the nights while she was thinking about Daddy and Beauty and all the kids at school and everything and crying by herself, she made a solemn promise to herself that the wedding would make her feel happy. It just *had* to.

And this morning Mommy seemed in a really good

mood, full of smiles, which she hadn't been lately. Maybe she had made herself a promise, too. She looked awfully pretty in her long shimmery red dress and the new dangle earrings. Lily had a new dress, too. Peacock-blue velvet with a sweetheart neckline, a real grown-up dress.

"I'll try not to cry any more, Mom," she said when they were both posing in front of the big mirror.

"Oh, Lily, my silly! We'll both do a lot of crying, I'm sure. Don't worry about it. Crying's good for the complexion, anyway."

"Oh, Mommy!"

"Scout's honor. And it'll make your eyes blue, too . . . well, all right, maybe not that. But it's awfully good for a sore heart, sweetie. So cry away; it's all right."

"Mom . . . ? I miss Daddy."

Her mother smoothed her hair. "I know, baby. And I hope, when all the . . . business . . . of divorce is settled, you'll see him a lot." She sighed. "Of course, it won't be the same as it was. But—we'll all be happier, I think." And she gave Lily a big smile. Lily tried to smile back. And then Mommy said: "And today's a wedding. We're getting a divorce, but our good friends are getting married. It all evens out."

Lily secretly thought that someone else's wedding didn't even out things for *her,* but she recognized that her mother was trying to make her feel better. So she gave her a fake smile and told herself again that the wedding would make everything feel different and be fun.

Well, the ceremony part was wonderful. It was in a judge's room somewhere, with big high windows and about a million red flowers that smelled beautiful and thick red carpets on the floor. Auntie Lee looked like a princess in her wedding gown. It was white satin with lace all over and pearls and about a million of the tiniest buttons she'd ever seen, all the way down the back. Auntie Lee was wearing a crown of pearls and a veil with lace on it down to the floor. Her bouquet was enormous, all different kinds of white flowers with satin ribbons that hung down—oh, it was exquisite! And Uncle Ben—! He had on one of those suits with the long tails, and a fat satin tie like a scarf with a big pearl pin, and a top hat, like a magician. Everyone was all dressed up and smiling, and it was really nice. When the judge said,

"You may kiss the bride," and Auntie Lee had to bend over so they could kiss, nobody laughed. Well, it wasn't funny; it was romantic. And then all the old people started crying a little—even Mom, who explained that everyone always cries at weddings. Why, Lily could not figure out.

And when they all came out of the building, Lily just had to stop and stare. Because the entire sidewalk and even some of the street, as far as you could see, was jammed with people, all mobbed together, shrieking and clapping and yelling. There was a bobby telling them to move back, please, and leave the wedding party some room.

"Why are all these people here?" Lily asked.

Her mother laughed and said: "Fans, baby. These are Auntie Lee's fans, come to wish her well."

"All these people?"

And her mother laughed again. "Auntie Lee thought she'd kept the wedding a secret! So these are only a *few* of her fans!"

Lily considered the masses of eager and excited, smiling faces. "You know what I want to be when I grow up? Famous!"

But by the time they walked to the waiting cars, she had changed her mind. The fans didn't just stand there politely. They kept reaching out and throwing flowers and rice and grabbing at you. And shouting. And taking pictures and yelling, "Over here, Lee!" and "Give us a smile, Miss Rivers!" and stuff like that. There were so many of them and they kept pressing forward, pushing and shoving each other. One of them stumbled and fell on the sidewalk, right in front of Lily, and had to be helped up. It was scary. She was glad to feel Mommy's arm around her shoulder the whole way, and when she saw the open door of the car, she nearly ran to it. And even then the faces crowded up, peering inside, asking each other, "Who *is* that?" Lily didn't like it, she didn't like it at all.

Mommy squeezed her shoulder and asked, "Still want to be famous, Lily Dilly?"

"Nope," she said.

And after that it was just noise, noise, noise, all the time. When they got to the hotel, there were more fans, squealing and waving autograph books. Lily put her fingers in her ears. And she wished she had kept them there because upstairs in the ballroom, the band was already playing. And then everybody crowded in and began talking all at the same time, pushing over to the big buffet table that was all along one wall and stretching their arms over her head to grab glasses of champagne from the waiters, who were walking around with big trays. And then that Angelo, that creep, came up to her and began annoying her.

"Mommy!" she whispered, pulling on her mother's hand. "I want that guy to stop bothering me!"

Her mother grabbed her hand tightly, too tightly. "Who?" she asked in a sharp voice. "Who's bothering you? Point him out!"

"Mommy! You're hurting me! It's . . . him!" And she pointed to Angelo. Her mother laughed and laughed. Well, it wasn't funny! It was dumb!

"Is that all?" her mother said, and all Lily could do to answer that was to give her a look of disgust. Well, if he came near her again, she'd kick him right in the shins!

Nobody seemed to see the little round table in the corner. Nobody knew she was even there. Being all alone wasn't as nice as she had thought it would be. Because, now that she was alone, she couldn't help remembering. Beauty's velvet nose and the way his ears pricked up when she walked into the stable. Her best friend, Samantha, who didn't even know she wasn't coming back. Daddy . . . even if he'd been away a lot lately, and then when he was home finally, all he did was tell her to leave the room. Still, she'd rather have him ordering her around than be here all alone in London, England, without a single friend and going to start some yucky new school tomorrow she just knew she'd hate. School! That made it all real. She'd been pretending that they'd pack up and go home tomorrow like all the rest of the guests. But now she *knew* they wouldn't! Tears threatened to fall, and she blinked as fast as she could and then stuck her fists into her eyes to hide the one or two that leaked out.

When she lifted her head up, the best man was standing there, looking very handsome, like a movie star, in his gray suit like Uncle Ben's. She was very embarrassed that he had caught her crying like a baby, but he didn't seem to notice. He bowed a little and smiled at her and said: "Excuse me, Lily. Are you waiting for someone, or may I join you?"

"How'd you know my name?"

He laughed and sat down next to her. "I always make sure to find out the name of a beautiful woman."

She squirmed a little. Grown-up talk sometimes made her uncomfortable.

"But I'm sorry," he went on, "we haven't been introduced. I'm Dan Copeland."

Lily instantly forgot all about being embarrassed. "You're the guy that crazy lady yelled at when Mom went to ree-*yoon*-yun!"

Dan Copeland laughed. "My claim to fame!"

"Uncle Ben told me she thought she loved you, and that's enough to make any girl crazy."

"Uncle Ben and I have always been very close friends. But that's going a bit too far, don't you think?"

Lily paused and then realized it was a joke. A grown-up man was making a joke with her. And she thought only Mommy did that.

"My best friend, Samantha, once did my math homework for me," she said.

"That's going a bit too far, too . . . but I remember math!" Dan Copeland laughed again.

"You knew my mother in college. She told me."

He got a funny look on his face, and then he smiled and it was gone. "That's right, I did."

She looked at him carefully, taking his measure. She wanted to ask him, but was a little afraid of how he would answer. What if he said it was none of her business? What would she say? But he was very nice and he didn't treat her like a baby. She decided to take a chance.

"Were you . . . were you one of my mother's boyfriends?" There, it was out. If he laughed at her, she would die.

"Yes, I was, Lily."

Lily leaned forward. "What was she like?"

He put a hand on the back of her chair and bent a little toward her. In a soft voice, he said: "Keep it just between us. She was lovely. She was smart. And she was very, very serious."

Lily stared at him. "Serious! My mom?"

"Does that seem so very strange?"

"Well, gee, she's so funny, usually."

"Your mom?"

"Well . . . *not* with Daddy. With Daddy she's kind of quiet. But Mommy and me, we always joke around a lot."

They were silent for a moment. And then he said, "You haven't eaten a bite."

Lily made a face. Just when he was treating her as if she were grown up, he had to go and talk to her like her father did.

"I'm not hungry."

"What? Not hungry at a wedding? My dear young lady, don't you know that's against the law? I hope the authorities don't get to hear about it. This is the finest food in London, and everyone must eat."

She had to smile. "I just don't feel like it." And then she saw *him*, that jerky Angelo, coming right toward them. "Oh, Lord, here comes that terrible boy again!"

Dan Copeland turned around, and when he turned back, she had the impression that he had just wiped a smile off his face. But she couldn't be sure. All he said was: "I'll save you from that terrible boy. We'll dance, and I hope *you* know the steps, because I don't."

He took her hand and they edged their way into the huge circle that sprawled all across the dance floor. Almost everybody was trying to get in to dance, and Auntie Lee and Uncle Ben were doing fancy steps and twirls in the middle. Dan Copeland's hand was firm and cool, and he smiled down at her.

"Look!" Lily said. "There's my mom, right across from us, with Auntie Lee's brother Carlos!" His hand tightened on hers for a minute and he got his steps all mixed up.

"See?" he said. "I told you I don't know the steps." But Lily got a funny feeling that it wasn't that. She glanced over at her mother. Wouldn't it be romantic if he had never married because he loved Mommy so much and she had married Daddy instead? But Mommy wasn't even looking at them. Carlos was whispering something in her ear and she was laughing like crazy. Lily wondered . . .

"Mr. Copeland?"

"Mmmmmm?"

"Are you married?"

He looked at her, kind of startled. "I *was*. But my wife died . . . a long time ago, Lily, so don't feel bad."

"Then you're a widower." So that wasn't it.

"I guess I am at that."

"Is that why you looked so sad?"

"Sad? Me? I'm happy-go-lucky, Lily! What makes you think I'm sad?"

"Before, you looked sad."

The music stopped, and everyone clapped and cheered and called for more.

"I'm tired," Dan Copeland said. "I'm not used to tripping the light fantastic. And don't forget, when I first came over to your table, you looked sad, too."

They began walking back. It was very nice, she realized, to have someone to *be* with. And he was neat.

"I guess I'm a little sad," she admitted. "See, my mom and dad are going to get a divorce."

"And that makes you feel bad. Of course it does. Makes it tough on you, doesn't it." They sat down.

And then it all came tumbling out. How she missed her old room and she'd never find someone like Samantha again, because she could talk to Sam about *anything* . . . and she was supposed to be in the school play in two weeks and now she couldn't . . . and everything.

Without her even thinking about it, she was holding on to his hand. "And—and my new saddle that Daddy just got me, now I'll never use it again. Beauty! My horse! Maybe I'll never see Beauty again, and . . . and I never even said goodbye forever!" It was just too much to bear. She began to cry, really cry, not like those little tears before. Ugh, it was so embarrassing, but she couldn't stop. Her nose was even running—gross!

"I hate it, it's not fair! My friends . . . a lot of my friends are divorced—I mean, their parents are, and they feel bad for a long time. But they don't have to go all the way across the ocean and live in a strange country . . . and we didn't even really *pack,* and my stuffed animals are all still there!"

He was so nice. He pulled his chair around, so that he blocked her from the rest of the room. Nobody could see her. He put an arm around her and patted her and said, "I know" and stuff like that. But mostly, he just listened to her, and it felt good to say it out loud at last.

When most of the crying was finished, he handed her a big white hankie from his pocket, and while she blew her nose, he said, "I know exactly how you feel, Lily. Once I had to be separated from a very dear friend, and there was nothing I could do about it. It just made me furious and sad and want to cry and cry."

"Really?"

"Really."

"A best friend . . . like Samantha?"

"A very best friend."

"What was his name?"

There was a long pause. And then he said: "Well, Lily, to tell you the truth, it was a lady."

Something in his voice made her look at him, and it came to her like a flash. "I get it! You mean my mom!" She was amazed to see his face turn red. "You're blushing! I'm right! You *did* mean my mom!" She craned past him to find her mother—to take a new look at her. Imagine, her mom had made this big strong man so unhappy he had wanted to cry and cry! It was incredible!

As a matter of fact, her mother was not far away, staring straight at them, a strange, sparkly look on her face. She was holding a telegram tightly in both hands. Lily looked right at her, but her mother's eyes were focused somewhere beyond, staring through her. As Lily watched, Mom frowned a bit, then smiled to herself. She glanced down at the telegram and then, suddenly, turned and hurried out of the room.

"Yes, it was your mother," Dan Copeland said. "But she married your father instead of me." He laughed. "The best man usually wins, you know."

Lily considered this. "But they're getting a divorce."

"Well . . . some people change, Lily."

"Daddy has changed a lot, all right. Always in Washington. What's so terrific about Washington?"

"Your father has a lot of business there."

"Yeah, but when I asked him, he just got mad. He's been getting mad a *lot* . . ." To her horror, tears welled up in her eyes again, and began to spill over. Dan Copeland immediately looked worried, and this only made her cry harder. "I heard . . . I heard Daddy say to Mom, 'I'll destroy both of you!' He *did!*"

Dan Copeland put an arm around her and patted her wet cheeks with his handkerchief.

"Oh, no," he said in a very certain voice. "He didn't mean it."

"He said it! He did mean it!"

"But he didn't mean *you,* honey. Look, I've known your father for years and years, and I'm positive he would never hurt you. He was just angry and said whatever came into his mind—you've done that, haven't you? Said things you didn't really mean, because you were upset?"

"Well . . . once I told Samantha I'd never be her friend again."

"And were you her friend again?"

"Of *course.*" She had to smile. "We're best friends. We'll *always* be best friends."

He gave one last wipe to her face and took her chin in his fingers, gazing deep into her eyes. "That's right, Lily. Some things are forever . . . the best always are." His eyes were warm and dark, a coppery brown like his hair, with little specks of gold. She thought they were beautiful. And he was so nice. Yes, she thought, he might just be Number One On The List.

After Mom had told her about the divorce and everything, she had thought and thought about it. Most of her friends got new fathers after a while, and she figured she might just as well start collecting her own favorite choices. Jerrod Waller had been the first. He owned the Mexican shop and he said funny things all the time. But she noticed that he watched her sharply all the time when she was in the shop—like she was going to break something, like she was a dumb little kid! The headmaster at the new school here was kind of neat. He had a wonderful English accent and he rode, too. His office was filled with trophies he had won at horse shows. But Mom hadn't seemed to like him very much. Lily liked Mr. Akkardijian just fine, but of course he was very old, and anyway, he already had a wife. Dan Copeland was the best one she had come across . . . and she had a feeling he still liked her mom a lot. He already liked *her,* Lily, so that wouldn't be a problem— And then she cut off her thoughts guiltily. She loved her daddy, even when he was being mean. But still . . . Samantha had told her, "They never get back together, you know. You can try and try and it doesn't do any good. When they say divorce, they mean it." And Sam ought to know; she had had three different fathers already.

"Feel better now?" Dan Copeland smoothed her hair; it felt good. She nodded and gave him a smile. "Ter-rific!" he said, and grinned back at her.

"You've got one, too!" Lily blurted.

"Got what, honey?"

"One dimple. Like me. See?" She poked at her cheek, making a smile for him.

For a minute he didn't say anything. And then: "Oh. Yes. And I can wiggle my ears. Can you?" And he *could* wiggle his ears. It looked awfully funny and she tried, but she couldn't do it.

The band played a fanfare then, and everybody had to stop talking while Auntie Lee took the mike and said she loved them all, and everybody cheered and clapped and yelled, "And we love you!" And Uncle Ben gave her a big smooch, like in the movies, right there in front of everybody, and there was more cheering.

Then Auntie Lee said: "It's time to throw the bouquet. All single women in this room who feel that Ben and I are setting a good example . . . all you gals who might want to trade your independence for a helluva man—but remember, this one's taken!" The rest of what she said was drowned out in laughing and shouting.

"Go on, Lily," Dan Copeland told her, grinning. "It's magic. Whoever catches the bouquet is the next bride."

Lily made a face. "*I* don't want to get married!" But even as she said it, the idea came to her. She didn't want to get married, of course not, that was silly. But what if, she wondered, what if she caught it for her mother? Lily knew magic worked. Any bouquet that beautiful, with that many flowers in it, had to have a lot of magic. And if she were the one to get it, it would be *her* magic. And she could use it whatever way she wanted.

"Oh, it doesn't really mean anything," Dan Copeland was saying. She smiled at him; obviously he didn't really know about magic. But she had it all figured out: If she caught the bouquet, then maybe . . .

"I want to do it," Lily said.

"Can you catch?" he teased.

Lily was indignant. "I'm very good at sports!"

"Okay, then. Let's go."

He took her hand and together they marched over to the stage. There were quite a few ladies there, all giggling and crowding around, but he made a path through them and put Lily right at the front. "Do your stuff, kiddo," he whispered, and she gave him a smile full of secrets.

Auntie Lee looked down and gave her a big wink. Then she lifted the bouquet over her head. Lily looked up, her tongue between her teeth in concentration, studying the huge cascade of flowers with its white satin streamers floating down. The drum rolled and the men shouted. And then Auntie Lee flung it out, straight at Lily. Oh, but it was too high! It was going to sail right over her head! If I catch it, Lily thought fiercely, then everything will be perfect. If I catch it, everyone will be happy. She forgot where she was, forgot the party shoes and the fancy dress. She balanced on the balls of her feet and sprang up, up, leaping into the air as high as she could. The streamers were floating by. She stretched, willing her arms to reach them, felt her fingers touching the ribbons, and then . . . she had caught it! A hand behind her tugged at it for a second, but *she* had caught it.

Breathless, she clutched the bouquet tightly in her arms. It was larger than she had thought, and heavier, and it smelled delicious, like a garden.

Everyone was applauding. She turned with her treasure and a flashbulb went off right in her face. Lily ducked her head and blinked, red and green splotches in her eyes. Where was her mom? Where was Dan Copeland? She had to find them. She squirmed through the crowd, blinking rapidly to clear her vision.

There was her mother, over by the doorway. And he was with her! He was bent forward and her mother's face was tipped up to his. She looked as if a light had been turned on in her; she glowed. She was smiling and smiling and talking very fast, and then Dan Copeland threw his head back and laughed. Was it working? Lily tightened her hold on the bouquet and wished with all her might. It had to work.

Dan Copeland stopped laughing and looked at her mother very seriously. For a moment they both stood very still, just looking at each other. Lily held her breath.

And then they reached out for each other, and then they were holding each other very close and kissing.

And then they pulled apart and looked around. Yes, they were looking for her. Now they saw her. They were smiling and smiling and they were both calling to her. Oh, they looked happy! It *was* working. Lily smiled to herself. How simple it was, to make everything come out right. You only had to know for sure what you wanted.

Women of all ages *can look and feel their best with these bestselling guides to wardrobe, weight loss, exercise and skin care.*

15   AL-30